Spirit Whispers

Mollie Moon

This book is a work of fiction. Names, characters, places and incidents are products of the author's imagination or are used fictitiously. Any resemblance to actual events or locales or persons living or dead is entirely coincidental.

Published by
Suka Press LLC
Carlsbad, California

ISBN 978-1-7368479 -2-3

Author Contact:
https://www.molliemoon.com

Cover by Joleene Naylor

Walk with the wind, brothers and sisters,
and let the spirit of peace and the power of love
be your guide.

– John Lewis

For my friends at the Healing Horse Ranch
and all horse lovers

Acknowledgements

I am deeply thankful to all who have helped and inspired me to write this book, which is a continuation of The Horseshoe Necklace, though it is not necessary to read them in sequence.

My thanks go to Enkhnaran Jargalsaikhan for sharing insights into the Mongolian culture and Jerry Meling for helping me understand the role of an outrider, though my characters and this novel are born out of fiction.

I am grateful for the time I got to spend with Nancy Stolz Petterson and her quarter horses at Airlie Farms and Lisa Meling during her horse training sessions.

I am grateful to Sheryl Marks Brown of Healing Horse Ranch, who graciously shares her knowledge and herd of therapy horses, allowing hundreds of people each year to experience the beauty of meditation with horses as well as other equine therapies.

Thanks to Sheryl's mare, Jane, who willingly lets me practice liberty work with her, although she often looks at me with her big, beautiful eyes, wondering what on earth I'm trying to ask her to do.

Thank you, Gail Chadwick, my longtime editor and friend, for your special skill in finding inconsistencies, suggesting rewrites, and fixing my punctuation.

My thanks also go to Joleene Naylor for help with formatting my books to make them publishable and, as always, for making the cover look beautiful.

Lastly, thanks to my friends and readers whose reviews and feedback are invaluable. You give me the enthusiasm to continue this writing journey and to develop the plot and the characters who pop up in my imagination. I hope you enjoy the twists and turns of this new novel as much as I have enjoyed putting them to paper.

Sincerely,
Mollie Moon

One

It was 2:00 a.m. in the quiet seaside town of Little Oaks. Everybody slept peacefully except one, tormented by recurrent nightmares that never seemed to cease.

"No," Emmy moaned, "please, no!"

With one quick move, the woman from social services ripped away the red-and-white striped comforter under which Emmy was hiding. Her belongings had been packed silently behind her back, immovably prevailing against the wall in two brown, rectangular boxes without an address. The woman forced a smile, but her green, catlike eyes stared at Emmy without blinking, leaving goose bumps rippling up and down Emmy's arms, as she peeked at the woman from under the comforter. The woman's pale lips formed two thin lines, barely visible, that didn't allow objection. Her dark-gray skirt was coerced tightly around her hips, and her matching blazer buttoned all the way to her throat. Her straight, light-brown hair had been pulled mercilessly into a tight knot, pinned in place on top of her head, exposing barely visible traces of blue veins on her temples.

"You must leave," the woman said. The three sharp words were pressed laboriously through the thin lips, each word separated from the other like jagged chunks of ice, cut forever from a glacier, plunging into the depth of the ocean and melting into the unknown.

"Where am I going to go?" Emmy stammered. Her dark round eyes were focused on the woman's stern, unpardonable face. Emmy's long, thick black hair was wildly spread on the pillow, surrounding her young face that had witnessed more tragedy than most.

"You must leave," the woman repeated more loudly. "You're coming with me." Her chilling voice echoed in the empty room, bouncing back from the barren walls, the words landing in Emmy's face like an unstoppable avalanche. Emmy cramped her hands around the comforter, but the woman pulled and pulled, leaning backward, pressing her rubber heels into the floor, her gripping, bony arms proving stronger than a bulldozer.

"No, please! Help!" Emmy shouted. "Help!"

Quietly, Baatar entered Emmy's room and sat on her bed.

"Emmy, wake up, you're dreaming."

"No, please, help!"

"Emmy, wake up. It's just a dream."

Slowly Emmy opened her eyes and, half-conscious, looked into Baatar's kind face. She focused on his dark eyes, filled with compassion. Her hands were stiff from clutching the comforter.

"Are you OK?" Baatar asked, his warm hand embracing Emmy's grip.

"Yes," Emmy said. She took a breath. "I'm fine."

"Do you want to tell me what happened?" he asked.

"I dreamed of when I was twelve and had to go to foster care after my parents and sister died."

He nodded. "Well, you're safe here, Emmy. You have a home now. Go back to sleep. We have a couple more hours."

"Thanks, Baatar," Emmy said. "I'm sorry I woke you up."

"No worries. Go back to sleep."

Baatar left the room, and Emmy petted Bruno, Baatar's

mutt, who lay alongside her, his head between her chest and armpit, his bushy tail covering her ankles. With half-closed eyes, his head popped up slightly. He yawned and licked his paw once, then his head landed back on the same spot, his eyes closing once again.

Emmy took a deep breath and looked around the room. The moon shone through the dark-blue curtains. Her college books were stacked on the desk next to her laptop. The picture of her deceased parents and sister, all three smiling, sat on top of the chest of drawers. The closet, she knew, held her few pieces of clothing, nicely organized. She listened attentively. There was no presence in the room.

Had the dream really just been a memory, or was it foresight, she wondered, *telling her she'd have to leave Baatar's cozy home? Was Jenna going to force her out?*

Things had fallen into place so magically last year when he took her in and saved her from homelessness. She didn't want to leave, not now and not for a long time. Baatar had become the dad she'd missed so much over the past six years. Through him, she'd gotten a job at the racetrack where he introduced her to his friends, including Manolo, who had taught her the ropes at the stables, taken her on a few dates, and introduced her to his own ponies, Diamond and Rush. She had a crush on him.

But Manolo had many fires burning. He'd told her he was going to take Diamond to the racetrack where he had signed up to pony, to guide thoroughbreds to the starting gate with his own working horse, four days a week. He'd done it before to make extra money. He was saving to go to farrier school and then get his master's degree. He was training his other pony, Rush, to see if he could enter him in the races. Emmy liked his ambition, but she'd like it even better if he arranged his life around her.

At a quarter to four, the soft sound of chimes spread through Emmy's room, and Bruno's ears pricked. Time to get up.

Emmy opened her eyes and stared at the stark white ceiling, which gave her a slight chill. It reminded her of nothingness, no home and no future, and made her tuck the comforter all around her shoulders once more, sticking both hands inside, and laying them on top of her stomach. "I hate changes," she whispered. "Everything's finally going well."

Bruno glanced at her from the corner of his eyes, lazily lounging a few more minutes after the alarm clock had admonished that the night was over. He lay on the bedspread against Emmy's slender frame, relaxed and trusting, smelling the scent of the teenager he'd learned to love, one of his legs dangling off the side of the bed.

Meanwhile, the master bedroom at the end of the hall remained quiet, though Baatar routinely woke up before four o'clock, when the night seemed only half over. His work at the racetrack demanded an early work schedule, exercising the thoroughbreds before the races, checking schedules, taking care of his ponies, and getting them ready for the patrolling job at hand. He didn't mind, though he wondered if his fiancée would get used to it.

He looked over at Jenna, sleeping peacefully next to him. She was a beautiful woman with a captivating smile. Her lively brown eyes had pierced his soul and drawn him in. What he uncovered in getting to know her was a compassionate heart, a creative mind, and a delightful physical connection he could describe only as heavenly. Sure, she could have strong opinions and a temper and didn't always agree with him, but he had his own flaws. He smiled.

He stared at her features, etched into his memory long

ago—her dark curved eyelashes, the slightly uneven brows, the straight nose that he found made her look aristocratic, her full red lips, her long dark-brown straight hair. His heart stirred. *If there were angels, she'd be one.*

Having Jenna live with him was extraordinary. Dating her back in Texas had been great, but the time together had been limited—a long weekend, a holiday, a short trip. Now, it would be different. They were getting married.

He got up and walked into the kitchen on bare feet to brew a cup of coffee. Emmy was already there, having a bowl of cereal.

"I'm so sorry I woke you up last night," she said. "I didn't realize I talked out loud."

"It was more like a scream, followed by Bruno's whining," Baatar said. He inspected her face with his piercing eyes. "I'm glad you're OK. Is Manolo picking you up today?"

"He said he would."

"Then he will."

Emmy headed out the door when she heard Manolo's truck arrive, and they took off for the racetrack stables for their morning shift. Some days, after his exercise riding was done, they worked side by side. Those were her favorite days. Some days their chores took them in different directions.

"You're hauling Diamond today?" Emmy asked, looking at the horse trailer hooked up behind Manolo's truck.

"Yes, we're joining the ponying team today." He smiled at her. "Diamond and I have worked together at the racetrack before. She's patient and confident, and can lead any thoroughbred to the starting gate, even when they're headstrong and resistant."

"I thought you wanted to focus on horse training?"

"I haven't given up on that, but it's still a bit sporadic until I've made a name for myself, and Rush is still very young. It'll be a while until I can enter him in a race."

"I see."

Emmy watched when Manolo maneuvered Diamond out of the trailer and into her stall.

"I've gotta report to Jack's stable for my chores," she said. "I'll see you later?"

"Yes, for sure."

But later didn't seem to be later that day. Emmy was busy raking, cleaning stalls, shoveling manure, carting it outside, hauling bales of hay. She got sweaty.

When she was at the end of her shift, she lingered. She went into the bathroom to freshen up. Her jeans were dusty, her T-shirt had sweat stains she couldn't hide. *I should bring a change of clothes*, she thought. She walked through the racetrack tunnel to watch the preparations for the first race of the day. Mario and Baatar were on the racetrack already, mounted on their ponies, awaiting the thoroughbreds as they were led onto the track.

Then she saw Manolo on Diamond, ponying a tall, flighty two-year-old thoroughbred, carrying an experienced, known jockey. *The owner must be rich*, Emmy thought, *if he can hire that jockey for this race.*

Suddenly the young thoroughbred shied and walked backward, his head held high, ears pinned back. It whinnied, its eyes wide-open. Manolo held the thoroughbred's reigns and didn't let him out of his sight. With experience and ease, he steadied the horse, calmed its gait, and directed it toward the starting gate. The horse was led in and the gate shut behind it.

And there, as Emmy had expected, was Savannah.

"That was awesome, Mano!" She blew him a kiss.

Manolo smiled. "Nothing to it."

"Don't downplay it," Savannah shouted across the racetrack. "You're a crazy, cool rider. You know how to handle the wild ones!" She picked up a thick strand of her sexy, blonde hair, draped it over her breast, and gave it a flipping toss toward her back with a broad open-mouthed smile.

Emmy wished a dust cloud would hit Savannah's face and shut her up. Instead, she saw Manolo smiling back at Savannah. Side by side, those two slowly rode their ponies back to the stables, like a young couple on a date they didn't want to end, their legs almost touching.

Mother Nature had been kind to Savannah, too kind. She was five foot eight, slender, and well-endowed. Her thick, golden-blonde hair was wavy and reached all the way down to her waist. Her skin was as white as a sandy beach in the Caribbean. She had small ears, always adorned with sparkly earrings that glistened in the sun. Her eyes were a mesmerizing, soft hazel with speckles of green. The freckles on her face only made her look more endearing. She wore a tight-fitting top, showing her cleavage as if it accidentally spilled out to her own embarrassment. It was intentional, of course.

Savannah was chatting with Manolo, laughing, showing her perfect, white teeth, reaching out with her free hand to touch his thigh. He seemed to listen, quietly engaged, sucking up the young woman's affection. Clearly, she charmed him, and he was eating it up. *Why does he do that when he pretends he's interested in me?* Emmy thought. *He seems sincere. Or is he playing games?*

Emmy looked down on herself, shamefully aware of her dirty jeans and sweat spots in her shirt. She was no competition. Manolo had it easy. All the girls liked him.

Emmy walked off when the pony riders were out of sight. She wondered what else Savannah would offer once she and Manolo were in the stable together alone. Emmy wanted to run over there and claim Manolo for herself, *but what could she say? What could she do?*

Instead, she took her backpack, filled with books and her laptop, and walked to the bus stop. The wind blew in her face, carrying particles of dust that made her eyes water. The bus ride from the racetrack to college took forever and gave Emmy way too much time to fantasize about Manolo and Savannah.

It took a whole two days until she saw Manolo again, after he had spent three hours galloping thoroughbreds for exercise in the early morning hours. He was carrying a heavy bale of hay to stuff all the slow feeders for the horses, his upper arm muscles showing.

"Hey, Emmy," he said when he saw her and approached her. He gave her a hug. "How're you?"

"Fine." She turned from him.

He looked at her. "What's going on?"

"Nothing."

"Are you in a bad mood?" he asked.

Emmy didn't respond.

"Did you have a fight with Baatar? Is Jenna not nice to you?"

Emmy took a deep breath. "No."

"No what?" he walked around, facing her.

"I'm OK." She looked down.

"Emmy, I know you. Something's bothering you. Will you tell me what it is?"

She shrugged her shoulders.

"Emmy, come on. We're friends."

"Everybody's your friend," she said.

Manolo put his hand on her arm. "What's that supposed to mean?"

"I watch you flirt."

"You do?"

"Yes."

"With whom?" he asked.

"Savannah."

"Ah, Savannah." He smiled. "She flirts with everybody. She always has. It's just who she is. You can't take it too seriously."

"How can I not?" Emmy asked.

"Are you jealous? Of her?"

She looked into his eyes.

Manolo grinned. "Come here, Emmy." He took her in his arms, and she sank into his embrace, scolding herself for not resisting.

"I've known Savannah for years," he said. "She's like a sister. She can be a brat. Her dad owns a couple of thoroughbreds. She's a rich, spoiled kid. She loves glamour. She loves attention."

"She's gorgeous," Emmy said.

"Yes, she is. And she knows it. And she plays it. I had a crush on her when I was nineteen. She laughed at me and went out with the son of an owner. Her father makes sure she meets the right kind of people in the right circles."

"But she seems to like you."

"She's just a friend, Emmy. We work together. I'm friendly to her, that's all. I'm not the kind of rich man she wants to cater to her. I have no interest."

"But…"

He gently laid his hands on the sides of Emmy's face and gave her a kiss. "I'm interested in *you*, Emmy. I like your company. I've shared my dreams with you. I've shown you my room. That's my secret hideout. I've introduced you to my ponies!"

"I can't compete with her," Emmy said.

"There's no competition."

"Can you teach me to pony?"

Manolo looked at her. "Emmy, it takes an experienced rider to do that job. But I can take you on a date. Would Friday night work for you?"

She hesitated.

"Please."

"OK." She nodded and smiled, but the hollow ache in her chest remained.

Two

Life had changed rapidly for Baatar and Jenna since their engagement. Baatar thought about the future, living together, making Jenna happy, having children, raising them.

Jenna had moved into his small house in Little Oaks, which was quite an adjustment from living in a three-bedroom, two-story house with Texas dimensions. Slowly, she was getting to know his friends and the neighbors, his job, the city, and of course, Emmy and Bruno.

She'd never had pets although she wasn't opposed to them. Bruno made getting to know him easy. He wanted food, treats, cuddles, and walks. He was a great listener when Baatar wasn't around, and he kept Jenna company when she was alone. Emmy, Jenna found, was a nice girl, and she didn't mind her staying at the house, although it took some getting used to living with Baatar and a teenager.

She had many things to think about—her future with Baatar, moving her business, having children. She'd wanted children for a long time. She'd envied her friend Amelia for getting pregnant. Now, hopefully, it was her turn.

After Jenna began to settle in, she thought it best to sell her house in Texas. There seemed to be no reason to keep it.

"Let me just fly out there and put the house on the market," she said to Baatar. "Would you mind keeping my living room furniture? I could have it shipped out."

"I've always liked your living room furniture, love," he said. "My furniture is functional, but it doesn't have that warm feeling of home you know how to create. Do you want me to come along?"

"No, honey, I can manage. I need to go through all my stuff and make decisions on what to let go of and what to keep. I'd rather just do it by myself."

While Baatar drove her to the airport, they talked about their wedding.

"I was thinking—we could just have a quick getaway with our closest friends," he said.

"Are you crazy?" She stared at him. "It's a once-in-a lifetime event! My family would go nuts if I eloped or celebrated with a couple of friends. I want a nice wedding, honey, with a beautiful, lacy dress and everybody present— your family and my family and all our friends."

He nodded. *Apparently, there was not going to be a discussion about this.* "What about our honeymoon?" he asked. "Do you have a place in mind?"

"Hmmm." Jenna said, pondering. "You always wanted to show me Alaska."

"Really? On our honeymoon? You don't want something more romantic? An island vacation? Something exotic? Hawaii?"

"I saw a brochure for a five-day Alaskan cruise," Jenna said. "Timewise that would work for us and I think we could make that quite romantic, don't you? A small, cozy cabin on a slick ship, you and me, being rocked by the waves, while we're drifting timelessly through the big blue Pacific Ocean?"

"Anywhere with you is romantic," he said and winked at her.

"I have the brochure somewhere," Jenna said and dug

through her purse, pulling out a picturesque, glossy brochure where she had circled the trip.

"I love the ocean," Baatar said. "The nature up in Alaska is breathtaking. But, love..." he hesitated. "I have to be honest with you. After working on an oil rig for a few years, and my friend Damdin's fatal accident, I'm not sure I could enjoy floating in the middle of the ocean in some small metal container."

"You mean a luxury cruise ship?" Jenna asked, with a smirk.

He looked at her, his eyes soft. "Would you be open to flying to Alaska and taking a road trip instead?"

"A road trip in Alaska? Isn't that dangerous? Aren't there grizzlies?" She swallowed.

Baatar smiled. "Yes, there are bears. But there are also big highways and cities and civilization."

"Where'd we go?" Jenna asked, her interest peaked.

He glanced at her. Her shiny dark hair reached down to her shoulder blades, and her full figure had always appealed to him. She had a natural, feminine beauty. "We could fly into Fairbanks, drive down to Anchorage, take a bay cruise, something like that?"

"Sounds intriguing."

"It'd be quiet, lots of nature and solitude. It'd give us a reprieve after we've had all the relatives visiting for the wedding." His skin prickled at the idea of a large wedding.

"Don't remind me!" Jenna rolled her eyes. "You have no idea what you're getting yourself into. You haven't met my aunts."

"And you don't know my Mongolian family," he said. "None of them speak English, so I'll be a translator twenty-four seven, not that I mind. I'm the one who left. I should welcome them here with open arms and be a good host, but it will be exhausting." He rubbed his chin. "So, you wanna go to Alaska?" He glanced at her.

"Let's."

They drove quietly for a while. There was no traffic early in the morning, but Jenna enjoyed how the scenery along the freeway changed, going from a flat landscape with lagoons to rolling hills, filled with colorful, picturesque small bungalows and the downtown skyscrapers ahead of them.

"It's strange, selling my home in Texas," Jenna said. "A part of me thought I'd live there till the day I die."

Baatar looked at her. His eyes saddened. "Would you rather live in Texas?"

"No, honey, that's not what I meant."

"You know I'd move for you," Baatar said.

"I like living in California with you. I love it here," Jenna reaffirmed.

He pulled into the parking lot at the airport and shut off the engine. As they walked inside the building, Jenna checked for the flight information and departure gate. He had his arm around her shoulder, carrying her bag.

"Come back quickly," he said when they reached the entry to the security gate, "or I'll have to come to Texas and kidnap you."

She smiled. "Selling the house shouldn't take me too long."

He gave her a tight hug and a kiss and waved goodbye as she passed through security.

He stood for a moment, almost paralyzed. He didn't want to see her leave, not even for a few days. He hated to be separated from her. It left a sore spot in his heart, filled with longing.

He turned and walked at a fast pace back to his truck and drove straight to the racetrack. *He'd said he'd move to Texas with her, but could he really? His place was here in Southern*

California now, with her. The lightness of the energy of this place had weaved into the fiber of his being. It had called him, rescued him, saved his soul. They'd become one. The horses were his kin; their greetings, their exhales, the look in their eyes that penetrated him like an elixir. He never talked about it. It was just a feeling, buried so deep inside of him that words couldn't reach it.

It was home.

"Saaral," he said when he approached his mare at the stable. "Jenna's gone to Texas, but only for a few days. She'll be back. We're together now, you know, for good. I'm gonna marry her."

He petted the mare, then walked over to Tsokhoor, his other pony, who tucked his head into Baatar's chest, and Baatar kissed his forehead and rubbed the sides of his cheeks. He fed both of them. "I'll see you in a little while."

Work was good. It demanded his focus and attention and kept his mind from wandering. He checked his schedule and walked over to Jack's stable, where the thoroughbreds were lined up for him to ride. The grooms had already fed them a light breakfast, then brushed and saddled up the horses going to the track. They walked the horses around the shed row to loosen any stiff muscles before Baatar showed up for their morning workout.

He galloped fifteen of them, giving them the morning exercise they needed. Each horse was different—some were not even two years old, hyper, and filled with anxiety, still scared of the noisy starting gate; others had years of experience and ran the racetrack like old pros, needing little to no guidance. Nonetheless, once he sat on their backs, they all demanded him to be fully present, an unspoken but sensible horse expectation.

Afterward, he went back to his ponies. He checked their feet and cleaned the frog, the triangular shape of the hoof, extending midway from the heels toward to toe, crucial for bearing weight, shock absorption and blood flow. Any debris, mud or muck stuck in it could cause infection and affect the health of the horse. He took the ponies out for exercise, one by one. He brushed them down, cleaned their stalls, and gave them some fresh hay.

He had a quick lunch and dressed in his official outrider uniform: blue jeans, white shirt, the red security vest, riding boots, and a black helmet. He saddled Saaral and met up with his colleague, Mario. Together, they worked the nine races for the day, ensuring that everybody on the track was safe, both humans and horses. If an accident happened, they were the first responders to help a jockey or catch a loose horse, but today, there were no incidents.

In the evening, he and Emmy took Bruno for a long walk.

"I'm gonna miss this," Emmy said.

"This?"

"Our walks with Bruno, our chats in the evening, you telling me what to do," Emmy said, smiling.

"You're an adult. I'm not telling you what to do," Baatar said.

"Your guidance," Emmy said quickly, "your advice. I'll miss that."

"I'm not going anywhere," Baatar said. "Are you?"

"You're getting married. You'll want the house to yourselves. Newlyweds. You'll have kids."

"One step at a time," Baatar said. "One step at a time, Emmy."

"I had an interesting dream last night," Emmy said, "before I had that nightmare. Are you planning to have kids?"

Baatar looked at her, his eyebrows raised. "Yeees," he

said slowly. "Jenna and I would like to have kids."

"I saw you having three," Emmy said. "Maybe I shouldn't tell you."

"Three, huh?" Baatar grinned. "I'd be OK with that. Boys or girls?"

"You really want to know?"

His lips puckered as he gave her a quick nod.

"Two boys and a girl," Emmy said. "That's what I saw."

He smiled. "And did they like horses?"

"Is that relevant? I didn't ask them." Emmy laughed. "I just saw three kids. I didn't get a rundown on their talents or interests. But given you'd be their dad and you own several horses, isn't it likely your kids would love them?"

"I hope so."

Baatar walked beside her quietly, thinking about Jenna. Like her, Emmy was of Mexican descent, yet so different. She was only eighteen, petite, her big, round eyes could be intense, sometimes expressing fear, sometimes anger, sometimes sadness. He knew she was highly sensitive. Having been orphaned at age twelve had forced her to grow up quickly, to adjust, conform, and reconcile with constantly changing living conditions, from social workers to foster parents, foster siblings, and roommates, all bringing challenging changes and instability into her young life.

Jenna's life had been so different, and it reflected in her personality. She'd grown up with two parents who dearly loved and protected her. With a musician for a dad, there'd always been music in her home, creating an atmosphere of happiness, comfort, and ease. With her dad from Puerto Rico and her mother of Mexican descent, she'd learned at a young age that there were different ways of life, different beliefs, different customs. She'd learned that one wasn't right and the other wrong, but that tolerance and respect blend them together. There'd been laughter, trusting relationships, dancing, freedom to decide who she wanted to be, what passion or interest she wanted to follow. She was still that way—a free spirit, emotional, passionate, creative, and filled with a love of life.

Three

When Jenna arrived in Houston, she rummaged through her belongings. She'd had many good times in this house. She met Baatar living here. They spent their first night together in this house. They cooked and danced and laughed together here with her best friend, Amelia, and his best friend, Damdin. Three days after Damdin died, Amelia had found out she was pregnant with his child. She'd moved in with Jenna, and they raised Damdin Jr. together, until Amelia met Wyatt and got married just four months ago. Of course, Amelia took the little boy with her. They called him DJ for short. The house had felt so empty, so lifeless.

And now Baatar had returned and confessed his love. She prayed silently and gave thanks to whoever made this happen, and she fell asleep in the dark.

Two days later, when she had made a list of what to sell and what to keep, her doorbell rang.

"Marty!"

"Jenna, I've missed you. I know you said you're dating someone else, but I hope you'll reconsider. May I come in?" He breezed past her before she could say a word.

He was six foot two and a bit heavyset, with a receding hairline and a big college ring on his right hand. He wore a suit with a white shirt and a blue tie, and custom-made shoes that were always polished to perfection. His face was clean-shaven, and his jaw pushed forward. He was a man who knew what he wanted, and he usually got it. He was a shrewd businessman.

"You and I, Jenna," he said, "we're perfect together." He swung his long arms around her and gave her a deep kiss. She struggled to free herself.

"Marty, I'm engaged."

"Surely you made a mistake," he said. "I forgive you for that. Jenna, we've always had such a good time together. You must feel it, too. You and I, we're meant for each other."

"Marty, please, I'm engaged to another man. It was nice getting to know you, but I've made my choice. Please understand. I've given it a try, but I just don't love you."

"What do you want?" he asked. "Diamonds? A bigger house? A boat? A new car? I can give you all of that."

"No, Marty. I don't want that. I've gotten engaged. I'm in love with Baatar. You should go."

"Jenna, darling, didn't you hear me? It's a mistake. You love me, and I love you."

"No, Marty. I love another man." Jenna stared at him.

"And where is that fella? I don't see him. Are you making him up? I'm here for you." He took her hair into his right hand and twisted it gently, then drew it into his face and inhaled.

"Marty, please. I'm moving to California. I'm selling my house. I'm gonna get married."

"We can move to California if that's what you want. Don't you like it here anymore? You and I together?"

"No, Marty. You and I—that's over. That no longer exists. There is no you and I."

"OK, I'll buy your house," Marty said. He looked around, estimating its value. "That way you can come home when this California fling is over."

"It's not a fling, Marty. I knew Baatar long before I met you. We dated for three years, and we've gotten back together. I told you that. I love him. I don't love you, Marty. I'm sorry. Please leave now."

"I'll buy your house," he repeated. "You just let me know how much you want for it. I'll be here when you return."

"Please leave now," Jenna said again. She managed to open the front door. He tried to kiss her once more, but she braced herself. "Goodbye, Marty."

"You're making a big mistake," she heard him say when she had already shut the door behind him.

She took a deep breath and peeked out the window to make sure he left. He was no longer in sight. He'd been a reasonable man when they dated. He could be a gentleman, although he'd always been a bit pushy, trying to convince her that his agenda was hers. But it wasn't. He was wealthy, a respectable businessman in the area. But no matter how much she tried to like him, her heart wasn't in it. It never had been, and that little voice inside her kept her from ever saying I love you.

She grabbed the phone to call Baatar, then decided not to tell him about Marty. *Baatar would get upset. Why alert him of something he couldn't do anything about?*

Instead, she called her dad. "I'm in Houston for a few days and hope we can see each other?" she said.

"That would be fantastic," her dad said. "I have engagements six nights a week now, playing the saxophone at a club. It's a nice place, you'd like it. You're welcome to come by, or we could meet earlier in the day? Perhaps for lunch?"

"Lunch sounds great," Jenna agreed. "Let's do that."

She contacted a real estate agent who made an appointment to come by in the morning. She'd barely hung up the phone when there was a knock on the door.

Marty, she thought, *not again*.

She opened the door and saw a man holding a big bouquet of flowers, his face covered behind them.

"Marty, don't," Jenna said.

"Delivery, Ma'am."

It wasn't Marty's voice. She accepted the bouquet from the young man and found a card inside.

"Te estraño," it said, "I miss you," signed by Baatar.

She smiled and picked up the phone.

"You miss me already?" she asked. "I just arrived in Houston a couple of days ago."

"You got the flowers," he said.

"I did. Thank you. That's very sweet of you."

"I do miss you, love. I hope you come home soon. And if I can help you with anything, just let me know and I'll make arrangements."

"I will," she said. "The flowers really weren't necessary, Baatar, but I love them."

The real estate agent came in the morning, as promised. While Jenna and she were discussing the market, the doorbell rang.

"Marty, I thought we were through," Jenna said rather coldly. "I really wish you would not come by any longer. Please accept my decision."

He peeked inside and saw the real estate agent and waved at her. "I'm interested in the property," he hollered.

"You must leave now," Jenna said and closed the door.

The agent looked concerned. "An old flame?" she asked. "Sometimes they can become pretty insistent. Is he nice?"

Jenna shivered. "He was always quite reasonable before I got engaged to another man."

Together, the two women cleared out some furniture

to stage the home nicely. "No clutter," the agent advised, "and no personal photos. You want the potential buyers to envision themselves living here."

Jenna agreed. She took down all her personal photos, even her favorite one with Baatar and her at the beach. Baatar called her every evening, and she told him about her progress.

"Should I come out?" he asked again.

"I don't think you need to," Jenna said. "I hope to get the place sold quickly. If all goes well, I'll return to California next week."

The open house was arranged for Friday, Saturday, and Sunday. Jenna met her dad on Friday for lunch and told him all about her new life in California. He'd always been a good listener, always encouraging, always proud of her.

"I hope you come visit us soon," Jenna said. "You'll definitely have to come to our wedding. Can you do that with all your engagements?"

"I'll make sure I can," her dad said. "I wouldn't miss your wedding. Your mother would have loved to see you getting married."

While the real estate agent showed her home on Saturday, Jenna met with her favorite cousin, Trisha, and asked her to be a bridesmaid. Trisha agreed wholeheartedly.

On Sunday, Jenna drove to Galveston, where she had lunch by herself, reminiscing about how she and Baatar had gotten engaged there on the beach.

When she returned a few hours later, the real estate agent awaited her, together with Marty.

"This gentleman has offered ten thousand above asking price," the agent announced. "I think you should take his offer."

"Let's discuss that in private," Jenna suggested. "I'd like to see what other offers may come in over the next couple of days."

"Jenna, you can't be serious," Marty said. "I'm meant to buy your house from you. For us!"

Jenna gave the real estate agent a long look.

"I'll think about it," she said. "Marty, you need to leave now."

Marty stepped closer, and Jenna stepped back.

"Please leave," she said again. He looked at the real estate agent, who had picked up her phone, ready to dial, then he looked at Jenna. "I love you, darling."

Jenna opened the front door. "Goodbye, Marty!"

He sighed, giving her a longing look, reaching out with his hand and blowing her a kiss, when she closed the door.

"He's such a nice man," the agent said, "and so generous."

"As I explained previously," Jenna said, "we used to date, but I'm engaged to another man. I don't really want to sell the house to Marty if there are any other reasonable offers. It's awkward. I don't want a business transaction between us. It doesn't feel right."

"I see," the agent said, "but it is the best offer."

That night around 11:00 p.m., when Jenna lay in bed, the doorbell rang. She didn't budge. Then she heard Marty's voice outside. He was throwing pebbles against her bedroom window.

She got up. "Marty, if you don't leave," she said through the closed door, "I'll call the cops."

"Jenna, darling, you're so confused," he said. "Open the door, and let's talk. Let me show you what you're missing."

Jenna picked up the phone. "I'm dialing the police now."

"OK, OK, I'm leaving. You're making the wrong decision, darling." His words were a bit slurred. Apparently,

Jenna after school. "I'm looking around."

"You can stay here, Emmy," Jenna said. "You can stay as long as you want."

"Thanks."

When Baatar returned from the racetrack, the living room smelled of Jenna. He'd always liked her cedar and pine furniture and the bright, lively colors of her rug, pillows, and blankets. The red sofa looked inviting as the centerpiece of the room.

He bent down and rubbed Bruno's belly. The dog showed his broad, content smile, with his tongue hanging out of one side of his mouth.

"Looks like somebody's taking good care of you," Baatar said. Bruno licked his hand profusely.

He walked over to give Jenna a hug and a kiss. "Do you like it?" she asked, looking around the newly furnished room.

"I love it."

After dinner, they sat on the sofa with a nice hot cup of tea.

"I had a long talk with Emmy," Jenna said. "She's worried she'll have to move. Did she tell you that?"

"She hasn't," Baatar said. "I don't mind her living here with us, do you?"

Jenna shook her head.

"I've gotten fond of Emmy," he said, reminiscing, "she's like a daughter to me and she's gone most of the time with work and going to college and dating Manolo. She has a good heart, but she had some tough teenage years. She just needs a little bit of guidance and a lot of love. And of course, her annoying persistence has brought you and me back together. I'm grateful to her."

Jenna nodded. "We should give her a home as long as we can."

"Yes." He remembered the accident that had brought Emmy and him together. *Accidents.* He wondered about them. *Were they really accidents or synchronicities—moments in life to halt our routines, to shake us awake, to give us an opportunity for change?*

Four

Baatar never thought arranging a wedding would be a big deal, not in America. In Mongolia, it was a big affair, involving not only two families, but often two clans, over great distances. Parents chose the spouse and arranged the marriage. Rituals abounded. The groom's brothers or other male family members visited the bride's home to bribe her and her family with gifts. A new *ger,* a round, tentlike home, for the couple was built. The bride and her clan traveled to the groom's home, which often could be reached only on horseback. The journey could take several days. Traditional Buddhist ceremonies were performed, a sheep slaughtered, and families gathered for a huge feast. Lingering celebrations followed.

Things hadn't changed much in remote places. But in the capital, Ulan Bator, modern marriages now took place at a wedding palace or a restaurant. City life was different, not the way life was when Baatar grew up on the Mongolian steppe with his nomadic family.

He'd imagined a quiet wedding getaway with Jenna, just him and her and a couple of friends. But she'd made her point that one couldn't elope with a woman of Puerto Rican and Mexican descent. Family was important and was to be included, family on both sides.

He called his parents, speaking with both his mother and his father, inviting them to the wedding.

"We'll get you and your wife traditional Mongolian clothing," his father said sternly and as a matter of fact. "She can bring her family. We'll make room. We'll help you with gifts for her parents. We'll slaughter a sheep and have lots of roasted mutton and *airag*, fermented horse milk, passed around the circle of family and friends. We'll build a new *ger* for you and your wife, and you can stay."

"Come home, Baatar," his mother pleaded. "It's been too long. Raise a family here with us."

Baatar took a deep breath. "I won't return to Mongolia," he explained patiently. "My life is in America, but I'd like you to come to my wedding, here in California. I'd like you to meet Jenna, see how we live. I'll pay for your trip. I'll pay for everything. Please come."

Eventually, reluctantly, they agreed.

Jenna had an easy, joyful call with her dad who was delighted and eager to attend the wedding. While Jenna's mom had passed, her aunts, uncles, and cousins were a lively bunch with lots of ideas and helpful suggestions of their own.

After their calls, Baatar and Jenna went into the sunny backyard and sipped refreshing iced tea.

"My mom's sister has a strong personality," Jenna shared. "She insists my mom would have wanted a Catholic wedding for me in a church, preferably in Texas. My dad's brother suggested we all come to Puerto Rico, and my mom's other sister would like us to marry in New Mexico."

"My parents expected me to marry, if not a Mongolian woman, at least in Mongolian style," Baatar said, "wearing traditional Mongolian clothing, with family members singing, dancing, and eating roasted mutton, with lots of *airag* being passed around the circle of guests."

"What?" Jenna asked, and they both chuckled.

"Jenna," Baatar said, taking her hand in his. "We're not

eighteen anymore, and our marriage wasn't arranged by our families. We marry because we love one another, not to keep up family traditions or cultural rituals. Let's do it our way."

Jenna smiled. "Yes, we'll do it our way."

Emmy came home late from class and saw the two still sitting in the backyard.

"Evening," she said, and plopped down on the grass next to Bruno. He barely lifted his head, sniffed Emmy, and rolled onto his back. She began to rub his belly, smiling.

"You're milking it, Bruno," she said. His eyes closed. He was relaxed, breathing contentedly, rocking gently from side to side with the circular movement of Emmy's hand on his belly.

The round, yellow moon with its shadowy landscape against the dark sky was a reminder of ancient stories of the man in the moon and gave the evening a dreamy atmosphere.

Emmy looked at the couple, and for a fleeting moment, saw a woman standing behind Jenna. She was shorter than Jenna, perhaps five foot two. Her black hair had streaks of red in it. She wore a dark red dress with a V-neck and small buttons down the front. She had creases on both sides of her mouth. Her eyes were hazel. She wore thick, dark-green eyeshadow and bright-red lipstick. Her hands touched Jenna's shoulders as she smiled down on her.

Emmy stared at the woman, intrigued. Then Emmy's eyes focused back on Baatar and Jenna, and the image of the woman faded.

"What's the matter?" Jenna asked. "You look like you've seen a ghost."

"I...uhm...I just...I think I just saw your mom."

Emmy described the woman she'd seen.

"That sounds like her," Jenna said. "She loved to wear makeup and color her hair. She always wore bright-red lipstick and dark red was her favorite color. Did she say anything? Did she give you a message?"

Emmy shook her head. "She just stood behind you with her hands on your shoulders, like she's watching over you. She loves you."

"I love her, too," Jenna said. "I'm so happy to know she's around. She knows I'm here now."

Emmy nodded. "It's nice to know the connection is still there."

As the week continued, Baatar and Jenna worked on their wedding preparations. Telling their families of their decision for the ceremony incited arguments and strong expressions of disappointment, followed at last by acceptance. Mario was to be Baatar best man, and Amelia Jenna's maid of honor. Amelia's son, Damdin Jr., now called DJ for short, was going to be the ring bearer.

Baatar's brother, still living a nomadic lifestyle, couldn't come. He couldn't leave a semiwild horse herd roaming the country by itself. Life couldn't be left to chance, not in Mongolia.

While wedding preparations occupied Baatar and Jenna's evenings, Baatar connected with Emmy at the racetrack stables during breaks.

"Baatar," Emmy called out, as he walked through the barn.

"How's it going?" he asked.

"Cody asked me to brush this mare here by the name of Beautiful Sunrise. I noticed she has a couple of rough patches on her coat, right here on the side. What causes that?"

Baatar stepped into the stall. He ran his hand over the

horse's coat, then ran his fingers down the first and last ribs on both sides. The mare lifted her right hind leg and stomped her foot.

"Could indicate abdominal pain," he said. "Make sure to tell Cody or the trainer if they haven't noticed it yet. They may want Gloria to check her out."

"What causes that?" Emmy asked again. "These horses are so well taken care of."

"Could be diet," Baatar said, "too much stomach acid, maybe an ulcer. Could be stress."

"Really?"

Baatar stroked the horse's neck. "Beautiful mare," he said, when he noticed Emmy's questioning eyes still glued on him. "You know that in the wild or on the pasture, horses graze all the time," he explained. "For you and me, our stomach produces acid only when we eat. For a horse, it's constant. When they eat, the food mixes with saliva, and that buffers the stomach acid. But when horses are stalled, the eating pattern gets disrupted. They may get two or three meals a day, and there are times in between where the stomach gets empty, but it still produces acid, which attacks the stomach lining or causes acid reflux, just as it can in people."

"Isn't that why we use the slow feeders?" Emmy asked.

"Yes, but as I said, there can be many reasons: stress, being hauled from racetrack to racetrack, a new stall, new smells, a new training schedule, loss of a stable mate she liked, or perhaps an injury—it could be anything."

Emmy nodded. "Stress, huh?"

"Now you understand why I like to have at least three trained ponies as catch horses for our work on the racetrack," Baatar said. "It's good to have backup and be able to switch them around—have two at the racetrack, one always on standby, while the others get a break for a while. We observe our ponies daily. When one develops a sore spot or becomes more rigid, or more sensitive, that's an indication that it needs a break. Each pony gets tired of working every day, you know. Then we take it back to the herd so it can remember what it's like to be a horse, to relax. In the pasture, it can graze all day in a natural environment. We take it for rides out in the country to feel the earth under its feet, smell trees, brush, meadows, nature."

"Like a vacation," Emmy said.

"Exactly. Time to recharge. When they've had time to relax, they rebound and are ready to work hard again."

Baatar turned as he heard Cody approach with Gloria, the stable's vet.

"Baatar," Gloria said with a big smile, "always nice to see my favorite outrider. How've you been?" She touched his shoulder and ran her hand down his arm.

"Fine," he said. "Busy with wedding preparations."

"Wedding preparations? Not yours?"

"Mine," he admitted.

"Who's the lucky woman? Do I know her?" Gloria asked, her eyebrows raised.

"Long-term friend from Texas," he said. "We've dated since before I came here."

"You never said."

A smile hushed across his face. He nodded politely and walked off.

"Getting married." Gloria looked at Emmy. "Did you know that?"

Emmy nodded. "They're in love," she said.

"Aha." Gloria turned to Beautiful Sunrise, checking her eyes, mouth, and coat, then listened to the mare's stomach with the stethoscope. She inquired from Cody what the mare was fed and how often and recommended keeping an eye on her; making her feed high in fiber and fat and low in starch and incorporating quality protein, vitamins and minerals. She also recommended a supplement.

"And if that doesn't work?" Emmy asked.

"Then we'll sedate her lightly and do a gastroscopy," Gloria said.

"A gastroscopy on a horse?"

"It only takes about half an hour to run an endoscope through a nostril down into the stomach," Gloria said.

"And if there's an ulcer?" Emmy asked.

"Then we'll give her medication to block the production of gastric acid," Gloria explained.

"You'd just give her a pill, like a person?"

Gloria laughed. "There's an oral paste that can be given daily, or we could give her an intramuscular injection once a week. After a month, we'd check with the endoscope again to make sure it worked."

"Thanks for the explanation," Emmy said.

"Lots to learn," Gloria said with a smirk, "if you want to become a vet."

Emmy took a deep breath and began cleaning the next stall. Being a vet would be fulfilling, she told herself, being able to help horses stay healthy and well. She mused about her role as a veterinarian at a racetrack, checking on thoroughbreds and ponies alike. She imagined herself carrying a medicine bag, but she wouldn't be as snippy as Gloria was so often, or would she? *What if someone else made eyes at Manolo in front of her? What if he became interested in someone else?*

"*Emmy.*" She heard her mom's voice and looked up. She noticed that the gate to Beautiful Sunrise's stall had become unlatched and the horse was already pushing against it to get out and roam. Emmy quickly pushed the mare back into the stall, bracing her thumb and index finger around the horse's face, about a hand's width above her nostrils, as Manolo had shown her. The mare obediently walked backward, and Emmy quickly secured the latch.

"Thank you, Mom," she whispered.

Back at home, Baatar and Jenna's wedding preparations continued.

In anticipation of Baatar's parents' arrival, Emmy, Manolo, and Jenna learned some basic Mongolian terms: *hello, yes, no, are you hungry, are you thirsty, bathroom, warm, cold, sleepy, thank you.* They practiced together, much to Baatar's amusement. It was a difficult language to learn, and it didn't help that it was written in either a squiggly traditional Mongolian script or Cyrillic, Russian script, none of which any of them could decipher. The rolling of the 'r' with the tongue came easily to all three, since they spoke Spanish, but some sounds deep in the throat were otherworldly. The word thank you alone was a tongue breaker: *Buy-rrrr-lala.* All three walked the hallways practicing.

Jenna made a thick quilt, with lots of batting inside, for Baatar's parents, with themes of horses and mountains and rivers, something useful they could take home. Mario's wife, Maria, and her girls made bolos, small bags made out of silk and white lace, filled with a horse charm for Baatar's background, a spindle for Jenna, and chocolate kisses. Each place setting would have a bolo for the wedding guests.

"What colors should we chose for the wedding?" Jenna asked.

Baatar looked at her with a blank expression on his face. "Colors?"

"For the decorations and the bride's bouquet," she explained.

"Oh."

"I love white," Jenna said, "not just for the dress.

White to me represents humility, sincerity, peace—all the elements that I think are important to bring into a marriage. Do you have a favorite color?"

"Blue," Baatar said.

Jenna smiled. "Why blue?"

"It's the color of the sky and the ocean, nature," he said. "In Buddhism, it represents tranquility, healing, and wisdom."

"Blue it is," Jenna said.

Emmy spent the evening quietly in her room, studying. She was grateful she could go to college. She crawled into bed and pulled the red-and-white striped comforter all the way to her neck when she heard a slight scratch on the bedroom door.

"Bruno?" She let him in, and he jumped onto her bed. Together, they fell asleep.

She dreamed of moving again. There were boxes stacked up in her room, filled with her books and papers and clothes. One box contained her photo album and candles. Her rug was rolled up and tied together, her comforter and pillow neatly folded up.

She'd be moving. She knew it without a doubt. Of course, she'd have to move. She couldn't expect Baatar and Jenna to share their two-bedroom house with her forever. She sighed, fighting back tears, as she stroked Bruno's head.

***

A day before the wedding, Baatar picked up his parents at LAX.

"I've got to go, love," he said and kissed Jenna. "I hope my parents won't be too much of a burden, living in our home with us."

"It's only for a week and if they're anything like you, I can't imagine them being a burden. After all, they made you. I'll get their room ready."

They had purchased a couple of extra mattresses to accommodate the visitors.

Baatar smiled and took off in a luxury rental car. He couldn't pile his family into the truck he used to pull a horse trailer. He drove to the airport alone, knowing they'd be chatting in Mongolian, and Jenna would feel left out. He waited in the reception area for quite some time, scanning the crowds arriving at the International Terminal from many different countries. He remembered there were long lines for customs and immigration.

Finally, he saw them and walked toward them. They looked tired. His mother cried as she hugged him tightly. He was surprised to see his sister, Narangerel.

It felt awkward, greeting them here in America. They wore Mongolian attire, a long overcoat called a deel. His father's was made of thick cotton; his mother's was made of silk, each tied with an embroidered sash. They looked so out of place. They'd never understood why he had left Mongolia.

Baatar stowed away their luggage, and they got seated in the car. "How was your trip?" he asked.

"Long, very long," his father said.

"Being in an airplane," his mother said, "was very scary. It rattled and sped upward like a rocket, and I thought it would burst. My ears got clogged up, and then I looked out the tiny window by my seat, and I saw the entire city below us. I could see the row houses and big, tall buildings, and the long gray streets, carved through them. Beyond, on the outskirts, were *ger* cities, one *ger* next to another, looking like round, UFO platforms from the sky. There was a lot of gray air, all misty, covering the city as though it wanted to make it obscure."

"Pollution," his father said.

"Then we flew higher and higher and pierced the gray air, and there was sunshine and blue sky. It was unbelievable."

"A long, long flight," his father said.

Driving down the ten-lane freeway, their eyes widened, watching the mega-size bulletin boards, the housing, and infrastructure so unlike Mongolia—the palm trees, standing tall like spires, with their leaves waving in the wind like greeting hands. The sun was midway on its circular journey across the horizon, illuminating the vast, flat, urban sprawl from LA to Long Beach and all the way through Orange County.

"The seats were uncomfortable," his mother continued, "but seeing you was worth the suffering." She updated Baatar on life at home, living in the city of Ulan Bator, the horse herd still kept by his brother on the steppe, his wife, and kids.

Baatar's sister, Narangerel, was quiet.

Baatar told them about Jenna, how they'd first met, how he'd fallen in love with her warmth and uncomplicated charm, how he'd lost touch when his friend Damdin had died, and how he and Jenna had gotten reacquainted this year through lots of prodding from Emmy. He couldn't wait to get them all introduced.

"But you already know all about them from my phone calls," he said.

His parents nodded and smiled, and said they looked forward to meeting everyone. His sister was listening, quietly.

Jenna had agreed to let Baatar's family stay at the house, although it was small and would feel cramped. She understood that a nomadic family wouldn't stay at a hotel in a foreign country, unable to communicate. After all, it was only for a few days. It didn't take much to persuade

Emmy to stay with Manolo for the week, also cramped, but neither of them was unhappy over the decision.

As Baatar arrived at home with his Mongolian family, he excitedly introduced everybody: Jenna and Emmy, his parents and sister, and, of course, Bruno.

Jenna and Emmy stuttered their newly learned Mongolian hello: *San Ban Oh.* Then there was complete silence. Jenna and Emmy reached out with hugs, which his parents didn't expect and stiffly endured. His sister shrieked back. She looked at Jenna as if she wanted to eat her alive.

Surely, Jenna thought, *that one's a dragon.*

Baatar looked in the circle and forced a smile.

"Let's sit and serve some cool beverages," he suggested. "I'll get the luggage."

The only one not awkward was Bruno; Baatar's parents and sister insisted he didn't belong in the house, but should be outdoors, and Baatar patiently explained that living arrangements in America were different. The dog was part of the human family.

Narangerel was wearing a wool dress, much too warm for California temperatures. Jenna took her aside and offered her various dresses but Narangerel shook her head. Only when Baatar stepped in, did she finally choose one of Jenna's soft cotton summer dresses, one of Jenna's favorites.

Jenna watched as Narangerel put it on and paraded the dress in front of her parents with a smile, then struck Jenna again with one of those I'll-eat-you-alive looks. *I'll have to launder that dress a few times to remove the evil,* Jenna thought, as she smiled at the intruder.

They all spent the evening in the backyard, where Baatar grilled steaks and translated back and forth, answering questions and giving explanations. They served the steaks with rice, tomatoes and cucumbers, vegetables Baatar's family knew and liked. The fresh baguette with butter was a big hit. They all loved Jenna's iced tea, and Baatar's father tried some tequila but admitted he much preferred *airag*, of which he'd brought two bottles along.

Throughout the evening, Jenna perceived that Baatar's mother was needy, needing Baatar's presence, his attention, and his opinion on everything. His sister was clearly a dragon. His father was quiet. Luckily, the wedding took place the very next day.

Jenna fell into Baatar's arms late at night when everybody had finally settled in. He didn't need words from her nor an explanation. He'd been watching the interactions and held her tightly.

"Jenna, my love," he whispered in her ear, "thank you for your patience. You're the number one in my life; you always will be."

"Has your sister always been a bit...sullen?" Jenna asked.

"No," Baatar said. "I'm surprised. She was a happy child. We rode together for hours. She loved her life. I wonder what happened. I've noticed she's not very friendly."

"Maybe she has a nasty husband," Jenna said.

"I don't know," Baatar pondered. "She's not said much since her arrival."

"Perhaps you should talk to her, see if you can help," Jenna suggested. "Give her a good experience while she's here."

"Yes, after the wedding."

"She looks at me as though I've kidnapped her children," Jenna said.

"I'm sorry. I'll talk to her," Baatar said. "Now, let's forget about the visitors and just be there for each other, shall we?" He smiled at her.

They'd just gotten cozy when there was a shriek, followed by hurried steps in the hallway. Their bedroom door flung open and Narangerel stood in the doorframe. She launched into a long, irritable speech in her gibberish that Jenna couldn't decipher. She stared at Baatar, then spewed more sparks in Jenna's direction.

Baatar said a few calm words in Mongolian to his sister, got up, and followed Narangerel, while Jenna watched. He returned with Bruno's bed and water dish and placed them on the floor in the master bedroom. Bruno stood behind him, his tail wagging.

"What happened?" Jenna asked.

"Bruno went to snuggle with Narangerel the way he does with Emmy," Baatar explained. Narangerel said she'd put him out the front door or I should lock him up. I told her the dog was a part of the family, as I've explained before. She was furious."

Turning to Bruno, he said, "you'll stay here with us for the next few nights, OK? You've done nothing wrong." He rubbed the dog and Bruno settled down in his own bed.

Baatar walked to the bedroom door and turned the lock. "I've never had to use this lock before," he said. He smiled at Jenna and crawled back in bed, hugging her tightly. "Now, where were we?"

Five

Emmy hadn't seen Savannah for a while because she'd chosen not to spy on Manolo any longer while he ponied. It came as a surprise to see Savannah stroll through the stables one morning.

"Savannah," Manolo said, when he saw her approach, "I'd like to introduce you to my girlfriend, Emmy."

"Hi!" Savannah said, inspecting Emmy, who had just put a rake full of manure on a cart. "You work here, too?"

Emmy nodded. "Hi, Savannah."

"Emmy's gonna be a vet," Manolo said, proudly.

"Really? That's cool," Savannah said. "I'm not sure I could handle treating injured or sick horses. I'll just ride them and leave the rest to others." She held a booklet from Harvard in her hands.

"Are you in college?" Emmy inquired, pointing at the booklet.

"I'll be heading to Harvard in the fall," Savannah said.

"Excellent school," Emmy said. "Have you chosen a major?"

"I like communication," Savannah said, "maybe journalism. My dad would like me to study international relations or business. We'll see. I'll probably go to England for a year, too. We still have some land there, and they've got horses there, too."

"Right," Emmy said as though she knew. "You're really beautiful; you look royal."

Savannah laughed. "Thanks! My grandfather in

England was an earl, so we have some of that family history. Anyway, I'll see you around," Savannah said and did her hair toss, glancing at Manolo to make sure he noticed.

"See," Manolo said, picking up the cart of manure to take it outside, "she isn't all that bad."

"I wish her good luck at Harvard," Emmy said, tossing her hair back with her chin lifted in the air.

Manolo laughed. "You girls!"

He introduced me as his girlfriend, Emmy thought. *Now it was official.*

With Baatar's parents going to occupy Emmy's room, Manolo offered for her to spend the week with him at his parents' house in Hillside Ranch, even if his room was tiny. They'd been getting closer lately, just the way Emmy had hoped, and she happily accepted his offer.

"Will you help me move?" Emmy asked when they were working side by side at the stables. "I feel this inner pressure to move. I keep dreaming about it."

"Sure," Manolo said. "Look at it as a new opportunity, meeting new people, making new friends. Sometimes it's good to get out of your comfort zone."

"Why do you say stuff like that?" she asked. "I hate changes, hate them!" She stomped her foot like a two-year-old while Manolo watched her silently. He took a black gelding and led him outside to give him a bath. He soaped him up good without looking up. Traces of the goopy soap trickled down the horses' flanks until Manolo washed them down with the hose.

Emmy sat down on a bale of hay in the barn. She didn't mean to be cross with Manolo. He'd done nothing wrong. She was mad at things shifting when they'd just become good. And she didn't want to hear stupid sayings like, "getting out of your comfort zone is good for you." It'd never been good for her. Ever!

Manolo allowed life to happen, she realized. He was too patient and easygoing. *How could anybody be like that?*

There were times when she got steaming mad at him for being quiet and accepting. He had a stillness about him that could drive her crazy. Why didn't he get upset at distressing situations? She'd even thought of walking out on him once if he weren't so handsome and kind and funny. He was a gentle soul. Rare. He was special.

She took a deep breath and walked out of the barn, taking a stance opposite the gelding, facing Manolo. He acted as if he didn't see her.

"I'm sorry," she said, pouting.

He glanced at her, across the horse's back, then focused back on the spray of water that bounced off the horse's coat, slowly trickling all the way down into the gutter.

"I said I'm sorry," Emmy said more loudly, staring at Manolo now, waiting for an acknowledgment of her peace offering.

He nodded slightly and continued hosing down the horse.

When Manolo closed the nozzle and placed it on the ground, Emmy turned and stomped off. With few steps, he caught up with her and gently touched her arm.

"Why are you upset?" he asked. "You said you want to move. There's always good and bad in a situation."

Emmy stood still, looking at him with her big brown eyes. Her long black hair was pulled back into a ponytail, a few strands clinging to her cheeks, blown there by a quick breeze and sticking to her sweaty face.

"Not always," she whispered, defiant.

"Come here," Manolo said, and held his arms wide open. He stepped closer. She looked at him and hesitated, then fell into his embrace. Another thing she loved about him. He didn't hold a grudge. He was an open book, which didn't mean he couldn't drive her nuts more than her dad ever had, or that older brother she'd imagined when she was young. That one had been perfect.

"I don't want to move," Emmy said. "I know I have

to, but I don't want to. I'll miss Baatar and Bruno and even Jenna."

"They're not going anywhere, Emmy," Manolo said gently. He looked at her, gently wiping the hair from her face. "You can see them anytime; you know that. And with the two married and wanting to get pregnant…" He didn't finish the sentence, just let it hang in midair. Emmy understood the rationale, all the justifications. But her heart wept.

People didn't understand. Change had meant the death of her parents and sister. Change had meant being shoved from one foster family to another. Change had meant having horrible, obnoxious, stealing Verena for a roommate. Change had meant living on the streets when foster care ended. Change was bad and frightening. There was nothing good about it.

"Am I too clingy?" she asked, lifting her head and staring into Manolo's eyes. She noticed the small mole on his cheekbone. She'd seen it a million times and still marveled at how perfectly it'd been placed on his boyish face, seemingly by accident, just to make one look at him more closely.

"You've had some tragic losses in your life," he said. "Of course, you don't want to be separated from people you've become fond of."

"So, you think I'm clingy?"

"I didn't say that." Manolo sighed quietly.

"You didn't say I wasn't either."

"Emmy," Manolo said, gently embracing her face with his hands, and looking straight into her eyes, "you're not clingy. You've become attached to Baatar and Bruno. Heck, I'm attached to them, too. They're very attachable people."

Emmy laughed. "Bruno's a dog."

"Dog, person, horse—you know they're all the same to me."

Emmy smiled. She reached up and gave Manolo a kiss. "I know." *Another reason why she loved him. She should make a list.*

Together they brushed down the gelding and moved him back into his stall.

"Let's go to Hillside Ranch for lunch," Manolo offered. She smiled. "OK."

In the car, they talked about the horses and their owners, the new racetrack rules, Manolo's training schedule with the ponies at home, and Emmy's classes. Manolo parked the car. They made sandwiches in the kitchen and headed upstairs to his room.

"We could talk to my parents, see if you could move in with us," he said, knowing full well Emmy was still mulling over the move in her head.

She looked at him. She didn't want to move in with *us*, she wanted to move in with *him*. But she knew it was too soon. Their love was too young. *Could love be too young?*

"There's not enough room," she responded, logically. "Your sisters already share a room, and your room is like a small closet." She scanned the few pieces of furniture, squeezed into these four walls. A twin bed, a tiny desk, tall bookshelves overloaded with books and magazines, a small, built-in two-door closet. They usually sat on the twin bed together or on the floor, with their legs pulled up. Sometimes they shared the bed, but it was tight. It wasn't a permanent solution.

There'd always been room for her at her own home way back when, a room planned to include her, to share with her sister. Memories—she loved them, and she hated them. They reminded her of what life could be like, with love and comfort and taking things for granted.

Manolo looked at his room and then at Emmy. "Yeah, I know, it's tiny."

"And Baatar's house is now too small for me to stay," Emmy said. "When I'm a vet, I'm gonna have a big house. Huge! One that'll have room for everybody, like a church."

Manolo put his arm around Emmy's shoulder. "We could build a room in the barn," he pondered.

Emmy looked at him. She knew he meant it.

"I'm not a horse. I'll have to look at the roommate ads," she said, when she saw a piece of paper on his desk with dates circled. She picked it up.

"You've got your confirmation from the farrier school?" She looked at him. "When were you going to tell me?"

"I told you a month ago," he said. "That's just the official paper."

Emmy folded it and placed it back on the desk. "How long will you be gone?"

"Only two months, remember? There are programs that last longer. I opted for a short program."

"Two whole months," Emmy said, her eyebrows shooting up, putting wrinkles on her forehead, her eyes ready to jump at his throat.

"Emmy, I'm gonna be just a bit up the coast."

"Five hundred miles up the coast, and I won't see you for two whole months." Her forehead relaxed, her eyes became darker, a shadow fell over her face.

"My parents often don't see each other for a few weeks," Manolo said.

"Your parents have been married for umpteen years and have raised five kids. You and I, we don't have that kind of history."

"Look," Manolo said, touching her chin with his hand, "I'm committed to you. Besides, I'll be surrounded by guys, horses, hammers, nails, iron shoes. It's not gonna be a romantic trip to meet girls."

The slightest of grins hushed over Emmy's face, momentarily. "You don't understand. I need you. Closely. I'm already losing Baatar."

"Even if you move, you'll still be in the same town, you still work at the racetrack three days a week, you'll still see him all the time."

"Whatever. You know what I mean. I'm losing my home all over again. I can't lose you, too."

"Emmy." Manolo took a deep, slow breath. "I get that.

But you can't let your history overshadow your life. Baatar and Jenna are going to be married. *You* brought those two back together. They love you. They call you their lucky star."

"Yes, and they asked me to move out."

"I believe you offered."

"It's getting too crowded." Emmy sighed.

"We'll find you a great new place to live, where you feel happy and make new friends. It's an opportunity, not a sentence," Manolo said. "Right?"

Emmy smiled. "You're right. See why I need you? You can put things in perspective for me. You see pink when all I can see is gray."

Manolo reached over and kissed her.

"And that," Emmy said. "I'm gonna miss that."

Manolo smiled, snuggled closer and then tickled her until tears ran down her face.

"That's what I like," he said, "you laughing." He gave her one of those boyish smiles, all smug and charming and irresistible.

Six

Baatar's house felt like an international hostel. Everybody was getting dressed in their fancy clothing amid a breakfast of noodles and meat. Phones rang and were answered; friends stopped by for last-minute directions. Somehow, miraculously, everybody made it to the wedding venue on time.

Jenna had chosen a beautiful, serene, secluded backyard in the country that offered a modern-day greenhouse turned wedding venue. It was large enough to seat fifty people, twenty-five on each side, with a walking path in between. The greenhouse was made of wood, painted white, with large floor-to-ceiling windows all around. White beams met at the center, above the aisle, giving it the feel of a small chapel.

The greenhouse was adorned with white daffodils, daisies, blue roses, and hydrangeas. Flower garlands in white and blue were draped along both sides of the aisle. The fragrance was heavenly. The big windows were covered with white transparent chiffon. White and blue balloons were tied at the entrance and white lanterns had been placed on each side of the center aisle.

There were lots of hand signals, people bowing, hands being shaken, until the guests were all seated. The best man, Mario, together with Jack, Cody, and Manolo were waiting on one side of the altar, across from Amelia and the bridesmaids: Maria, Emmy, and Trisha. The priest awaited the couple.

Baatar walked down the aisle on a white rug with both his parents by his side, who wore their traditional Mongolian attire: long coats made of silk, colorful and beautifully embroidered, and special for the occasion. In Mongolia, his father would have led the wedding ceremony, but he had gracefully agreed to step aside. The white rug, however, was a must, symbolizing that the marriage would be pure as horse milk, the staple of the nomadic life.

Baatar wore a black suit and white shirt with a silver tie, the first time in his life he'd ever dressed in a suit. He felt awkward. He'd much rather have worn his blue jeans and black leather jacket, but Jenna wouldn't have it. His stomach felt hollow, his heart beat faster than usual, his eyes were focused on the back of the greenhouse.

A hush went through the crowd when Jenna arrived. Her dress was magnificent, white lace upon white lace over a white silk underskirt, perfectly hugging her body. The dress showed her tanned shoulders and in the front, her cleavage. She looked like an angelic being, as she slowly floated down the aisle, her dad by her side, while a piano played the traditional wedding song in the background. Her black hair was sophisticatedly pinned up under a lacy veil. She carried a bouquet of flowers, white and blue, to match the chapel's decorations. She also carried a fan, a Puerto Rican tradition symbolizing good luck. Her father's face was somber.

When Jenna arrived at the altar, her father went to the side to sit, and Jenna handed her bouquet of flowers to Baatar's mom, who gave her a big smile. The priest spoke a few introductory words about the value of marriage and motioned for the couple to exchange their vows. Just then his mother got up, placed the bouquet of flowers into his father's lap and ran outside.

Baatar looked concerned. He looked at his father who motioned for him to wait. They waited patiently until his mother rushed back to her seat a few minutes later and took the flowers back to hold them. She smiled at the couple.

Jenna reached out her hands to Baatar and he gently held them in his.

"I believe," she said, looking at Baatar and not seeing anyone else at that moment, "that every good and unexpected gift is given to us from above. You, Baatar, are such a gift to me. You're my soulmate, the one to whom I can reveal the innermost secrets of my life. With you, I feel sheltered." She took a deep breath. "I promise to cherish you always," she said, her voice shaking, "to embrace you with patience and understanding in good times and bad, in sickness and in health. I look forward to discovering together the mysteries of our lives, our different backgrounds, and the intricacies that make us who we are. I promise to keep your heart safe. I give you my love, myself, and all of me. You, Baatar, are the love of my life."

Baatar didn't take his eyes off her. He couldn't have, even if he wanted to. He felt as though he was in a different world, transformed, filled with light. He squeezed Jenna's hands and then his eyes. His lips puckered slightly. He cleared his throat and swallowed and took a deep breath.

"Jenna," he said, "today I promise you my love. I promise to dedicate myself completely to you with body, speech, and mind. I embrace our differences. I shall know myself as you, and you as me. I will care for you and respect you. I will forgive any hurt and be responsible for my actions. My senses are filled with your beauty, endlessly. I bow deeply before you. May our love be never-ending."

There were sniffles in the audience, tissues were silently being exchanged, eyes wiped quietly. A woman blew her nose. The priest looked at the best man for the rings. Mario motioned toward the back of the chapel.

On cue, a little two-and-a-half-year-old boy, dressed in white, began to slowly march down the aisle, proudly smiling to the people on both sides. On his little extended forearms, he carried two wedding bands placed on a light blue, velvet pillow.

Once again, Baatar's mother stood up and rushed down the aisle to leave the ceremony. Turning his head and watching her, instead of his steps, DJ tripped and fell on the white rug. The crowd breathed in deeply. Baatar's mother was gone.

DJ stood up, picked up the rings off the floor and held them tightly, one in each hand. He kicked the velvet pillow aside and ran full speed the rest of the way, fully focused on his destination. People giggled, including Jenna and Baatar.

At the altar, DJ proudly held both rings up to the priest, who asked him to give them to Baatar and Jenna. DJ obliged.

Just then, Baatar's mother returned, rushing back to her seat. Baatar glanced at her for a moment and she shrugged her shoulders apologetically.

The couple exchanged the rings and the priest announced, "You may now kiss the bride."

Baatar gently removed the veil from Jenna's face. They looked deep into each other's eyes and kissed.

DJ sat down next to Amelia and his stepdad, Wyatt.

The priest stepped aside, and a Mongolian Buddhist officiary took his place, greeting the couple. He washed their hands with blessed water as a symbol of coming clean into the relationship. He then addressed the couple, as well as the crowd:

"The need for love is universal," he said. "It is the foundation of human existence. We give and receive. We live and die. Life is circular, just as the rings this couple has exchanged form a circle."

He looked at Jenna and Baatar. "Cherish the good," he said. "The Buddha said, 'in the end, only three things matter: how much you loved, how gentle you lived, and how gracefully you let go of things not meant for you.'"

He put a hand on each of their heads and recited scriptural passages over the couple in Mongolian. He paused and looked at them. "Perfect your kindness and compassion toward all sentient beings," he said. "Be free from hatred and envy. I bless you with health, happiness and a long life."

As the wedded couple walked out of the greenhouse, the crowd clapped and cheered. They tossed rice over the newlyweds as a symbol of good luck, fertility, and abundance. Some rang small bells, dispelling any negativity.

Baatar officially accepted Jenna's last name, Flores, a minor detail he didn't share with his family. Why upset them? Jenna and he had discussed this in detail. Nobody could pronounce or spell his Mongolian last name; people had enough difficulty with his first name. They lived in America, not Mongolia.

Outside, round tables and chairs awaited the guests. Each table was decorated with a floral centerpiece in white and blue, with a white candle in the middle. The white china plates, neatly arranged on the table, contained a bolo for each guest. Jenna walked to each table to light the candles.

Baatar spoke with his mother and learned that the trip and excitement had caused intestinal upset she couldn't quite control. She apologized.

He hugged her. "I'm sorry, why didn't you say something earlier? We'll get you some medicine." He asked Emmy to take care of it, and she and Manolo drove to a nearby pharmacy and delivered the medicine to Baatar's mom.

The wedding feast began with food for all tastes. The crowd was relaxed, perhaps due to the abundance of tequila, vodka, and sangria. Baatar and Jenna danced a traditional waltz, which Mario had taught Baatar at the stables, much to their friends' amusement. Then Baatar danced with his mother, and Jenna with her dad. Soon everybody was dancing. Jenna's dad was a favorite among the ladies.

After the couple cut the wedding cake, Jenna's dad appeared with his saxophone. His music went under the skin, right into the heart. It broke down all language and cultural barriers. An atmosphere of lightness and ease spread through the crowd. Even the waiters and caterers stopped in their tracks to listen.

When Baatar and Jenna finally returned home, to honor his family's traditions, the couple circled their home three times for good luck, before they entered, and jumped over a pile of burning wood in the backyard, symbolizing a blessing by the fire god to make the couple's future as bright as a flaming fire. His parents nodded contentedly.

"I'm a bit tipsy," Baatar admitted, smiling at Jenna.

"Tipsy or drunk?" she asked.

"Tipsy," he said. "I know you never liked me getting drunk."

She smiled as they slipped under the covers together, husband and wife.

***

The next day, Jenna got to spend time with Amelia and

her new husband, Wyatt. She told them how much she had enjoyed DJ's performance at the wedding ceremony. Amelia smiled. Wyatt though wasn't pleased. The boy needed to learn to focus and not get distracted.

"He's only two and a half, honey," Amelia said.

"He's old enough," Wyatt responded with his deep, stern voice.

Amelia and Jenna's eyes met, shortly, and Jenna saw a painful hush cross her friend's face. DJ sat quietly, obediently, not stirring, as was expected by his stepdad.

Mario had invited everybody to his home where Baatar's family got to meet his and Mario's spare ponies as well as Sunny, the white stallion Baatar had chosen as a wedding present for Jenna, who'd been gelded shortly thereafter, and had quickly found his place in the herd. Baatar's father checked out the horses, one by one, and approved of the choices.

Emmy played with DJ who seemed lost in the crowd, being the only toddler. She took him for a walk to the pasture to see the ponies. She liked DJ. He was a little shy but trustingly slipped his little hand in hers. He looked like Damdin, whose picture Baatar had shared with Emmy last year on the Day of the Dead, when she'd put the pictures of her deceased family amid candles on her chest of drawers.

DJ had thick black hair and slightly slanted dark eyes in an oval face. He smiled easily, except, as Emmy had noticed, when his stepdad, Wyatt, approached. Wyatt seemed to be a nice enough man and quite charming, Emmy thought. He was blond and blue-eyed, reminding Emmy of her old boyfriend, Paul. Wyatt was tall and slender, perhaps six foot three. His hair was cut military style. He had a long, thin nose and very thin lips. He was clean-shaven, and his face looked haggard and bony. He had noticeably big hands.

After watching the ponies, Emmy took DJ to play on the swing, Mario had once built for his kids. She'd seen his youngest, Miguel, use it at times. The swing hung from a big oak tree that provided wonderful shade during a warm, sunny California afternoon.

At six o'clock, Wyatt came to pull DJ away. "Enough playtime," he said to the little boy. "Look at your clothes. Your pants are dirty. Shame on you." He took the little boy by the hand and dragged him along, pulling hard on his little extended arm until DJ fell.

"Watch your step!" Wyatt said and slapped DJ on his bottom. DJ looked down and walked faster, as fast as his little legs would permit. Amelia ran after Wyatt, trying her best to catch up on her high heels, and the three left together. Jenna was in the kitchen and didn't get to say goodbye.

Amid the celebrations, Baatar observed his sister. She wasn't the way he remembered her. She'd always been cheerful. He remembered her big smile when they rode together as kids. He remembered how babbly she'd been. Now she sat aside, quietly, her eyes cast downward, her lips closed, her face sullen.

"Talk to her," Jenna encouraged Baatar. "Perhaps there's something that concerns her. Maybe you can help her while she's here."

Baatar took her aside. "Narangerel," he said, "tell me what's bothering you. You've always been so happy. What's wrong? Tell me, please."

"I don't see you in years and now you want to be the understanding brother?"

He looked at her, his eyebrows raised.

"You should've never left," she blurted out. "You hurt us, and look at you now, living in a foreign land, marrying a foreign woman, having children far away from home."

His mouth puckered. "The only thing I regret is that I never told you that I love you," he said.

"Love. You leave those you love?"

"Narangerel, I didn't leave you because I didn't love you. I left because life in Mongolia is harsh and difficult. I wanted to explore if life somewhere else was easier. I didn't leave because of you. I left because of me."

"Selfish."

"Yes, it was selfish," Baatar agreed, "but I don't regret it."

"So, you're still selfish; nothing has changed," she said.

"I have changed," Baatar said calmly. "Life changes us all, don't you think? Each experience, each person we meet, each tragedy has an impact. You have four children. Wouldn't you say each child has taught you something about yourself, about life, something you didn't know before? Perhaps something you didn't expect?"

"I didn't leave home," Narangerel said. "My life's been steady, as expected. I married, I had children, I live close to our parents."

"Are you happy with your life?" Baatar asked.

"Of course I am."

"So am I," he said. "So, we both walked our path and we both were blessed with a good life."

"But you left," his sister said, "just like that."

"Narangerel, I was seventeen. I was a kid. What are you angry about?"

"Nothing. I can't wait to get back home. I don't like your wife or your friends."

"What's not to like?" Baatar asked.

"They're not like us."

"Isn't that the beauty?" Baatar asked. "To meet people who are not like us? To discover something new, something different? To learn new ways and see life from a new perspective?"

"No."

"Life is full of possibilities," Baatar said, "and full of challenges. I'm glad your life gave you what you wanted, and my life is giving me what I want."

"You just took it," Narangerel said.

"You're still angry, and I don't know why. Did I take something away from you?"

"*You*," she said. "You took *you* away from me, from us. Don't you get that?"

Baatar looked at his sister. "I see," he said. He bowed his head and looked down, then looked up straight into her eyes. "Narangerel, why can't you just say that you miss me? Why make it sound like an attack?"

He took her into his arms and held her tightly. "I've missed you, too," he said. "I've missed seeing you grow up. I've missed seeing you fall in love. I've missed seeing you get married and have children. I'm very, very sorry. I'll be better about staying in touch. Do you want to go for a ride?"

She nodded.

Baatar saddled up Sunny, Jenna's horse, and handed him to his sister. He knew Narangerel was an exceptional rider, having grown up with horses just like him. He saddled up Kheer for himself.

They returned after riding and talking for three hours, sharing about their past, their choices, challenges they each met. Afterward, everything about her changed. Narangerel smiled. She rubbed the horses and helped clean them after the ride. She helped feed them. She rejoined the crowd for a barbecue, and the Mongolian family members tried s'mores for the first time in their lives.

Narangerel was chatty. She told her parents all about

her day, and late at night, she called her husband and children.

It was already dark when they all returned to Little Oaks, and Jenna found peace and quiet walking Bruno by herself. She just had to get away for a little while. Having the Mongolian family in the house was, to say the least, annoying. It felt like living in a *ger*. Not that Jenna had experience living in a *ger*, but she thought that's how it would feel.

There were people everywhere, in the living room, in the bathroom, in the hallway, in the kitchen, in the bedroom. There was no privacy, absolutely none. They'd barely knock and step inside. Clearly they weren't used to privacy. The mother was needy, having more questions and concerns than anybody could have, and the sister had been grumpy for days. Only the father seemed quiet and content.

Jenna wondered if that's where Baatar had gotten his stillness—observing the horses in the wild with his father, listening to the sounds of the steppe. If only she could understand their language, Jenna thought, but all she could do was smile and say, hello, are you hungry, are you thirsty? How hungry and thirsty could anyone be? She'd been smiling so much her cheeks hurt. *Only five days*, she kept telling herself. Luckily, they wanted to stay for only five days.

She couldn't relate to the food they liked, the way they drank their tea, nor the way they talked. And *airag* was entirely disgusting; not that she liked vodka or tequila either, but *airag*? An acquired taste, Baatar had explained. Acquired. Admittedly, she couldn't relate to his family. *How could she love her man and despise his family so much? Only three more days.*

Jenna suggested she'd show her father and two aunts, who had decided to stay for a few days, around town and

Baatar agreed. When Jenna left to meet her family, he decided to give his parents and sister a behind-the-scenes tour of the stables and the racetrack facilities and explain his job.

His father immediately got involved, walking the ponies, riding in an unfamiliar saddle, brushing, feeding, cleaning. He carefully and thoroughly examined all the riding equipment, the saddles, the halters, the bridles. "Different material," he said. "Everything's different, but it works." He slapped his son on the shoulder, smiled, and gave him approving nods.

Baatar's mother also loved the ponies and her son's work and asked to see him in action. His family willingly got up with him before four o'clock the next day and accompanied him to the racetrack. While Baatar always had a special bond with Saaral, his gray mare, his father and mother both took a special liking to Tsokhoor. His father joined the exercise riders on Tsokhoor, and Narangerel rode Saaral. Baatar stayed behind with his mother, watching.

"This is the greatest gift you could give them," his mother said. "They've wondered about your work, having only three or four horses. Now they understand. Now we all know how you live. We've worried about you all these years, especially after Damdin died and you returned to a foreign land, all by yourself. We couldn't understand why you'd do that, how you could possibly leave your family, your home, your land."

"Can you understand me better now?" Baatar asked.

"I see you happy, and that makes me happy," his mother said. "I see you found a wife. I'll always miss you, but Jenna is a good woman, and you have good friends. I cannot understand their language, but I can read their eyes. I hope you'll have children." She looked up at the sky and then back at Baatar. "I like the weather."

He hugged her tightly. "Thank you, Mom. I know I've caused you pain. I'm very sorry."

She nodded.

His father and sister returned from exercising the ponies. Before they dismounted, Baatar took several pictures of them. They liked the American saddle, very different but comfortable, they said. They marveled at the racetrack, sending horses in a loop instead of riding cross-country.

"Everything is so urban," Narangerel said. "Big grandstand seating, restaurants, decorations, a designated winner's circle." She took pictures of everything to show her family and friends. Baatar explained the racetrack rules, his job as an outrider, and the betting. Since they all decided to stay at the racetrack for the day, he was happy to dress up in his work attire to join Mario for their outrider duties. He waved at his family from the racetrack, while they sat in the grandstand and watched.

On their last day, Baatar offered to take them on a scenic tour, but all they wanted to do was be with Baatar and his ponies, and stay to observe the crowds that went wild, and listen to the cheers that could top the noise of a county fair. On the drive home, Baatar took the coastal road and stopped at the beach. They all took a walk with their feet in the ocean, and he took pictures.

Meanwhile, Jenna showed her dad and two aunts the marina, the Bazaar del Mundo in Old Town, Coronado Island, Balboa Park, and La Jolla. On their last evening, they decided to dine at the Rockin' Baja Lobster Restaurant in the Gaslamp District.

"Too bad you didn't marry a nice Mexican man," Aunt Aurelia whined. "Somebody who understands your culture."

"Baatar is the most understanding man I've ever met," Jenna said.

"It's best to marry your own kind, sweetie," Aunt Aurelia insisted. "My late husband was such a gentleman."

"Uncle Juan was a womanizer," Jenna stated, annoyed.

"Jenna!" her dad admonished.

"Now, dear, don't you like our Mexican food so much better than that mutton they served?"

"Aunt Teresa, we all love the food we grow up with," Jenna said. "Americans love burgers, we love tamales, Mongolians love mutton. We can't judge others if we've never lived under their conditions, can we?"

"I wouldn't want to live in Mongolia," Aunt Teresa said, "I hear it gets really cold there."

"That wasn't my point," Jenna said.

"I wonder what your children will look like," Aunt Aurelia continued. "Don't you wonder what your children will look like?"

"I think we'll have beautiful children with big hearts and happy smiles," Jenna said.

"There's prejudice, you know," Aunt Aurelia pointed out. "I'm just saying. Kids with slanted eyes, there's prejudice."

"Aunt Aurelia, California isn't the South. People from all over the world call California home. Besides, there's prejudice against Mexicans as well, and blacks, and the poor, and the homeless."

"We're not homeless," Aunt Teresa said, appalled.

"I thought you'd be happy for me," Jenna said, looking in the round, "that I found someone I love, that I found someone who supports me and wants to build a future with me. I'm really disappointed by your attitudes."

"Jenna!" her dad whispered, looking at her sternly, with a fold between his eyes.

They had a couple of drinks, which seemed to ease the tension, and Jenna returned them all safely to the hotel.

Looking back, the week was a blur. There were goodbye hugs and tears when the families left.

"I'll miss them," Baatar said when he returned from LAX.

"Me, too," Jenna said.

"But they are a handful," Baatar added.

"That they are, all of them," Jenna agreed, when there was a knock on the front door.

"Emmy, you have a key," Baatar said when he opened the door.

"You're newlyweds!" Emmy said, looking at the two with a big smile on her face. "Do you have a room available?"

"Yes, we do, and it's all yours."

Emmy quickly moved back into her room—for now. They all had some iced tea together and Emmy shared her experiences with DJ and Wyatt.

"He slapped the little boy for not walking fast enough?" Baatar asked in disbelief.

"Yes," Emmy confirmed. "I couldn't believe it. Maybe he just had a bad day."

"Wyatt or DJ?" Baatar asked.

"Wyatt."

Jenna listened, taking note. She remembered the expression of pain she'd seen on Amelia's face. Perhaps she'd just imagined it.

Quiet returned to the home. Bruno peacefully snored once again in the hallway and on the sofa, uninterruptedly. Jenna and Emmy cleaned the house like never before, and Bruno snuggled next to Emmy at night. Jenna pulled the honeymoon itinerary from the fridge and began to select clothes to take along. She was excited. Alaska awaited. Their new life together could begin.

Seven

Emmy and Manolo took Jenna and Baatar to the airport and promised several times to take care of Bruno and the ponies. They waved goodbye as Jenna and Baatar headed to the terminal for their flight to Alaska.

As planned, the couple flew into Fairbanks. Sleepy from the trip, which lasted all day, they checked in at Pike's Waterfront Lodge, right on the banks of the Chena River. It was the perfect start for an Alaskan vacation. The lobby entrance was inviting with a wood-burning fireplace that created an overall warm, cozy welcome. The lodge had an authentic Alaskan feel to it with original canvas art depicting Alaskan nature scenes. The personnel were friendly. Jenna was delighted at the lodge's décor, including a life-size polar bear.

They had reserved one of the lodge's cabins.

Outside the lodge were quacking ducks by the river, that flowed smoothly at a pace of its own, with a well-visited dog park nearby. The eyes drank in greens in various shades all around—tall, dark green pine trees surrounding juicy meadows any horse would have treasured. The mountains, dark against the blue sky, rose high in the background. The sky was a deep, crisp blue and the air so clean one could see for miles.

Baatar and Jenna had dinner sitting on the restaurant's deck, overlooking the river. It was a picture-perfect setting.

Baatar chose fresh Alaskan salmon, Jenna a different kind of fish, Alaskan-style.

"It was so nice to reconnect with Amelia and DJ at the wedding," Jenna said over dinner. "I miss them. Amelia lived with me, you know. When she realized she was pregnant, she moved in with me. Then she had the baby and they stayed with me for two years. We always joked that little DJ had two moms and no dad."

"So, he's attached to you, too," Baatar said.

"I was like a second mom to him," Jenna reminisced. "A two-year-old can be rambunctious, but I enjoyed every moment of it. He was so curious, had his little hands into everything. He had his stubborn moments, but at the end of the day, all he wanted was to be cuddled and loved. Of course, when Amelia and Wyatt got married, Amelia and DJ moved in with him."

Jenna looked at Baatar. "My house felt so empty. I felt lonely. And then out of the blue, you reappeared and made it all better."

Baatar took her hand in his and squeezed it.

After dinner, on their way back to the cabin, Jenna cleared her throat several times.

"Are you OK?" Baatar asked.

"I'm fine, honey."

They settled in the cabin, decorated with a big dark wooden four-poster and thick white goose-feather bedding. A large picture of grazing moose hung over the bed. Opposite was a big solid dark wooden chest of drawers with a seventy-inch TV. The bathroom was clean and had a shower and a big tub—Jenna's kind of rustic. She lay on the bed and looked at Baatar as he unpacked.

He was a handsome man, a head taller than her, slender and muscular, well-built. His hair was thick and black, and his eyes even darker than hers. They were kind. He wasn't much of a talker, but she'd learned to draw things out of him, and he'd learned that she wasn't a horse and preferred words for communication. She knew his beauty went beyond what she could see.

They took a bath and Jenna kept clearing her throat.

"Jenna," Baatar said, "something's not right."

She touched her throat. "I have this sensation that something's stuck in there," she admitted. "It hurts when I swallow. I thought it'd go away."

"Did you get chilly on the airplane?" he asked.

"No, I was fine then."

"Do you think you're coming down with something? A sore throat?"

"It feels different. There's a sharp pain when I turn my head to the right." She clutched the front of her throat.

"Perhaps we should have it checked out," Baatar said.

"It's past ten, Baatar, and we're in Alaska!"

"We're in Fairbanks. They have emergency rooms here."

"I don't know; I don't want to ruin our honeymoon." She held the front of her throat as she cautiously swallowed, then cleared her throat again.

"Did the fish you ate have bones?" Baatar asked, looking at her.

"Yes, but I removed them."

"Could you have swallowed one?"

"I don't think so." She cleared her throat. "Now I'm getting scared, honey. What if it gets worse, and I can't breathe? And we're way up here!"

He looked at her and studied her face. "Let's have it checked out," he said. He stood up, dried off, and got dressed.

"Now?"

"Yes, now."

Reluctantly, Jenna got dressed.

They drove to a nearby hospital. The emergency room was crowded. There was a man with a wound on his arm that had bled through the bandage, a mother rocking her screaming baby, a constantly coughing teenager, someone with a knee injury, a man with a bleeding head wound, and several people who just sat quietly.

Jenna filled out the paperwork and they sat down on cold, uncomfortable chairs amid the chaos, waiting with the others.

"Maybe it can wait till tomorrow," Jenna said, clearing her throat.

"We're here now."

Two and a half hours later, Jenna was led into a treatment room. A nurse took her vitals, which were normal. The ER physician asked a few questions and looked into her throat, then ordered X-rays be taken. There was a wait for the X-ray machine.

At one thirty in the morning, the doctor returned with the results. He showed Baatar and Jenna that a fish bone had indeed lodged in her oropharynx, and he explained that it most likely would not spontaneously expel or be dissolved. He suggested removing it, and Jenna agreed. She looked at Baatar with fearful eyes.

"I'm right here with you," he said, holding her hand.

She received a local anesthetic and a light sedative medication. The doctor used a video laryngoscope and alligator forceps to remove the fish bone.

While Jenna lay still, Baatar wanted to flee the scene. He hated hospitals, the smell of chloroform mixed with sterilizing cleaners made him nauseous. The medical equipment looked like torture instrumentation; the beeping noises were irritating at best.

He held Jenna's hand and said, "You're doing great,

love," while he stared at the floor. In an attempt not to throw up, he thought of galloping his pony.

"There it is," the physician said and proudly held up the fish bone as if he'd just caught it in a wild stream. Jenna felt immediate relief.

They returned to their cabin around three thirty in the morning.

"I hope this wasn't a bad omen," Jenna said.

"What do you mean?" Baatar asked, uneasy.

"For our trip," she said.

"It was just a fish bone, love, and it's been removed. Everything will be fine. You wear a horseshoe necklace. It brings you luck!"

"Yes, it does," Jenna said, as she sank into the fluffy featherbed and almost immediately fell asleep.

A bad omen, Baatar thought. *Had it been a bad omen?* He'd had injuries up here in Alaska, when Damdin and he were hiking or skiing. His stomach cringed, as he thought of his deceased friend. His mind was taken back to their life together and Damdin's sudden death. Baatar had not been able to talk about his grief for a long time afterward. It had felt like a perpetual lump in his throat. *Perhaps the fish bone incident was an omen after all? Was there something left unspoken between Damdin and him?* He felt a strange sensation, as though his heart skipped a beat, like a twitching muscle, followed by a feeling of dread that flooded his entire body. He took a deep breath, trying to shed those thoughts in a desperate attempt to fall asleep.

But sleep didn't come.

***

Back in Little Oaks, Emmy and Manolo were busy taking care of Baatar's ponies and Bruno. Emmy had Baatar's house to herself, which was nice for a change.

After class, she sat at the dining table checking out room rentals on the *roommate wanted* list online and wrote down a few addresses while Manolo brushed Bruno's scruffy fur.

"What exactly is this guy?" he asked.

"A mutt," Emmy said, not looking up.

"He looks like a wheaten terrier and lab mix, doesn't he?"

"Uhu. Will you check out these places with me?" she asked, showing Manolo the list. "They're all in Little Oaks, which is promising."

"Are you sure you want to do this? Without first asking Baatar?" Manolo asked.

"He's too kind to throw me out," Emmy said. "Believe me, I don't want to move, but I know I have to. My dreams have been very clear."

"OK, if that's what you want to do," Manolo said.

Together, they headed out in his truck. The first target was a room rental in an old neighborhood, by far the most affordable, with no kitchen privileges. The house had been around for some time, witnessed by the large, overgrown trees all around the premises. A thick hedge surrounded the house and it's beige color was fading. A bald man opened the door. He wore slippers and looked unshaven.

"Hi, sir, we're here to answer your ad. You're offering a room for rent?" Emmy asked politely.

"Hattie!" The man disappeared, the door slowly closed on a hinge mechanism. Emmy and Manolo waited patiently. At the last minute, the door swung open again from inside. A tall, sturdy woman looked Emmy up and down, then stared at Manolo.

"The ad says female only," she said.

"Yes, ma'am, I'm the one looking for a room to rent," Emmy explained. "My name is Emmy." She reached out her hand, but the woman didn't budge. Instead, she looked

Manolo up and down, then said sharply, "we don't allow that here."

"What exactly do you mean?" Manolo asked.

"That," the woman said plainly, waving her hand toward Manolo. Looking distinctly at Emmy, she asked, "do you want to see the room?"

Emmy looked at the woman's stern face, her immovable posture, standing in the doorway like a prison guard.

Manolo nudged Emmy to take a look at the room, when Emmy asked the woman, "you mean you don't allow love in your home?" Emmy's voice was friendly, matter-of-fact, curious.

Manolo bit his cheeks.

The woman's shoulders stiffened above her rigid, steel-like spine. Her eyes spewed like fire hoses, her neck froze in place. "How dare you?" she spouted.

"I chose love," Emmy said and smiled. "I hope you find a good match."

Emmy turned and Manolo slipped his hand in hers as they walked to his truck. The entrance door slammed shut behind them with a bang.

"Welcome to prison camp," Emmy said as they sat in the truck. "Would you like to see your cell?"

They giggled. "We don't allow that here," Manolo imitated the woman, waving his hand at Emmy, then leaned over and gave her a kiss on the cheek. "I'm glad you decided against it."

The next address was a townhouse. The area wasn't plush but acceptable, during daylight hours. Emmy knocked on the door and a friendly redhead opened. She was around Emmy's age.

"Hi," Emmy said, "I'm responding to your ad for a roommate."

"We just filled up," the girl said.

"I see," Emmy looked at Manolo, disappointed, and they turned.

"We only have one more address to check on," Emmy said.

They arrived at a larger house, close to campus. It was painted white with blue shutters and a blue front door. A young woman opened the door.

"I'm Carla, please come in. This is my brother, Mark."

"You both live here?" Emmy asked.

"Yes. It's a four-bedroom house and we'd like to have two roommates," Carla explained. "We'll each have our own room upstairs and share the living room, dining room, and kitchen. We even have a washer and dryer. Do you want to see the rooms?"

Emmy nodded and they all headed upstairs. "We have one unfurnished and one furnished room," Carla said. "Your choice."

Emmy looked at Manolo. "I'm sure Baatar lets you have the bed and desk," he said. "They'll need to furnish a nursery sooner or later."

"Do you allow boyfriends to come over?" Emmy asked.

"Sure," Carla said. "Mark's got a girlfriend, too."

"The unfurnished room," Emmy said. She looked at Manolo and he nodded.

"We're all set then," Carla said. "You can move in on the first. We just need the first month's rent to hold your spot."

"Fantastic!" Emmy beamed. She handed Carla the money she'd brought.

She took Manolo's hand as they walked to his truck. He squeezed it. "They seem nice," he said. "Let's celebrate!"

They picked up Bruno and went to the dog beach, where they let him retrieve a wet toy from the ocean over and over, with a big smile on his face.

"I love animals," Emmy said. "They're so carefree."

"They are special," Manolo agreed.

It was the middle of the month, which meant Manolo would be there for only two more weeks before he headed to farrier school. He kept quiet about it, but Emmy counted the days with a very prickly knot in her stomach.

Emmy texted Baatar, attaching a video of Bruno at the beach.

"Thank you, Emmy! Miss you," he texted back.

Eight

The night had been short, a little too short, but Jenna woke up full of enthusiasm. She kissed Baatar good morning and he sleepily opened his eyes.

"How're you feeling?" he asked.

"Great!"

"Is your throat OK?"

"Perfect. I can't wait to get on the road."

He took the hint and got up.

Alaska time seemed slower than California time. Instead of cars on ten-lane freeways rushing by, Baatar and Jenna sat at the breakfast table outside the Pike Waterfront Lodge. They watched the flow of the river, trustingly following its destination without any resistance. Trees stood like guards, protecting its path. Slowly, the couple perused the landscape from their table, watching a moose across the river.

"So, we're heading to Denali"? Jenna asked.

"Right after breakfast," he confirmed. "It's about a three-hour drive."

Jenna dived into the tour book she carried everywhere. *"Denali is the highest mountain in North America,"* she read aloud and looked at Baatar. "Who knew? *The Denali park and preserve is larger than the state of New Hampshire and offers a mix of forest, tundra, and glaciers. In the winter, Denali offers dog sledding, cross-country skiing, and snowmobiling."*

She looked up. "Dogsledding would be fun," she said, with melancholy in her voice, "but I'd rather not be here in the winter."

"It gets pretty cold," Baatar said.

They packed up and headed on the road.

"I can't wait for us to have kids," Jenna said. "I was ready three years ago but then…anyway, there's no reason to wait, is there?"

"I can't think of any," Baatar glanced at her.

"When we have kids, do you think we should find a bigger place to live?" Jenna asked. "I don't mind doing my sewing in the garage for the time being, but if a baby comes along, where are we gonna put him or her?"

"We have plenty of time to think about it," Baatar said, "nine months, right? Once you're pregnant."

"Yes, but I wouldn't want to consider a move while I'm highly pregnant," Jenna said. "My house in Texas is sold and gave us a nice down payment for a bigger place."

"You'd like a bigger place now?" Baatar asked.

"I'm just thinking ahead."

"I have savings, too," Baatar said, "and if we sell my house as well, we can definitely afford something spacious. What would you like?"

"I don't know," Jenna said, "a three-bedroom would be nice, or if Emmy will stay with us, a four-bedroom? One for us, one for her, one for the kids, and an extra one for guests."

"And your sewing projects," Baatar said. "Wouldn't it be nice to have your own space for that? Where you can design and sew at your leisure?"

"Yes, that would be fantastic."

"I like Little Oaks," Baatar said. "It's closer to the ocean than Hillside Ranch and closer to the racetrack. We'll just have to see what's available, what we can afford, and decide how and where we want to live."

Jenna nodded. "I like the idea of being close to the ocean."

"Let's explore the market when we get back," Baatar suggested.

"I'd love that." Jenna didn't mention she already had snooped around online, out of curiosity.

They arrived at Denali National Park and checked in at the Grande Denali Lodge for a private cabin, which was a five-minute trail walk from the main lodge. The cabin was small but sturdy, with log furniture and cedar plank walls, which gave it a rustic feel. The floors were made of wood, with thick carpets on each side of the king-size bed. A window overlooked a small veranda. There was a log-burning fireplace in the room and a small bath with a shower.

"Time for our tour at the sled dog kennels," Jenna said, after they had stopped for lunch at the Black Bear Restaurant. "I can't wait to see them."

They hiked about a mile and a half uphill to reach the kennels.

"Hi, I'm Danny. I'm a ranger and one of the mushers," a young man introduced himself. "Alaskan huskies and rangers work together to protect the park. We call the dogs our bark rangers. Let me show you around."

"We need bark rangers who are smart, people oriented, and hardworking," the ranger explained. "As you'll see, the dogs come in different sizes and colors, but all Alaskan huskies have long legs for breaking trail through deep snow, tough feet, and a thick coat to keep them warm. They have the ability to independently make decisions when they lead a team on a trail. Both the physical and mental characteristics of these dogs are important for success during sledding. We breed one litter of puppies a year."

"How do you train the puppies?" Jenna asked.

"They play with the older dogs and get long daily walks. As winter nears, they get to race on trails. When they're adults, they get mixed with the older dogs to pull a sled. We take them on short trail rides first until their bodies get strong and they learn the trails. In the winter, the dogs pull sleds all the way to the Toklat River."

"How far is that?" Jenna asked.

"About sixty-five miles one way. You can go there by bus in the summer, but in the winter, the roads aren't plowed."

"And the dogs really like to work that hard?" Jenna asked.

"Alaskan huskies are working dogs," the ranger explained. "They love to problem-solve and to find a route on a trail in the winter."

"How do you keep them busy when there's no snow?" Jenna asked.

"During the summer months, we train them for their winter tasks. They learn directional commands, and how to run at a trot. The trot reduces injuries when they cover long distances. Let me show you," the ranger said.

He walked over to one of the dogs. "This is Cookie, one of our seasoned sled dogs." He led her to the training ground. "We train them by running through cones and poles. Look at her gait. It's a beautiful trot, just what we want. Good job, Cookie."

Next he took her to a wobble board. "We train the dogs to balance on these," he said. "When they shift their weight, it causes their wrists and feet to flex. That's a great strengthening exercise for the muscles and tendons."

"I did that exercise once in physical therapy," Baatar said, "when I had injured my ankle."

"Yes," the ranger said, "it's the same concept for us as for the dogs. The stronger our muscles and tendons, the less inflammation and fewer strains we get." He gave Cookie an assuring pet when she jumped off the wobble board.

"Up," he said, and Cookie lifted herself on her hind legs. "This is part of our strength training," the ranger explained. "In this exercise, they use their core to balance on their back legs. That strengthens the chest, back, and hindquarters, and all the muscles they need to pull a sled. This helps prevent pulling injuries. Good job, Cookie."

Next, he had Cookie roll over with her paws sticking up in the air. "And this," he explained, "helps us to examine their paws for soreness or to put on booties when the ground becomes too cold. The booties prevent ice balls from forming between a dog's toes."

Jenna laughed. "That's so cute."

"Yes," the ranger said, "it's cute and very functional, and we try to keep all these exercises fun for the dogs. In the wintertime, we leave home for one to four weeks at a time. On the trail, each dog gets his or her own spot to sleep. They dig into the snow to create their own cozy bed. When they return home to their straw-filled houses, they cherish the luxury after weeks of working on the trails."

They thanked the ranger and hiked back to the Denali Visitor Center.

"I could see you doing something like this," Jenna said, "being a musher."

"Training the dogs would be fun," Baatar admitted, "as would the sled tours. But living in Alaska for good, in this cold climate with its extreme seasons? Would you like that?"

"Absolutely not," Jenna said.

They had a cup of coffee and a snack, and in the late

afternoon, they drove the fifteen miles to Savage River for a walk, during which they saw a great variety of birds, marmots and Dall sheep. Seeing a caribou was the highlight of the drive.

"Are you hungry?" Baatar asked.

"Tired and hungry," Jenna said.

"Me, too."

They headed back to the Denali Visitor Center, listening to the radio, when after a couple of miles, the car slowed, then stopped.

"What's the matter?" Jenna asked.

"I don't know." Baatar popped the hood and examined the engine while Jenna stood next to him. She shivered in fifty-degree weather.

"I think it's the battery," he concluded.

"The battery?" she asked in disbelief. "In a rental car on a remote road in Alaska?"

"It can happen," Baatar said, calmly.

"It can happen? Are you out of your mind?"

"Don't worry, love. I have Triple A," Baatar said. "Let me give them a ring."

He placed the call and was told someone would come out in the next hour or so.

"See," he said to Jenna, "not so bad," when she pointed across the street and expelled a gut-wrenching scream.

Baatar looked up and saw a bear, walking down the road. It was approximately two hundred feet away. It was an adult black bear, alone, perhaps a three-hundred pounder. The bear stopped. Jenna kept screaming.

Baatar covered Jenna's mouth with his hand and dragged her into the car, as though he was going to kidnap her. He shut all windows and doors, and turned to her, putting his index finger against his own mouth. "Let's not startle the bear," he whispered. "Let it mind its own business and walk away. Screaming may trigger an attack. They can be unpredictable."

Staring at the bear, then at Baatar, Jenna whispered, "Don't you ever treat me like that again!"

He looked at her. "I'm very sorry, Jenna," he whispered. "The bear was walking away from us. Your scream alerted it of where we are, and it turned toward us. You've gotta stay calm, love. Bears can run as fast as a racehorse, and we don't have a gun."

"You're telling me we have no defense?" she whispered, still staring at the bear. "Didn't I ask you if going on a road trip to Alaska was dangerous? And you said no!"

"I didn't think a rental car would break down and leave us stranded."

"You didn't think!" she fumed.

"Are we having our first fight?" He observed the bear, then looked at Jenna, then glanced back at the bear.

She didn't respond.

"Please don't be mad at me. I panicked." He looked at her with pleading eyes.

"*You* panicked? *I* panicked."

"Peace?"

"What are we going to do if the bear comes closer?" Jenna asked.

"Being in the car is our best defense," Baatar said.

"And that should calm me down?"

The bear had turned in their direction, moving toward them for about thirty feet. It sniffed, paused, then turned again and walked down the road. They both followed it silently with their eyes for quite some time, until eventually the bear turned into the woods.

Baatar leaned over to give Jenna a kiss and there

seemed to be no objection. He kissed her. Then he kissed her a little more deeply. She put her arms around him and drew him closer, and they forgot all about panic and Alaska and bears, when suddenly there was a bang on the car.

They froze.

They looked at each other. Neither of them budged.

"Need some help?"

A tall, bulky man in his fifties with a long beard down to his chest stared at them through the driver's side window with a big grin.

Baatar opened the window. "Yes, sir, yes. We didn't hear you coming."

The man grinned, looking down on Baatar, as he got out of the car. He stood a head taller than Baatar.

"We'd seen a bear and felt best to hide in the car," Baatar explained.

The man stood and grinned.

"Anyway, I think the battery went dead," Baatar said. "Can you recharge it or tow us?"

"Lemme check." The bulky man stuck his head under the hood. "Best to replace it altogether out here," he suggested. "I have this model in my truck."

He changed the battery while Baatar and Jenna waited, then they followed the man's truck all the way back to the Denali Visitors Center.

The couple stopped at the Alpenglow Restaurant for dinner. The dining room offered spectacular views with daylight available almost around the clock, while they dined on moose burgers with home fries and the house special salad.

"What else can go wrong?" Jenna asked. "Like I said, maybe the fish bone was a bad omen?"

Baatar looked at her. "Let's just trust the bad luck is over," he said and forced a smile.

They ended the day with a romantic two-some that started with a bubble bath, jazz music and a glass of wine. Being in an intimate cabin in Alaska fulfilled what a honeymoon promised. Baatar sat on the bed, opposite her, and took her hands in his. "Your eyes have such a luminosity," he said in a low voice. "They brighten the world and make the sorrows more bearable." He blinked. "Your face reflects the warmth and grace of your soul, and your body the softness with which you walk this earth. It's such a privilege to be with you."

"I'm very happy to be here with you, too," she said, "to build a future together, a family."

"We can start on that right now," he suggested with a smile on his face. He leaned toward her and gave her a long kiss. "Unless you've got something else planned."

"Planned?" Jenna asked. "We're in a cabin in Alaska, alone." She looked at him. "I assume we are alone without any beasts lurking around in the dark? And I've always wanted a little Sophie."

"A Sophie, huh?"

"Yes, a little girl with pig tails."

They were together again, Baatar thought, relieved, *and they'd have kids*. He moved closer to her and allowed the evening to take its course.

Late that night, in his dreams, he saw Damdin. His friend looked at him with sad eyes. Baatar saw scenes from when they were back in Texas, when Damdin dated Amelia. The two of them had wanted to get married but it never came to pass. Baatar saw images of his own wedding and wondered if Damdin had been present. Amelia had been there, together with their son, DJ. Baatar awoke to a sudden loud blow that reminded him of the explosion that had taken Damdin's life.

He sat up in bed, staring into the darkness. The room was quiet; Jenna fast asleep. *Why did he have that dream? Was there a message?*

Nine

He awoke again when Jenna stirred and sat up in bed. He looked at her and cocked his head. "Are you ready for breakfast?"

"Yes, let's get going. We have a big agenda today."

He put his arm around her as they walked the short trail from the cabin to the main lodge for breakfast before getting on a tourist bus for a tundra wilderness tour.

"The Denali Park road is ninety-two miles long," the tour guide explained. "It runs parallel to the Alaska Range."

The road was narrow with sharp curves, as one would expect in the Austrian Alps or the Rockies. It offered constantly changing scenery, from mountainous terrain to quiet lakes and steep cliffs. They admired the snowcapped Denali, whose top was surrounded by a protective layer of thick clouds, as if it were too sacred to view.

In the elevated regions, they saw golden eagles, soaring high in the sky, carried by the wind, motionless and effortlessly. Watching them was hypnotizing, taking the mind into an empty space where all thoughts dissipated, and one's soul hovered in a place of peace and silence.

Jenna turned toward Baatar and, picking up their earlier conversation, said, "What's your philosophy on raising kids? What's important to you?"

"I think the parents make the rules and stick to them. If mom says no, then dad says no, and vice versa. Being consistent is key, just like when you train a horse."

"You compare raising kids to training a horse?"

"Don't you think it's similar?" Baatar asked.

"I've never trained a horse."

"You watch and observe to see what their natural strengths are and encourage them," Baatar explained. "If they show a behavior you don't like, you discourage it."

"I've watched DJ for a couple of years, you know," Jenna said. "Smart little boy, but around two years old, he started to pout, stomp his feet, and tell us no."

"Well, that's a typical two-year-old, isn't it?" Baatar said. "What did you do?"

"I talked to him a lot," Jenna said, "and if he did something inappropriate, I diverted his attention. Do you believe in spanking a child?"

"I don't like the idea of using physical force," Baatar said. "At two, kids just want to establish boundaries, don't they? I think consistently telling them what they are allowed and not allowed to do is the best method, even if it takes a lot of patience, just like with a horse." Baatar looked at Jenna and grinned. "And giving them age-appropriate consequences if they disobey, like a timeout for a young child, restrictions to something they like to do for an older one. But most of all, give them lots of love. Always."

"Is that how you train your ponies?" Jenna asked.

"Yes. Love, consistency, and rewards for good behavior."

"Is that how your parents raised you?" Jenna asked.

He smiled. "My dad was strict. We knew very well what we weren't allowed to do. Of course, living on the Mongolian steppe or even in the village, where we went to school, there wasn't as much luxury and diversion as kids have here. There wasn't as much temptation. Life was much simpler. I'd like to teach our kids about horses, so they learn to take responsibility, to have respect, to care for someone or something other than themselves, to learn humility. Those things are important to me. What about you?"

"I'd like to allow them to find out who they are," Jenna said, "and where their own interests lie. My dad was pushed very hard as a child to go into construction, his dad's career. But all my dad wanted was to play music. It caused a lot of fighting between him and his parents. They kept telling him the life of a musician was ludicrous. He was bound to be poor. Yet he became a jazz musician. To this day, he loves his job. He always provided for our family. He made a lot of people happy with his music. So, finding out who you are and living your own life—that's important to me—but I'm not sure how to teach that to a child."

"I believe kids learn much from mirroring their parents," Baatar said. "It's how all the animals teach their young. They copy what they see. They repeat what they hear. They learn as they grow, and we can encourage them. What's the one most important thing to you in your life?" Baatar asked.

"You," Jenna said spontaneously, as the bus came to a sudden halt.

"Not to worry," the bus driver said. "It seems the engine is overheating. This hasn't happened before."

The passengers exited the bus and stood on the roadside, as the bus driver talked on the phone and poured cold fluid into the radiator. "Not to worry," he kept saying, while he desperately waited for the engine to cool off.

Jenna looked at Baatar. "No omen?"

He shook his head. "Let's not go there."

She stomped her feet and rubbed her hands. "It's cold," she said.

He put his arms around her and rubbed her back.

"Let's go sit in the bus. There's nothing we can do to help the driver out here."

"All I really want is love," Jenna said, as they got seated in the bus. "Being there for someone who's also there for me and exploring life together. And you?"

"What's important to me?" he repeated her earlier question. "Love, compassion, friendship, a spiritual connection. Those are my most basic needs. To know I fulfill what I came here to do, whether that is to be a good spouse, a dad or a friend. I was taught to honor nature, the earth, and all its living beings, not only humans."

After nearly an hour, they continued their tour and stopped once more at a turnout for a scenic view. They stepped off the bus, and the driver pointed to a clearing at a distance. They watched a grizzly bear momma and her two cubs, who followed their mom closely.

"What a sight," Baatar said. "We're so afraid of them but they don't gather in groups and come into our cities to devour us or shoot us with guns. They're very content to live their lives out here in their own habitat."

Jenna nodded.

They stepped back onto the bus and the tour continued. "I see a lot of abuse in our world," Baatar said, "unfairness, disregard, disrespect, and I hope to have the courage to make things right, even if it's just for one person or one animal."

Again, they were pushed backward into their seats as the bus came to a sudden halt. The tires crunched on the gravel road when a lynx, with its unmistakable pointed ears and long legs, was crossing the road. All eyes were on the animal. Cameras clicked, before it disappeared in the thicket. Excitedly, Jenna looked at Baatar and he nodded in acknowledgment.

On their way back, as they drove through the forested

area, they sighted a black bear.

"Black bears are common across many areas of Alaska," the ranger explained. "They are smaller than a grizzly, but they can get up to three hundred pounds. All of them have an incredible sense of smell. They are usually solitary animals."

Jenna shuddered. "One better not be coming close to our cabin tonight," she whispered to Baatar.

He took her hand in his.

The bus rattled back. The crowd had turned quiet, tired from the long trip.

"That was the most incredible day ever," Jenna said, as she lay down on the bed after dinner, yawning. "I've never seen so much scenery and wildlife. I think my senses are on overload."

"It was a wonderful ride," Baatar said, leaning against the credenza that held the TV. "Do you want to go for a little hike?"

"A hike? Are you crazy? I'm exhausted. All I want is a nice bath and a good night's sleep."

Baatar looked at her. "Are you serious?"

"I'm dead serious."

"OK, why don't you take a nice hot bath, and I'll go for a run," he said.

"Honey, we've been gone all day. It's 9:00 p.m."

He took a deep breath. "Jenna, love, I'm used to physical labor. I ride horses several hours a day. Today, I sat on a bus. You don't want me pacing the room all night 'cause I can't sleep, do you? I need to get out and run."

"Isn't that dangerous out here? At night? You saw the bears!"

"I don't think so. Besides, it's still light out. We're in Alaska."

"If something happens to you, I'll be hysterical," she

said, staring at him.

Baatar smiled. "I'll be careful. I'll take my phone with me. Go and take a bath. I'll have a run."

"I can't change your mind?"

"No."

She sighed. "OK."

Baatar walked outside. It felt good breathing the cool, fresh air. He walked fast onto the trail, then he began to run. *He couldn't believe he was back in Alaska.* He'd often thought of returning to this place again, this beautiful, uncivilized, unspoiled land. He loved the trees, the mountains, the wildlife, so unlike any other place he'd been; *if only there weren't that nagging feeling inside of him.*

The climate and the surroundings reminded him of his younger years, spending them with Damdin. An anxiety came with it that he hadn't experienced for a long time. It felt as if his long-gone friend wanted to tell him something important, but the channel of communication was off. Deep in his stomach, Baatar felt a sense of doom.

He ran a couple of miles in one direction, then stopped for a short break, taking in the scenery. He heard bird calls and looked up. He stared into the trees, green against the blue sky, amid silence. At a fork in the road, he turned right and continued to run. With his feet hitting the ground, his legs took on an automatic rhythm, like a loping horse than could run for miles. When he heard cracks in the woods, he stopped and listened. He wondered if Jenna had been right. Running alone in the woods wasn't the smartest thing to do. He thought of Damdin, Amelia, and DJ. He didn't want to father a child and not be there for his wife and kid.

The sun had set, and it was getting dark. Best to get back to the cabin. He turned around and ran back, imagining Damdin was running beside him. He felt strangely sad. There was a sense of obligation, as if Damdin expected something from him. "I couldn't rescue you," Baatar said. "I wish I'd been there to rescue you."

When he got back to the fork in the road, he couldn't remember which way to go. It was getting quite dark. He decided to turn right.

After half a mile, he felt as though he was running in a dark, thick fog. "Wrong way?" he asked, as if talking to Damdin. He took a few deep breaths, then turned around, took the left turn, and headed back to the cabin. It was hard to see the path. There were cracks in the woods every so often, not caused by him. He ran faster, breathing heavily, and relieved when he saw the lights of the lodge.

When he arrived, he felt better physically, but the mental strain still remained.

Jenna was all relaxed, lying in bed with her tour book when he walked in. She greeted him with a big smile, and he leaned over and gave her a kiss. "Thank you, love."

"For what?"

"I needed that run. I'll take a quick shower. Don't fall asleep." He winked at her.

"I'm not *that* tired."

He got cleaned up and nestled into bed with her.

"Tomorrow we're heading to Anchorage already," Jenna said. "I can't believe how quickly the time is passing. Have you read up on Anchorage? There's so much to see there."

"Yes, way too much to see in one week," he said, staring into space.

Jenna looked at him closely. "Baatar, what's bothering you? When you get quiet like this, something's on your mind. You feel withdrawn."

"I'm so sorry, please forgive me."

"There's no need to apologize, honey. I want to know what's burdening you. Whatever it is, can we tackle it together?"

He looked at her. He loved looking at her face. Her eyes were curious but underneath the curiosity lay warmth and understanding.

"Do you think grief ever ends?" he asked. He looked at her closely.

Jenna shrugged her shoulders. "Does love ever end? I still miss my mom since she died last year," she said. "I often picture her. I talk to her as if she were here, as if she could hear me. I dream of her. I think grief is as much a part of life as love is. You love, you grieve—like two sides of a coin. You can't have one without the other."

Baatar looked at her and nodded. "And it's cumulative," he said. "We grieve all losses, not just people; things we've left behind, places, experiences, health, youth, animals, the things we love, anything we've become attached to."

"Are you in a sad mood?"

"Melancholy," Baatar admitted. "Alaska brings back a lot of memories."

He looked at her, his eyes holding sadness. "I don't know how to explain it," he said. "It feels as though I'm thrown back in time. The climate, the air, the trees—it all reminds me of when I first came here with Damdin. It was a tough time, working in the mine. It was hard labor. It was dangerous. I was young, and I was frivolous with my life then. I think of Damdin a lot and all the things I left behind."

"Sometimes you have to leave the familiar to gain new experiences," Jenna said.

Baatar nodded. "Of course, you're right, love." He looked at her and smiled.

"But that's not what's bothering you, is it?" Jenna asked.

"No." He sighed, and looked down, then glanced at her again. "You'll think I'm crazy."

"Spit it out."

"I feel like Damdin wants to tell me something. I feel his spirit so close. It feels like he wants to share something really important, but I don't know what it is. I just can't grasp it."

"Do you think we're in danger, and he wants to warn us?"

"No. It doesn't feel like it's about us. It's about him, but I can't figure it out." He looked at Jenna's frightened eyes. "Please don't worry, love. We're safe here. I shouldn't have told you."

"Of course, you should tell me! Whatever it is, I'm here with you, and we're in this together."

"Thank you."

"And I don't think you're crazy," she said.

He leaned into her and gave her a peck on the cheek.

"Do you think we should buy a gun?"

"No." He cracked up. "Look, we're not going to be devoured by a bear."

They talked about their impressions of the day. "It's such a shame we've lost touch with the earth," Jenna said. "Dogs on leashes, cats locked up in homes, birds in cages, fish in tanks. That's our world. And there's such a mind-boggling world of wonder out here—all those animals living their purpose—the beavers, the wolves, even the bears! They keep the earth in harmony and look at what we do with it, we plaster it with cement; pollute the air, the rivers and oceans; and call that civilization, like it's a good thing. Progress."

Baatar nodded. "Animals kill to stay alive, humans kill and dominate out of greed. Let's teach our kids to be respectful of the earth and all its creatures."

Jenna nodded in agreement.

"Come here, beautiful," he said, and drew her close. She felt his strong arms wrapping around her and forgot all about the bears and dangers and let herself fall into his caress and the bliss of the moment.

Ten

Emmy wanted to call Baatar and tell him of her plans to move, but she didn't want to bother him, not on his honeymoon. She was a grown-up, she told herself. She had to take matters into her own hands, make her own decisions. Instead, she texted Baatar: *Bruno and the ponies are fine.*

She promptly received a return text: *Tx, Emmy!*

She sighed. Honeymooners.

After Baatar and Jenna had a leisurely breakfast, they packed up the car and headed south.

"Glenn Highway," Jenna said, following the road on the map. She looked out the window and smiled. "I love these trees. It feels like traveling through a fairy tale. Have you seen those small lodges that pop up every so often? Must be some solitary-minded people living in this area. Could you live this remotely?"

Baatar grinned. "Love, I'm a nomad."

"Right. I can't imagine living like this," Jenna said and smiled at him.

They took a guided tour of the Matanuska Glacier. The path started on a low angle, then became steeper. The sound of walking on the crunching ice was hypnotizing. There was silence all around them, except for feet stomping on the ice. They stepped across deep, blue crevasses, where Baatar held her hand. Every so often, a rock dropped into a bottomless hole, sending echoes across the glacier and chills down Jenna's spine.

"It's all so dreamlike," Jenna said. "I can't believe I'm really here. I've walked a glacier!"

"And you have pictures to prove it," Baatar said, as they both sipped a hot cup of coffee at the nearest lodge.

"Honestly, I don't really like places where there's no food nearby, no stores, no restaurants, and my hands and feet are freezing cold. Don't you find that creepy?" She looked at Baatar.

"It's certainly different," he said, diplomatically. "I find it fascinating. I really enjoyed it. I don't mind the cold. Hot sand deserts would frighten me—that blistering heat that eats you up."

"I definitely wouldn't care about that either," Jenna said.

"Are you ready to head down to Anchorage?" he asked.

"I'm ready for a nap."

"You can snooze in the car if you want," he offered. "The drive should take us another three hours from here."

After a while, he noticed her steady breathing. The tour book lay in her lap.

His thoughts drifted as he drove the highway in a southerly direction, passing gorgeous landscape with spectacular views of ragged mountains and valleys lush with green trees as far as the eyes could see. He passed through Chickaloon and Palmer, the small town of Wasilla, known for its past gold rush days, while he thought of his ponies and his friends in California.

Baatar's heart had found its home in Little Oaks. He liked being in charge of his horses, instead of the horses being in charge of him, deciding where to go next. Following a herd of horses on the Mongolian steppe had been his ancestors' established way of life, feeding on the mares' milk and whatever food the women managed to make with it. And although he'd grown up there, surrounded by his family, and his father and uncle had taught him everything he knew about horses, he never missed it as he now missed his ponies and the camaraderie at the racetrack stables.

He missed Emmy, although he'd known her only for about a year. *He'd never before had a younger person look up to him, rely on him, ask his advice. He liked it. It made him feel valuable.*

He watched the rental car's gauge closely, indicating he was about to run out of gas. He prayed silently he'd make it to the next gas station or Jenna might have another breakdown. Luckily, he made it. He refilled the gas tank to the top while Jenna kept sleeping peacefully.

She awoke when he stopped the car in front of the Copper Whale Inn in Anchorage in the late afternoon.

"You shouldn't have let me sleep," she said. "Did I miss anything?"

"You looked like you needed the rest, love," he said, "and you didn't miss anything, except that super large grizzly a few miles back."

"What?"

"I'm kidding." He laughed and she nudged him in the side with her elbow.

"Let's check in."

The Copper Whale Inn had lush gardens all around it with views across the Cook Inlet.

"I'm utterly fascinated with Alaska," Jenna said. "I knew it would be a unique experience, honey, but this is way beyond what I ever expected."

Baatar nodded. "And we've seen only such a tiny portion of it."

They had dinner and called it a night.

As Jenna snuggled close and fell asleep quickly, he stared through the gap in the curtain. It was light outside for a long time. He saw pictures in his mind, pictures of gold mining days, taking the lift down into the depth of the mountain, working in darkness with heavy equipment, sweating and swearing. He remembered hikes he and Damdin took and the boat trip where they saw whales for the first time. And then they went to work at that godforsaken oil rig in Texas because he, Baatar, couldn't take working in the darkness of the Alaskan mountain any longer.

His heart was heavy. He could almost feel Damdin's presence in the room. He could see his face so clearly. *"What do you want me to do?"* Baatar asked quietly into the silence of the room. He felt sadness, helplessness, anxiety, as he had when he dislocated his shoulder snowboarding years ago and Damdin had rushed to camp to get help for Baatar, while he'd been stranded in the wilderness, listening to each tiny noise with hyperactive senses. *But why these feelings now? It felt as though Damdin was asking him for help. Help with what?*

He fell asleep in the early morning hours.

Baatar and Jenna spent most of the next day at the Alaska Native Heritage Center to explore ten thousand years of history of Alaska's indigenous people who lived on hunting moose, beavers, and ducks; fishing the rivers; and gathering berries and herbs in the forest. They harvested whales and other marine mammals. They cherished self-sufficiency and hard work, respect for others, and love for children. They believed everybody has a special gift, and they highly respected their elders.

"I like their traditional values," Jenna said. "Don't you? Their traditions hold such wisdom. It feels like we've lost a lot of that."

Baatar nodded. "I like the sentiment that each person has a special gift, and I appreciate their respect for animals and nature. They are who keep us alive."

"I love what we've seen and experienced here," Jenna said, "but I do like our civilized world. I can't imagine living in a remote cabin in the woods and having to hunt for food and kill the animals with my own hands."

"It's a rough existence," he agreed. "Nonetheless, we're so much more connected with everything than we think, and we need to take care of each other."

"I admire how you took in Emmy," Jenna said. "There aren't a lot of people who would have done that. As a matter of fact, I don't know any."

Baatar smiled. "There were odd circumstances around that. It kind of fell into place. The accident. She wore a horseshoe necklace, just like you. She was young and orphaned like Damdin. She was homeless, and I had a spare room." He looked at Jenna, almost apologetically.

"You have kind eyes," she said, "a reflection of who you are."

"You flatter me. What values of the Alaskan natives spoke to you?" he asked.

"Accept what life brings you," Jenna said, "because you can't control many things. I'd like to control everything but how much control do we really have? I struggle with patience, with allowing life to unfold as it should."

Baatar looked at her. "I struggle with loss," he said. "It really affects me when someone close to me dies, human or animal."

"We'll support each other," Jenna said, and he nodded.

At night, Jenna quickly fell asleep. He looked at her. *What a lucky woman; sleep came easily to her. She wasn't pestered with haunting thoughts.*

He wasn't used to having so much leisure. If he didn't occupy his mind with things to pay attention to in the moment, it seemed to drift to the past, rechew old stuff he thought he'd long since digested, like a cow's stomach, rechewing it for a second time, although he hadn't had this issue in California. It was time to get back home. *Jenna seemed to be relaxed, to enjoy Alaska, enjoy him. Why was he plagued by thoughts and memories that had no place with him and Jenna on their honeymoon? He'd just have to stop thinking.* Slowly he drifted off the sleep.

He had visions of riding his motorcycle from Texas to California. It had been the most solitary time in his life. He saw Saaral, who had beckoned him in his dreams then. He saw images of DJ at the wedding, when he slipped on the rug, carefully picked up the wedding rings, and proudly delivered them; and he saw Damdin watching his son from afar.

On their last day, Baatar and Jenna headed down the Seward Highway to catch a glacier cruise through Prince William Sound.

"Look at these views!" Jenna exclaimed. "Wow!" They saw harbor seals and sea otters as the catamaran majestically glided through the pristine water and fjords.

"Prince William Sound has a total of three thousand eight hundred miles of coastline," a forest ranger aboard the ship said proudly. "The Sound has an abundance of marine and coastal life, a rain forest, and one hundred fifty glaciers."

Once more, they saw black bears, perusing the shoreline and foraging on shellfish.

"How many black bears are in Alaska?" a guest asked.

"We estimate about a hundred thousand," the ranger said.

Jenna shuddered.

The highlight of the tour was a pod of humpback whales, three adults and a baby. The young whale swam close to its mother. They touched one another with their flippers, just like a mom touches her baby's arm as a sign of affection. Jenna had tears in her eyes. She barely listened to the ranger, as he explained, "Humpback whales are powerful swimmers. Watch how they use their tail fin that propels them forward. The tail fin is called a fluke."

Baatar and Jenna stood for nearly twenty minutes witnessing the family of whales.

"It's such a spiritual experience," Jenna said.

"The ocean definitely feeds my soul," Baatar agreed.

"It holds such power, and yet it carries such serenity. It reminds me in some ways of the vast grasslands of Mongolia. They just are, you know… Nature lives its own life. We're so ignorant of it. It has an existence beyond our short lifespan. The steppe and the ocean each are like a cradle that allows life to be experience in all its variations."

"You can be so poetic," Jenna said.

Baatar grinned. "Doesn't it stir something in you?"

"I just want to know what the whales talk about," Jenna said.

Baatar shook his head. *"I'm hungry, mom. You wait till the family is ready to eat, but I'm hungry now, mom."*

"Nice try, Baatar. I bet they have poets among them, too."

"It'd be nice if we could live with them in their environment, with plenty of time to observe, to get a feeling for what they talk about. I imagine they hold a lot of wisdom."

"Like a herd of horses?" Jenna asked.

"Yes."

They headed back to Anchorage for dinner and stopped at a tourist shop where Baatar bought Jenna an eighteen-inch, caramel-colored stuffed bear with a cute, sideways smile, for memories.

"I love him," Jenna said. "Look at his tiny eyes and big feet, and he's so fluffy. Look, he even has pads and claws on his feet!"

"And he's not scary," Baatar said. They purchased two smaller ones, one for Emmy and one for DJ, to hold in reserve should he come to visit them again.

Jenna carried the big bear like a young child in her arms when they left the store. "Oh, I wish we could stay longer," she said.

"So, you do want to move into one of those remote cabins?" Baatar teased.

"Never!"

Their return flight home was uneventful.

Being back in Little Oaks with the horses and his normal routine, Baatar started to sleep better. Gradually, he began to think less about Damdin and more about his ponies and the racetrack. Exercise riding took roughly three hours in the morning, and meeting with trainers and taking care of his ponies drew him back fully into the present. Entering the stables with their well-organized stalls, with the sight, smell, and sound of horses, chewing contentedly from their haystacks, made him happy. He was grateful Jenna had settled in, and he avoided any talk about living in Texas.

Jenna loved working from home and being her own boss. She quickly found ways to adjust the house to her needs. Having her sewing studio in the garage wasn't ideal, but she made it work. When the weather was nice, which she found was most of the time, she opened the garage door wide, which provided natural light, fresh air, and an opportunity to meet the neighbors who walked their dogs or were out for a quick jog in the morning.

Once she threaded the needle, aligned the soft material under the sewing machine, and heard the rhythmic humming as a seam took shape, the little nervous twitch she'd been feeling at the top of her stomach disappeared. Fabrics, taffy, lace, patterns, and yarn filled the garage. She was cautious with the needles so none would land on the floor for Bruno to step on.

The dog was always by her side. He lazily lay on his bed that she moved next to her, and they both got in the zone. With the sun shining and the palm trees stroking her cheeks with a gentle breeze, Jenna even began to design dresses again, one for Maria, one for Emmy, and one for Amelia.

"What do you think of these two colors together?" she asked Bruno, and he willingly sat up and sniffed them for approval. When she designed a new pattern, he put his head on the edge of the table, and she lifted up the paper for him to see. Sometimes, she explained to him why she wanted a pleat here and a pocket there.

Baatar and Jenna connected by phone in the afternoons to discuss their schedules and what they might enjoy for dinner. Sometimes they cooked together; sometimes they ordered in.

The evenings at home were couple time. Back in Texas, three years ago, they'd gotten into the habit of reading books together—one chapter at night, and sometimes two on a rainy day. One read aloud, and the other listened. Now they took up the habit again. On worknights, they had dinner, followed by a walk with Bruno, and then snuggled up on the sofa to read. Some evenings turned romantic.

Eleven

It was only a quarter to four when Emmy awoke to the smell of coffee. How she loved that. Even when she had to move, she would always associate the smell of coffee with Baatar, her rescuer, her adopted dad. Sleepily she headed to the bathroom for a quick pee stop, then headed into the kitchen. She couldn't believe her eyes.

Breakfast was served and there was a birthday cake in the middle of the table with nineteen burning candles.

"Make a wish," Baatar said.

"How'd you know it's my birthday?"

"Guys talk too, you know," he said, smiling. He and Jenna exchanged looks.

"Manolo," Emmy said, and Baatar nodded slightly.

"Make a wish before we burn down the house," Jenna said.

"Did you make this cake?" Emmy asked, and Jenna nodded.

"Thank you. OK, let me think. This is important," Emmy said. She closed her eyes and smiled, then blew out all the candles.

"This is for you," Baatar said, and handed her a little red box.

"Thanks." Emmy sat down at the table and carefully lifted the ribbon. She pried the box open with her fingertips. There, in the middle of the box, embraced by a tiny, red velvet blanket, lay a bar of gold. Emmy stared at it, then looked from Baatar to Jenna and back at the box.

"You can't," she said, her mouth wide open. She stared at him. "Baatar, this…I can't believe…you're giving this to me?"

"It's yours, Emmy," he said.

"But, but…it's your keepsake! Didn't Damdin give you a wooden box with seven pieces of gold as a reminder of the seven years you two worked in the gold mine in Alaska? The box that sits on top of your chest of drawers?"

Baatar nodded. "Yes, but I've got plenty of keepsakes left, Emmy," he said. "Our getting married changes your life, too, and you're growing up. We'd like to give you more freedom. It's time you had your own car, don't you think? This should give you the means to pay for one."

Carefully, Emmy lifted the gold bar out of the box. It weighed heavier in her hand than she'd anticipated. It was solid gold. She flipped it over and held it into the light, then tenderly placed it into the box, tucking it back into its red velvet bedding like a young, lost kitten being returned to its mother.

"But it was a gift to you from Damdin," she argued once more.

"This one isn't from the wooden box he gave me," Baatar said. "I have a few more of those gold nuggets tucked away. Would you rather I gave you the cash?"

"No, I love it!" She stared at him again. "It's so unique. It's so precious, so memorable. I don't know that I'd want to turn it into cash and spend it. Thank you, Baatar. Thank you!" She stood up and hugged him, then hugged Jenna, too.

"Emmy, money is there to be spent," Baatar said. "You can't hold on to everything. Life is impermanent; you know that."

"And this is from me," Jenna said and handed Emmy another box with a ribbon. Carefully, Emmy opened it and found inside a beautiful summer dress, made of a colorful cotton print in white, blue, and green, with dark-blue edges.

"Did you make this?" Emmy asked.

"Yes, I did, and I hope it fits."

"Let me try it on!" Emmy disappeared in her room and returned with the new dress on. It fit her perfectly. She swirled around in the living room. "It's so pretty, Jenna. I love it. Thank you." She hugged Jenna. "You're the best people I've ever met in my life," Emmy said. She picked up the red box again and stared at the gold.

"Don't let Manolo hear that," Baatar teased.

"Can we have some cake for breakfast?" Emmy asked.

"You can have anything you want. It's your birthday," Jenna said.

They had a piece of cake and Emmy changed back into her work jeans before she and Baatar headed off to the racetrack at four twenty in the morning.

"Baatar, you're the kindest man ever," Emmy said in the truck. "I can't believe you gave me such a huge gift."

"You should have your own car," he simply said. "You're in college. You work. You commute."

"It'd be fantastic to have my own wheels," Emmy said, "but I still can't believe you gave me gold. I can't wait to tell Manolo. Can you drive a little faster?"

Baatar grinned.

Emmy scooted on her seat. "Come on, Baatar!"

"We're almost there."

Emmy flew out of the truck and ran into Mario's trailer.

"Manolo? Manolo!"

"Good morning, birthday girl," Manolo said and gave her a big kiss. "Happy birthday!"

Mario chimed in. "Happy birthday, Emmy."

"Thank you. Mano. Do you know what Baatar gave me?"

Manolo looked at her.

"Gold, Mano, he gave me gold, real gold! So, I can buy a car. Baatar used to work at a goldmine. In Alaska."

Manolo and Mario nodded. They looked at Emmy and grinned.

"You knew?" Emmy asked. "He told you he'd give me gold for my birthday? And you kept it quiet?"

"It was a surprise, babe." Manolo gave her a hug and a peck on the cheek. "I've got something for you, too, tonight. But I've got to go exercise riding now and then work at the stables. We're having dinner together, right? I made reservations."

Emmy nodded. "I'll wear my new dress that Jenna made," she said, excitedly. She watched as he put on his boots and helmet and headed out the door.

"See you in a bit."

She walked over to the barn and started cleaning stalls. She talked to the horses and told each and every one of them about her birthday present. She even walked over to Tsokhoor and Saaral to tell them, although they weren't on her list of chores.

Gold.

At six o'clock, Manolo picked her up at home. She was wearing her new dress, which he admired. They drove to a Mexican restaurant. They had dinner reservations, like grown-ups. The waiter took them to their table and brought the menus. A live mariachi band played Mexican music, the type of music Emmy's parents had loved, the music she listened to as a little girl at home. And now she was an adult, having dinner with her boyfriend. How much she would have liked to introduce Manolo to her parents.

She knew they would have liked him, welcomed him into their home with open arms.

The waiter came and lit a candle at their table.

"What's on your mind, birthday girl?" Manolo asked.

"Gold," Emmy said, "buying a car. Do you think I should buy a car? Do you think it's a hint they want me to move out? I haven't even told them I found a place."

"Emmy," Manolo lay his hand on hers, "I think Baatar's trying to make your life easier. He'd never kick you out of his house, you know that. You still take the bus from the stables to college and back home. It takes forever."

"You're right, I'm just anxious with the weird dreams I've had. So, you think I should buy a car?"

"Absolutely. Don't you?" Manolo said.

"I've not thought about it. I didn't have that kind of money."

"But now you do."

"Will you help me find something reasonable?"

"Of course, I'll help you, Emmy. We'll all help you if you want. And you should really tell Baatar and Jenna that you've found a place to move to. It's not fair to leave him in the dark."

Emmy nodded. "I know. But once I tell them, it's real."

"Emmy, it's already real. You paid for the first month's rent."

She sighed.

After dinner, they checked on cars online—new ones, used ones, coupes, hatchbacks, trucks.

"I like the coupes," Emmy said, "nice and easy to drive. I have no need for a truck."

"Let's go test drive some this weekend," Manolo suggested, and Emmy enthusiastically agreed.

"I have a present for you, too," Manolo said, "but I

didn't want to carry it into the restaurant. I have to give it to you at home."

"Dinner was enough of a present," Emmy said, "my favorite food, your company, and car searches!"

He smiled. "You're being too easy on me, sweetie. Come." He stood up and reached out his hand, and she took it. They drove to Hillside Ranch, where they ran into Ariana, Manolo's oldest sister. "Emmy, happy birthday!" she said. "We'll have to get together again soon."

"Yes, thanks, we will," Emmy said. "You'll have to update me on your experience at the hospital."

"I'm just a nurse's assistant until I get my degree," Ariana said.

"It's a great career. You'll help people every day," Emmy said. "I admire that."

"I try."

Emmy followed Manolo upstairs to his room. On the bed was a big box, wrapped in horseshoe gift wrap with a big red bow on it.

"Happy birthday, Emmy!" Manolo said.

"Wow, that's humongous!"

"Open it."

She looked at Manolo, then at the box. "This is huge," she said again, "and so pretty." She took a picture.

"Open it!"

"OK, OK." Slowly she unwrapped the paper, which revealed a cardboard box. She looked at Manolo again, then opened the lid.

"Cowboy boots!"

"Riding boots," Manolo said. "I hope they fit. They're your size. I want to teach you riding, I mean, real riding, not around an arena or on an old trail horse. You could help me with the horse training; we could go out on rides together, exercise the ponies, see how they do."

Emmy held both boots in her hands, then hugged them. "Mano, I don't know what to say. They cost so much. They're beautiful. Thank you!"

"Try'em on."

She sat on the bed next to him and pulled on the boots, then walked around the small room and leaned over to give him a kiss. "They fit me perfectly!"

"Phew," he sighed. "Good. Come, let's go outside for your first riding lesson."

"It's already dark and I'm wearing a dress."

He smiled. "The ponies don't mind."

"Oh, wait, I have my jeans and a shirt in the car." She changed quickly, and they walked over to the pasture. "You've got choices," Manolo said. "Which one do you want? Kheer, Sunny, Rush, or Skittles?"

"I don't know. Sunny is too young and rambunctious; I'd be scared riding him. Kheer seems OK. Rush is still quite young, too, right? You're preparing him for the races? Maybe Skittles?"

"Good choice," Manolo said. "Skittles is much older than Rush. She has a very kind nature, and she's smart. She wants to please. She won't buck you off."

"Skittles it is then."

They saddled her up together and Manolo gave Emmy a leg up. He showed her how to safely mount and how to adjust the cinch if it were too loose. While he had Skittles on a longe line, he let Emmy ride in the arena and taught her how and where to use pressure with her weight, her thighs, her knees, and her ankles.

"Look straight ahead and keep your body posture straight and confident," he said. "Hold on with your thighs instead of relying on your hands and arms. Put only the tips of your boots into the stirrups for better control." He let her go from a walk to a trot and back to a walk.

"I love Skittles!" Emmy said, smiling. "She's so steady. I barely have to do anything, she reacts so quickly."

"Yeah, Skittles is a great pony to learn on. Once you feel more confident, you can ride other ponies to get a feel for how different they are, different temperaments, different reactions. Ready to go on the trail?"

"I'm ready when you are," Emmy said, proudly sitting on Skittles, looking down on Manolo.

He brought a couple of bottles of water and put them in a saddlebag, then put a bridle on Rush and opened the gate for the ponies to go through.

"The ponies love these rides as much as we do," he said. "They get to go out in nature, feel the environment, clear their minds, and digest the training they've received during the week. Walking on firm ground strengthens their muscles and bones, tendons, and ligaments. Running up and down the slopes, they have to engage their hindquarters, just like we engage different muscle groups when we hike up a hill. Being out on the trail helps them to focus. They see very well in the dark."

They reached the top of the hill and went from a walk to an extended trot when Skittles' head shot up. She reversed gear and walked backward into Rush, much to Rush's discontent. He bit her, but it was just a warning bite and didn't injure Skittles.

Emmy held on tightly. "What spooked her?" She looked at Manolo.

"See the feral cat sitting in the bush? See its green eyes?" Manolo said. "Look at it and tell Skittles it's OK. Let her know it's nothing to be afraid of."

Emmy did as told, and Skittles calmed down.

They rode for another ten minutes and dismounted when they reached a clearing. The ponies began to graze next to them, and Manolo retrieved the water bottles for

Emmy and himself.

"Will you teach me more about horses? I still know so little," Emmy said, as they sat down.

"Sure. When you want to work closely with horses, it helps to understand the nature of the horse, the way they think," he said.

"How do I learn to think like a horse?" Emmy asked.

Manolo pondered. "Try to see life from their perspective. As a herd animal, a horse depends on others for survival, and for that reason, there's safety in numbers. Every horse knows that. And from a horse's perspective, its main job is to stay alive. That's it. That's a lesson they've learned and passed on from generation to generation through centuries of living in the wild. The best way for them to achieve that goal is to live within a herd and to graze all day to store energy, which they may need at any given moment to get away from a predator, should one show up. So, they try to expend as little energy as possible because they never know when they may need to run for their lives, right?"

"That makes sense," Emmy said.

"And within the herd, there are leaders. Often it's a lead mare, someone who the rest of them think will help keep them alive if there's a threat. When there's a really large herd, there may be passive leaders as well, horses that some others find dependable and reliable."

"OK."

"As horsemen, when we train a horse or work with a pony on a daily basis, it's our job to become the kind of leader to whom they run for help when they need it. We need to give them the assurance they can rely on us and accept our help if they feel threatened. A horse sees something as harmful and wants to flee, or it's not harmful, and the horse remains calm. There's no middle ground for a horse. For them to trust us with their lives, so to speak, we need to know what may startle them and how to calm their fear."

"How do you do that?"

"The first rule is to stay calm yourself. I believe in a crisis situation, any horse would rather follow another horse than a person. It's their instinct. But when you train a horse in a round pen, for example, and it's just the horse and you, it'll try to become your friend if that is its best option to stay alive and safe. It does what you request. Horses are smart that way."

"How does that help me when I ride?"

"When you ride, you take on the role of a trustworthy partner. You're present and aware at all times; you listen and watch for anything that may startle your horse; you watch its demeanor, its ears, its eyes; you feel if there is any tension manifesting in the horse's body. And it helps to ride with the horse, not just on the horse."

"What do you mean?"

"You're partners; one trusts the other and vice versa. Don't treat your horse like it's dumb. It has a brain, a mind to think, eyes and ears to be alert. It's intelligent. A horse's sight and hearing are far better than ours. For example, when you look ahead at where you're going, the horse picks up on that. Trust it to get there. We don't have to kick them and force them to do it our way. Any slight encouragement usually works. When we have a purpose and direction, they understand that. They're sensitive and intuitive. They like to be our partners. It's much easier riding a horse when you're one with it, trust it, let it know you two are in this together, than when you want to dominate it."

"Is that what Baatar and your dad do as outriders?"

"Yes, absolutely. They've chosen ponies with a calm

disposition, who are willing to watch and run to catch a loose horse at a moment's notice. Pony and rider both approach the loose horse together. The pony knows how fast it'll have to run and how close it needs to get to the loose horse, so the outrider can catch it."

"I never thought of it that way. I thought you had to control the pony constantly."

"Well, you do, and you don't. You train it so it understands your commands, but you don't want to overtrain or ask it to do things your way when it can figure out the best way all by itself."

Emmy nodded and snuggled closer to Manolo. "It's getting a bit chilly," she said.

He put his arms around her to keep her warm. "I love you," Manolo said. "We've never talked about being exclusive. Our relationship developed so naturally, but I'd like to make it official, you and me, Emmy."

"What do you mean? Of course we're together. I love you, too, Mano. You know that."

He nodded and gave her a peck on the cheek. "You're pretty young," he said. "I don't want to pressure you with any kind of commitment. You want to go to college, become a vet. I don't want to hold you back."

Emmy looked at him.

"I want to give you time, Emmy, but I also want you to know that I'm committed to you with or without a marriage license."

"A marriage license, Mano? I'm not ready for marriage."

"I know, Emmy," he said. "I know. I just wanted to let you know where I stand."

All lights in the house were off when they returned home, except for the porch light. They tiptoed upstairs like thieves and quietly closed the bedroom door.

"I had such a beautiful day today," Emmy said, "with so much excitement. It was incredible."

"The day's not over yet," Manolo said, and helped her out of her new riding boots. "Let's give it a nice ending."

***

The following day, Manolo dropped Emmy off at the bank to exchange the gold for dollars. It wasn't as easy as she expected. The teller stared at her as though she were a thief and went to fetch a manager. That manager fetched another manager. They both stared at her. They tested the gold to make sure it was real, weighed it, and did some lengthy calculations of its worth, while Emmy patiently sat in an upholstered chair, being stared at by other customers, the tellers, and the managers. *What was their problem?*

Eventually she established an account, as they suggested, so she wouldn't run around with thousands of dollars in her pocket. It seemed reasonable. Her parents had had a bank account. Now she had one, too.

As promised, that weekend she and Manolo went car shopping together. She wanted one in blue, her only requirement, while Manolo checked engines and maintenance records. After test-driving several cars, they decided on a small two-door coupe in her favorite color, blue.

Emmy proudly drove it to Baatar and Jenna's house and gave them a ride. Jenna admired the color, Baatar checked the engine. Both of them seemed happy with her choice.

That night, Emmy dreamed of stuffing all her belongings into her new blue car and driving off, carrying everything into the new white house with four bedrooms and three roommates. *Why do I have to leave when I love it here?* she thought, when her Mom appeared before her. "It's time," she simply said. "You're growing up, Emmy. It's time for a new experience."

But Emmy didn't want a new experience. She wanted no changes, and above all, she wanted Manolo by her side, not at some farrier school five hundred miles away.

SPIRIT WHISPERS | 117

Twelve

Although Baatar was surprised at Emmy's sudden decision to move, he agreed for her to take the bed, desk, and dresser, plus all the accessories—the curtains, the rug, and the pillows—and Jenna supported her by packing up some towels and dishes.

As planned, Emmy moved out on the first of the month, with the help of Manolo and Baatar who carried the heavy furniture and loaded her bike into Manolo's truck, while Emmy put the lighter boxes into her car. They caravanned to the new house together and unloaded.

"Our door's always open," Baatar said when he left. "Don't be a stranger."

Emmy nodded, then ran to him and swung her arms around him. "I'll miss you," she said, "I really will."

"I'll miss you, too, Emmy," Baatar said. "You let me know if you need anything, anything at all. You can call me anytime." He looked at her with his dark eyes that looked so much like her dad's. She nodded. "I'll see you at the racetrack."

She smiled. "Yes, for sure."

Manolo helped her unpack her belongings. They had a quick dinner at a fast-food Mexican restaurant, and he drove her back to the new house. It had gotten dark outside.

"I've got to go, Emmy," he said, taking her hand. "I've

got to go home and pack. I'm leaving early in the morning."

"I know," she whispered. She looked down, holding on tightly to his hand.

"Emmy, the program at the farrier school takes only a couple of months, and I need to advance my career. We'll both be studying, and you'll connect with Baatar at the stables. We'll be in touch daily."

She forced a smile. She couldn't speak with that knot in her throat that would have made her all emotional and teary-eyed. She swallowed and looked at him. They hugged and kissed, and she got out of the truck. She waved goodbye until the truck was no longer visible, tears flowing freely now, but at least he didn't see them.

He was gone. She stood at the curb in the dark for a minute or two, looking up in the sky, which was covered with clouds. Not a star was visible, not even the moon.

She headed into a house of strangers.

Alone.

There was no dog. There was no smell of horses, no obnoxious wrestling match on TV to which Baatar fell asleep on the sofa, no familiar street on which she'd grown up. No neighbors she knew.

She should be happy, she told herself, but she felt like someone who'd been pushed, or worse, voluntarily jumped out of a moving train. She swore at herself under her breath for her utter stupidity as she headed upstairs to her assigned room.

She sat on her bed and caressed the red-and-white striped comforter, filled with the smells of home. She put Mom, Dad, and Cecilia's photo on her dresser and stared at pictures of Manolo on her cell phone until the battery turned the screen black.

There was only one place where she would find solace:

the cemetery.

Even though it was late and dark, she rode her bike to the cemetery. She could find her family's grave in her sleep now, she'd been there so many times. She stared at the gravestone, as if looking at each of the engraved names could make them come to life. Mateo Sanchez, Sofia Sanchez, Cecilia Sanchez.

She sat down and leaned her head against the gravestone, and her tears flowed. "Mom," she whispered, "Mom, I feel so alone."

Her chest felt constricted as if her meal had gotten stuck in her heart. She breathed into it, breathed into her grief that she felt would never end, when a light became visible, encircling her Mom.

"Emmy, all will be good," Mom whispered. "There's a reason for everything. Trust. You're the chosen one."

"What do you mean, Mom?"

"Life is a special gift, Emmy. You have talents inside you. You'll meet people, learn, work with animals, express your love. Trust what is, Emmy."

"I don't understand, Mom. What people?"

The apparition gradually disappeared, and Mom was gone.

Emmy sat quietly, as if in a daze, staring into nowhere in the dark, eerie cemetery. She took a deep breath and stood up and noticed that her chest felt warm and open. The pressure was gone.

"I love you," Emmy whispered. "I miss you." She traced each name on the gravestone with her fingers once more, then turned.

As she walked down the dirt path, pushing her bike to the road, she had a strange sense of being observed. "Mom?"

There was no sign of Mom. Emmy looked all around

in the silence of the cemetery. A slight breeze brushed her face and she got chills. She scanned the area again slowly. There was nobody, nobody visible. "Mom?" Emmy asked again. But Mom had left. "Hello?"

There was no answer.

She rode her bike to her new home, all the while feeling as though someone was following her. But there was nobody in sight.

She didn't sleep well in the new house. She listened to the unfamiliar sounds, the hum of the refrigerator that sounded all the way up to her room; doors opening and closing; chatter in the hallway; muffled laughter from an adjacent room. It all reminded her of when she was in foster care—six years of misery, although here she had her own room.

She remembered sharing a room with Verena, her latest foster care roommate, who lied and stole and put her down in front of others. Oh, how Emmy had despised her. Instinctively, she touched the comforter next to her leg where Bruno used to snuggle against her. She listened deep into the night for the dog's breathing. She stared at the picture on her dresser, barely visible in the dark, and at the curtains that shed no light into the room. She asked for guidance, repeatedly. *Why was she here?*

She was grateful when the alarm chimed to end the anguish of the night. She ate a bowl of cereal in the strange kitchen, alone, and drove her new car to the racetrack. Her mind wandered. She pictured Manolo standing at the entrance of the barn, with his arm leaning against the doorframe, so she could see his physique outlined against the sunny courtyard.

"*Emmy,*" her mom's voice was clear and pronounced. Emmy slammed on the brakes. She'd not noticed the light turning red, when a big rig rattled through the crossing, bringing her back to full awareness instantly. She took a deep breath. "Thank you, Mom!"

She turned and barely made it through the yellow light at the corner before she reached the racetrack premises and parked her car.

Turning off the car's engine and the lights, she sat in the dark for a moment, reminiscing about the time she drove to the racetrack with Baatar three times a week. Although he was a quiet man, she'd always felt good sitting next to him in his truck. He exuded calmness. He could shed frustrations by galloping fast around the racetrack or running at the beach, and then he was done with it. She admired that. Her coping mechanism was to brood. She wanted to talk about the same thing incessantly. Her stomach churned, and her gut cramped up. Things nested in her.

She made her way to the barn and cleaned a couple of stalls, then walked through the racetrack tunnel to get a glimpse of Baatar. He was galloping around the track, glued to one of the young bay thoroughbreds as though they were one. She had wished for a long time that she could ride like him. Now she just wanted to be in his presence.

She walked back into the barn to continue her chores. Her stomach growled as if it resented the cereal she'd eaten. As she approached a usually friendly mare, smiling and talking with her softly, the mare pinned her ears, lifted her head, and walked backward, backing away from Emmy.

"What's wrong, Maya Lou?" Emmy asked. "Did something spook you?" Emmy looked around but didn't see anybody. "Maybe a mouse?" She scanned the hallway and stall but didn't see or hear any commotion. "Silly girl," Emmy said to the mare. The horse still looked agitated.

Emmy sighed anew and continued with her chores, disrupted by a couple of trips to the bathroom to flush away a bout of diarrhea. She wondered if she should go to Mario's RV trailer after the exercise riders returned just so she could hang out with Baatar for a while. But she had plenty to do and decided to be a grown-up about her girly moods. She could be sad by herself and didn't need the guys mocking her, which they'd probably do.

Ten o'clock came around and she washed her hands and sat down to eat the sandwich she'd brought. Peanut butter and jelly, not the type of thick, juicy turkey sandwich Manolo made. She stared out onto a stack of hay that'd been delivered in the parking lot. She sipped water. Her stomach growled again, then her gut made some obscene digestion noises. She was grateful she'd not gone to see Baatar after all.

To appease herself, Emmy decided to say hello to Baatar's ponies, Tsokhoor and Saaral. Both were nibbling hay from the hay sack when she approached them.

"Hi, my lovely friends," she said with a big smile, and reached out to Saaral, but the gray mare immediately raised her head and widened her eyes.

"What's wrong?" Emmy asked. She took a step back and headed toward Tsokhoor with a smile, but he walked away from her, facing the back of the stall.

"Why are you being mean to me today?" she asked aloud. She stood immovable, staring at the ponies.

"Who's being mean to you?"

Emmy's head swung around. "Baatar, I didn't hear you come in."

"It's good to see you, Emmy," he said with his usual, soothing voice, and put his arm around her shoulder. "What are the ponies telling you?"

"I said hello, and Saaral raised her head and widened her eyes, and Tsokhoor walked away." Emmy pouted.

"And why do you think that is?"

"I have no idea," Emmy said. "I approached Maya Lou earlier and she was mean, too."

"Come," Baatar said with a slight move of his head, and Emmy followed him outside.

"Sit," Baatar said and pointed to a bale of hay. He sat down next to her. "Tell me what's going on with you."

"I don't know," Emmy said. "The horses are mean to me today."

Baatar turned to face her and looked at her quietly. "You know the horses are highly sensitive to our emotions, right?"

Emmy nodded.

"They mirror what's going on inside of us that we try to cover up."

"I'm not mean," Emmy said, a little annoyed.

"When three horses turn away from you, do you think all three horses have a problem today?"

Emmy shrugged her shoulders. "I don't know. Maybe it's the weather."

"I don't think it's the weather," Baatar said. He looked up, scanning the racetrack, which was still enmeshed in a little bit of fog, as on most mornings. It felt comfortably cool. There was no breeze.

"The feed?" Emmy asked.

"Nope."

"Then what is it?"

"What's going on with *you*, Emmy?" Baatar asked. "I know you. Something's bothering you. If you approach the ponies when you're angry inside, they can feel that; even if you smile at them as if nothing's wrong and cover up your true feelings, they'll react. If your stomach is upset, they feel their stomach becoming upset."

"How'd you know my stomach is upset?" Emmy asked.

Baatar smiled. "It was just an example. Why's your stomach upset?"

"I don't know."

"You know you can talk to me about anything."

"I don't really need anything." Emmy looked down and sighed.

Baatar patiently sat and waited. "Emmy, talk to me."

"I think it's because Manolo's gone, and I live with these strange roommates. I feel stranded and alone, although I shouldn't feel alone because I have three roommates, and I'm going to school with other students, but somehow it's affecting my stomach, and it's making all sorts of weird noises."

"Are you feeling sick?" Baatar asked.

"No, I just miss him."

"He just left yesterday."

"I know." Emmy looked at Baatar. "It's stupid."

"Feelings are always stupid," he said. "We can't control them well. They do what they want with us."

"But you're always calm," Emmy interjected.

"Me? Remember how miserable I was when I thought I'd never see Jenna again? And how I turned to vodka after the wildfires killed a couple of horses?"

"Oh, yeah."

"Emmy, we all go through highs and lows, and the horses are specialists in picking up how we feel. So, when you have an upset stomach because you're sad, they pick up on that. So, they say, *Hey, you smiled, but you have an upset stomach. There's something wrong. Don't smile at me and give me an upset stomach.* So, they turn away.

"So, what's your suggestion?" Emmy asked. "Are all the horses gonna be mean to me for the next two months?"

Baatar smiled. "Well, I hope you won't be upset for

two months because Manolo and you will connect and talk. And he'll be back. But with the ponies, you have to be authentic."

"I don't know what you mean."

"When you smile but you're upset they say, *Look, she smiles, but there's something not right with her. I'm not going to want anything to do with that. Something's off.*"

"You mean I should tell them I'm upset?"

"Yes, be honest with them. They know anyway. You can't cover up how you feel in front of a horse. Let's give it a try," Baatar suggested. "Come."

They walked back into the barn.

"Tell'em," Baatar said.

Emmy approached Saaral, who continued pulling hay from the hay sack. "Hi, Saaral," Emmy said. "I'm upset today because Manolo left for school and I feel lonely."

Saaral chewed contentedly, her eyes focused on Emmy. She continued to pull hay and chew. Emmy stroked her neck, and Saaral continued to eat.

"No way," Emmy said, perplexed. She walked over to Tsokhoor and repeated her confession. She rubbed his forehead, then looked at Baatar. "I can't believe it. It works! They just want me to tell them how I really feel?"

"That's the secret."

Emmy smiled. "I'm gonna have to go to Maya Lou, too."

"When are your classes today?" Baatar asked.

"Four to seven this afternoon."

"Would you like to join Jenna and me for dinner tonight? I'm sure Bruno would love to see you, too."

"Really?" Emmy's face lit up. Then she became serious again. "I don't want to disturb you."

"You won't disturb us, Emmy. You're my daughter, remember?"

Emmy smiled. "I'd love to come."

The chores became easier. Maya Lou didn't mind Emmy telling her about being upset, and strangely her stomach settled and didn't make weird noises anymore.

Over dinner, Jenna and Baatar told Emmy about their house-hunting efforts.

"It's exhausting," Baatar said.

"I think it's fun," Jenna said, full of excitement. "We're preparing to have a family. We're looking at some properties in Little Oaks."

"Really?" Like what?" Emmy asked.

"Three to four bedrooms, a little more inland," Baatar explained, "with more room, perhaps a pool. I won't be able to walk to the beach any longer."

"Oh, what a sacrifice," Emmy teased.

"If we get a four bedroom, we'd have an extra room," Jenna said, "but you're nineteen, you may not want to live with us any longer. After all, you decided to move."

"Only because this house is fairly small," Emmy said, "and I didn't want to impose; you're newlyweds!"

Baatar smiled. "*We* don't want to impose, Emmy. We're planning on having kids and kids are noisy. They can be demanding. Sometimes they cry at night. That may not be the type of environment you want to live in."

"I'd love to live with you and Jenna and your kids."

Baatar acknowledged it with a quick nod. "Give us some time," he said. "It may take us a few months to find the right place."

Emmy felt better when she drove to the new house in her lovely, blue car. Perhaps, she thought, it was just going to be a temporary arrangement. *It was dumb to move. Why'd she ever do that?*

Thirteen

Two days later, when Emmy came home from class, a tall brown backpack blocked the hallway. She heard chatter from the kitchen.

"Emmy, come here," Carla hollered.

Emmy stepped into the kitchen to meet a smiling young man. He was about six foot three. His head was crowned with thick dark-blond hair, bleached on the top layer. His skin was fair but tanned, his nose and cheeks slightly burned, like those of a surfer who'd enjoyed the waves a little too long. He was wearing shorts and a T-shirt with sleeves hugging strong upper-arm muscles. He had defined, Nordic features with a narrow straight nose and a square jawline. His striking gray-blue eyes looked pale like the sky on a hazy day and penetrated Emmy to the core.

His arms and legs seemed extraordinarily long and were covered with blond hair. His chest hair protruded from the V-neck of his T-shirt. He had broad shoulders. Emmy could easily picture him lifting a heavy wooden canoe and carrying it on top of his head, balanced solely by his strong arms. She imagined him shirtless, chopping wood at a cabin in the forest.

"Hi, I'm Axel." He stretched out his big hand.

"Hi," Emmy said and shook it. "Are you visiting?"

"I'm from Haugesund," he offered.

"Excuse me?"

"Haugesund," he repeated. "We have a Marilyn Monroe statue."

"I'm not familiar with that place," Emmy said.

"It's a beautiful place, yes?"

"Where is it?" Emmy asked.

"You don't know Haugesund?" he asked, his pale eyes taking on a surprised look. "Haugesund region in northern Rogalund."

Emmy shook her head.

"Norway."

"Oh, you're from Norway! Are you a student here?"

"Yes, I study engineering. I got the room opposite from you. We'll be sharing the bath, yes. OK with you?"

Emmy swallowed. "Sure, as long as we're not using it at the same time."

He smiled. "It's OK."

"No, that wouldn't be OK with me," Emmy said.

"I mean it's OK. We won't use it together."

"Don't you just love international students?" Carla asked, glancing at Axel. "They're so interesting." She sat with her elbow on the table, her chin resting in the palm of her hand, as she stared at Axel, admiringly. But he only had eyes for Emmy. Emmy glanced at Carla and wondered if she was interested in Axel. It sure seemed that way.

"Welcome," Emmy said to Axel, then headed upstairs and looked at pictures of Manolo. He'd be gone for two months. Sixty days. She picked up her phone and called him.

"Mano, are you settling in?" she asked.

"Hey, Emmy," he said. "I was gonna call you, too. Wanna hear my training schedule?"

"Yes."

"Listen to this," he said. "Anatomy, confirmation and biomechanism, hoof mapping and distortion analysis, dissection lab, forging techniques, anvil usage, radiograph analysis."

Emmy laughed. "Sounds like training in an ancient torture method."

"No kidding," Manolo said, "but I hear the horses they use are well behaved. I think the teachers are pretty good; a couple of big guys. I'm gonna have to do some weightlifting."

Emmy laughed again. "You're plenty strong."

"And how are you?" he asked.

"I'm all right."

"It's nice to hear your voice, Emmy. I'm gonna head to dinner. I'll talk to you soon."

"OK."

"Kisses," he said and hung up.

She did her homework, biology, with lots of reading and memorizing. Around 9:30 p.m., she headed downstairs to the kitchen and was surprised to see Axel sitting at the table by himself. Emmy took some OJ from the fridge and sat down.

"Tell me about life in Norway," she said. "What's it like there?"

"What do you want to know?"

Emmy shrugged her shoulders. "Anything," she said. "What does your hometown look like? What university do you attend? Do you have siblings?"

"Oh, you *are* interested," Axel said and sat up straight. He placed both forearms on the table and leaned toward Emmy. His blue eyes seemed bigger than before, a watery blue, translucent and mysterious.

"Norway's in Scandinavia. You know Scandinavia, yes?"

"I generally know where it's located, " Emmy said.

"Many Norwegians live in the southern part," Axel

explained. "My family, too. It's warmer there, more people. Norway is a long country, you know, like California, long and skinny, yes. It faces the ocean in the west and has land barriers only in the east."

"What land barriers?""

"I mean borders, yes," Axel corrected. "Finland and Russia."

"I see. So, Norway has lots of coastline like California," Emmy said.

"Yes, but it's much colder. Norway is far north, yes, parallel to Alaska, but we have the stream, so it's not as cold as Alaska, except past the Arctic Circle, yes. That's where the Sami live, you know, reindeer herders."

"Reindeer herders?" Emmy smiled. "Is that where Rudolph came from?"

"Rudolph?"

"The red-nosed reindeer," Emmy said.

"No. That's an American tale."

"Do your cities look like ours?" Emmy asked.

"Kind of," Axel said. "Most of our homes are made from wood, like yours here, except commercial buildings, of course. And we don't have a lot of skyscrapers. It's more European, yes."

"And your family?" Emmy asked. "Is everybody blue-eyed?"

"Yeah, we're all Nordic," Axel said, looking into Emmy's dark eyes with a grin. "We go back to the Vikings. You've heard of the Vikings, yes?"

"An old seafaring people that had a bit of a rough reputation," Emmy said, "kind of like Genghis Khan in Mongolia."

"Ah, yes. You know Genghis Khan." Axel's eyes widened in excitement. "Yes, Vikings were tough. Big, strong guys," he said, "like me, yes."

"And the women?" Emmy asked.

"I have two sisters, both younger, nice," Axel said.

"And the Viking women?" Emmy asked. "How were they?"

"Tough, I suppose." Axel grinned again. "Fighters. Loving their men. Norway was the first country to have a female president. We have equal rights. We value our women, better than here, yes?" Axel said.

He reached out to Emmy and put his hand on hers. "You're very pretty. I like your dark eyes and long black hair. Not many women like you in Norway. I appreciate it. Beauty. You want to come with me to Norway, yes?"

Emmy retrieved her hand and laughed. "I don't even know you."

"We get to know each other here, yes?" Axel said.

"Tell me about your sisters."

"Two girls," he said. "Fifteen and seventeen. Nice."

"Do you do stuff together?" Emmy asked.

"Yes. We ski a lot and hike, and in the summer, we go swimming, yes. My family has a cabin in the mountains. Most Norwegians do."

"Can everybody go to college?"

"Lots of questions," Axel beamed. "You like to know Norway, and you like to know me, yes?"

"We're roommates," Emmy said. "We should know a little about each other."

"Yes." He smiled at her for a little too long, looking into her eyes. He blinked slowly. "Everybody goes to school for ten years, from six to sixteen. If you add another three years, you can take an exam and go to the university."

"So that's what you did?"

"Yes. University of Oslo. I study engineering. That's a good career in Norway. We have lots of natural resources, oil and gas, hydroelectric energy, metal products, ships, yes."

"Is the economy stable?" Emmy asked.

Axel laughed. "Of course! Norway is in the top ten countries for per capita income. We have one of the highest standards of living in the world. Life is good in Norway, yes. Great social benefits, free healthcare, good state retirement. Nobody starves or is homeless. Not like here, yes?"

"How many people live in Norway?" Emmy asked.

"Over five million."

"So, there aren't very many people. California has almost forty million, the United States many more. It's difficult to compare social structures when the population is so different."

"You're defensive, yes," Axel said.

"You just can't compare the two countries when the conditions are so different," Emmy said.

Axel's face grimaced and a thick fold appeared above his eyes. "What are you saying?"

"All I'm saying is it's easier to govern five million people in Norway than over three hundred million in the United States."

"Come, I'll show you pictures, yes?" Axel pulled out his phone and shared pictures with Emmy.

"This is Haugesund," he said, showing her a picture of a beautiful, coastal city with a population of a hundred thousand people and a landscape with rocky heather moors to mountains, fjords, and waterfalls.

"Haugesund is known for trade," Axel explained. "It was a big power center during Viking Age, yes, and still has many reminders of Viking history. We have a history center where kids can dress up as real Vikings, and we have a reconstructed Viking farm with teachings about Viking way of life."

Emmy listened patiently.

"We used to have an abundance of herring, big export industry. We also make ships. The shipping passage by Haugesund was known as the way to the north, yes, what we call the North Way. That later became Norway, yes, the name of my country.

"And this is our cabin." He showed Emmy a picture of a small, wooden log cabin in the mountains, surrounded by spruce and pine trees. He also showed her a picture of his two sisters, who looked very much like him. Their skin was pale like his. They wore thick turtleneck sweaters in the picture. They both had very light-blonde hair. They had oval, narrow faces with prominent refined noses, and deep set, pale blue eyes.

"You're from a beautiful country," Emmy said. "I love the forests and the fjords. It's very unique."

"Norwegians are unique," Axel said, "just like me, yes?" He smiled at her and didn't take his eyes off her.

His pale-blue eyes drew her in. She'd seen blue eyes, like Paul's, her old boyfriend, but never ones as pale as Axel's. "The color of your eyes is unusual," she said.

"Thank you. I'm strong, too, yes," Axel said and pushed up the short sleeves of his T-Shirt to reveal his upper arm muscles. "I could lift you." He stood up and walked toward Emmy, his long arms reaching for her.

"That's OK," she said quickly and blocked him with her hands.

"We can make tacos together sometime, yes?" he suggested.

"Yeah, sure. I better go now. I've got some more studying to do." She ran upstairs, while he lingered in the kitchen.

Fourteen

The next day, Emmy connected with Ariana, Manolo's oldest sister, as promised a while back. They were the same age, and both had prior medical experience, Emmy from working at a doctor's office for a few months, and Ariana from working as a nurse intern at the hospital.

"What's new at the hospital?" Emmy asked. "Do you still like being an intern?"

"I do and I'm learning a lot," Ariana said. "My biggest challenge is to not get personally involved. I feel sorry for the old folks who have no visitors. I feel sorry for the kids whose parents can come only once a day or less. I feel sorry for people who have cancer and have to spend weeks at the hospital. I have to cut out my feelings and be in neutral and just do my job. That's really hard."

"I don't know if I could do that either," Emmy said. She told Ariana all about her new roommate, Axel. "Do you want me to introduce you to him? He likes girls with dark hair."

"He likes you?" Ariana asked.

"I think he generally likes girls with dark hair," Emmy said.

"I just started seeing Justin," Ariana explained. "He's a radiology technician at the hospital."

"Do tell," Emmy said, and Ariana shared all the details.

Emmy checked her phone various times a day and was

delighted when Manolo texted her, even if it was just a quick hello.

A few days went by before Emmy ran into Axel again in the kitchen shortly before dinnertime. Spontaneously, they decided to make tacos. While she prepared the tacos, he began to snap pictures of her.

"Hey, what are you doing?"

"Pictures to send home," he said, innocently. "They like to know what I do and people I meet."

Over dinner, Emmy told Axel about the loss of her parents and sister when she was twelve. She told him about how she met Baatar and his ponies and how he saved her life.

"What do you study?" Axel asked.

"I want to be a veterinarian, a vet," Emmy said.

"Vets make a lot of money in Norway," Axel said. "Like maybe a million NOKs before taxes."

"How much is that in dollars?" Emmy asked.

"I think ten NOKs is about a dollar, yes?"

"Seems earnings might be similar here," Emmy said. "But I don't want to be a vet because they make a lot of money. I want to be a vet because I love animals and want to work with them closely, keep them healthy."

"The best known school is the Norwegian University of Life Sciences," Axel said. "It houses the School of Veterinary Science, yes. It's a tough school to get into. Five to six years of studies, and only seventy students per year are accepted, yes. It's tough."

"Vet schools are competitive here, too," Emmy said. "But that doesn't keep me from going for it."

"You're competitive," Axel said. "I like that. I like you."

"Axel, I have a boyfriend."

"That's OK," he said. "I have a girlfriend in Norway,

but she's far away, and I'm here with you." He placed his big hand on hers, and Emmy pulled her hand back. "Let's just be friends, OK?" she said.

"Why?"

"Because I don't want another boyfriend."

His shoulders slumped and his face saddened. "I'd be good to you."

Emmy couldn't help but smile. "Thank you, but all I can offer you is my friendship."

She went upstairs and called Manolo, and they chatted for a long time. He told her about the school, the premises, and what he was learning. She updated him about the stable and school. She never mentioned Axel.

A few days later, she invited Baatar and Jenna over for dinner, and they accepted. Emmy was happy to see them both, and had asked Carla if Bruno could come, too.

She received big bear hugs from Baatar and Jenna, though Bruno was the most exuberant with his melodious greeting, rubbing her legs, licking her hands, and requesting a belly rub. Emmy laughed and obliged. She gave Bruno a big bone and served Baatar and Jenna homemade empanadas with rice and a salad, when Axel appeared.

"Hi, Axel," Emmy said. "This is my adopted father, Baatar, and his wife, Jenna."

"Very nice to meet you," Axel said and shook hands. He petted Bruno on the top of his head, but Bruno growled. "He's probably just protecting his bone," Emmy said, when Axel sat down at the table as though he'd been invited.

"I've invited Baatar and Jenna for dinner so they can see my new home," Emmy explained, but Axel didn't stir.

"Are you both from here?" he asked.

"No," Baatar said, "I grew up in Mongolia, and Jenna grew up in Texas."

Jenna motioned for Emmy to get another plate.

"Don't you have homework to do?" Emmy asked Axel with a hint in her eyes.

"I can do it later," he said. "So, you're both foreigners like me. Mongolia, that's as cold as Norway, isn't it?"

"Axel, Texas is in the United States," Emmy interjected.

Baatar looked at her. "Yes, Mongolia gets very cold in the winter," he said.

"And you guys have lots of horses, don't you? Isn't it famous for horses, yes? Small and sturdy, just like Norwegian horses, yes?"

"I've never been to Norway," Baatar said. "You have small, sturdy horses?"

"Fjord horses," Axel said, "from the mountains in Western Norway. They are agile and very strong, yes. Farmers have used them for hundreds of years. They have a good temperament."

Axel looked at Emmy and smiled, and she politely smiled back.

"We think they came from Asia, probably related to yours, yes?" Axel looked at Baatar. "Vikings used them in war, like Genghis Khan. Mongols and Vikings are strong men, yes." Axel winked at Emmy.

"It's quite possible the horse breeds were related originally," Baatar said. "Do you ride?"

"Oh no, not me. I like ships. I want to be an engineer."

Emmy reluctantly placed another plate on the table, and Axel served himself generously. "I have two sisters," he said. "Girls are fun."

"Girls are *fun*?" Emmy mocked.

"Pretty, yes," Axel corrected himself, and stared at Emmy with his pale-blue eyes, blinking slowly.

"How's life different in Norway?" Jenna asked.

"Most of us live in the south," Axel explained. "The north is cold, arctic, yes, with northern lights in the winter. We have oil and gas, which has made the country rich, yes. We are very emancipated." He smiled. "Men and women in Norway are equal. Some men raise kids, women work." He took another helping of the empanadas. Emmy couldn't understand how he could talk so much and eat so much all at the same time.

"We don't eat out a lot," Axel said. "We prefer homemade food."

"Do you cook, too?" Jenna asked.

"Yeah, I can cook, but I prefer not to. Emmy's a good cook. We're getting close." He smiled at Emmy, then shoved another big bite of empanadas into his mouth.

"He means we're getting to know each other as roommates," Emmy said.

After dinner, she showed Baatar and Jenna her finished room. "It looks pretty much as it did at your house," Emmy said. "Thanks again for the furniture and everything."

"Of course," Baatar said. "That's the least we could do for your new start. Do you like it here?"

"I miss you guys and Bruno," Emmy admitted.

"But people here are nice to you?"

"A little too nice." Emmy grimaced. "Axel doesn't seem to know personal boundaries."

"He seems quite taken with you," Jenna said.

"He has a girlfriend in Norway, and I'm with Manolo," Emmy said, "and I didn't think he'd butt in as he did this evening. I can't stand that."

"But otherwise, he's respectful?" Baatar inquired.

"He flirts, but he doesn't attack me, if that's what you mean."

Baatar grinned. "Good. You let me know if I need to

have a word with him."

"He's pumping iron in the backyard," Jenna said, "right outside your window. He's really trying to impress you, Emmy."

"He does that every day," Emmy said. "I don't care. Tell me about your plans. Do you have plans?"

"We're settling in, finding our new routine after the wedding and the honeymoon," Jenna said. "I'd like to grow my sewing business, and Emmy, please come and visit. You're part of the family."

Emmy texted Manolo and told him about her dinner with Baatar and Jenna, and he responded with a thumbs-up. Most days, they kept their messages short. His schedule was busy, with long hours of instruction and practice time. He didn't say it, but Emmy could tell he missed home as much as she missed him. She didn't want to whine and vent when he was far away. Instead, she updated him on the horses at the stables, shared funny stories, and told him which new thoroughbreds arrived. Manolo, in turn, told her horse jokes and what he learned. They kept it light and fun. She finally mentioned Axel to him, as a sideline.

On the way home from Emmy's place, Baatar was quiet. Seeing Axel, as outgoing as he was, trying to make friends in a foreign country, reminded him of Damdin. Baatar hadn't thought of his deceased friend since he'd had those strange sensations and dreams up in Alaska during the honeymoon. He still didn't know what that had been about.

In the early morning hours, before waking, Jenna heard Baatar moan in his sleep. She sat up and looked over to him. The room was dark. She heard him breathing heavily as though he was in pain. He was drenched in sweat. "What?" he moaned in his sleep. "What?" Then he awoke.

Jenna switched on a light. "Baatar, are you OK?"

He glanced at her and got up and went into the bathroom. She heard the toilet flush and then the faucet. He took off the T-shirt he'd been sleeping in, which was soaked, and returned to bed.

"What happened?" Jenna asked.

"Nothing," he said, "just go back to sleep. It's too early to be up."

"Honey, what's going on? I can't sleep like this."

"A bad dream," he said.

"A nightmare?"

He glanced at her and gave her an almost imperceptible nod. "It was my friend Damdin again," he said. "We were on the oil rig together, and I saw smoke, then flames. I didn't see him getting injured, I just saw him staring at me with these pleading eyes. I kept asking him what he wanted but he didn't speak. There was this urgency in his eyes, like he wanted me to do something. But I don't know what."

She nodded.

"Jenna." He looked at her. "It felt so real. It was so damn real."

"But you weren't on the oil rig when the explosion hit that killed Damdin. You had the day off and were on land."

"Yes, but in my dream I was there."

"Have you ever had nightmares like that before?"

"No."

"It must have a meaning," she said.

"Yes, but what? What does he want me to do?"

"I don't know, Baatar."

"The look on his face—it reminded me of a time when he and I were in Alaska," Baatar recalled. "The only time he ever looked at me that way."

"What happened back then?"

"We'd been hiking, and he slipped and slid down a slope and twisted his knee. He was in a lot of pain, and I didn't want to leave him out in the wilderness, injured, by himself. I supported him and he limped along. At times, I practically carried him. We both weren't sure we'd make it back to camp. We were exhausted and thirsty. Sometimes we weren't sure we were even walking in the right direction. It got very late, but we made it. He was scared, although he joked through clenched teeth the whole time. But his eyes couldn't lie. He was in a lot of pain. There was fear. His eyes could never lie."

Baatar rubbed his face and closed his eyes, trying to recall the dream and its message, but to no avail.

"Maybe Emmy would know," he said, glancing at Jenna. "She has visionary dreams sometimes."

"Really?" Jenna asked.

"Yes, she sees her deceased mother, and sometimes she gets messages."

"Right. She saw my mom once when we were sitting in the backyard together, remember?"

Baatar rubbed his eyes. "Let's try to get some more sleep."

Jenna switched off the light. The room was dark again. Baatar tried to imagine Damdin, to see if he could connect, see if his friend would tell him what was so urgent, but the connection was gone.

The next time he ran into Emmy, he asked her about any recent premonitions. He tried to sound casual.

"Premonitions?" Emmy asked. "I had a dream where you and Jenna raised three kids, but I guess that'd be sometime in the future, and I already told you about it." She smiled. "Is something on your mind?"

Baatar told her about his dream.

"I wonder if he tried to warn you of something?" Emmy questioned.

"It felt more like a plea," Baatar said, "like he wants me

to do something, like…rescue him.”

"Rescue him from what?"

"I don't know. That's why I'm so puzzled."

"Give it some time," Emmy said. "Maybe he'll come to you in another dream; maybe he's just preparing you for something to come. I know how frustrating it is when they look at you, or they talk, and you can't hear them. The only place…" She looked at Baatar and bit her lips. "The only place I can hear my mom is at the cemetery."

"I can't fly all the way to Mongolia to sit by Damdin's grave," Baatar said.

"I know. I'm just saying that's what seems to work for me. I only found out by accident, and I haven't shared this with anybody."

"So, you can actually talk to your mom and get information?" Baatar asked.

"Yes, but only in the cemetery when I visit her grave."

"Will she give you answers about friends, too?"

Emmy smiled. "You want me to go to the cemetery and ask my mom what Damdin wants from you?"

Baatar shrugged his shoulders, then slowly nodded. "It was so real, Emmy. It was so damn real."

"I'll see what I can do," she said, "but don't expect too much."

She went to the cemetery that evening but didn't get a message about Damdin for Baatar. All she got was that strange sensation that somebody was watching her. For a moment, she wondered if it could be Damdin, but she discarded that thought. It didn't feel like Baatar's friend. It felt different.

Fifteen

Jenna began to love her life in Little Oaks. When Baatar was at the racetrack and she was alone at home, her creativity rekindled. She started to draw designs again, as she had a few years back—dresses, skirts, blouses, jackets, or a pantsuit, nothing too fancy, but pretty and unique. Saxophone music was playing on the radio, and Bruno was by her side, when Baatar came home. He took off his boots at the front door.

"Hi, honey." She lowered the volume on the radio.

"Hi, my love." He roughed up Bruno's fur and greeted her with a kiss. He picked up three pieces of paper from the table and held them up into the light. "Jenna, what are these drawings?"

"I'm just piddling around a bit," she said.

"These are beautiful. Look at these dresses. Jenna, you're talented. You should have your own fashion line."

Jenna looked up. "Baatar, that's what famous designers have. I'm just a seamstress."

"Look at these," he said, as she gently took them from him. "You're more than a seamstress. You have an eye for beauty."

"I'm happy you think so," she said.

"Have you ever thought of becoming a fashion designer?"

"Honey, I just piddle around. I've never been to

fashion school."

"That doesn't diminish your talent," he said. "You can't learn vision and imagination in school. You can learn technique, but not this."

"You're being very kind."

Baatar sat on a chair, still eyeing the drawings. "I'm not saying it to flatter you. I really mean it. If this is something you enjoy, I support you 100 percent in exploring it further. I don't want you to feel you're here to support me. I want you to thrive and be happy, follow your passion."

Jenna smiled. "I have followed my passion." She looked at Baatar. His face was tanned from being in the sun all day, although the mornings had been a bit foggy. The fog from the ocean cleared up by midmorning.

Baatar's hair was cut short, the way he liked it since he was wearing a security helmet half the day. He was still wearing his white shirt and blue jeans, part of his outrider uniform, that she knew would end up in the hamper later today. He usually left his red security vest, helmet, and chaps in Mario's RV trailer.

Baatar put his hand on Jenna's. "You moved to California for me. You sold your house. You gave up a lot. I'm willing to give, too."

"I know," Jenna said. She gathered her drawings and put them into a little pile. "I think my focus will be on homelife for a while."

"But you love your business," he argued, "and it's growing."

"I do. I love working with my hands and creating pretty things. And I realize there may be more money in fashion design, but also a lot of stress. I like the handicraft. I like being my own boss and choosing my own customers."

"I'm not concerned about the money," Baatar said.

"I'm concerned about you feeling fulfilled."

"I'm happy with my life, honey. What I'm trying to say is," she looked up at him, "our family is growing."

"What do you mean? Is your dad coming to visit? Does he want to stay with us?"

Jenna placed her hand on her stomach. "I'm pregnant, Baatar. We're gonna have a baby."

"Really? You're pregnant? Already?"

He jumped up, flung his arms around her and lifted her into the air. He swirled her around three times, then let her back down. He took a step back and looked at her. His face was serious. "How are you feeling?"

She laughed. "I feel fine."

"You're not sick? Nauseous?"

"Not so far."

"And how far along are you?" he asked.

"Only six weeks. I just found out this morning."

"I've got to call my folks," Baatar said, "they're gonna be so happy. What time is it in Mongolia now? We should have a barbecue, invite all our friends."

"Hey, slow down, cowboy," Jenna said. "Baatar, we better not spread the word yet. Things can still go wrong, you know. It's my first pregnancy."

"What do you mean, go wrong?" He sat down at the table, staring at her.

"Any miscarriage usually happens in the first trimester," she explained, and sat down across from him.

"And how usual is that?" he asked, concerned.

"I think there's only a 10 percent chance, but I'm already in my thirties. I just don't want to alert the whole world yet; maybe give it another month."

"OK." He took her hands and pulled her into the living room. He hugged her tightly, then turned the hug into a slow dance. "Can we tell Emmy?" he asked.

"I suppose, she's part of the family."

"And Mario?"

Jenna cocked her head and slowly shook it from side to side.

"You're the boss," he said. The radio music was soothing, and they danced for quite a while.

"I just don't know what to do with myself," Baatar said. "Do you want to go out to dinner? We need to celebrate. Where'd you like to go?"

"How about that little outdoor garden restaurant where we can bring Bruno?"

"OK."

Baatar took a shower while Jenna cleaned up her design papers and sewing utensils. She put on a summer dress, refreshed her makeup, and pulled up her hair.

"Come on, Bruno," Baatar hollered as he walked into the living room fifteen minutes later in shorts and a T-shirt. "Are you ready, love?"

Jenna nodded, and he took the leash off the credenza as Bruno came running. "You lucky dog."

The garden restaurant was in walking distance. It was a beautiful evening, just the two of them and Bruno, sitting under the canopy of palm trees, each table lit with a candle, and a big hedge all around the small premises for privacy. They had a view of the ocean with the sun setting while they dined. It was peaceful, romantic, and cozy. The waiter even brought a bowl of water for Bruno, who received a few morsels of meat from Jenna's and Baatar's plates. The evening air was filled with the fragrance of night-blooming jasmine.

After dinner, they took a walk by the ocean, hand in hand. It was low tide, and flat rocks, black like onyx and the size of stingrays, cowered on the sand, motionless, like sleeping sea turtles, observing the world around them silently. The waves were exceptionally low and calm, gently gliding onto the beach and tiptoeing back into the sea. The usual crowd of thirty or more surfers, pushing their boards into the waves on a summer evening, were absent. Only the ocean, the sand, and the setting sun were present.

"I feel so helpless," Baatar said. "With you being pregnant, I want to help, but I don't know what to do."

"You're doing everything right," Jenna said. "Your joy and excitement over the news was the best gift you could give me. And you were part of this, too, you know. I didn't get pregnant by myself. Now…" She paused and looked at him seriously. "I do expect you to be with me during the delivery and once the baby's born, there'll be plenty you can do to help."

He nodded. "We're in this together all the way. I've always wanted a family."

When they returned home, Baatar walked straight into the kitchen, where a wall calendar hung by the fridge. He took a pen and put a big star on today's date, then counted forty-five days and put the word "NOW."

"You're a crazy man, Baatar," Jenna said, laughing.

"I'm gonna be a dad!" Beaming, he said, "I didn't think it would happen so quickly, love. We're a good match."

After they'd gone to bed, Baatar suddenly sat up as if he'd been stung by a bee. "We need a bigger house!"

"Let's talk about it tomorrow," Jenna whispered, half asleep, and he settled down, his eyes wide open, imagining what their life with a child might be like.

Sixteen

Baatar looked for Emmy at the racetrack stables. "Emmy, I've got news," he said, then hushed himself and looked around to assure nobody else was present. "We're gonna have a baby."

Emmy smiled. "Congratulations, Baatar, that's wonderful news. You must be stoked."

"We are," he said. "We're very happy. But you can't tell anybody yet, not Manolo, not Mario, not Jack, nobody, OK? Jenna wants to make sure it…it… You know what I mean?"

Emmy shook her head.

"She says things don't always go smoothly during the first pregnancy."

"You mean she could still lose it?" Emmy asked. "I'll say a prayer for you two so everything will go well." *She wondered if this was why she had to move, to make room for the new baby.*

Emmy did her chores and went to school, then to the library to study. Sometimes she didn't even want to be in her room at the new house. It was awkward with Axel stalking her. She returned home late and went straight to bed. She pulled out pictures of Manolo and stared at them, then dialed his number.

"Emmy!"

"Hi, Mano, did I wake you?"

"No, I'm just getting settled in. Long day. What's up?"

"Nothing, really. Work, school, and Axel hanging on me like a sloth in a tree, staring at me with his big baby-blue eyes. Sometimes I wonder if I should just give in and be nice to him."

"You still making tacos for him?" Manolo asked.

"I'm not offering any free meals or any leisure activities to Axel," Emmy said. "He's a nice guy and his foreignness is intriguing, those pale-blue eyes have something, but…"

"Do those blue eyes lure you in?" Manolo asked. "Didn't Paul, that guy you told me about, also have striking blue eyes? The one that went to Harvard?"

"Yes," Emmy admitted. "Blue eyes have something, don't you think?"

"Don't know. I'd rather date a girl with sparkling brown eyes who wants to be a vet," Manolo said.

"You're just saying that to flatter me."

"I miss you," he said. "I can't wait to hold you in my arms again. You tell that Axel guy to find someone else, will you?"

"I will. I'm really not interested in him as a boyfriend. He's just obnoxious."

"Good. Emmy, I'll be back home soon. I love you."

"I love you, too," she said, holding her phone close to her ear.

"Kisses."

Emmy was wide awake. She longed to see Baatar and Bruno, but she couldn't bother the newlyweds with their baby news, and besides, it was past ten. Instead, she rode her bike to the cemetery. She knew it was an unusual time to go there, but she just had to get out of the house. Besides, there'd be no visitors at the cemetery this late at night to bother her.

She brought flowers and placed them on the ground,

then sat with her back against the gravestone and closed her eyes. She took a few deep breaths and pictured her mom until her image appeared and became stronger.

"Mom," Emmy said, "I miss you. I've told you about my move. I live with roommates now, Carla, Mark, and Axel. It's an OK arrangement. I have my own room, but there's no dog. You know what I really miss? Driving to the racetrack with Baatar in his truck early in the morning. I know it's silly. Sometimes he didn't say a word, and I still miss him. I invited Baatar and Jenna for dinner."

Mom listened quietly.

"Manolo went up north for school," Emmy continued, "for two months. And I'm stuck all by myself with roommates." She sighed.

"Be patient, my girl," Mom whispered. "Trust. I'm proud of you. You've made so much progress. Every person we meet teaches us something, good or bad."

Emmy nodded. She stroked the gravestone as her mother's image faded much too soon.

Emmy stood up and walked away slowly. She continued to feel a presence though Mom had left. As Emmy looked around, she noticed a figure following her. Emmy immediately turned around and faced it. The ghostly woman was short and petite, perhaps five foot one, with lush auburn hair and big green eyes. She wore a long dress with beads and frays. The dress covered the woman's feet. She looked misplaced.

"Who are you?" Emmy asked.

"I'm Thessaly," the appearance said.

"I don't know you, Thessaly."

"I need to talk to you," Thessaly said, as she floated closer.

"I don't know you," Emmy repeated. "Why are you following me?" She felt a hand on her shoulder that made her shiver.

"You know Axel," Thessaly said. She spoke English with an accent. Her appearance blushed. "Axel and I are lovers."

"Lovers?" Emmy asked slowly. She stopped to get a better look at Thessaly. "As far as I know, Axel has a girlfriend in Norway. Are you that girlfriend? Did you die?"

"Axel and I are lovers," Thessaly repeated. "We lived together in Ireland. He was my husband, a farmer, but he died young. I came to California during the big move. And now Axel's come here. I've called him, and he heard my call."

Emmy sat down on a bench in the dark, and Thessaly hovered in front of her.

"He heard your call?" Emmy asked. "You're not real, are you? I mean, you're a spirit? You're actually dead? And why can I hear you when I can barely hear my mom?"

"I need you to connect with Axel for me. I've called him and he came," the appearance said.

"You want me to give him a message from you?" Emmy asked.

"No message. He needs to be loved. I called his soul. I want to be close to him," Thessaly said.

"You somehow manipulated him to come from Norway to California?" Emmy asked, baffled.

"I want to be close to him," Thessaly said again.

"Look, I'm not here to play matchmaker between the two of you," Emmy said. "I suggest you go ahead and connect with Axel directly, OK? And leave me alone."

"No, I can't," Thessaly said. Her voice quivered. "I've tried. That's why I need you. You're open. You can hear me. You can love him for me."

Emmy stared at Thessaly. "What?"

"I need you to love Axel for me," Thessaly said.

"Are you out of your mind?" Emmy shrieked. "Look, Thessaly, I love Manolo. Besides, I have school. I have homework. I work at the racetrack stables. I have obligations. I have no time for this. Please leave me alone. Find someone else. I've got to go."

Emmy stood up but Thessaly stood in her way. "No time?" Thessaly said. "What do you know about time? Axel and I were both born in Killarney, in Ireland. We met in elementary school, and I never let him go."

"Thessaly," Emmy said, "Axel is from Haugesund, Norway."

"Yes, now, yes," Thessaly said. "But when we were together, when we were married, he was born and lived in Killarney. He loved me from the day we met."

Thessaly was floating slightly off the ground. "We were only seven years old, but I knew how to get him to protect me. And when we were teenies—well, you know what to do to make a boy come around." She giggled, and her energy expanded and turned pink.

"Look," Emmy said firmly, "that life is over. You have to say goodbye. You have to let go."

Emmy picked up her bike and started to ride away from the cemetery as fast as she could. She turned a couple of times to the appearance and shouted, "Thessaly, I *cannot* help you! Please leave me alone."

Emmy was relieved when she arrived at the house, alone. She slept poorly for the remainder of the night. She studied all morning and went to school in the afternoon but could barely concentrate. Another night with little sleep followed, and she got ready for work as soon as the alarm clock chimed. She was happy to see Baatar among the exercise riders and decided to see him at Mario's trailer later for their usual coffee break around ten.

Baatar was still adjusting to the baby news. While he

galloped the fifteen thoroughbreds assigned to him, he told the news to each of the horses. In his head, he talked with Damdin. If he'd still be here, they'd celebrate together, drinking *airag* until their heads would spin. They'd make plans on how to raise their kids together, give them a good home, teach them the right values. Respect, honoring parents and elders, resilience, humility. They'd teach them to ride and take responsibility for the well-being of a horse, for its needs. They'd teach them to read and interpret horse language.

Emmy gave him a hug when they met up. They had coffee together, and he talked about his and Jenna's plans. Buying a bigger house had become more imminent, getting a nursery ready.

"And you?" he asked, "everything OK?"

"Everything's as good as it can be," Emmy said. That wasn't a lie. She chose not to talk about her ghost experience or obnoxious Axel, who still ate her food when she left some in the fridge, or *accidentally* brushed against her in the hallway, or happened to urgently need the bathroom when she'd just stepped out of the shower. "I still love my car," she said instead, and he smiled.

"I'm happy we can help each other," he said.

When Baatar arrived at home at 6:30 p.m., he heard voices inside the house. As he entered, he was practically overrun by a little boy, who quickly backtracked to a corner, standing very still, his eyes shut tightly.

"Say hi to your uncle Baatar," Amelia coaxed him, but DJ didn't move. His eyes remained squinted shut.

Baatar walked over to him. "DJ." He lifted the boy up and gave him a peck on the forehead. "What a surprise." He let the boy down and greeted Jenna with a hug and a kiss, then reached out to Amelia who was sitting on the sofa, petting Bruno, who also stood in line for a greeting from Baatar, tail wagging.

"A surprise visit?" Baatar asked, as he bent down to pet Bruno.

"We cooked for you," Amelia said, and pointed to the dining table, which had been nicely set with dishes, napkins, and candles.

Baatar looked from one woman to the other. "Do I have time to shower and change?"

"Of course." Jenna smiled at him. "You go get washed up and we'll put the finishing touches on the meal."

Baatar walked into the bedroom, passing the hallway and noticing a suitcase in Emmy's old room. Something was up. *Amelia wasn't known to just pack a suitcase and go on a spontaneous trip. She was more of the planning type, but there'd been no call, no announcement, as far as he knew. And her looks?* It struck him then.

He stripped down and placed his dirty clothes in the hamper. The shower felt good. The warm water was soothing on his back and shoulders. Sometimes he didn't realize how much strain he accumulated in his muscles throughout the day. Jenna's warm hands had become a welcome treat. She should've been a massage therapist with those hands of hers—well, she was now. He smiled. The hot shower poked at the sore spots and eased any stiffness in his back.

He shut off the water and used his hands like a squeegee on his arms and legs before he dived into the oversized towel to dry off. The house smelled of garlic, onions, and sesame oil. *Mongolian beef?* His mouth watered. He liked things a bit spicy, as did Jenna, but not so Amelia. *What were the ladies up to?*

He dressed in shorts and a T-shirt, his regular evening attire. There was no need for shoes and socks in the house.

As he opened the bedroom door, he saw DJ sitting in

the hallway, gently stroking Bruno's belly. "You like Bruno?" Baatar asked and crouched down next to DJ.

Bruno lifted his head, then it popped back down.

"Good doggie," DJ said and continued the petting.

"Yes, he is," Baatar said. "Come, let's eat. It smells heavenly, and I'm hungry. How about you?"

DJ nodded and ran into the dining room.

"Let's wash your hands first," Baatar said and grabbed DJ who froze in place.

"Go with Uncle Baatar and wash your hands," Amelia said.

DJ looked at her, then lowered his head. He didn't move.

"Come," Baatar coaxed him, but DJ stood in place, his eyes squinted shut. Baatar looked at Jenna.

"Come with me," Jenna said, and DJ trustingly put his little hand in hers. Jenna washed his hands and told DJ that his uncle Baatar was a very nice man.

She served the food. Baatar had been right. It was Mongolian beef, one of his favorite dishes.

"So, ladies, what's going on?" Baatar asked.

Jenna looked at Amelia, and Amelia looked at Jenna, taking a deep breath. Quietly, Amelia stared at her food. She bit her lips.

"Wyatt isn't treating DJ very nicely," Jenna said. "Perhaps we should discuss it later when he's in bed?"

Baatar nodded. "How's life in Arizona?" he asked instead.

"We've been settling in nicely," Amelia responded and smiled. "I love the house, the neighborhood, and the small town. I thought Arizona would be superhot, but Prescott is at a higher elevation. We have trees. It's quite lovely, and a small-town setting seems really nice for raising a family." Her voice drifted slightly.

"And you're pregnant," Baatar said, looking at Amelia.

"How'd you know? Is it that visible?" Amelia blushed. "I'm only in my fourth month.

"Are you excited?" Baatar asked.

"Yes, very. Wyatt wants a boy, his own boy, as he keeps reminding me." She smiled awkwardly. "I'd be OK either way. I just want a healthy baby. You know," her face lit up, "the pregnancy makes me happy. I guess I'm producing a lot of happy baby hormones or something. I could sing and dance all day."

"Yummy," DJ said and smiled when he'd managed to stab a carrot onto his fork and held it up in the air.

"You like carrots?" Jenna asked, although she still knew it was DJ's favorite vegetable. The little boy nodded and stuffed it in his mouth, chewing contentedly.

"And what if it's a girl?" Baatar asked, looking at Amelia, "Will Wyatt be OK with that, too?"

"I'm sure he will be," Amelia said. "He's a good guy, you know. He just hasn't adjusted to having an adopted son yet."

"Did he adopt DJ?" Baatar asked.

"No, not legally. He didn't want to."

After dinner, they all went for a long walk with Bruno. DJ trustingly put his little hand into Jenna's and trotted along. They walked all the way up a steep hill from where they could see the full panorama of the Pacific Ocean as the sun was setting. Baatar lifted DJ onto his shoulders so the boy could see better. "Look at all that water," Baatar said. "Isn't that just beautiful?"

DJ lifted his outstretched arm and pointed it in a half circle. "Water!" he said.

"One day we'll all go to the beach together, and you can stick your feet in the ocean," Baatar said. "Maybe tomorrow."

DJ was quiet.

Amelia gave DJ a bath when they returned home.

Baatar looked at Jenna. "They're planning to stay?"

"Yes, I hope you don't mind. She called me this morning. She sounded so desperate I couldn't say no. It's just for one night. I meant to call you to explain, but it wasn't something I could explain quickly."

"Trouble in paradise?" Baatar asked.

Jenna nodded. "It's not as perfect as Amelia had hoped. Seems Wyatt's not open to raising DJ. He treats him worse than a dog. It's quite sad. He knew Amelia was coming with baggage."

"We all come with baggage," Baatar said.

DJ came running into the living room in his puppy pajamas, smelling of soap.

"Good night!" he said quietly and fell on his knees next to Bruno, then snuggled up next to the dog, with his head on Bruno's back.

"Good night," Baatar and Jenna said, and Amelia scooped up DJ to tuck him in bed.

"Auntie Jenna," DJ shouted, "no, Auntie Jenna!"

"You want Auntie Jenna to tuck you in?" Amelia asked.

"Yes, Auntie Jenna!"

Amelia gave Jenna a pleading look.

"Come on," Jenna said and picked up DJ with her left arm around the boy's waist and carried him into Emmy's old bedroom. The boy squealed with laughter.

She tucked him in, then read him a bedtime story. Within minutes, DJ was fast asleep.

"Thank you," Amelia said when Jenna stepped back into the living room. "He adores you."

Jenna took a seat on the sofa, next to Baatar. He looked at Amelia. "Tell me what's going on."

Amelia sighed and took a sip of juice. She pulled up her legs and hugged her knees. "It's Wyatt," she said. "He's not treating DJ well."

"Tell us more."

"He scolds him constantly. He spanks him unnecessarily. He tells him he's stupid all the time. DJ cries in his crib quietly at night. He tries to get Wyatt's attention, brings him his slippers, but then Wyatt doesn't want them and pushes him away. He tells DJ things like 'you'll never do anything right.'" Amelia took another sip of juice.

"DJ brought him a glass of beer the other night," she continued, "and it spilled when he placed it on the table. Wyatt smacked him in the face. He told him he was a stupid ass. DJ's two and half. He tries. Of course, he'll make mistakes. I worry so much about him. It's become quite apparent that Wyatt doesn't want him. But I love DJ. I want to protect him. Wyatt thinks there's nothing wrong with how he treats DJ. He says he's not his own blood; he'll be tolerated, but he'll never love him. I really don't know what to do."

"Are you worried he'll mistreat his own child, too?" Baatar asked.

"No, he keeps saying he wants his own child, not another guy's, not a *half-breed*. But he knew I had DJ when we got married. And now I'm pregnant with his child."

"Do you want me to talk to him," Baatar suggested, "man to man?"

"I don't think that'll do any good. He's a bit controlling, you know. He wants things his way. I think if you talked to him and he found out I shared about our personal life with you, it would just make things worse."

"Then what can we do?" Baatar asked. He put his arm around Jenna.

Amelia looked at Jenna.

"Maybe…DJ could stay with us for a little while?" Jenna suggested.

Baatar's eyes widened. He stared first at Jenna, then at Amelia. "You want your son to live with us? What good would a little while do if the guy's a jerk?"

Jenna gave Baatar a long, concerned look.

Amelia started to cry. "I don't know what to do. I just want to protect DJ."

"And if you left your husband?" Baatar asked.

"Baatar, I'm pregnant with his child!"

"And if he's abusive to that child, too?"

"Then I…" Amelia sucked up her nose, "I know he wouldn't make it easy. Right now, I just want to protect DJ."

"This is a big step," Baatar said. "I think Jenna and I need to discuss this in private. There's a lot at stake here. We don't want to shove DJ back and forth. He needs a steady home."

Amelia cried. She blew her nose and wiped her eyes. More tears flowed. Baatar stood up and put his arms around her, and she sobbed into his shoulder.

"We're your friends," Baatar said, reassuringly. "We'll find a solution together."

Seventeen

After they settled in bed, Baatar and Jenna agreed that DJ could stay with them temporarily, until Amelia had sorted things out with Wyatt.

"And you really don't mind?" Baatar asked. "You know I'm gone all day and the main burden falls on you."

"I don't mind. I've missed the little guy," Jenna said. "It'd be fun to have him around for a while."

In the quiet of the night, Baatar lay awake, thinking of his friend Damdin, of their crazy times together in Alaska and Texas; their travels through Russia, when they were mere teens. He wondered if the vivid dreams about Damdin had to do with DJ. *Did Damdin want Baatar to help find a solution for DJ?* He stared at the ceiling in an attempt to connect with Damdin, but to no avail.

Damdin and he had been together through thick and thin. And now? What could he possibly do for the boy? And what about Amelia? She gave birth to DJ. He was her flesh and blood. Baatar couldn't move to Arizona to help protect the boy, and he couldn't get between Amelia and Wyatt. He didn't know Wyatt, didn't have a right to interfere.

Baatar remembered Jenna telling him that she had partially raised DJ. She was attached to the boy. She'd missed him, but now she was pregnant with a child of her own.

Baatar closed his eyes and took a deep breath, once more trying to call upon his deceased friend. *Talk to me,* he pleaded quietly, *please!* But there was no dream, no vision, no voice, only the quiet of the night.

Baatar got up at 3:45 a.m., as he always did. He showered, gave Bruno some fresh water and a treat; Jenna would feed the dog later as was their new routine. She was a nurturer. Baatar quietly brewed some coffee and warmed leftover rice and beef in the microwave when a small figure showed up in the doorway.

"DJ, why are you up already?"

From a distance, the little boy quietly observed every move Baatar made.

"Don't you want to go back to bed?" Baatar asked. "I have to leave for work, but I'll be back tonight."

Without a word, DJ turned and disappeared in the bedroom.

While Baatar was at work, Jenna had a long conversation with Amelia. They discussed all sorts of possible scenarios. Amelia could visit Baatar and Jenna once a month with DJ to give the boy a reprieve. She and Wyatt could see a counselor, but Amelia had already tried that path and lost. A final temporary possibility might be for DJ to stay with Baatar and Jenna and visit his Mom in Arizona regularly, or Amelia could come to California as often as possible to see her son. Possibly, DJ could move back with her once the baby was born to see if Wyatt would treat him better. Or Amelia could divorce Wyatt and raise her child alone. She could move to California, so they could all help each other.

"I love him," Amelia said. "I love my husband. I know it's crazy, but I do. And I also love DJ. What am I gonna do? I don't want to be raising my children alone. It's too hard, being a single mom. I just don't know what to do. I know I can't do it alone." Tears welled up in her eyes.

"We're here to help," Jenna assured her. "Let us know what we can do to help."

"Yes, I know," Amelia said, crying. "It's the hormones, all the crying is just the hormones."

Amelia had planned to stay for a day, but it turned into three. She'd just wanted to get away, to clear her head, to get advice. They took DJ for a walk with Bruno every evening, peacefully, telling stories, laughing. They went to the beach together to see the ocean, and Baatar told DJ stories about his real dad, the wonderful man Amelia had built up in little DJ's head as a hero.

Wyatt was getting anxious, calling Amelia several times that evening, demanding that she come home. She quickly packed and made reservations to fly home the next morning. Although she tried to be as quiet as possible, DJ awoke. "Go back to sleep, honey," she whispered. "We're going home tomorrow, go back to sleep." She kissed his forehead.

DJ sat up in bed and looked at his mom, then quickly scooted out of the room and ran into the living room. He clamped his little arms around Jenna's leg as tightly as he could. "Auntie Senna," he cried. "Auntie Senna and Boono. Mommy, stay here!"

Amelia rushed into the living room, fell to her knees and did her best to pry DJ's arms off Jenna's leg. "We have to go back home, DJ. Your new daddy is waiting for us. He loves us," Amelia argued. "We can come back to visit sometime, but tomorrow we have to go home."

"Auntie Senna," DJ cried. "Mommy, stay with Boono and Auntie Senna."

"Baby, we can't. We've got to go home."

Amelia took DJ into her arms, where he sobbed so heavily that his entire body shook.

They left the next morning.

Jenna and Baatar talked about DJ after he left and wondered what their own children would be like. What if they had a girl, and what if they had a boy? No matter, they'd love them. They'd teach them about life, they'd travel with them to meet all their relatives, to show them the world with its different landscapes, cultures, people, languages, and lifestyles. It was fun to dream and plan.

While Baatar and Jenna imagined what their lives would be like as parents, Emmy had her own issues at hand. She stayed out of Axel's sight as much as possible and hadn't had any strange ghost experiences for a few days. *At least the house wasn't haunted*, she thought.

She decided to go back to the cemetery. She just wanted to talk to Mom. As she arrived at her parents' grave site, before she could even connect with her mom, Thessaly awaited her.

"What are you doing here? Go away!" Emmy said angrily.

"It's so miraculous that you can hear me," Thessaly said, seemingly sitting on top of Emmy's family's gravestone. "I've been waiting for you."

"You've been waiting for me for a week?"

"Time has no meaning in my life," Thessaly said with a sweet voice.

"You're not alive," Emmy said. "Thessaly, you're dead. You need to go where you're supposed to go." Emmy took a deep breath and sighed. "Mom! Will you please help Thessaly?" She called out, but there was no sight of Mom.

Thessaly hovered closer. She was almost touching Emmy now. "I was mean to him then," she whined, picking up the conversation where they had left a week ago. "I judged him. I told him he was a failure, he wasn't a man. He had no courage. So, he enlisted and went to war to prove to me how courageous he was. He was killed in action. Do you understand? I was horrified. I caused his death. I searched for him for a long, long time, and now I've found him again. I must make amends."

Emmy stared at Thessaly. "If you were born and lived in Ireland, why did you move here anyway, way back then?" Emmy asked. "Why didn't you stay where he was buried, and you could be together when you died? In that other...sphere?"

"Haven't you heard of the Irish potato blight?" Thessaly asked, her energy flickering.

"I have not."

Thessaly's body lowered until her face was level with

Emmy's. "There was a series of famines in Ireland. About a million people died, and almost as many decided to flee. Many immigrated to America then."

Emmy listened patiently.

"Axel and I were born in 1901. His name was Liam then. He inherited a potato farm from his parents. There were seven brothers, and each inherited the same amount of land. Our farm was very small. We had a baby and not enough to eat. Then typhoid, cholera, and dysentery broke out. Our girl died. She was only two."

"I'm very sorry," Emmy said.

"It was misery. Do you understand?" Thessaly asked, lifting her head, her big, green eyes staring at Emmy. "Then the first World War broke out. Axel left for war and was killed. And I was left behind with no future. So, I left with my parents for America."

"Did you get remarried?" Emmy asked.

"No," Thessaly said. "I felt ashamed. I was supposed to be Axel's wife. We were supposed to grow old together. He wasn't supposed to die so young. I want those remaining years with him. And you can help me. You and I, we can love him together."

"Are you insane? No, Thessaly!" Emmy said, "We will not! Look, my parents died young too, and I cannot make them come alive as much as I want to. It was fate."

"It wasn't Axel's fate," Thessaly insisted. "I judged him. I must make amends."

"What makes you think Axel is your...your reborn Liam anyway?" Emmy asked.

"I recognize his soul," Thessaly said. A soft smile came over her lips.

Emmy sighed. "Look, Thessaly, if you were alive, I'd send you to therapy, but since you're actually dead..."

"You'll help me then!" Thessaly completed her sentence. "Oh, Emmy, thank you. You're my savior. I knew I could count on you because you lost your family. You understand!"

"No, Thessaly. I can't be your savior." Emmy's voice grew louder. She looked around to see if any real people were around but didn't see anybody.

I don't want to be involved," Emmy said. "I don't even know what to think of your story. I mean, anybody could invent a story like that."

"He loves potatoes," Thessaly said, "and he loves tacos. When he eats garlic, he gets hiccups, and he's allergic to avocados. He gets hives. And he's jealous; he gets very spiteful when he's jealous."

"Really," Emmy said, mocking Thessaly.

"Trust me," Thessaly said, "check it out if you need proof. I thought you were compassionate. You talk to your Mom and she's a spirit, too."

"My mom watches over me," Emmy said. "She raised me. We have a close connection. That's very different."

"You're the only one who can hear me," Thessaly said again, "and I can tell you can see me, too. You're gifted. You're a bridge between two worlds. It's your obligation to use your gift for good, to help lift sorrow and spread love. I need you, Emmy. Love never dies, even when we're physically gone. I thought you understood that."

Of course, Emmy understood that. She remembered how much she'd wanted to have a dad and how Baatar had taken on that role for her. When she had no one, Baatar had offered her a place to belong, and more than that, he called her his daughter. She loved him for that. *But she couldn't help a dead person reconnect with her husband from another era.*

"Please go home," Emmy said. "I only come here to talk to my mom. Do you understand? Exclusively to my mom."

"I don't have a home," Thessaly said. Her eyes filled with tears.

That stung. Emmy searched the row of graves where her family was buried and read every gravestone, but there was nobody named Thessaly. She searched further rows, until six rows back, she found it. Thessaly was still following her.

"There," Emmy said. "That must be your grave. The gravestone says, "Thessaly Flynn, born May 1, 1901, deceased February 15, 1970. You've been dead for over fifty years. Why aren't you in your grave? Isn't it time for you to go to heaven?"

"You don't speak with your mother that way," Thessaly sneered and sat on top of her gravestone. "Axel got to come back, and I didn't. It wasn't fair. I can only be with him through you."

"No!" Emmy said. "I'm not getting in the middle of this. And besides, I don't believe in reincarnation, so you go back into your grave, and I'll go home."

"We don't really live in those graves," Thessaly reproached Emmy. "That's only for the physical body; you know that. The soul separates. I'm waiting for a new body. Let me borrow yours."

"That's out of the question!" Emmy looked at Thessaly. "Doesn't your soul have a place to go? My Mom doesn't just hover around here. Don't you have things to do? Become an angel? Sing to the harp? Watch over somebody?"

"I watch over Axel," Thessaly said.

"Is that your job? That's the official role you were given? Or are you stalking him?" Emmy asked.

"I'll come home with you," Thessaly suggested. "That way I'm close to him."

"Don't you dare," Emmy said. "I'm leaving now, and you stay right here, or go wherever your soul is supposed to be, but don't follow me."

"You're mean," Thessaly said, pouting.

Emmy turned on her heels and walked off. She turned once more and shouted, "You stay here!"

She saw Thessaly standing by her grave, forlorn, her luminosity had taken on a reddish hue, as if she were angry. Then her appearance faded more and more.

Emmy rode her bike home, shaking her head and laughing on the way. *How could she connect with a ghost? Axel's ex-lover? From a different era?* She laughed heartily. It felt unreal, as though she'd made it all up. *She could only see and speak with Mom, end of story. That young woman had been the strangest hallucination ever.*

"That's all I need," Emmy said aloud as she pedaled down the road. "An angry ghost." Perhaps, she'd ask Mom to keep Thessaly in check...if Thessaly ever got out of the way and let her speak with Mom again.

When Emmy arrived at home, she felt extremely tired, much more than usual, as if Thessaly had zapped all her energy, *but that couldn't be, could it?* She had trouble pushing open the front door. It was past midnight. The door seemed to jam, when Axel opened it from the inside, and Emmy fell into his arms accidentally.

"Excuse me," Emmy said. "The door jammed."

"It's OK." He smiled big. "I catch you any time. You need a hug, yes?"

"No, I don't need a hug. I just need to go to bed and get a good night's sleep."

Slowly, he released her. "I hug you any time," he hollered, as she climbed the stairs.

She had to admit, the hug had felt good, even if it hadn't been intended. Despite his height and big muscles, he was gentle, warm. She'd felt safe with him for a moment.

As she closed her bedroom door, she quickly brushed those thoughts aside. She couldn't wait for Manolo to come home. She wondered if she should tell Baatar and Jenna about her strange meeting with Thessaly.

Better not.

Eighteen

Three days after Amelia left, Baatar had another nightmare. He saw DJ being beaten, cowering in a corner, scared to look up. He saw bruises on the little boy's back. He saw fear in his eyes. Then DJ's face switched to Damdin's. They looked so very much alike, father and son. Then all Baatar saw was Damdin's eyes—eyes that held a lifetime of a message; eyes that had followed him for years of journeying from country to country and state to state. Eyes that had laughed and cried with him. Now they were filled with sorrow and pain.

Baatar awoke and sat up in bed, drenched in sweat once again. *He couldn't tolerate it. He couldn't bear a young boy being beaten and traumatized for life, not if he knew; not if he was Damdin's son.*

In the morning, he shared his dream with Jenna. She was concerned and promised to speak with Amelia to see if Wyatt was still mean to DJ or if things had changed.

She didn't reach Amelia. She left a voicemail message. And a text. And another voicemail message.

The next day, there was a call, a desperate call. Amelia had misplaced her phone the day before, she said, when things had been bad. Wyatt had beaten DJ when he'd thrown up in bed. DJ had bruises on his back, and Wyatt threatened to beat him with his belt if he'd continue to be a pest.

Amelia sobbed.

That night, Baatar and Jenna drove to Arizona. Amelia packed a suitcase for DJ to visit Auntie Jenna for a few days while she would have a serious talk with Wyatt. Jenna again pressed for marital counseling for the two of them, and Amelia promised to address it again. She agreed; things couldn't continue as they were.

DJ didn't seem to mind the long road trip in the middle of the night. He fell asleep in the truck. At home in Little Oaks, Baatar carried him into the house, while DJ peacefully slept in his arms. As Jenna prepared a bed for him, Baatar laid him on the sofa, where DJ continued to sleep, his feet tucked into Baatar's thigh and his head resting on Bruno, who'd also jumped on the sofa.

Jenna didn't mind taking care of DJ. In the following days, Jenna and DJ took a walk with Bruno, then went to the beach, where he tirelessly played in the sand. They had a chocolate ice-cream cone in the afternoon before they went home. Jenna cooked while DJ quietly played with his toys or with Bruno. She made sure DJ got to speak with Amelia every day. After all, she was his mom—his real mom.

"DJ would blow kisses to Amelia and tell her a highlight of the day. "Mommy, come," he'd say and run off to play again.

"Short attention span." Jenna smiled.

"He's two," Amelia said. "Thank you, Jenna. You're like his second mom, always have been. I'll talk to you tomorrow."

"Have you had a talk with Wyatt?" Jenna inquired.

"I tried."

"Will he go to counseling? Did you find a solution? He's got a serious problem."

"Not yet. I'll keep trying."

"Mommy, come," DJ requested again the following day.

"I'll come see you soon, baby," Amelia promised.

Jenna kept asking Amelia what she and Wyatt had decided, but there was always an escape, an excuse, a delay, and never a clear answer.

The first few days in Little Oaks, DJ clung to Jenna. He followed her everywhere. He was shy. When Baatar came home, DJ quietly huddled in the corner.

"Do you want to go for a walk with Bruno?" Baatar asked, trying to make DJ feel more comfortable.

"Auntie Senna," DJ whispered.

"OK, why don't we all go together," Baatar suggested. Throughout the walk, DJ clung to Jenna, his little hand tightly pressed into hers.

At night, Baatar read him a story and DJ listened intently. He loved the pictures Baatar showed him. "All right, little boy, time to sleep," Baatar said and tucked him in. When he switched off the light, DJ began to cry.

"Auntie Senna."

Jenna came to kiss him good night. "Mommy," he'd say.

"Your mommy is coming to see you soon," Jenna said.

The next day, Jenna showed DJ pictures of Tsokhoor, Saaral, Kheer, and Sunny and told him everything she knew about horses. "They come in different colors, just like people," she said. "Some are tall, and some are short. They have a big head and a mane and a tail. They love to eat grass. Uncle Baatar works with horses."

"Horsies," DJ said, pointing with his little fingers at the horses in the pictures.

"Uncle Baatar works at the racetrack where the horses run really fast. The fastest one wins," Jenna explained, and DJ listened quietly.

"On the racetrack, Uncle Baatar watches to make sure everybody is safe," Jenna said. "Would you like to go and see the horses and see Uncle Baatar at work today?"

DJ nodded. Jenna packed a small backpack with water, a snack, and carrots.

The little boy was very excited to see the horses and Jenna pointed out Baatar. "See, there he is, on that gray horse. See him? He's wearing a red vest and a black helmet. The gray horse's name is Saaral."

"Saaral," DJ said.

"Yes, that's right. Look at the jockeys who ride the racehorses. Their saddles are very small, and they sit up very high. It's a dangerous job, and they can fall. The horses run close to each other and can get injured. Uncle Baatar makes sure everybody is safe."

DJ watched closely as the racehorses were led into the starting gate. His body jumped when the starting gate flung open with a loud smack. He followed the horses around the track, with the jockeys on top, standing in their saddles. Some jockeys used a whip to spur on their horses.

"Uncle Ba hit horsies?"

"No," Jenna assured him. "Never. Uncle Baatar is here to help. He watches for any accidents. If a jockey or a horse fall, he helps them."

"He doesn't hit the horsies?" DJ asked again.

"No, DJ. Uncle Baatar doesn't hit horses or children or anyone else."

When the winning horse was led into the winner's circle, Baatar and Mario sat on their ponies, side by side, quietly watching the ceremony until everybody left the track.

In between races, Jenna and DJ walked to the tunnel and Baatar stopped Saaral to chat with them. He dismounted and held Saaral by the reins. "Hi, you two, I'm so happy to see you. DJ, this is Saaral. She is my friend. We work together. Would you like to get to know her?"

DJ stared at Saaral.

"Make a fist and let her smell you. Yes, right there, hold it right up to her nostril." Baatar showed him how and DJ followed his directions. Saaral sniffed, then exhaled.

DJ giggled. "He breathe on me."

"That means she welcomes you," Baatar said. "Horses know each other by smell. When she breathes on you, it's like she's shaking your hand."

DJ giggled again and held up his little fist to Saaral again.

"I brought carrots," Jenna offered. "Would you like to give her one?" She looked at DJ, then reached out and gave Saaral a small carrot, which the pony graciously took and chewed.

DJ giggled.

"Now you," Baatar said and put a carrot in DJ's hand. "Hold your hand out flat so she can take it from you."

DJ looked at the carrot, then at Saaral, and ate the carrot himself.

"I know, she's big but she's very gentle," Baatar explained. "Look." He gave Saaral another carrot, and the pony took it and chewed. "Just hold out your hand and feel her muzzle," Baatar suggested.

"Does he bite?"

"No, she won't bite. Her muzzle is very soft, like soft lips."

DJ held out his hand and squealed with laughter when he felt Saaral's soft muzzle. Immediately he reached into the bag with carrots and offered Saaral one, which she gently received.

"Horsie." DJ laughed. "Horsie."

Baatar looked at Jenna and they both smiled. "I have to

go," he said. The next race will be starting. He crouched down and looked at DJ. "Saaral and I have to go and work," he said. "We'll see you later." He winked at Jenna and mounted.

"Bye, Saaral," DJ said.

Just as he mounted, two dolled-up women in high heels walked up. "See, that's the one I told you about," one of them said, pointing at Baatar. "Isn't he handsome?"

Looking at Baatar, she asked, "Can we take a picture of you?"

"No, ma'am," Baatar said, "but you can take a picture of my pony."

They pushed Jenna and DJ out of the way and snapped pictures. He looked at them sternly. "That's my wife and son," he said. "You're being very rude."

The women stared at Jenna and DJ and giggled as they walked off.

After the races, when Jenna and DJ arrived at the stable, Baatar was already brushing Saaral. The dinner buckets, full of grains and molasses for Tsokhoor and Saaral, sat in front of the stalls.

Baatar stopped brushing and walked out of the stall to greet Jenna and DJ.

"Does that happen often?" Jenna asked, "women wanting pictures of you?"

"Jenna, they were drunk," Baatar said. "It means nothing." He gave her a peck on the cheek and turned to DJ. "This is where Saaral and her friend Tsokhoor stay when we're not working," he said. "These are their rooms."

DJ looked up at Tsokhoor who stretched his neck out over the gate and sniffed.

"Welcome," DJ said.

Baatar smiled. He crouched down so his face was on level with DJ's. "There are some rules when we're around horses," he said. "First, you need to wear a helmet for safety." Baatar put his helmet on DJ. It covered his entire head and forehead. He could barely see. "We'll have to get you one that fits," Baatar said.

DJ stood still.

"No running in the barn," Baatar said, "just walk calmly and speak with a low voice."

"Why?"

"Horses have very good hearing, much better than ours. When they hear loud voices, they get startled."

"Startled?" DJ asked.

"Fearful," Baatar said. He lifted DJ on his arms so he could more easily reach the ponies. "You've already met Saaral. This is Tsokhoor. Feel his coat," Baatar encouraged. "Feel how soft it is." He showed DJ how to run his hand down Tsokhoor's neck.

DJ giggled. "Horsie," he whispered.

"That's good," Baatar said. "He can hear you well."

DJ touched Tsokhoor again with his little hand.

"Do you want to feed him a carrot? Horses love carrots. It's like candy for them."

DJ nodded.

They fed both Saaral and Tsokhoor the remaining carrots. While Baatar finished brushing Saaral, Jenna held on to DJ and answered his many questions. He watched as Baatar gave both ponies their dinner buckets, refilled their hay sacks and gave them fresh water. "When horses are in a pasture, they graze all day," Baatar said, looking at DJ, "but in the stable, we feed them hay."

"Why?"

"Grass cannot grow in the barn. The barn is like a house."

DJ nodded. He got to touch both ponies before they left, and Baatar removed his helmet.

"Let's wash our hands before we leave." They all washed their hands and Jenna helped DJ dry his on a paper towel.

Quietly, on the way to the car, DJ slipped his hand into Baatar's.

Emmy came over for dinner that evening. She arrived just as Baatar helped DJ put on his shoes for a quick walk with Bruno. Bruno was already waiting by the door, his leash in his mouth. He scratched the door with his paw, and DJ laughed. "We're coming, Boono!"

Emmy walked into the kitchen to see if she could help Jenna with dinner and set the table. She looked over at Baatar and DJ. For a moment, she saw a young man standing in the corner, watching. He had a smile on his face. As she stared at him, she realized he was the man from the picture Baatar had placed on her altar on the Day of the Dead last year. It was Damdin, DJ's dad. He glanced at Emmy, and she noticed he had that same intense look in his eyes that DJ had—the kind of piercing look that gave her the impression he saw more deeply than most. She smiled in acknowledgment. Then his image faded. She wanted to tell Baatar, but Bruno had managed to pull both him and DJ out the door. *She'd tell him later*, Emmy thought.

Jenna updated her on everything that had happened with DJ.

After dinner, Jenna gave DJ a bath, and DJ let Baatar tuck him in for the night.

"A big breakthrough," Jenna said when Baatar joined her in the living room.

"The ponies won his heart," Baatar said.

"I think you did, too."

Baatar leaned over and kissed her. "It's nice having kids around," he said, "to witness how curious they are and experience everything with innocent eyes."

"You're a patient teacher," Jenna said. "You'll make a great parent."

"Together with you."

"I saw Damdin," Emmy said.

"Damdin?" Baatar asked, looking at her. "What do you mean?"

"I saw him just for a moment when you put DJ's shoes on earlier. Damdin was standing in the corner, watching the two of you. He has these piercing, dark eyes and an oval face. I recognized him from your picture."

"He's checking up on me?" Baatar asked.

"I think he's watching over his son," Emmy said. "He was smiling. He seems happy that you're taking care of DJ."

Baatar nodded. "So, our house is haunted? Jenna's mom, Damdin, any other residents we should know about?" He grinned.

Emmy laughed. "I don't know. It doesn't seem they live here. Perhaps they just come to say hello sometimes, making sure you guys are OK. Does it bother you?" Emmy asked.

Baatar shook his head. "But do tell them not to disturb our privacy!"

"I don't think they would," Emmy said, laughing, "but yes, sure, I'll try to strike up a conversation with ghosts, whom I don't know, at your house, when I can't even communicate with my mom unless I'm right by her grave." She paused for a moment, listening into the house, remembering Thessaly.

"Everything all right?" Jenna asked.

"Yeah, fine," Emmy said quickly. "By the way, my mom never gave me any messages from Damdin for you, Baatar."

"I think his message has been received," Baatar said

and smiled at Jenna. "We're just waiting to hear from Amelia what she and her husband have decided. I hope they go to counseling, so we don't have to send them the cops or social services someday."

Jenna continued her online meetings with Amelia, which seemed to be getting shorter.

The following evening, Baatar walked in with a children's helmet and a gray, stuffed animal. "I got you a gift," he said to DJ and the boy came running.

"Horsie!" he said and hugged the stuffed animal.

"You'll have to name it," Baatar said.

"Saaral," DJ said.

"I guess that's a good name," Baatar agreed. He put the helmet on DJ, and it fit him well. When Baatar tried to take it off, DJ ran off. He wore the helmet in the house and later on their walk with Bruno.

Baatar insisted he take it off for dinner, and DJ reluctantly did. Then he put it back on. He insisted he sleep with it and started to cry.

"We'll keep the helmet right by your bed," Baatar said. "When I'm off work on Monday, we'll go visit Kheer and Sunny, two other ponies. They're in a pasture, and you'll need to wear your helmet to see them."

"Pomise?"

"Yes, I promise. But now you've got to go to sleep."

As promised, on Monday afternoon, Baatar and Jenna brought DJ to Hillside Ranch, where they were invited to Mario and Maria's home for a barbecue. Mario's daughter, Tina, volunteered to play with DJ, and they found games to play in the backyard. Then Baatar and Jenna took DJ to the pasture to meet Kheer and Sunny, and Baatar put the helmet on DJ.

"Horsies," DJ said and held out his hand.

"Let them smell you first," Baatar reminded him, and

DJ stretched out his little fist. Kheer breathed in deeply and then exhaled.

"Welcome," DJ said.

"Yes, good, you remember that means she welcomes you. Do you want to sit on her?"

"Like Uncle Ba?" DJ asked. Wearing the helmet, DJ bent all the way back to look at the horse, then Baatar."

"Yes." Baatar put a bridle on Kheer. "Do you want to ride her with me?"

DJ nodded.

"OK." Baatar lifted DJ on Kheer's back and mounted her himself, with DJ sitting in front of him. He held DJ with one hand and the reins with the other. "We'll ride very slowly," he assured Jenna.

The little boy giggled when Kheer began to move.

"Horsie," he said. He turned around to look at Baatar with a big smile. Then he waved at Jenna and howled with glee. He petted Kheer while they slowly rode in a circle.

When Baatar stopped Kheer to dismount, DJ shouted, "More!"

"Quietly," Baatar whispered to DJ. "Remember, they have really good hearing."

"More," DJ whispered.

Baatar grinned and they rode a few more rounds together.

"Looks like he's a natural," Jenna said when they were done.

"What did you expect?" Baatar said, smiling. "He's part Mongolian. It's in his blood."

"I thought you said his dad was never a good rider?" Jenna said.

"He lost in competitions with me, but he could certainly ride."

Jenna chuckled. "I see."

"It's kind of fun having DJ visit us for a few days, isn't it?" Jenna said at night after DJ had gone to bed, with his helmet right by his side. "It gives us some time to practice."

"Time to practice?" Baatar asked.

"Practice parenting skills."

"You think this is practice time?"

"Yeah, don't you?" Jenna asked.

"I have a feeling he's here to stay," Baatar said.

Jenna looked surprised. "I can't imagine Amelia would let him stay with us for good. I think she has a lot on her plate with Wyatt and her pregnancy and living in a new town where she doesn't know anybody but him. But that'll change in time."

"Yes, probably. I'd hate to see DJ go back to a stepdad who abuses him though," Baatar said.

Jenna nodded. "I don't mind him being here for the time being, even if we didn't expect an instant family. Do you mind him being here?"

"I don't mind at all. I *will* have an issue with him returning to Wyatt unless he'll make some drastic changes in how he treats the boy," Baatar said.

Jenna called Amelia every day. "Have you and Wyatt seen a counselor?" she asked.

"No," Amelia admitted. "He refuses to go. Things haven't changed yet. I don't know what to do. I know he'd beat DJ into obedience." She began to cry.

"Or worse," Jenna said. "Amelia, you have to find a solution. DJ's your son. He needs his mom."

"I know," Amelia said, swallowing. "I know. But at least he has you. You're kind of a second mom to him." When she had herself under control again, she video chatted with DJ. She told him how much she loved him.

After ten days, Amelia came to Little Oaks for a day to check on DJ in person. She hugged and kissed him and told him over and over how much she loved him. Then she left.

The few days of DJ staying with Baatar and Jenna turned into a week, then two, then three.

Baatar and Jenna adjusted to their new situation. Mario's daughter, Tina, came over in the afternoon to play with DJ, so Jenna could pursue her sewing business and fulfil orders she'd taken on.

***

Baatar shared his situation with Emmy, who wanted to help as well. She still slept poorly at the new house. While she waited for Manolo to return, she wanted only to study, get good grades, learn about horses, and be there for Baatar and Jenna, except now she struggled with her new acquaintance, Thessaly. She wondered if Thessaly had indeed followed her to the house, made herself invisible, and manipulated things? *Could a ghost do that?*

One evening, when Emmy took a shower, she heard her mom's voice. *"Emmy, watch out!"* Then the lights turned off, and the room was dark. Emmy thought it was Axel, trying to be funny in his own way.

"Not funny, Axel," she said aloud, but there was no response.

"Carla!" she hollered, but again, there was no response. The room was pitch black. Emmy turned off the shower and touched with her hands along the wall to the towel rack and then the door, trying to find the light switch. Just as she approached the door, the lights went back on, and Axel stormed into the bathroom.

"I heard you calling out—everything OK?" he asked, staring at her. *"Hello!"* he said with a big smile.

"Get out!" Emmy shouted at him. "The lights went off."

"It was a fuse. Carla was blow-drying her hair, and I

made popcorn in the microwave. Overkill," he said, with a smug grin on his face.

"Get out!" Emmy said again, now holding a towel in front of herself. *She should have locked the door.*

"I grew up with two sisters," Axel said, "no big deal."

He turned, and Emmy shut the door behind him, this time locking it. Shampoo dripped from her head to her shoulders, slowly running down her back, giving her a creepy feeling. She felt a slight breeze pass her, then it was gone. *Thessaly?* Emmy thought. Hesitantly, she stepped back into the shower and rinsed off.

She barely slept that night, dreaming of Thessaly and Axel with herself in the middle, being pulled and pushed, which was not a good place to be. In her dream, she ran away, leaving the two to be on their own, but they couldn't communicate. She saw Manolo at a great distance and couldn't get to him.

The week dragged on. She went to the racetrack early for her shift and worked hard, harder than usual, carrying heavy bales of hay until she was out of breath. She told all the horses about being haunted, and how lucky they were that no ghosts pushed them to do things they didn't want to do.

Emmy called Manolo's sister, Ariana, and they spoke for a little while, but Ariana had volunteered for a double shift at the hospital and couldn't meet.

Finally, on Thursday, Emmy drove to the cemetery. She ran through the rows of graves and stopped at her family's gravesite. She leaned against the gravestone, as usual, and closed her eyes, focusing on connecting with mom. Her chest warmed, a sign that there was a connection. She could feel her mom's love, and then she could see her image.

"Hi, Mom, I'm always so happy to see you. I love you,"

Emmy whispered.

"I love you, too, Emmy."

"Mom, did you see that spirit that followed me the last couple of weeks? Her name is Thessaly, Thessaly Flynn. She is buried a few rows down."

"I didn't see her. What about her?"

She says she knows Axel, my new roommate from Norway, but she knew him in a different life when they were married in Ireland. Do you think that's possible? Is she fibbing to me?"

"Anything's possible, Emmy," Mom said. "There's so much more to life than your five senses permit you to experience. When your soul is freed from the physical world, you realize there are many dimensions."

"But do you think people get reborn into a new life?"

"I don't know, Emmy."

"If this ghost is going to haunt me, can you stop her?"

"I don't think I have a right to interfere in someone else's life," Mom said.

"But you'd be protecting me, and she's dead."

"I'll always protect you, Emmy, but I don't have the right to interfere in another soul's life. Perhaps send her a healing prayer?"

"OK, I'll try that. Mom, that whole moving-out thing turned out to be a disaster. Look at the mess I'm in. Why'd I do that?"

"There's a reason for everything, Emmy. Be patient. You're guided. Trust."

Emmy sighed deeply. "Thanks for connecting with me. I need you very much."

"I love you, Emmy." Her mom's appearance faded.

Emmy ran back to her car as fast as she could. There was no sign of Thessaly. *Perhaps she'd found someone else to bug,* Emmy thought, *or she'd changed her mind about Axel, or she actually listened and went to where she was supposed to be.*

Driving home, Emmy felt lucky to be alive. Thessaly had a miserable existence. *She isn't here and not there,* Emmy thought. *She's in limbo; she's stuck.* Emmy felt sorry for her, but Thessaly didn't really matter. Manolo would be coming home in a week.

Nineteen

DJ was slowly getting used to living with Baatar and Jenna. One evening, on a rainy day, he was cranky. He'd not been able to run and play outside as usual. Jenna and Baatar cooked together, and he set the table, then asked DJ to put away his toys.

"No!" DJ shouted. "I want to play."

"You can play again tomorrow," Baatar said. He sat on the living room floor with DJ. "Let's put away your toys. You're a big boy. You can do that."

"No," DJ said again.

Baatar looked at DJ and reached his arm out for the toy basket that sat on top of the sofa. Immediately, DJ crouched down. He remained motionless and quiet.

"DJ?" Baatar asked.

The boy remained crouched down, immovable.

"Come here, DJ."

DJ remained crouched down, his head bent down to the floor.

Baatar looked at Jenna.

"DJ, come here," he said again calmly, but the boy remained motionless.

Baatar picked him up and sat down on the sofa, putting DJ in his lap.

"Auntie Jenna," DJ whined and squirmed to get away.

"Aunt Jenna is right there," Baatar said calmly, but this

is between you and me. DJ, I understand that sometimes you don't want to do something. That doesn't mean I'm gonna spank you. But we do have rules for you. Your Aunt Jenna and I set the rules, and you need to obey them. Do you understand that?"

DJ looked down.

"And if you're naughty and don't obey, we may punish you, but we won't hurt you or beat you, do you understand that?"

DJ listened quietly.

"OK, let's shake hands on that," Baatar said.

They shook hands.

"Now, we've made a nice dinner. It smells really good, and I'm hungry. But before we eat, you'll have to put your toys in the basket. Will you do that, please?"

DJ nodded. He slid off Baatar's lap and quickly put all his toys in the basket.

***

Every Monday, Baatar took DJ to Hillside Ranch to ride the spare ponies. DJ proudly wore his helmet around them at all times. He listened and obeyed. He helped feed the ponies carrots and added a ladle of supplements to their evening feed. In the arena, Baatar rode Kheer and put DJ on the pony with him, as his own father had done. Baatar remembered feeling majestic then, sitting on top of a horse like his father, and learning to intuitively sense the horse's motions and moods.

Baatar enjoyed passing on what he had learned at a young age—the knowledge that stayed with him all his life and made him who he was. Respect, humility, and resilience were values a Mongolian boy on the steppe learned naturally. He'd have to teach them to his kids in a world that was kinder to children, and to adults, for that matter. Living in a *ger,* with only life's essentials during harsh winters, and being dependent on a herd of wild horses for sustenance, was very different from living in Southern California, with pleasant year-round temperatures, and the Pacific Ocean as one's playground. Teaching good values in this environment wouldn't be as easy, Baatar knew, but he'd try.

***

He saw Emmy during her shifts at the racetrack and was proud of her work ethic.

"Baatar, will you take a look at this horse, please? He's different," Emmy said as he walked by.

"Different how?" he asked.

"His head is down. He's not eating, and usually he can't get enough."

"Has he been pawing or sweating? Does he have an elevated heart rate? Those can be signs of colic."

"No pawing or sweating, I think," Emmy said.

"Let's feel his pulse." Baatar found the artery under the horse's jawbone and pressed lightly on it. Come, feel it," he encouraged Emmy. "Run your finger along the bottom of his jawbone until you feel a small, firm cord. Do you feel it?"

"Yes." Emmy smiled.

"Look at your watch's hand and count his heartbeat for fifteen seconds, then multiply by four."

"Forty-eight," Emmy said.

"I counted that, too. A normal pulse reading would be between thirty-six and forty beats per minute. He might be in pain. We should have Gloria check on him. Look, he's pawing."

"Oh, right. He was lying down when I walked in," Emmy said, "with his head turned around toward his belly."

Baatar nodded. "Best to get Gloria to check him out."

"But you think it's colic?"

"I do, but I'm not the horse's owner, trainer, or the vet. Best to get the official diagnosis."

Emmy nodded. "Should I wait for the trainer?"

"I'd get Gloria now."

Emmy found Gloria, and she came and listened to the horse's belly with her stethoscope. She took his temperature and vitals and diagnosed colic.

Emmy smiled. *The horsemen knew their stuff. She trusted Baatar's opinion, even if she had to get Gloria's official diagnosis.* She was learning so much from Baatar and Manolo. She was counting the days until Manolo's return. Five more days.

On occasion, Emmy managed to free some time to babysit DJ in the afternoon before school. She enjoyed playing with the little boy. It gave her something to do besides think about Manolo not being there, or avoiding Axel, or fretting about Thessaly. Baatar had built a sandbox in the backyard, where DJ loved to bake imaginary cakes and fill at truck with sand and unload it. Emmy taught him a song that she and her sister Cecilia had learned as young children. Now she sang it to DJ, and he learned to sing along.

But the playtime didn't solve Emmy's real problems.

She drove to the house where she lived and studied. She felt hungry and cooked some chili. Just as she finished cooking, Axel showed up, looking at her with his pale-blue puppy eyes.

"I'm staaaarving," he said. Longingly, he looked at the stove.

"Perhaps you should buy some food?" Emmy suggested.

"Emmy, please! I'm so hungry and this smells so good. Chili?"

Emmy stared at him. She rolled her eyes as she took a second bowl out of the cabinet and filled it up for him.

He gave her a kiss on the cheek. "I like dating you," he said. "You're a good cook. He took a bite of chili, then licked the spoon from all sides and looked up. "And pretty," he added.

"Axel, we're not dating," Emmy said.

They talked about their classes and instructors, college life in Norway and California. Emmy picked up the empty dishes and rinsed them when Axel approached her from the back. His long arms slung around her waist like a boa constrictor, his hands clamping tightly in front of her stomach. For a moment, she enjoyed his embrace, then she became agitated.

"Axel," she said politely, "would you please not hug me?"

"Your hair smells good," he said, ignoring her request. "Peach?" he guessed.

"Axel, please take your hands off me." She embraced his wrists with her soapy hands and pulled his hands apart.

"Nice grip," Axel said, smiling. He stroked her hair.

"Axel!" Emmy turned around and stared at him with a quick, heavy exhale, her eyes enlarged, her face serious. "I'm together with Manolo."

"It's OK," Axel said, "he's away."

"He's attending a training, but he'll be back soon, and I'm not looking for an affair."

"Affair," Axel said, "I'm not an affair. I'm Axel from Haugesund. Don't you want to explore? Norwegian style?" He blinked at her slowly. His pale blue eyes looked as innocent as can be. "Build international relations?" He added, smiling from ear to ear, raising and dropping his eyebrows three times in a row.

Emmy sighed. "No, thank you."

"I thought Americans were friendly," Axel said, "welcoming, especially in California. I like you. Don't you like me?"

"I like you as a friend."

"I like more," Axel said.

"Axel, give it up. This isn't going anywhere. Perhaps you're interested in Carla? She doesn't have a boyfriend, and I think she likes you."

"But I like you."

"I don't know how you see things in Norway," Emmy said, frustrated. "From my perspective, both people have to want the relationship."

She turned and walked away, while Axel lingered in the kitchen, watching her legs as she walked up the stairs.

Twenty

DJ had been living with Baatar and Jenna for a month. After dinner, Baatar helped him take a bath, brush his teeth, and tucked him in bed.

"Daddy," DJ said.

Baatar picked up Damdin's picture, which he had placed on DJ's nightstand, and held it up to him. "This is your daddy," Baatar said, "and you have a stepdad in Arizona."

DJ shook his head. "Daddy." He looked straight at Baatar.

"DJ," Baatar sat on his bed, "your daddy had an accident and died. But he watches over you all the time, and when you close your eyes, you can feel his love in your heart. Try it, close your eyes."

DJ closed his eyes.

Baatar put his hand on the boy's heart. "Can you feel it? Do you feel the warmth?"

DJ nodded.

"And if you could hear him, he'd say, "I love you, DJ."

The boy smiled.

"And when you see a cloud in the sky, he's riding on the cloud, and he's sending you a big smile."

DJ giggled.

Baatar withdrew his hand and the boy looked at him. "Daddy."

"I can't make your daddy come back, but I'll do everything I can to be like a daddy for you."

DJ stood up in bed and gave Baatar a hug.

"I love you, DJ," Baatar said, holding the little boy in his arms. "Do you want to hear a good-night story?"

DJ nodded.

"OK, lie down. Let me see. Once upon a time, there was a little boy named Damdin. He was born in Mongolia in the springtime, just when the snow started to melt, and the grass sprouted and grew, and the grasslands began to be green again. There were lots and lots of green slopes, big, juicy meadows. The little boy grew up in the country with his parents and horses in all colors, and big white sheep, and little goats, and he had a big, fluffy dog."

"Boono!" DJ said.

"Yes, a big, fluffy dog just like Bruno. And together they ran in the grasslands every day. They watched the horses and the riders, many riders and many horses. And when they got home, after a long day of playtime, his mom gave him a warm cup of milk and fed him rice pudding."

Baatar looked at DJ who'd fallen asleep. Baatar switched off the bedside lamp and sneaked out of the room. The baby monitor would alert him and Jenna of any trouble.

Baatar walked into the living room. "Did you hear him?" he asked Jenna.

"Sounds like he wants you to be his daddy," she said and smiled. "Yes, I heard him."

"What can I tell him?" Baatar asked. "I'd love to be his dad, but we can't take him away from Amelia. She's his mother."

"I think what you told him was the right thing," Jenna said. "You'll do the best you can to be like a daddy to him, and that's all you can do. I just don't know if a two-year-old can grasp that."

Jenna continued every day to connect with Amelia so DJ could see his mom and chat.

Amelia was happy that DJ was loved and safe. "I miss him," she said to Jenna, "but I don't miss the cries and the threats and Wyatt scolding and spanking him all the time. Wyatt's been so loving and understanding without DJ here. I don't know why he has such a short fuse with the boy. Thanks for taking care of him. Doesn't Baatar get annoyed with DJ?"

"No, Baatar's very patient with him," Jenna said. "It's just who he is. Besides, I think DJ reminds him of Damdin. They did so much together. There were like brothers. They truly cared for each other."

"Yes, I remember," Amelia said. "Life with Damdin would have been so different, well, at least I think so. Wyatt says it's easy to idealize someone when they're gone. I keep talking to him about DJ. Wyatt knew I was coming with a child. He just doesn't feel close to the boy and thinks DJ shouldn't be his responsibility."

"Mommy come," DJ requested.

"I'll come see you soon, baby," Amelia promised.

But one week led to another and another. She came after another three weeks had passed, then six, always without Wyatt, who didn't feel like spending the weekend in a crowded house. Nobody spoke about counseling any longer. It was futile.

"I'm getting so pregnant," Amelia said to Jenna. "Look at me. I'm approaching my sixth month and wobble like an elephant. I won't be able to travel for a while."

"What are you saying?" Jenna asked.

"I won't be able to come and see DJ for a while."

"You want him to stay with us? Wyatt hasn't changed his mind about him?"

"He hasn't. And I don't want him and DJ alone at home while I'm in the hospital delivering a baby. Those two alone in the house would really worry me. You do understand, don't you? Do you mind?"

Jenna shook her head. "We don't mind, but DJ's your son, Amelia; he misses you."

"I know," Amelia said. "I miss him, too. But I know he's safe with you."

Jenna couldn't imagine giving her child away to someone else, not even Amelia. The thought of seeing her own child only on a computer screen or the phone, to not cuddle and hold him and kiss him good night, to watch him learn and grow, would be unbearable. "We'll do the best we can with him," she assured Amelia. "Do you see this as a permanent solution then?"

"I don't know." Amelia's eyes watered. "I never thought his dad would die on me. I can't see into the future. I don't know how my life with Wyatt will turn out once we have our own child. What would you do?"

"I don't know," Jenna said, truthfully. "I just think I couldn't bear not being with my own child. I don't know how you manage."

"I couldn't do it without you," Amelia said. "I feel like life screwed me, you know. I'm trying to make the best of what I've got."

Jenna nodded. "Just give DJ a lot of love when you're here. He needs that."

"Of course, I will."

***

As DJ became more settled in Little Oaks, his facial muscles began to relaxed. He no longer cowered in the corner when Baatar came home. He smiled more. He learned to say *I'm sorry* when he did something wrong and to say *no* when he meant it. He could laugh with abandon.

He ran faster than a bullet train and squealed when being caught. He loved to play hide-and-seek and sleep with Bruno by his side. But being a two-year-old, DJ was also high-spirited.

Whenever time permitted, Jenna took him for long walks or to a nearby playground where he could use a swing and a slide. When Jenna took a break from sewing, they went to the beach together where he played in the sand, and they explored the waves together, gathered seashells or rocks, and built sandcastles. One afternoon, he ran ahead.

"DJ, stop. Wait for me," Jenna said. But DJ wasn't listening. He ran as fast as he could. Jenna ran after him when suddenly he fell. He started to cry. She reached him a few seconds later.

"DJ, did you get hurt? Let me see."

"Ow," he cried and held his leg. His knee was scraped.

"We'll have to clean and dress that," Jenna said. "We'll have to put on a Band-Aid."

"Mommy," DJ cried.

"Yes, I understand, at moments like this you want your mommy. But Mommy isn't here right now, so you'll have to trust me. It's just a scrape. I promise it won't hurt."

She was about to turn around to go home when a lifeguard reached them.

"Can I help?"

"We need to clean his knee and get a Band-Aid," Jenna explained.

"Come with me," the lifeguard said. He lifted DJ onto the back of his truck and brought out hydrogen peroxide and a first aid kit.

"You're a brave boy, aren't you?" the lifeguard asked. "Like a hero."

"My daddy's a hero," DJ said. "He's from Mangolia."

"Oh," the lifeguard said in admiration, "he must be a very strong and courageous man."

DJ nodded.

"Does your daddy know how to ride a horse," the lifeguard asked, "if he's from *Mangolia*?"

"My daddy rides on a cloud," DJ said.

"That's very impressive. You must be very proud of him."

DJ nodded.

"Do you have kids?" Jenna asked.

"Two."

When the lifeguard tried to clean the wound, DJ shouted, "No, Auntie Jenna!"

The lifeguard smiled and handed the wipe to Jenna, and she carefully blotted the wound and put a Band-Aid on it.

"You have a very nice aunt," the lifeguard said. "You better mind her."

DJ nodded.

"No more running off without me, OK?" Jenna confirmed. "We're a team. We work together. Shake on that?"

They shook hands and went to the beach where they built a sandcastle, and DJ ran back and forth to the ocean to fill and refill the mote with water. Afterward, he was tired enough to take a nap.

That evening, Baatar was sitting in the living room when he observed DJ and Bruno interact. DJ had been petting Bruno when the dog got up and walked away.

"No," DJ said, "stay." He pulled Bruno by the tail and Bruno turned around and snapped at DJ. Baatar jumped up but Bruno hadn't hurt DJ in any way. The dog had merely given DJ a warning to set boundaries.

"Bad dog," DJ shouted and wanted to hit Bruno, when

Baatar caught his little hand in midair.

"Sit down, son," Baatar said and picked up DJ to sit on the sofa with him.

"Bad dog," DJ repeated.

"No," Baatar said calmly, "Bruno is not a bad dog. Bruno is not a toy. When you pet him, and he has enough, he has the right to walk away. You, DJ, need to respect Bruno. He's always there for you. He plays with you. He watches over you. He takes walks with you. He protects you when you sleep. But he's not a toy. Do you understand?"

DJ shook his head. "Bad dog."

Patiently, Baatar explained again. "When Bruno wants to walk away, you need to let him walk away. When you pull on his tail, you're hurting him. His tail is very sensitive. Bruno defended himself because you hurt him. And he didn't hurt you back. He startled you, but he didn't hurt you. He only let you know it's not OK to pull his tail. You need to apologize to Bruno for hurting him."

DJ pouted.

"Did you want to hurt Bruno?" Baatar asked.

DJ shook his head.

"But you did."

DJ was quiet.

"Bruno is such a beautiful dog and such a great friend. What do you say to a friend when you've hurt him?"

"I'm sorry," DJ whispered.

Baatar lifted DJ off his lap and motioned for him to go to Bruno.

DJ stood and looked at Baatar. Baatar nodded at him again and looked over at Bruno. "Poor Bruno's hurt."

DJ walked over to Bruno and said, "I'm sorry, Boono." The dog lifted his head and licked DJ's hand.

Baatar walked over to both of them and crouched

down. "It's nice to have a friend, isn't it?" he asked.

DJ nodded.

"Come, we'll take him for a walk."

Baatar put the leash on Bruno and took DJ by the hand as they left.

"It's easy to respect a horse," Baatar said to DJ outside. "Horses are big and powerful. But it's important that we also respect those who are smaller than us. Every living being has feelings. They all feel pain, even the little ones."

Even a dog?" DJ asked.

"Yes, even a dog."

"Even a bird?"

"Yes, even a bird."

"Even a butterfly?"

"Yes, even a butterfly."

When they returned home, DJ was a good boy again. Baatar walked into the kitchen and pointed at the calendar, then looked at Jenna. "Today's the day," he said, pointing at the word NOW he'd written down a month ago. "Everything good?"

"Everything's good."

He hugged Jenna and swirled her around, then bent down and said to Jenna's stomach, "Hello, Sophie."

"You remember that?" Jenna asked.

"Of course, I remember. So, I can tell all our friends and my folks now?"

"Yes, honey, but we don't know if it's going to be a boy or a girl yet."

"But it's safe to spread the news?"

She nodded. "I think so."

That evening, Baatar called his parents, his sister, and his brother to tell each of them about Jenna's pregnancy. They were happy for him, they said, and expected updates and pictures.

"That's a given," he said.

Baatar waited until around ten in the morning, when everybody was gathered in Mario's trailer, to spread the good news. Mario, Cody, and Jack congratulated him on the pregnancy and inquired about Jenna's well-being.

"She's fine," Baatar proudly announced. "Mom and baby are fine."

"And DJ?" Mario asked. "What's his situation?"

"We'll see," Baatar said. "We'll just have to wait and see."

Twenty-One

Emmy didn't have time to stop by the trailer, but she already knew about the pregnancy. She stopped in the bathroom to put on her new dress and some lipstick, and then she headed to the airport to pick up Manolo. She parked her car and walked all the way to the arrivals terminal.

Then she saw him.

"Before you stands a professional farrier," Manolo said. He looked like he'd just stepped out of a cowboy movie. He wore a dark-blue-and-white-checkered, long-sleeve shirt and a brown leather vest with the farrier school's logo, blue jeans with a brown belt and silver buckle, and leather boots. He'd grown stubble as if he'd been on a cattle drive for a week. The dark stubble enhanced his features and made him look more grown-up, more manly. His hair had grown and his bangs, although pushed to the side, kept falling into his face, but the small mole on his cheek hadn't changed, just like his bright, contagious smile.

"Mano!"

He dropped his bag and wrapped his arms around her.

"Hi, beautiful," he gave her a kiss. "I know, I need a bath and a shave."

"You look great," she said. "I'm so happy you're home. Don't ever leave me again. Aren't you glad to be back home?"

He looked into her eyes and smiled. "I am now. How are the ponies?"

"Everybody's fine," Emmy said.

"I think my arms are two inches longer and my hands have grown," he said, holding them up for Emmy to investigate.

"You're funny," she said. "They're the same as always; maybe a little brawnier."

He chuckled. "It's been a workout."

They drove straight to Emmy's new residence.

"I'm making tacos," she said, "just for you. I've missed you so much."

They walked into the house and Manolo dropped his bag by the door. Emmy walked ahead of him, looking over her shoulder. "Come in the kitchen," she said, when she slipped on a rug and Axel caught her in his arms.

"*Hello!*" Axel said with a big smile.

Emmy struggled to free herself. "Since when do we have a rug there?" she asked. Her face flushed.

"I bought it and just placed it down," Axel said. "My contribution, yes. I just couldn't take my eyes off it when I saw it in the store. You like it?"

"I slipped on it," Emmy said, reproachfully.

Manolo stood next to her. "Are you OK? Did you get hurt?" he asked.

"I caught her," Axel said with a big grin. "She's safe with me."

"Yes, I noticed," Manolo said. He gave Axel a long look. "Thank you."

Emmy gave Manolo a kiss and introduced the two men.

Axel sat down at the table while Manolo walked over to the kitchen counter with Emmy. She had already prepared all the fillings for the tacos, and they heated the tortillas together.

"Please sit down," Emmy said to Manolo.

"Taco Friday, just like home," Axel said. "Norwegian special. For me."

"No, not for you," Emmy said. "For Manolo, my boyfriend."

"We have Taco Friday in Haugesund," Axel said to Manolo. "We eat tacos at home, just like here."

"Maybe we can share with him," Manolo whispered to Emmy. "He's foreign. He probably doesn't have a lot of friends here yet."

"He hits on me," Emmy whispered back. "I don't want to feed and encourage him."

"Really?" Manolo glanced at Axel.

"Today I'm making lunch just for Manolo," Emmy said to Axel.

Axel looked at her with his big blue eyes and didn't budge from the table.

Manolo felt bad and looked at Emmy with pleading eyes. She sighed and placed the tacos on the table, but before Axel could grab a taco with his big hands, she slapped a couple big dollops of avocado on each of them.

"No!" he shouted. "Not that icky green stuff. I don't like it."

"What's not to like?" Emmy asked, observing him closely. "It's my grandma's recipe."

"It gives me bumps," Axel said, "on my skin. Red bumps."

While Emmy and Manolo ate in the kitchen, Axel didn't leave the room. He sat at the table, staring at Emmy, watching every morsel of food that went from her plate into her mouth.

Emmy sighed and looked at Manolo. "Do you want to

eat upstairs in my room?"

Manolo blinked at her and slowly shook his head. "It's OK, Emmy. "Let's go upstairs after we've eaten."

He was kind, Emmy thought, too kind. "Sounds good," she said. She stood up to refill their water glasses with a pitcher when she felt a push and accidentally poured the water all over Manolo's lap.

He pushed the chair away from the table and looked at Emmy with wide eyes, his forehead wrinkled.

"I'm so sorry," Emmy stuttered. "It was...I got this push." She ran into the kitchen and got a dish towel to help dry off Manolo's jeans.

"What's going on with you?" he asked.

"I'll tell you upstairs," Emmy said. "I'm really sorry."

They finished their tacos while Axel kept talking about his engineering classes. Emmy got two bowls and spoons and opened the fridge. She looked for the vanilla pudding she'd prepared earlier. She turned to Axel.

"Have you seen the pudding I made?"

"The yellow jiggly stuff?" he asked.

"Yes."

"I shared it with Carla. It was really good."

"Axel, you can't just keep eating my food without asking."

"Oh, here." Axel put three dollars on the table.

"I'm not asking you to pay me," Emmy said. She blushed. "I'm asking you not to eat the food I make unless I offer it to you."

"She's blushing," Axel said, looking at Manolo. "So cute and defiant. She likes me."

Emmy's eyes widened. She took a deep breath and exhaled heavily.

"Emmy," Manolo said, "let's go upstairs." He closed the bedroom door and looked at Emmy. "You want to tell me something?" he asked and sat down on the bed.

Emmy sat down next to him. "I love you, Mano," she started.

Manolo looked at her. His eyes were dark, focused. She could see his long black eyelashes with every blink. He listened quietly.

"I know this is gonna sound weird," she said.

"You love Axel, too?" Manolo suggested.

"No!" Emmy sighed deeply. "You know I go to the cemetery to visit my parents' grave, right?"

Manolo nodded.

"Because that's the only place where I can actually communicate with my mom."

Manolo nodded again.

"But lately…"

"You don't hear her any longer?"

"No. Lately there's been this…this apparition. I see a young woman but she's really dead. I mean, she's a spirit, like my mom, and she lives there in the cemetery. It seems she's kind of stuck in place, like she's stuck in the past, in her mind, you know. She heard me talk to my mom and somehow I can hear her, too, and now she's become a problem."

"A problem?" Manolo asked. He looked in Emmy's eyes.

"I'm not making this up. Do you think I'm making this up?"

Manolo cleared his throat. "I believe you," he said. "Go on."

Emmy stood up and walked back and forth. "So, this young woman, her name is Thessaly, she claims she used to be married to Axel in another life." Emmy glanced at Manolo to see if he still followed her. "And in that life she says she judged him and told him he wasn't very…very manly. So, he went off to war to prove himself to her."

"Aha."

"And he got killed."

"I see."

"Mano, I'm just telling you what she said. So, after the war, she came from Ireland to the US and lived here for the rest of her life. I saw her grave. It's just a few rows behind my family's. Thessaly Flynn."

"And what do you have to do with her?" Manolo asked.

"Right. She feels horribly guilty because she was so judgmental and nasty to Axel, and now she wants to make sure he's loved. Nonjudgmentally, you know. Unconditionally."

"And what's your role in this?" Manolo asked.

"I don't know, Mano. She has it in her head that she wants to love him through me. She follows me around. She trips me. She pushes me into him. It's like she moved in here, but she's made herself invisible. She's using me just like she said she would. It's all very odd. I've told her to leave. I prayed. I can't get rid of her. When I spilled the water earlier, I felt this uncontrolled push. She manipulates me. I don't know how to explain it. It's so weird. Manolo, you've got to help me, please!"

"Maybe you should just move out."

"I've signed a six-month lease."

"So, you want to be here with Axel and this ghost?"

"No."

"Axel seems to like you without any help from the other side," Manolo said. "I don't care much for the way he stares at you."

"And I don't like how he devours everything I cook. He just assumes he's the center of the universe. How can anybody be so insensitive? I tell him no and he thinks it's a come-on."

Manolo grinned. "Emmy, come sit down."

He pulled her close and gave her a kiss. "You could stay with me until we find you something else."

"I don't know."

"You'd rather stay here?" Manolo asked.

"No. I don't know what to do. Have you ever been stalked by a ghost?"

Manolo shook his head. "But I hear it can happen. My grandma knew how to deal with that sort of thing. She knew some effective prayers. She could make potions and saged the house all the time. But she's gone and nobody learned it from her. They say she was gifted."

"You've got to be kidding me," Emmy said, her mouth open.

He shook his head.

"Do you think I should talk to Baatar and Jenna? There's got to be somebody who can get rid of a clingy ghost."

"And Axel," Manolo said.

"I can handle Axel and tell him to butt out. It's the ghost who's causing all the problems. You wanna spend the night?"

Manolo smiled, when they heard a knock and voices in front of the door.

"Emmy, open up we know he's in there." It was Carla's voice.

Emmy and Manolo looked at each other. "Huh?" Emmy opened the door.

"He stole my wallet," Carla said. She looked at Manolo. "How dare you steal my wallet?"

"What?" Manolo asked.

"I was looking for it all over the place until Axel suggested to look in your bag that you left sitting in the hallway. You didn't even try to hide it. My wallet was right on top when I opened your bag.

"I didn't take it," Manolo said calmly.

"You stole my wallet!" Carla shouted. "Get out of here. You're a thief."

"You're crazy," Manolo said.

"Get out!" Carla shouted, "and don't come back. We don't have any tolerance for thieves."

Axel stood right behind Carla. "I told you he was trouble," he said, batting his pale-blue eyes at Emmy.

Emmy looked at Carla and Axel. "Manolo and I were together the entire time. He didn't steal your wallet, Carla. He couldn't have."

Manolo shook his head and walked down the stairs, and Emmy ran after him. "Wait, Mano!"

He grabbed his bag and left the house.

Emmy ran outside. "Mano, please wait." As she caught up with him, he turned toward her. "I thought they were decent people," he said. "I was wrong."

"How do you think her wallet got into your bag?" Emmy asked. "You were first in the kitchen and then upstairs with me."

"Perhaps you should ask Axel," Manolo said, "or your weird ghost."

"You think I'm making her up?" Emmy asked.

"No." Manolo sighed. "Emmy, I'd really feel better if you'd come home with me tonight. I don't like you staying here with people who lie and accuse me of committing a crime in their house. What kind of place is this?"

Emmy's eyes widened. "Thessaly told me that Axel gets very jealous, and when he gets jealous, he gets spiteful," she said. "Let me get a few things. I'm coming with you."

They left together. As Manolo backed out of the

driveway, Emmy began to cry.

He stopped the car. "Emmy."

"I miss my parents, and I miss Baatar," she said. "When I'm alone my life just sucks. Living with these roommates is like living in foster care. I had a roommate there, too, Verena, who stole and lied. It's just a repeat. I need a real home. I know I'm an adult now, but I really need that."

"Emmy," Manolo said, "why didn't you tell me how bad the situation here has become for you? You should've told me all along."

"I didn't want to bother you. You were busy."

He looked at her, studied her face. "Emmy, you're more to me than a friend. You don't bother me. You can tell me anything. You don't have to pretend or hide things from me. I love you. You're the most important person in my life; don't you know that yet? I'd do anything for you."

Tears welled up in her eyes.

"We could have found a solution together," he said, "even if I wasn't here. We have resources. You're not alone, Emmy." He leaned over and gently wiped her tears.

"Oh, Mano, I've missed you so much." She flung her arms around him, and he held her tightly, stroking her hair. "Everything will be OK," he whispered.

"How can everything be OK when I live with lunatics and am stalked by a ghost?"

Manolo grinned. "That's a good question."

"It's not funny."

"I agree. You wanna go home with me or go for a surprise visit to Baatar and Jenna?"

"Both." She sucked up her nose.

He kissed her on the cheek, then drove straight to Baatar's home. He parked the car in front of the house. It was 9:30 p.m.

"He gets up before four," Emmy said. "It's his bedtime."

"Not today. Come." Manolo took her hand.

Jenna brewed some tea for everybody while Emmy told Baatar all about Axel and the new addition in her life, Thessaly, the ghost.

"At first I was kind of happy I could see and hear her like my mom," Emmy explained. "I didn't realize she'd become such a problem. She's ruining my life. What can I do?" She looked at Baatar while Jenna distributed the tea mugs.

"I'm not an expert on ghosts but I could have a word with Axel and set him straight," Baatar said. "And if living with those roommates turns into a problem, we'll find a better solution for you."

My mother could talk to ghosts," Jenna said.

"She could?" Baatar's, Manolo's and Emmy's eyes landed on her.

"Yes. It wasn't something she talked about. As a matter of fact, she kept very quiet about it. Only immediate family members knew. Perhaps you can find out more about this spirit?" Jenna suggested to Emmy. "Question her. When did she live? Where did she live? What was her relationship with Axel in that life? Why does she want you to be the go-between? And for what purpose?"

"She's been quite clear," Emmy said. "She wants to possess me so she can make love to him."

"That's very invasive," Jenna said.

Emmy nodded. "It feels like she's taking over my life, and I don't know how to get rid of her."

"How long has this been going on?" Jenna asked.

"Over a month."

"Oh my, over a month! So, she's become quite attached to you."

Emmy nodded.

"This is serious," Jenna said. "We need to find a *curandera*."

"That's what I've been thinking, too," Manolo agreed.

"A *curandera*?" Baatar asked.

"Yes," Jenna said, "someone who can get rid of the ghost."

Emmy sat up tall. "Really? You know someone like that?"

"I don't know anyone here," Jenna said. "My aunt Teresa may know someone in Texas."

"My mom may know someone," Manolo said. "Or Ariana, my sister. I think they know a woman who's performed a *limpia* at a friend's house."

"A *limpia*?" Emmy asked.

"A purification—cleansing a house to get rid of a spirit or energy that is negative or intrusive," Jenna explained.

"And you're only telling me now?" Emmy asked, looking at Manolo.

"So much was happening all at the same time at your house," he said, "we just had to get away from that place, and I needed a bit of time to digest it all."

"What if she's here clinging to me now?" Emmy asked. She strained to look over her right shoulder, then left, and patted and brushed invisible things off her dress with her hands.

"Usually they stay near their source, so her energy's probably strongest around Axel and the house you both live in," Jenna said. "If you want, we can make you a bed on the sofa. You can stay here tonight."

"And we'll be buying a bigger house soon," Baatar added.

"Emmy can spend the night with me," Manolo said. He looked around. "If that's OK."

"You're adults, you don't need our permission," Baatar said, smiling. "It's up to Emmy."

"I'd love to spend the night with you," she said and gave Manolo a peck on the cheek. "And thank you, Baatar and Jenna, that we could bother you so late at night."

"I'm glad you came over," Baatar said. "It's always good to find a solution together. We're your family, Emmy."

Emmy and Manolo left, and the house became quiet.

"A *curandera*?" Baatar asked Jenna again when Emmy and Manolo had left. "Tell me more about that."

"A spiritual healer," Jenna said. "They're very common in our Latin culture. They know how to purify negative energies, they cleanse and bless houses, they help in all kinds of situations. They know special, powerful prayers, herbs, potions, incense, sage."

"Like a holy man or woman," Baatar said. "We have those in Mongolia, too. They use prayers, herbs, massage, and rituals to cure illness. They have a strong spiritual connection. Some have healing hands, some know how to set bones. Nomads also use what we call *dom*, comfort medicine."

"Comfort medicine?" Jenna asked.

"Yes." Baatar smiled. "Ancient customs based on folklore, old family remedies that are supposed to help. For stomach trouble, skip a meal. If you feel restless and can't sleep, count your breaths."

"Like eating chicken soup when you have a cold," Jenna said.

He nodded. "Our cultures aren't all that different, are they?"

While Baatar and Jenna settled in for the night, Manolo and Emmy drove to Hillside Ranch. The house was dark already when they arrived, another family with an early schedule. They tiptoed upstairs like thieves and quietly went to bed, sleeping arm in arm, which made Manolo's twin bed big enough for two.

They spoke with Manolo's mom in the morning, and she promised to find a *curandera* to help Emmy.

Emmy and Manolo worked at the stables together again. She'd missed him there, even though she had shifts only three times a week. Working with the horses felt good. The work was much the same every day, unless there was a horse with an injury that needed special attention. Being with the thoroughbreds and the ponies calmed Emmy. The horses were her therapy. Looking into their eyes touched a place deep in her heart that made her feel understood. Hearing them chew hay had a hypnotic effect, soothing all senses. Listening to their hooves, as they walked down the hall or around the shed row, was comforting. Their mere presence brought harmony and peace. Emmy didn't even think about Axel or Thessaly or Carla, accusing Manolo of being a thief.

While Emmy awaited updates on the *curandera* from Manolo's mom, she avoided the house as much as possible. She drove to the racetrack stables early in the morning, and straight from there to college. She studied at the library or locked herself in her room. She avoided the kitchen, living room, and dining room. She avoided Carla and Mark, and above all Axel. She was hesitant to go to the cemetery now that she knew how cunning and unpredictable Thessaly was.

Baatar continued to make a point to casually run into Emmy at the racetrack stables, though she knew it wasn't a coincidence. He always had an encouraging word for her, a compliment, a wink, a quick hug. "How's my daughter today?" he'd ask. He found ways to get Emmy smiling. "Any problems?" And then he'd invite her to join him for a cup of coffee in Mario's RV trailer.

It was clearly a man's trailer, with dirty boots by the door, leather leggings on the cot, dishes piled up in the sink, phones and wallets on the table, mixed with a belt, a pair of socks, and a bag of horse treats. She sat down on the cot when Baatar handed her a mug of coffee, and Mario walked in.

"Hi, Emmy, did Maria call you already?"

"No, why?"

"She found a *curandera*. We think she's very experienced and can help you."

"Thank you, Mario!"

Emmy called Maria while she walked back to the stables to finish her chores. Manolo was working closely with the onsite farrier, and Emmy hadn't seen him yet today.

"Her name's Pia," Maria said and gave Emmy the phone number. "She comes highly recommended and is expecting your call."

Twenty-Two

When Jenna was in her sixteenth week of pregnancy, she and Baatar went to the doctor's office together while Emmy babysat DJ. The nurse took the vitals, which were all good. Then the doctor came to perform the ultrasound.

"Mrs. Flores," she said, "how've you been?"

"I feel fine," Jenna said. "I had a little bit of nausea for the first couple of months but not lately."

"You're lucky," the doctor said and smiled. "No pain, no bleeding?"

"None," Jenna said.

The doctor squeezed some gel on the ultrasound wand. "It's going to be a bit cold." She gently moved the wand across Jenna's abdomen. "There it is," she said.

Baatar and Jenna stared at the monitor, watching that tiny being, seemingly curled up. They could clearly see the baby's outline.

"Looks a little like an alien, doesn't it?" Jenna said.

"It's so miraculous," Baatar said, not taking his eyes off the monitor. "Can you tell from the image whether it's a boy or a girl?"

The doctor looked more closely and changed the angle of the wand when the baby moved a little. "Looks like it'll be a girl," she said. "We can check again in a couple of months to confirm, but I'm quite sure."

"A Sophie." Baatar smiled. "That what we want." He

squeezed Jenna's hand.

They took a walk along the beach together, just the two of them, followed by dinner. They talked about their future and decided to make a point to always have special dates without the kids, no matter how much they loved them.

Emmy had already fed and bathed DJ when they returned home. They thanked her and she headed to her roommates' house.

"Time for bed," Baatar said to DJ. "Come, I'll tell you a story."

"Yeah." DJ smiled.

Baatar winked at Jenna and followed DJ into the bedroom. He tucked him in and told him about his dad's great sense of adventure and courage, how he traveled from Mongolia all the way to America, over mountains and hills, through forests and rivers, until DJ's eyes closed, and he fell asleep.

Baatar returned to the living room and sat down next to Jenna. "I thought DJ would spend only a few days with us until things had calmed down at Amelia's house. It's been three months. What's the situation? Did she convince Wyatt to seek counseling? We haven't seen her in six weeks."

"He still refuses," Jenna said. "He's become quite outspoken that he doesn't care much about DJ. Amelia is worried his demeanor toward DJ will never change. Some men just don't have a big heart. Can you imagine being stuck between two people you love? It must be hell on earth."

Baatar looked at Jenna, and she glanced at him from the side. "I'd really like to read the guy the riot act," he said.

"Baatar."

"It's not right," he said. "The poor boy. It's not his fault his dad died."

"Maybe he's not such a poor boy," Jenna said.

"What do you mean?"

"He's got you," Jenna said. "He's got us."

"What good can we do when he returns home and then comes to see us every so often to lick his wounds while Wyatt abuses him on an ongoing basis?" Baatar asked.

"Perhaps we could consider…"

"Consider what?" Baatar asked.

"Taking him in?"

Baatar pondered for a while. He stared at Bruno.

"Like you did with Emmy," Jenna said.

"Emmy's an orphan," Baatar said. "She had nobody." He paused and stared into space. "I wouldn't mind raising DJ, but I don't want to burden you. You have your career, your passion, working as a seamstress. I'm gone for many hours a day, sometimes I travel for work and am gone for a few weeks. The burden would fall on you, and you're pregnant, too."

"It wouldn't be a burden," Jenna said. "I've always wanted kids. And Damdin and Amelia and us, we were all friends. As you said, it's not DJ's fault that Damdin died. It was a horrible accident. Amelia and I have been friends since kindergarten. She and DJ lived with me for two years. It'd be an honor raising her son."

Baatar looked at Jenna. "I love you, you know that?" he whispered. "But if DJ stays here with us, for good, I won't give him back. He's not a horse one sells, or a guitar one lends to a friend for a while. He's a little boy. He's my best friend's son. I can't raise him for a few months or a few years and then have to let him go back. I'd grow too fond of him. I'd want to adopt him."

"I'm not sure Amelia would stand for that," Jenna said. "He's her son."

"But she's willing to pass him to us so he can be safe, grow up in a safe environment," Baatar said.

"Yes, but he's still her son. She's his mother. She's not just going to give him up," Jenna said. "Just imagine how Amelia feels, having to let go of her own son to keep him safe."

"She has other options."

"You mean leaving Wyatt and raising her two young children by herself?" Jenna asked.

"For example."

"Perhaps she's not strong enough to do that. Not every woman can," Jenna said.

Baatar looked at her without a blink. "Could you?"

"I could, and I would," Jenna said without hesitation. "But I'm a born nurturer, and Amelia is Amelia. She needs validation. She needs a man in her life. She doesn't want to be a single mom. I don't think she can." She paused and let it sink in.

Baatar rubbed his chin. In the semidark room, with the moon shining through the curtains, he looked at his friend's picture, the one where Damdin held a bar of gold in his hands. Jenna had placed it on the mantle next to their wedding picture.

"Why couldn't you stay?" he asked him. "Why'd you have to make things so complicated?"

Jenna smiled. "He's giving us a chance to prove that we're his friends," she said. "We can do this. We can help his son."

Baatar was quiet.

"What do you think Damdin would want you to do?" Jenna asked.

Baatar took a deep breath. "I think he's already made that clear, haunting me in my dreams."

He stood up. "I need a run."

He put on his running shoes and headed toward the beach. He loved Jenna. He loved their life together, but sometimes he just needed to be alone, run, and clear his head.

He ran a few miles and sat down on the cool sand. It was dark. The half-moon, halfway along its heavenly journey, reflected its light on the water. *Was he just half a friend?* Baatar wondered. *Why did he want to put his own conditions on raising DJ? Damdin had been more than generous with Baatar. He'd taken him under his wing, taught him about traveling and living abroad. He'd rescued him a few times, without conditions, when he'd been injured or down in the dumps. He'd changed his life to accommodate Baatar's needs more than once.*

Damdin was dead, died in a fire on an oil rig where the two of them had gone so Baatar would feel better. And now, Damdin's little son was down in the dumps. Baatar knew only too well what that felt like; to be rejected. He remembered when he'd tried to buy himself free from his guilt for having left his parents and siblings in Mongolia. He'd sent a lot of money for his parents' retirement, and his father had rejected it. He remembered Narangerel's coldness toward him until he reached out to her and they talked, brother to sister. He knew what rejection felt like, and he was sure it was as painful to a two-year-old as it was to a thirty-year-old. Damn.

He pulled off his shoes and waded along the shoreline with his feet in the waves. The salty ocean water was soothing, splashing his feet and ankles, coming and going. Life was like that, he knew. We all come and go—the circle of life. And sometimes we get to connect with old soul friends, like Damdin and Jenna. *What was his role in all this?* he wondered. *Certainly, he had enough love in his heart to raise his friend's son.*

It seemed Amelia almost pleaded for him and Jenna to take DJ in. But what if he was only on loan? Moving to America had changed him, Baatar thought. *He took on Bruno when his owner was taken to a nursing home and could no longer take care of him, and now he couldn't imagine life without the dog. And the ponies? He talked to them every day. He confided in them. They'd become family members. He wasn't just fond of them, he'd fallen in love with them, and Emmy and Jenna and DJ. He never realized how attached he got to the people around him, the ponies, even the dog.* The painful loss of his friend still lingered in his heart.

Clinging was useless; he could never make DJ his own, or force him to stay, not Damdin and not DJ. Life threw hurdles in our path, challenges, and we could all only give what was asked in the moment. There were no long-term guarantees in life. He knew all that. Why was he so damn selfish? Of course, he could raise the boy for however long his help was needed. He and Jenna would have their own kids soon, and even with them, there were no guarantees for a long, healthy, and happy life together. There was only hope and trust. Had he and Jenna married three years ago, as planned, they'd probably have a little DJ of their own already anyway.

Baatar put his shoes back on and ran home through the deep sand.

"Well?" Jenna asked as he entered the house.

Baatar stood in the hallway. "I'm sweaty."

"Come and sit," Jenna said and motioned for him to sit next to her. She looked at him. "And?"

"I'm a selfish bastard," Baatar said. "Of course, I'll take care of DJ, whether it's now, for a few months, a few years, or forever. And you won't mind for sure?"

Jenna smiled. "I love you, and I love DJ," she said. "With each family addition, my heart will grow a little bit bigger."

"How'd I ever deserve you?" Baatar asked and gave her a hug and a kiss.

"Jenna wrinkled her nose. "You're sweaty."

"I told you," Baatar said and grinned on his way to the shower.

Twenty-Three

Pia, the curandera, and Emmy connected by phone, and Pia invited Emmy to come to her house. After class ended at 7:00 p.m., Emmy drove to Pia's home, a small back-alley cottage in a cul-de-sac in the old part of town, hidden behind a tall, brown wooden gate with planks that had seen better days. The rusty lever at the top loosely held the gate in place. Emmy peeked through a gap in the fence and saw a yard with colorful flowers. She carefully lifted the rusty lever and let herself in. The door squealed.

Inside the front yard of the cottage, Emmy was greeted by a big black cat with emerald-green eyes and long fur, sitting on the porch. The cat followed Emmy's every step as she walked toward the cottage, nervously clearing her throat. She rubbed her itchy nose. As she lifted her fist to knock, the door flung open.

"Emmy, I'm Pia. I've been expecting you. Please come in. Pepe, you come in, too." The cat hunched his back, sat up, and followed Emmy into the house.

The aging cottage had two small rooms, one to each side of the entrance, with low ceilings and crooked floors. The wooden planks moaned under Emmy's light weight, giving her the feeling of having stepped inside a century-old wooden-hulled ship. There was a dark-red velvet sofa, slumped in the center, with rounded arms on each side, held in place with studs, neatly applied in an arch formation from the bottom up, each stud about an inch from the next. It appeared they once had been golden, but like an old treasure buried for too long, they had lost their original sparkle.

The sofa lured Emmy with welcoming soft pillows in red, lilac, purple, and maroon. A colorful, woven Mexican blanket embraced the length of the sofa's back. Bundles of herbs hung on the wall over the sofa and along the doorway to the kitchen. White crystals, emerald stones, and a large sky-blue celestite geode watched her from a small round glass table. Seven white burning candles illuminated the room from the windowsill, throwing shadows on the walls, and reflecting the colors of the crystals, giving the room the appearance of a small, sacred ancient chapel.

A tarot card deck was laid out on a small square table in the adjacent kitchen, which Emmy could see through the open doorway. An old-fashioned brass kettle sat on top of the stove, next to a small pot in which Pia had boiled some herbs. A raven cawed from the rooftop, leaving Pepe unfazed. He had rolled up into a bundle of fur underneath the small, glass table.

"Please, Emmy, have a seat," Pia said, pointing to the sofa. "Have you ever seen a *curandera*?"

Emmy shook her head and sat down as told.

"I can see and talk to spirits," Pia said, "like you. Don't be scared of it, or them. It's a special gift. It's probably something we've studied and learned throughout the millennia. Some people study art, some music. You and me, we've learned spirit communication."

Sitting on the edge of her seat, Emmy crossed her ankles. She looked at Pia. It was hard to decipher her age. She had long, black hair with gray roots showing. She was missing two upper teeth on the side of her mouth. The skin on her arms and hands was wrinkled and her veins protruded like roots of ancient trees pushing their way out of the earth's surface. She had long fingernails, painted in a maroon red, matching the same color on her lips. She had long, curved, black eyelashes, and her eyelids were covered with emerald-green eye shadow, matching the color of Pepe's eyes.

The black dress she was wearing covered her plump figure. It was cut out of one piece of material without any pleats for a waist and had a big, round neckline. The opening was crowded with several necklaces, one made of rose quartz and another of amethyst, joined by a third made of wooden beads, with a large wooden cross dangling in front of Pia's stomach. It reminded Emmy of a rosary. Pia's fingers were decorated with numerous silver rings. She wore a wide silver bracelet with a big turquoise stone in the center.

Pia had dark, warm eyes that reminded Emmy of Baatar. She wore a lacy purple shawl around her shoulders, and her feet were bare. "A sign," Emmy thought, remembering how her mom always walked barefoot in the house.

Pia looked at Emmy. "Tea?" she asked.

"That would be lovely."

Pia poured water from the brass kettle and returned with two purple, ceramic mugs. A fresh scent of lemon filled the room.

"Herbal tea is healing," Pia said, as she placed the mugs on the coffee table. She sat down and looked closely at Emmy.

"You've had much tragedy in your life," she said. "I can see it in your aura and your eyes. You're an old soul. You see and hear things to which other people don't have any access. You're very gifted; you just don't know it yet. You don't own it yet. Things will get better for you, much better. You'll live a long and happy life."

Pia took a sip of tea. "Tell me about the ghost. Somebody's bothering you?"

Emmy nodded and told Pia all about Thessaly and the problems she'd been causing for Emmy with Axel.

"I see," Pia said, and nodded. Her eyes were filled with empathy. She stared into a candle flame as if she could see life's mysteries in it. Then she looked at Emmy. "Don't be afraid," she said. "We will do a *limpia*, a purification ceremony. It should help detach the ghost from you and protect you in the future. There are other more powerful measures to get rid of a ghost, but most of the time, a *limpia* will take care of the issue."

"Will it hurt the ghost? I mean, will it hurt Thessaly?" Emmy asked.

"You're worried about hurting a ghost who's causing problems in your life?" Pia smiled.

Emmy shrugged her shoulders. "I can see and hear my mom, and I can see and hear Thessaly. I don't want them getting hurt. And I feel sorry for Thessaly for being stuck with her guilt. She can't let go."

"You're empathic," Pia said. "You feel others' pain and emotions. You can use this gift for healing in the future. You'll help many. But you haven't claimed your power. Come back when you're ready. I'll teach you. It'll be a remembrance of what you already know. You've known it in other lifetimes."

Pia shifted in her seat, which made the candles flicker. The cat's tail swished. Emmy quietly observed, as Pia took a deep breath. "The *limpia* will help Thessaly to move into the light. It'll help both of you. Are you Catholic?"

Emmy nodded.

"Let's pray together," Pia said. "We will say three Hail Marys and then the Lord's Prayer three times, followed by three more Hail Marys. Then I will do the *limpia*."

Emmy nodded. They prayed together.

Pia asked Emmy to stand up, while she lit sage and used a large feather to cleanse Emmy's energy field with the smoke, from top to bottom and all around. She hummed a tune and spoke some special prayers, invoking cleansing and healing, asking the angels to help Thessaly to disconnect from Emmy, to heal Thessaly's past, to heal her guilt and fear, and to lead her into the light, to guide her spirit home.

Emmy stood with her eyes closed, imagining Thessaly's spirit moving up into heaven, away from earth and far away from Emmy. She felt a quick movement from bottom to top in front of her stomach and heart. She felt a slight breeze, though all windows in the cottage seemed to be closed. For a moment, she felt lightheaded, then she felt a tranquility settle over her that she hadn't felt in a long time.

"You may sit down," Pia said and walked into the kitchen.

Emmy sank into the kind old sofa that had witnessed a great many rituals in its life. Pepe woke up and jumped next to Emmy on the sofa. He purred loudly, as he kneaded her thigh, when Pia returned.

"I've prepared a special potion for you in this spray bottle," Pia explained. "Take it home and cleanse your environment, particularly your room, and every corner of the house in a clockwise motion. Leave one window cracked open so the ghost can escape if a part of her is still there at the time of the cleansing. Then close all windows and doors for twenty-four hours and shut her out for good. Say the three prayers again after you've cleansed the house."

Emmy nodded. They finished their tea while Pia told Emmy about her family. She'd raised four children. They were all grown up now, each successful in the world. She was proud of them. Her husband had died a year ago, so now she was alone with Pepe.

"I go to the cemetery, too," Pia confided. "I like the peaceful setting, and I talk to my José the way you talk to your mom, although he's near me all the time, even here. Do you feel his presence?"

Emmy shook her head.

"Well, he probably doesn't want to scare you off," Pia said, smiling. "You've had enough of ghosts for a while."

"But I'll still be able to see and hear my mom?" Emmy asked.

"Of course, you will. You always will. You're gifted. Your powers will increase in time. Where did you get that horseshoe necklace?" Pia asked.

"My parents gave it to me for my twelfth birthday," Emmy said.

"Where'd they get it?" Pia asked.

"I don't know."

"It's a special necklace," Pia explained, watching it closely. "It wards off evil spirits."

"But I'm wearing it all the time, and I've still been haunted by Thessaly," Emmy said.

"Correct," Pia said. She took the wooden cross that hung from her neck into her hand and squeezed it. "Emmy, Thessaly is obnoxious but not evil. You're protected. You're very lucky. Evil spirits cannot approach you. That necklace protects you."

Pia gave Emmy a rose quartz bracelet to wear for additional protection and balance. "Should you still feel Thessaly coming around, you say three Hail Marys," Pia advised, "and call me if there are any more problems."

"Thank you, Pia," Emmy said. "I've brought some cash. I don't know how you're paid."

"It's all been taken care of," Pia said.

"But I don't want Maria to pay you for helping me."

"Maria didn't pay me," Pia said. "It was a young man named Manolo."

Emmy smiled. "Manolo," she said and shook her head.

"He's like my José," Pia said. "There are some good souls on the earth, and he's one of them. Hold on to him if you can."

On her way home, Emmy called Manolo and told him all about Pia and the *limpia*. She thanked him for paying Pia. "I owe you," she said.

"I love you," Manolo responded.

Back at the house, Emmy cleansed her room with Pia's potion. She knelt down and said the three prayers. In the middle of the night, when everybody was asleep, she sneaked through the house and blessed and cleansed every corner with the special potion, just as Pia had instructed her.

Things shifted after that. Axel was still big, blue-eyed Axel, lurking in the hallway or kitchen, longing for attention. But there were no more surprise rugs in the house to slip on, no more lights that suddenly turned off, no more brushes of energy against her face, no more doors jamming so Axel could catch her.

Emmy's initial excitement about the house had completely vanished. She didn't want to spend much time there. She despised Axel, although she realized Thessaly had initiated most of his come-ons. Moreover, she hadn't developed a friendship with Carla or Mark, and had no desire to do so, not after Carla accused Manolo of stealing. *She'd have to ask Jenna about her progress with the house-hunting.*

Twenty-Four

At the stables, Emmy watched Baatar as he walked from thoroughbred to thoroughbred, looking into their eyes, checking their stance, stroking a neck here, rubbing a face there, whispering in an ear.

"A newcomer?" he asked the trainer, Jack, when he noticed a nervous gelding in a new stall.

"Yes, arrived today," Jack said. "The owner is..."

"I'm the owner," a heavyset man said. "Jones." He stood six foot four tall, wore a fedora, and looked down on Baatar and Jack.

"Hi, Mr. Jones," Baatar said and held out his hand. "I'm Baatar, one of the outriders here. I like to get acquainted with all the horses before the races."

"A rule keeper," Jones said, sarcastically. He stared down on Baatar before he reluctantly shook his hand. He had a sturdy grip. "He's here to win, not to keep rules," Jones said, pointing at the gelding. "Cost me a bundle. Supposed to be first-class."

"Well, he's a mighty fine horse. Good luck with him," Baatar said, nodding toward Mr. Jones before he continued his walk through the stable.

Emmy met up with Baatar in Mario's RV trailer. "Baatar, how can you be so patient?" she asked, as she stomped inside.

He looked at her as if he didn't understand the

question.

"*Jones*," she imitated. "I wanted to make faces at that man, kick his shin, give him a piece of my mind. People like that bring out a temper in me."

Baatar grinned slightly. "Not everybody has a temper, Emmy. That's not one of my flaws."

"Right," Emmy said. "You drown your sorrow in alcohol, I mean, you have in the past. With vodka." She plopped onto the cot and looked at Baatar. "I'm sorry, I didn't mean to say that."

Baatar looked at her, calm and composed. He smiled genuinely. We have a saying in Mongolia, "*'It's easier to catch an escaped horse than to take back an escaped word.'*"

"I'll remember that. I'm really sorry, Baatar. I didn't mean to offend you," Emmy said.

He nodded and looked at Emmy. "Coffee?"

"Yes, please."

"Drinking isn't the best reaction to a crisis, is it?" Baatar said. "Men in Mongolia drink. It's sort of a coming-of-age ritual. You have to prove that you can hold your liquor and the more you can drink, the more respected you are. It's like an honor code. If you don't join in, you're not accepted. I found the same to be true in Russia and in Alaska and in Texas. There's a lot of drinking here at the racetrack. Drinking a lot means you're a real man. The more stamina you have, the higher your ranking."

Emmy listened.

"But it's stupid," Baatar continued. "You're right, in the past, I tried to drown my sorrows with alcohol. I tried to escape my nightmares, my sorrows, my anger by getting drunk. But every time the hangover passed, and I was sober again, the inner struggle was still there, haunting me, staring me in the face. The drinking did nothing. It didn't help me. It didn't solve anything. Did I ever apologize for that phase after the fires when I lived in a stupor?"

"You did," Emmy said.

"I'm not doing that anymore," Baatar said, "the drinking. It's senseless."

"But when you guys meet on Tuesday night to play cards, isn't that one of those drinking nights?" Emmy asked.

"Yeah, sort of," Baatar admitted, "but I don't drink much any longer. I'll have a drink or two and watch the others get drunk."

"And they let you?"

"They tease me for being a lightweight, a fool in love, but the drunker they get, the more they don't pay attention to me. I've had long conversations with Mario about it. He generally agrees with me that getting drunk is stupid—on a logical, rational basis, he agrees. But he still thinks bonding with the guys means getting drunk. A lot of men see it that way. It's just part of male bonding."

Emmy looked at him, her eyebrows raised. "But why?"

"I don't know, Emmy. Sometimes people do things because they've always done them. There's an unwritten male code. It seems living through misery together makes us feel manly." He grinned. "It's been passed down for generations—fighting wars, trying to find an escape from the physical and mental struggles. Booze and women have been our solace for so long." He smiled sheepishly.

"But how'd you figure out that it's stupid?" Emmy asked.

"It took me a long time to get it."

"You're only thirty-six, Baatar."

"Almost thirty-seven," he said.

"Oh geez, you're practically an old man," Emmy teased.

"I know Jenna doesn't like it when I get drunk," he

said, looking at Emmy. "And I love her, and I don't want to mess it up. My life without her was OK, it was various shades of gray. But with her, it has a golden glow. It's magnificent. I can't really describe it. More coffee?" he asked.

"Yes, please."

He got a refill for both of them. "I grew up in simple circumstances," Baatar said. "We didn't have much, but we had all we needed. Now I have more than I need and I'm grateful, in my heart, you know."

"But how do you keep so calm? Don't people drive you crazy sometimes? Joneses?"

Baatar pondered for a moment. "Detachment," he said, as if that explained everything. "I was taught to detach when I was a little boy, not officially, not in a class. My father taught me to clear my mind, you know? To breathe in and out and just allow life to flow through me. Don't get attached. Don't let people get to you too much."

"What do you mean, don't get attached?" Emmy asked.

"Don't have a preconceived idea of what life should be like, of what people should be like. You allow life to unfold at its own pace; let people surprise you," Baatar said. "When you grow up on the steppe in Mongolia, there's a lot of solitude. You observe, you listen, you become centered. There's no distraction. Land and sky. All that nature all around you creates a calm mind. It's my natural state of mind. I may get melancholic, I may struggle with loss and grief, I may have my deceased friend try to give me messages, but I've never had a temper."

"Can you teach me?" Emmy asked. "I mean, I'm grateful for what I have, too, but I have this inner pressure to do more, to want more. And people get to me. Verena drove me crazy, and Axel. Too much noise around me, and I feel disoriented. My mind gets on overdrive, and it won't shut up."

"I wanted more once," Baatar said, "when I was young."

"What changed?" Emmy asked.

"Life changed me. Tragedies, accidents, death. They taught me not to take people for granted, not to chase after external gratification. We chase after things in the external world when all we really want deep inside is love and acceptance."

"But how do you find that?"

"You adjust your thinking. You approach people and situations with kindness instead of competition. You put yourself into someone else's shoes, someone else's circumstances. You try to see life from their perspective. You give them all the love you have inside of you. You understand rather than judge."

"And if you don't have enough love inside?"

Baatar smiled and looked at Emmy. "I think you have an overabundance of love," he said. "The heavens are always open. The earth nurtures us. You have a notable spiritual connection, Emmy. Your mom watches over you. She has more love for you than you can imagine, and so does your dad. All you need to do is close your eyes and feel that spiritual connection. Feel it inside. Don't focus on what you don't have. Focus on what you have. You're very gifted, Emmy. You're a very special young woman, and you are very much loved."

"You embarrass me."

"I thought you asked me how to become aware of that love inside?"

Emmy grinned and looked up at him, noticing her bangs needed trimming. *How trivial I am,* she thought. "Thank you, Baatar."

Baatar shook his head, smiling. "Let's get back to

work."

Two hours later, she stepped out of the barn for lunch and sat on a bale of hay when Baatar approached again. "Mind if I sit?"

"Please," Emmy said and moved aside to make room. "I usually have lunch here with Manolo," she said, glancing at Baatar, but he's been glued to the farrier. "Do you want some of my sandwich?"

He shook his head. "You seem sad today," he said. "I noticed it when we were in the trailer."

Emmy nodded. "I don't like living with roommates. I want to be able to go to the cemetery and talk to my mom's spirit, but I'm worried Thessaly may still be there. Why is life so difficult sometimes?"

"I've told you before, Emmy. I think we're here to learn. Life holds lessons for us."

"I don't mind going to school to learn, and I don't mind taking care of horses and shoveling their manure, so I can learn about them. But I don't like all that other stuff."

"The stuff that pushes your buttons?" Baatar asked.

"Yes!"

"Nobody likes it; but therein lies the lesson, doesn't it? Experiencing things that are completely against our nature. Losing a best friend, losing your family. Watching an innocent young boy beaten—the things that make us want to shout and scream; things that are so disturbing that they force us to act."

"Losing my family caused irreparable damage," Emmy said firmly.

"And it made you who you are today," Baatar said.

Emmy glanced at Baatar and exhaled loudly with a puff of disgust.

"I know it hurt," he said, "but it taught you to live with and learn to tolerate people you didn't care for. It taught you to know yourself, to know your limits, to do everything you can to fulfil your dreams. And it gave you visionary abilities."

Emmy bit into her sandwich and chewed.

"If with all the indescribable pain we experience, we can come out of that darkness and love and see the pain in another, that's tremendous human growth," Baatar offered.

"I don't care about human growth," Emmy said.

Baatar looked at her. "Every sacred text, every scripture teaches that," he continued. "All sacred texts teach us to develop understanding, compassion, to relieve suffering and reach out in service to one another. None of these sacred writings talks about becoming the greediest, most self-centered, domineering and controlling person in the world."

Emmy grinned. "Darn."

"So, our job is to love and serve. You ready for that?" Baatar summarized.

"No."

He smiled and stood up. "I see. You're not ready. There're a few stalls that need cleaning."

She followed him with her eyes, as he walked back into the stable. He was a simple man, just like he said, wearing blue jeans, a plain T-shirt, and riding boots. But his heart was something special, and as much as she rebelled against him challenging her, she couldn't help wondering if she could indeed take on that job, to love and serve. But then she thought of Jones and Verena and Paul.

No way!

Twenty-Five

DJ was playing in the sandbox in the backyard, in full view of Jenna, while she was fixing lunch when the phone rang.

"Jenna, he's here! My new boy is here!" Amelia said, full of excitement.

"You had your baby? I thought you were due in a month," Jenna said. Why didn't you say? I would've come to help. Do you want me to come to Arizona?"

"No, it's OK," Amelia said. "Wyatt's helping me. He's very happy to have a boy—his boy," she corrected.

"And DJ?" Jenna asked, looking at the little boy, contentedly filling sand into the bed of a plastic truck. What about DJ? Should I come and drop him off? Introduce him to his little brother?"

There was silence.

"Amelia?"

"Yeah, I'm thinking. I'll be able to go home in a day or so, but I'm a bit sore from the birth, you know. I don't think Wyatt will be able to manage me, the new baby, and DJ. You know how he is with DJ."

"Amelia," Jenna said, wondering how best she could formulate her question without sounding insulting, "do you ever want DJ to return to your home with Wyatt?"

There was a long silence.

"We really need to discuss this, Amelia, but probably

not on the phone today. Baatar and I don't mind raising him, we've discussed this," Jenna said, "but Amelia, we need clarity. We need to plan our future a bit, too, you know. We love DJ, and we'll take care of him, but we need to make a more permanent decision for the boy's sake."

There was silence on the phone, followed by suppressed sobs.

"Amelia, I didn't mean to upset you. We don't mind helping, but we need to know. It's been a few months." *There, she'd said it, gentle or not,* Jenna thought.

"Yes, yes," Amelia whimpered between sobs. "It's just the hormones, you know. I easily weep these days. I don't want to burden you."

"DJ's not a burden," Jenna said.

"I'll always be grateful to you," Amelia whispered.

Jenna took a deep breath. "How's your baby?" she asked.

"He's beautiful," Amelia said. "He's got Wyatt's features and a head of blond hair."

"Have you decided on a name?"

"Yes, Wyatt Jr."

Jenna smiled. "I can't wait to see you and meet your new baby. Let me know when you're up for a visit and we'll all come over. Then we can discuss DJ's future in person. As I said, we're happy to have him, so don't worry about anything. Just recover."

"You're the best friend ever," Amelia said.

They hung up.

Jenna stared at DJ who was pouring the sand back from the toy truck into the sandbox. He was a cute boy. As little as he was, he reminded her of his dad, Damdin, the way he looked at her. He had deep set, piercing eyes, hooded, with dark eyebrows. In the quiet of their house and the peaceful setting of the backyard, with Bruno by his side, he seemed to be recovering from the abuse of his stepfather. She even thought at times she could see the boy's mischief coming to the surface. He could be charming and seemed to know how to wrap people around his little finger.

She was glad she'd been resolute with Amelia, who'd been avoiding the topic, stalling any conversation that had to do with the boy's future. But Jenna and Baatar weren't going to be a casual, temporary drop-off place. They wanted to give DJ a real home.

A month passed before Amelia was open to a visit, although Jenna had pushed for it a few times during video conferences between DJ and his mom.

Baatar, Jenna, and DJ left for Arizona on Sunday evening around six o'clock, after the last horse races had been completed. Emmy had happily accepted to stay at the house and take care of Bruno.

The roads were clear, and they arrived in Prescott shortly after midnight.

Amelia welcomed them with Wyatt Jr. in her arms, a tiny little bundle, wrapped in a diaper and a light-blue onesie. "Here he is," she said proudly and let her visitors adore him.

DJ had fallen asleep in the truck, and Baatar held him in his arms. "Perhaps we can go inside?" he asked.

"Oh, yes, of course." They hugged and kissed as friends do, and Amelia took Baatar into the children's room. Baatar placed DJ in his old crib and Amelia gave him a kiss. The boy didn't wake up.

"Where's Wyatt?" Jenna asked.

"He's sleeping. He works, you know," Amelia whispered. "He needs his sleep. Would you like some coffee?"

"No, thanks," Jenna said. "We've had a long day and a

long drive. We should get some rest."

"Yes, of course," Amelia said. "Let me show you our guest room and the bath. Wyatt's bought us such a beautiful house." She smiled shyly.

"She feels distant," Jenna said to Baatar when they were alone. "What happened to my best friend? We used to be so close. We talked about everything. We grieved Damdin's death together and your disappearance. I was there when she gave birth to DJ and the two of them lived with me for two years. And now she barely acknowledges DJ and talks about that...that new husband of hers like he's some superhero—a man who rejects his wife's own son!"

"Shhh," Baatar said and hugged Jenna tightly. "She's under a lot of pressure, Jenna. Did you see the look on her face? Her eyes are full of pain and sorrow, although she manages to put on a smile."

"I didn't notice. I'm just angry at her. How can she disassociate from her own son? I just don't understand it."

"I think she doesn't have much choice," Baatar said. "As you yourself reminded me, she's never been independent like you, and Wyatt's an ass; we know that."

"He is," Jenna agreed. "I'm not sure I can be civil with him when we face him tomorrow."

"Yes, you can," Baatar said. He looked into her eyes, "because you're bigger than him. Let's just focus on DJ and his well-being, OK?"

Jenna took a deep breath. "I love you, Baatar Lkhagvasüren," She kissed him. "Let's get some sleep."

They awoke around six thirty when they heard voices. Baatar decided to take a shower before getting dressed for the big talk. Jenna pulled on a robe and meandered into the kitchen, which she found empty, except for a few breadcrumbs on the counter and a half-full coffee maker, filling the air with the delicious fragrance of fresh coffee. She breathed in deeply, as though it could give her the patience and tolerance she needed to face the jerk.

Jenna sat down at the kitchen table when Amelia walked in, all dressed up pretty, with blush, soft eye shadow, mascara, and full red lips, holding Wyatt Jr. in her arms.

"Where's Wyatt?" Jenna asked. "I thought I just heard him."

"Oh, sorry, you missed him. He just left for work. He's quite busy these days."

Jenna swallowed. "I see. How's DJ?"

"I haven't heard him yet," Amelia said. "I assume he's still sleeping. Do you think I should check on him?"

Jenna took a deep breath, holding her tongue. Just then, a little two-year-old boy appeared in the doorway, holding a stuffed horse in his arms. He walked straight to Jenna and hugged her leg. She put him on her lap. "Good morning, DJ. Are you hungry for breakfast?"

He nodded.

"Does he like oatmeal?" Amelia asked. "Or toast?"

"Oatmeal or cereal," Jenna said. "You know what he likes."

Amelia said nothing but started to prepare some oatmeal. "And Baatar?" she asked.

"Eggs and toast," Jenna said. "I'd like that too, if you have it."

"Yes, we do."

"Why don't I make breakfast, and you rest and take care of the baby," Jenna suggested. "You've hardly had any sleep last night. Does Wyatt Jr. still wake you up?"

"Every two hours." Amelia cuddled Wyatt Jr. and smiled at DJ. "You remember this house?" she asked.

DJ watched her closely with his dark, piercing eyes. He

nodded slightly. "It's a nice house, isn't it?" Amelia said.

DJ looked at her. "Mommy," he said.

Amelia stroked his head. "I love you, sweetie."

"Bad house," DJ said.

Baatar walked into the kitchen. "Do I smell breakfast?" he asked. He kissed Jenna and gave Amelia a peck on the cheek, then rubbed the top of DJ's head. "How's our boy today?" he asked.

DJ gave him a big smile. He held Saaral, the stuffed horse, tightly in his arm.

Jenna served coffee and gave DJ his oatmeal and a glass of milk. "Here you go, DJ."

"Amelia," Baatar said, looking at her, holding her newborn, "we need to talk, I mean seriously talk. I thought Wyatt was going to be here for this?"

Amelia bit her lips. "He's at work," she whispered.

"You know I loved my friend, Damdin," Baatar said, "and I know you loved him. DJ's your son. It seems Wyatt has no room for him in his life, but Jenna and I do. I'd like to adopt him."

Jenna stared at Baatar.

"I realize that may not be what you want, Amelia," Baatar continued. "I'm just being honest with you. If we raise him, I'd like him to be a full member of our family. I don't want to force something on you that you don't want, but I think it would be best for the boy and for us."

Amelia scratched her ear, then rearranged the blanket around baby Wyatt.

"Amelia, how do you feel about this?" Jenna asked. "Do you think Wyatt will ever change his attitude toward DJ? Or would it be best if he stayed with us for good?"

Jenna expected rage, fury, sobs, despair. But Amelia just sat there, holding on to her baby, while DJ was quiet, sitting tensely, holding on to his stuffed horse.

"You'd be OK with that?" Amelia finally asked, not looking up.

Jenna put her hand on Amelia's. "Amelia, are you aware what we're proposing here? DJ would stay with us for good. We'd be his parents, legally. Of course, you could come and visit anytime, but we'd raise him as if he were our son. You don't have any objections to this?"

There was a long silence while Baatar and Jenna ate.

"Amelia?" Baatar asked. He looked at her intensely.

She looked up. "I can't bear the thought of my child being beaten and abused," she said. "If you guys are willing to…" She looked down.

"We're more than willing," Baatar said. "We'd be delighted. We'd love to adopt and raise DJ, but can *you* live with that decision, Amelia? This is a huge decision!"

She nodded. "He seems happy with you," she said, "safe."

"We'll do the best we can to keep it that way," Jenna said.

DJ climbed onto Baatar's lap, his hands wrapping tightly around Baatar's neck. Baatar put his hands around DJ and held him.

"But you'll have your own child soon," Amelia said, looking at Jenna.

"Yes, in a few months," Jenna said, rubbing her belly. "We're excited, and we're happy to take care of DJ, too. He's a good boy."

"He looks good with you," Amelia said. "He looks like he's part of your family," as if this would make the decision to give away her son any easier. "Wyatt's blond like me. DJ would be an outsider. He'd always be an outsider."

Baatar swallowed. His eyes narrowed, his jaw tightened. He took a deep breath. Then he relaxed and looked at Amelia. "You're right," he said. "DJ's one of us." He smiled and winked at DJ and the boy smiled back at him.

"Saaral wants to go home," DJ said.

"Saaral?" Amelia asked.

"He named the stuffed horse Saaral," Jenna explained. "It looks like one of Baatar's ponies."

"I see," Amelia said. She smiled at DJ.

"You must think I'm heartless, Jenna," Amelia said, rubbing the table with her hand, wiping invisible crumbs off it. "I'm a lousy mother."

"We think you want to protect DJ," Jenna said, "and we'll give him the home you can't give him. We'll treat him like our own son."

"You're angels," Amelia said, "true angels. I'll miss him but I know he's in good hands with you, better than here with me. He's almost three, and he calls this the bad house." Her eyes watered. "He remembers."

"Come and visit often," Jenna said. "You're always welcome."

Amelia nodded.

Jenna fussed over Amelia's new baby while Baatar put their overnight bag in the truck.

"Let me do the dishes before we head back," Jenna said.

"No, please, let me do that," Amelia insisted. "You have a long drive home."

"Amelia," Jenna said as she hugged her goodbye, "you're my best friend. Let's continue our friendship, remain open, talk regularly, OK? I miss that."

"I feel so ashamed," Amelia admitted. "I feel so ashamed for what I'm doing, for what I'm asking you to do. DJ reminds me of Damdin all the time. I have such regrets."

"Regrets that you got pregnant by him?" Jenna asked.

"No, regrets that I'm failing to be a mother to his son,

that I'm not as strong as he was. Wyatt wanted me, but not DJ, from the moment we met. I didn't want to see it. I was so desperate to be with a man."

"I understand," Jenna said. "We understand. You're in a tough spot."

Back in the car, Baatar and Jenna continued the discussion. "I still can't believe she can let go of her own son," Jenna said, "but I'm glad you were clear with her, very clear."

Baatar looked in the rearview mirror to see if DJ was listening. The boy was looking out the window, but it was quite apparent he heard everything, young as he was.

"Amelia's always been different from you," Baatar said. "From the get-go, she went for the chief. Damdin was a charismatic leader; Amelia the follower. Damdin liked to make the decisions, and she went along with it. Wyatt makes decisions, and she agrees. She's never been a fighter. She doesn't have your backbone, your independence. She suffers in silence. If she left Wyatt, she'd be lost."

"Sadly, I think you're right," Jenna said. "When Damdin died, she found shelter with me. I became her therapist, her nurturer. I took charge. She's never been one to take initiative, to find her own path. I don't think she has the desire."

"At least now we have a clearer path ahead of us," Baatar said. "I do think it best that we adopt DJ. What if he needs to be vaccinated, see a doctor, go to school—we'd have to get Amelia's consent for all of it. Adopting him will give us rights to make the decisions parents make."

Jenna nodded.

"Damdin Flores," Baatar smiled at Jenna, "sounds good to me."

That week they purchased new furniture for DJ's room, a small bed, a chest of drawers, a shelf for toys and books, and a small table and chair. He'd been sleeping on the guest mattresses they had acquired when Baatar's parents visited, but DJ no longer was a guest. He was their son.

Amelia came to visit two months later. Jenna had prepared all the papers to initiate the adoption process and Amelia signed all of them, no questions asked.

That night, Baatar had a dream. He was with Damdin. They were back in Alaska at the gold mine. It was their last day there, because Baatar had become tired of working in the dark tunnels underground. Damdin handed him a wooden box with seven bars of gold, one for each year they'd endured working at the mine. "You take good care of this," Damdin said, smiling. "And you take good care of my son," he added, holding DJ by the shoulders. He let go of the boy, directing him toward Baatar. "I'm grateful," he added.

They hugged and Baatar nodded in agreement. Damdin gave him a big smile. Then he turned and walked away, and Baatar knew he'd not see his friend again for a long time.

Twenty-Six

Emmy was on her way to class but a construction zone on her usual route to the local college forced her to take a detour. *Life had gotten so much better*, she pondered. *She'd not have any more run-ins with Axel; he'd completely backed off. And Thessaly had disappeared from the house, and there had been no more strange happenings. Pia was amazing, or her prayers, or her potions, whatever it was. She'd have to write Pia a thank-you note.*

Emmy was driving through unfamiliar streets, following the detour signs, looking for a bite to eat. She had enough time for a quick sit-down dinner before the three-hour class that started at seven. At the next corner, she saw a fast-food restaurant and turned into the parking lot.

"One loaded burrito please," she ordered and sat down to review her notes from the last class.

"Loaded burrito," the waitress said as she put the food in front of Emmy, then stared at her for a moment. Emmy looked up.

"Verena? I almost didn't recognize you without the…uhm…you look so different."

"Boring?" Verena asked.

"Normal," Emmy said. "What are you doing here?"

"Short form," Verena said, "Tony's in prison for trading with narcotics, burglaries, a holdup with a weapon, resistance to the police. I got away with parole. I wanted to go back to the city, but my parole officer felt I should live in a calm and peaceful environment. I live in a halfway house. There're strict rules. The parole officer showed me my dad's records. He was a criminal. They say I have to get my act together, or I'll end up like him."

"Verena!" a voice came from the kitchen.

"I've got to go work. Customers. Would be nice if you came around sometime."

Emmy ate her burrito quietly, thinking about those awful two years in foster care, living with Verena as her roommate. *Why would she want to come around for her? She who stole from Emmy, belittled her, mocked her. She who broke into Baatar's house, together with her criminal husband, and stole Baatar's keepsake last year, the box with seven pieces of gold from Alaska. She'd probably also taken the hundred-dollar bill from the jar on the kitchen counter. Verena and Tony, the awful couple who'd caused havoc at the racetrack, where they let thoroughbreds run wild during official races, risking lives, while they stole money and jewelry from the racetrack's cash office and store.*

Luckily, the cops had found and returned Baatar's keepsake box.

It was odd seeing Verena like this, in jeans and a T-shirt, without heavy makeup, striking red lips, and fake eyelashes. Her hair was no longer dyed. She wore no pointy, red, acrylic fingernails. Her well-endowed bosom was no longer squished into a see-through blouse that was two sizes too small. She wore regular tennis shoes instead of lacquered, red, four-inch heels.

Luckily, Verena didn't work the counter at the restaurant but was somewhere in the kitchen, so Emmy didn't have to be friendly and say goodbye.

For a few days, Emmy's life took on some sort of normalcy between working at the stables, doing homework, going to school, and spending as much time as she could with Manolo. While working at the stables, she watched Gloria, the vet, as she diagnosed a fetlock injury on one of the thoroughbreds, when Baatar walked by and pulled Emmy aside. "Lunch in Mario's trailer?" he asked, casually.

Emmy nodded. "See you around noon."

They were alone in the trailer, which didn't happen often.

"Anything new going on with you?" Baatar asked, as they sat down at the small table, both unwrapping their sandwiches. He took a hearty bite.

"I ran into Verena, remember her?" Emmy asked. "My old foster care roommate who stole your box of gold and burglarized the racetrack?"

"The name sounds familiar," Baatar said with a grin.

"How can she be back in my life, Baatar? I'm in serious trouble if that's the kind of people I attract into my life. I finally got rid of Thessaly, the ghost. And now I'm being haunted by Verena? Luckily, her boyfriend was put in prison for quite some time. He was trouble. All I need now is to have Paul reappear. Remember Paul? The track and field athlete who stole my heart with his steel-blue eyes and wealthy lifestyle?"

"Harvard, wasn't it?" Baatar said. "I thought his going to Harvard was the biggest draw."

"Shut up!" Emmy said, smiling. "You're supposed to forget those things. You threw him out of the house, remember, 'cause he was rude and disrespectful."

"How could I ever forget," Baatar said.

"And then you lectured me."

"I didn't lecture you," Baatar said. "I may have shared my thoughts."

"Aha," Emmy said. "Yes, you definitely shared your thoughts." She grinned. "And I was grateful," she quickly added.

You wanna come over for dinner tonight? You know we've adopted DJ. We bought some new furniture for your old room."

"I'd love to see it," Emmy said.

"OK, seven o'clock tonight. But first, let's get back to work."

Emmy pulled into the driveway to Jenna and Baatar's house just as she saw Baatar's truck approaching. They went inside together, where they were greeted with melodious licks and happy yowls from Bruno. DJ came running with his stuffed toy horse to Emmy, and she admired it greatly. Baatar greeted Jenna with a kiss.

"Welcome home," Jenna said and gave Emmy a hug. "We're having enchiladas suizas and rice with a green salad, and if we're not all completely stuffed afterward, we may have to add dessert."

"Oh, what a horrible prospect," Emmy said and laughed.

They talked about day-to-day happenings at the racetrack, at school, and Jenna's sewing business. She'd gotten three new customers in one week by word of mouth. Jenna shared how she and DJ had been to the playground, and DJ learned how to ride a seesaw. DJ proudly gleamed.

Emmy told them all about Pia, the *curandera*, and her cat, Pepe, who Emmy thought was doing half the work, although neither Pia nor he'd ever admit it. "I haven't seen Thessaly since," Emmy reported, "and there haven't been any strange run-ins with Axel. But I'm a bit worried about going back to the cemetery. I miss connecting with my mom there."

"I'll go with you if you want," Jenna offered.

"You would?"

"Of course."

"Thank you. Maybe I'll carry Pia's potion with me when we go."

"Won't harm," Jenna agreed.

It was almost bedtime when Emmy left. She decided to stop at the market on her way home so she could make a sandwich to bring to work the next morning.

She'd barely set foot in the store when she heard a familiar voice, addressing her from behind.

"Hi, gorgeous! How ya doing? I haven't seen ya at the restaurant. Time for another burrito soon?"

Emmy froze in her tracks and slowly turned to face Verena.

"Shopping for yummies, too?" Verena asked. Her basket was filled with strawberries, blueberries, bananas, spinach and kale. "It's so nice to see ya, Emmy!" Verena leaned in for a hug and Emmy stepped back just in time to avoid a close encounter.

"Smoothies?" Emmy asked, looking at Verena's basket.

"Yeah, trying to live healthy. I've got nothing to offer besides being pretty, so better keep that up."

Emmy looked at Verena.

"I should've listened to ya," Verena said. "Learn, ya know. I can barely read, and I'm horrible with math, so I can only work in a kitchen."

"It's never too late to learn," Emmy said.

"Easy for you to say."

"Looks like you're turning your life around," Emmy said, trying to be polite.

"Really?" Verena asked with a huge smile. "I've been trying, but I didn't know it showed. Hearing it from you means a lot. I'm divorcing Tony. Who wants to be married to a jailbird?" She laughed a little too loudly. "And I've stopped smoking; that's why I'm chewing gum all the time."

The more Verena talked, the closer she got to Emmy's face. Emmy leaned back but the distance between Verena and her didn't seem to diminish.

"I've got to go," Emmy said.

"OK, thanks again, Emmy. Maybe we can hang out sometime?"

Emmy couldn't wait to get out of the store. Verena followed her to the cash register, but luckily Emmy was first in line. She paid quickly and left. She sprinted to her car and took off. She parked in the driveway at the house and headed upstairs to her room. There was no sight of Axel.

She sighed deeply as she sank onto the bed. *Please don't let Thessaly come and haunt me anymore,* she prayed. *First Axel, then Thessaly, and now Verena? Enough already.*

***

As promised, Jenna accompanied Emmy to the cemetery. "I've always liked the peace and quiet at cemeteries," Jenna said, as they approached the rows of graves. "Our dead friends don't talk much."

Emmy turned and stared at Jenna.

"I mean, usually," Jenna said. "Do you see or hear Thessaly?"

Emmy clutched Pia's potion inside her pocket and shook her head. She knelt down and touched her family's gravestone, closed her eyes and said a prayer. Then she saw her mom in soft pastel colors as though she was standing behind a door of frosted glass.

"Mom," Emmy whispered, as the appearance became clear. "I've missed you."

"Thessaly's gone?" Mom asked.

"I hope so," Emmy said. "I saw a *curandera.*"

"I've been watching over you," Mom said, smiling. "I

saw you visit Pia. She's very much in tune with us spirits. You can trust her."

Emmy pulled Pia's potion out of her pocket. "I do," she said.

Mom nodded. "She will teach you. The more you learn to heighten your energy vibrations, the easier you can talk with spirits."

"I don't want to talk with spirits," Emmy said. "Talking with Thessaly was a nightmare. I want to talk only with you!"

Mom nodded. "For now, yes. When you're ready, Pia will be a good teacher."

"For what?" Emmy asked. "I want to be a vet."

"All animals have spirits," Mom said, "including the horses you like. Listening to their spirits will help you tune into them, hear them, understand their worries and upsets, know what they need."

"I never thought of that," Emmy said.

"You're gifted, Emmy," Mom said. She gave Emmy a big smile, and slowly her image faded.

Jenna had taken a walk and found a bench nearby, closing her eyes and thinking of her own mom, when Emmy quietly approached her.

"All good?" Jenna asked, and Emmy nodded. She told Jenna all about her mom's message on the way home. She'd be communicating with animals, with horses, her life's dream.

Twenty-Seven

"You haven't had a horse lesson in a while," Manolo said to Emmy at the racetrack stables. "Are you ready for a challenge?"

"Yes," Emmy said, "challenge me."

"OK, we have three new thoroughbreds," Manolo said. "Let's check them out. You tell me what temperaments they have."

Emmy smiled as they walked to greet the new horses.

"May I introduce you to Ms. Wow the Crowds?" Manolo asked.

Emmy greeted the horse, letting it smell her first. She gently breathed into its nostrils. The horse reacted with an exhale. Emmy walked around the horse, checking her coat. She petted her neck, withers, and Ms. Wow the Crowds lifted her head. Emmy stroked the horse's legs, and the horse lifted a foot, then placed it back on the ground. Emmy looked into the horse's eyes and observed her lips and ears. She carefully watched every move the horse made. Then she looked at Manolo. "Looks good to me," she said, smiling.

"Temperament?"

"A little skittish, a bit nervous perhaps, timid. She hasn't quite settled in yet."

Manolo smiled. "All right, let's walk over to Super Charger."

Emmy laughed. "Those names—where do they get them?"

"From very hopeful owners." Manolo chuckled.

"Hello, Super Charger," Emmy said and repeated her greeting ritual. The horse looked at her with a raised head as though he was in charge. She stroked his neck, and he shook his head. As she walked around him, he stomped his feet twice. His ears were pinned backward. "I hope he has a strong groom," she said. "He looks very bold to me. Fearless and in control. Kind of scary."

"And the last one," Manolo said, as they approached Winning Willy.

"I love him already," Emmy said.

"Why?"

"I can't say. He has such an air of a prince, but a humble one. I feel like he has a sense of humor. Look at his eyes and the way he nibbles at my shirt. Emmy greeted and checked him as she had the others, and Winning Willy stood relaxed and nibbled on his hay. His ears followed Emmy. "He's so easygoing," Emmy said, "like he can't be bothered with anything. I wonder how he performs."

"He's a fast runner," Manolo said. "Out on the turf, he's very focused. I watched him this morning. He gets the job done, and then he's happy to be back at eating hay."

"I'll clean his stall anytime," Emmy said, "but Super Charger?"

Cody's taking him on," Manolo said. "He's very experienced and won't let the horse bully him. But you know, a horse senses your fear."

"Yeah, I know," Emmy said. "I've got to work on that. Isn't it weird that the owners don't ride their own horses? Isn't the greatest pleasure in having horses to have a close relationship with them? To ride them? Feel that interspecies connection?"

Manolo smiled. "You think too much."

"Why have a horse if you don't ride it and enjoy that connection?"

"For some people in the racing industry, a horse is an investment," Manolo said. "Entering the horse in a competition and earning money, that's the owner's enjoyment."

Emmy wrinkled her nose.

"And if it weren't, we'd all be out of our jobs."

"Right."

"Wanna help me train a pony at home?" Manolo asked.

"I'd love to." Emmy's face lit up.

"OK, how about Thursday afternoons? You don't have classes until seven, right?"

"Yup." Emmy smiled.

Thursday came, and they met at 1:00 p.m. and ate Manolo's homemade, thick, juicy turkey sandwiches before the training began.

"I've been training Rush to listen to word commands," Manolo said. "And I want to see how he reacts to someone else. Will you help me with him?"

"I'll do whatever I can."

"Thank you. I need someone to ride him so I can watch his reactions. And then we can ride a couple of the ponies together for exercise."

"OK," Emmy said as they entered the arena where Rush was waiting.

"Let's check his feet first," Manolo said.

"Why do you have to do that every day?" Emmy asked.

"They can develop thrush," Manolo explained.

"What exactly is thrush?" Emmy asked.

"Thrush is an infection of the frog inside the hoof," Manolo explained. "It's caused by bacteria. Whether they're on the pasture or in a stall, muck and dirt can get stuck in the hoof and get infected."

"But Rush is on a huge, beautiful pasture!"

"Bacteria can develop quickly, although you're right, horses that live in dirty stalls or in a wet pasture are at higher risk. Still, if a horse's feet get packed with dirt or manure, an infection can develop and eat at the frog tissue. You'd smell it when you clean the hoof. There may also be a dark coloration or black secretion at the edges of the frog. If you catch it early on, you can clean it up and apply some iodine to clean the affected area. All that needs to be carefully applied so it doesn't hurt the neighboring skin."

"So, to prevent it you have to clean the feet regularly?"

"Yes, and it helps to exercise or ride the horses daily. The movement keeps their feet healthy."

They saddled up Rush together, and Emmy rode him, while Manolo gave him word commands.

"I'm not a good rider," Emmy lamented. "Really, I don't know how to ride."

"You've made a lot of progress," Manolo said. "Remember to sit straight and confident, use the muscles in your thighs, your knees, lower legs, and ankles." He showed her how to hold the reigns and how the pony reacted to the slightest shift in her weight in the saddle. "Some of the movements are subtle," he said. "It takes practice. You're doing well."

Afterward, Manolo saddled up Sunny and they went on a trail ride together.

"How'd you learn all these training methods for the ponies?" Emmy asked.

"My mom taught me a lot, and my dad, Baatar, and Jack. I'm from a family of horsemen, you know that. My grandfather learned very different training methods when he was young and working at cattle ranches," Manolo said. "Attitudes toward horses were different then. A horse was seen as a tool more than a living being with feelings of its own. Nobody had a horse as a companion. Their value was in being a working horse."

Emmy listened quietly.

"They subdued them with force. They pushed a horse to the ground, sat on it for a while, bound its legs so it couldn't get up or move until the horse gave up all resistance. Now we know what damage that causes to the horse, but back then they didn't. They thought they were doing what needed to be done, just like kids were beaten into submission when they disobeyed."

"My parents were beaten when they were kids, too," Emmy said.

"Nobody thought of the horse," Manolo continued. "They were treated like an object."

"Like women in some cultures," Emmy said.

Manolo looked at her.

"Don't look so shocked," Emmy said. "It's true, and you know it."

He sighed and weighed the information, his brows lifting as his head bent slightly to the left. "Anyway," he said, "good trainers involve the horse. They consider its personality, its strengths and weaknesses, likes and dislikes. We partner with the horse," Manolo gave Emmy a long look, "as we do with our women."

Emmy laughed. "That's good, Mano. That's a really good approach. What does it do to a horse when you force it to the ground and sit on it?"

"It kills its spirit," he said, pensively. "They're prey animals, right?"

Emmy nodded.

"In the wild, when they're hunted and forced to the ground by a predator, it means they're being killed. I imagine their soul leaves the body, so they don't feel the predatory bite that kills them. There've been some studies around that. Many animals seem to do that. But with a training style like that, they're not actually killed. They become subdued, traumatized, like a zombie. No more pain, no more joy."

"That's sad," Emmy said.

"It is. Like I said, people didn't know better then. My dad wouldn't do that to a horse, neither would Jack or Baatar. We've learned."

"Is that why you're interested in working with the disabled? Veterans or kids? To heal their spirits? You've told me you'd like to do that someday."

Manolo nodded. "Horses have an inner antenna for what we need," he said, "unless we've screwed them up with our forceful demands. All horses aren't the same, of course, they're not all equally good at helping a human in need, but you can tell which ones are, and wouldn't it be a shame not to let them? Some people visit hospitals with therapy dogs. I'd like to put those, who need healing, on a horse."

Every Thursday, Manolo and Emmy trained the ponies together. After a while, it became clear to Emmy that Manolo masqueraded her private riding lessons as training for the ponies, and she loved him for it.

When Manolo accepted a new gelding for training purposes, she watched.

"He looks wild," she said.

"He's not been trained well," Manolo explained. "I wonder if he was abused, definitely not treated well and not trained well."

"Did you buy him?" Emmy asked.

"No, he belongs to one of Cody's friends," Manolo explained, "a family with a couple of kids. They bought the horse four months ago, but they don't know how to handle him. When they approach him, he runs away."

"Don't you use a lead rope to teach him?" Emmy asked.

"Watch," Manolo said. "I really like this technique. When you force a horse, it obeys you out of fear. Instead, I want to earn the horse's trust. Once he trusts me, he'll do anything for me. He'll respect me. He'll accept me as a leader. This is similar to Monty Robert's join-up technique."

"But he just keeps running in circles," Emmy said, "and then he stands in that corner and does nothing."

"Yes, I give him that corner to feel safe," Manolo explained. "That's his space to go to, his safety zone. I control the rest of the arena."

"So, you only use the rope to make a noise to direct the horse?"

"Yes. See, I let him run for a while, then I get in his way and make him change direction. Let him run off the fearful energy. Now he goes in his corner to rest and think whether he wants to accept me. See how he chews? He's thinking. So, I give him time to think."

Manolo approached the horse and stroked his neck and shoulder, then his face. "Good boy," he said. The horse's ears flicked toward him. Then it lifted its head, turned, and ran. The scene repeated three more times.

Back in the corner, Manolo rubbed the horse's face and ears, and stroked his withers, back, hips, and legs. The horse lowered its head and neck and chewed. "Good boy, Connor," Manolo said and mounted the horse bareback. He rode him through the arena, and the horse obliged his commands.

"That's amazing," Emmy said. "Look at him. He no longer spooks. He listens to you."

"Sometimes a horse just needs to run off stored

energy. It's like shedding unwanted emotions."

Emmy thought of how Baatar ran at the beach for that.

"Then they need clear instructions," Manolo said. "Each one's different. This one wasn't trained well, so he made his own rules. Horses are naturally fearful, and who knows what this one's been through. If you speak their language, they usually react in a positive way. This gelding has to learn that humans are above him in hierarchy. He knows he's bigger than me. He knows he's stronger. But if I show him that I'm in control, then he gets it."

"How do you do that?" Emmy asked.

"I've controlled the space around him just as a lead mare would do in a herd. I've shown him that he's safe with me. The horse's main goal is to survive, to be safe. Horses who get abused may obey but they don't feel safe. I want him to trust me. It's all about trust."

"Just like with people," Emmy said. "If the trust in a relationship is gone, the relationship is broken."

"Exactly." Manolo dismounted and walked over to Emmy. The horse followed him closely, without a lead rope.

"Looks like you've got a new friend," Emmy said.

Manolo smiled. "Yeah, he's a good horse. He rubbed Connor's neck and face. "He learns quickly. I'll want to saddle him up and take him on a trail ride, see what he does out there. I've got to make him safe to ride before I turn him loose on the family and kids. You wanna go out together? You could ride one of the ponies?"

"I'd love that."

"You wanna ride Diamond?" Manolo asked.

"OK." They saddled up Diamond together and Emmy fastened the cinch, then checked the length of the stirrups.

"What did we forget?" Manolo asked, looking at Emmy.

"Saddle pad, saddle, bridle," Emmy checked and looked at Manolo and shrugged her shoulders.

"We need to check her hooves."

"Oh." Emmy stood close to Diamond's shoulder and facing toward her rear, used a hoof pick to clean her hooves while Manolo watched.

"Good job," he said. "Ready?"

Emmy nodded.

Manolo gave her a leg up and then mounted Connor. "OK, let's go."

They started off slowly, letting the ponies walk up the trail until it leveled off. "Ready for a trot?"

Emmy nodded.

"Giddyup!"

Manolo let Emmy ride in the front so he could watch and make sure she was safe. Diamond knew the trail. She'd been on it many times.

"Ho," Manolo called out, and both horses stopped. "Emmy, your cinch isn't very tight; does the saddle feel a bit loose?"

"Yeah, actually, it does."

Manolo dismounted and tightened it for Emmy, and Connor took the opportunity and ran off.

"Oh no!" Emmy shouted.

"Let me go and catch him." Manolo took Diamond and raced after Connor. He caught him within half a mile and returned to Emmy. "Looks like I'm not done with the training," he said and smiled.

"Yours or the horse's?" Emmy teased.

"Yeah, I know, that was stupid not to tie him up."

"But Diamond wouldn't have taken off," Emmy said.

"Right, because we're bonded."

They rode for an hour, and Connor was very responsive to anything Manolo asked of him—slowing down, speeding up to a trot or a lope, and coming to a halt.

"So, we'll have to make sure not to leave him without supervision out on a trail," Manolo said, as they returned home.

They gave both horses a bath since it was a hot day. "I think once Connor feels at home with his new family, it'll become less of an issue. He just doesn't feel he belongs yet."

Manolo continued the training with Connor in the arena for another couple of days, then had the owners come, including their two children. Each of them got into the arena to work with Connor under Manolo's supervision, until the horse was relaxed around all the family members. Manolo had both children take turns riding Connor in the arena while he observed. The family was thrilled. Connor's behavior had shifted dramatically for the better.

"You've done great," the husband said, shaking Manolo's hand. "Our neighbor has a troubled horse; won't obey any commands. May we recommend him to you?"

"I'd be delighted," Manolo said. "Just have him call me. And for Connor, please make sure not to leave him unattended on a trail ride. Tie him up when you dismount. He doesn't quite feel home yet."

"We'll be sure to do that."

Twenty-Eight

"How's your work at the hospital going?" Emmy asked Manolo's sister, Ariana, while she and Manolo were fixing enchiladas in the kitchen. "Do you like being a nurse?"

"I do," Ariana said. "It's interesting but also sad."

"Sad?" Emmy asked.

"You see these sick people," Ariana explained, "and hear their stories. There's an old woman with no family; she's lonely and scared. Then there's this young guy with leukemia who needs a bone marrow transplant, but neither of his parents is a match, and he has no siblings. His name was put on a waiting list, but it may take too long to find him a match. He's only nineteen. Rich kid. Track and field athlete at Harvard and then wham."

Emmy swallowed. "Track and field at Harvard? Why wouldn't he be in a more renowned hospital if his parents are rich?"

"I don't know," Ariana said. "I think he was at first, but his mom wanted him local, I have no idea why. She doesn't work. She comes to the hospital in her yoga outfit." Ariana laughed. "Can you believe it? Your son's dying of leukemia and you do yoga?"

"Maybe she needs it to not go insane," Manolo said.

"I know a guy who had a scholarship for track and field at Harvard," Emmy said. "We were in junior high together. His name's Paul."

"Paul," Ariana said. "Yeah, that's his name."

Emmy's face lost all color. "That's horrible. It must be him."

"He's actually not a nice guy," Ariana said. "He's spoiled rotten. He commands us around all day long; constantly rings us for something trivial—to fluff up his pillow, to pour him fresh water when he has a bottle of mineral water sitting right by his bed. He's not so weak he can't pour a glass of water. Most of the staff don't care too much for him."

"Still a poor chap," Manolo said, "to be so young and so sick. There's no cure?"

"Not without a bone marrow transplant," Ariana said.

"All that potential for a great future," Emmy said, "and he may not make it?"

"His mom's weird," Ariana said. "She's very aloof and on a strict schedule; it seems her social calendar's more important than her son. At the same time, she's super protective of him, pampers him like he can't blow his own nose. I've never met his dad."

"I don't think he was ever close to his dad," Emmy said, reminiscing. "His dad works all the time. He travels a lot. I don't think he was there for his son growing up."

"I'd rather have less money and a loving family," Manolo said. "I loved it when dad took me riding when I was little. I loved hanging out at the stables with him. I watched him for hours. Just being around him made me happy."

"Yeah," Ariana said. "I do feel kind of sorry for that spoiled brat. He doesn't even know what he's been missing. Maybe with a different dad he'd not turned out as awful."

"Awful?" Emmy asked.

"Self-centered," Ariana corrected.

"I wonder if I should visit him," Emmy thought aloud.

"Really?" Manolo asked, looking at Emmy. "That's that blue-eyed guy you had a crush on, right?"

"We went out a few times when I first moved back to Little Oaks," Emmy said, "but I don't love him or anything like that. He mocked me when I told him I wanted to be a vet, and yes, he did have striking blue eyes." She looked at Manolo and smiled.

"Blue contacts," Ariana said. "He wears striking blue contact lenses and lightens his hair like a girl. Without his contacts, his eyes are brown. His hair is brown, his skin a little lighter than mine. Otherwise, he looks just like one of us."

Manolo chuckled. "So, he's vane, too."

"Are we making way too many enchiladas?" Emmy asked, looking at the dish as it filled up.

"There can never be too many enchiladas in this house," Manolo said. "Watch'em disappear."

He put the dish in the oven, and as the smell began to fill the house, people started showing up and sitting at the table. Ariana brought a big jug of water, and little Miguel was told to set the table. Mario was home from the racetrack. His other two daughters, Tina and Daniela, came running. Under Mario's watchful eye, everybody respectfully waited for mom.

Manolo had been right. Thirty minutes later, the enchiladas had been devoured.

"I'd like to have a big family," Emmy said and was surprised when all eyes landed on her. She blushed. "I mean, it's fun when we're all together," she said quickly.

"Yes, it is," Manolo said and put his arm around her. "Family's great."

***

When Baatar entered Mario's trailer close to 10:00 a.m.,

looking forward to a nice, strong cup of coffee, he found Mario sitting on the cot, quietly staring in front of him.

"Hi!"

"Hi."

No coffee had been made yet, so Baatar filled the coffee machine. Mario didn't budge.

"What's wrong?" Baatar asked, while he fiddled with the coffee maker.

Mario stared at the floor.

"Mario!"

"What?" he looked up though his eyes seemed far away.

"What's going on?" Baatar asked.

"Nothing."

The coffee brewed, spitting and spewing like a misfiring motorcycle. Baatar patiently waited for the last few drops to filter through and filled a couple of mugs. He walked over to Mario and stared at him.

"When I had nothing going on a while back," Baatar said, "you gave me a hell of a time. Spit it out. What's going on?" Baatar sat down on the cot next to Mario and handed him the coffee.

Mario glanced at Baatar, took the mug, and stared at the floor again.

"Maria?" Baatar asked.

Mario shook his head.

"One of the kids?"

Mario shook his head.

"Work?" Baatar asked.

"Nope."

"One of the ponies?"

"No."

"You've made a bad bet and lost all your money?"

"Shut up, that's stupid."

Baatar sipped his coffee. "You're having an affair?"

Mario looked up. "Worse."

"Worse?" Baatar asked.

"I have a son."

"Yes, I know. You have two sons, Manolo and Miguel." Baatar looked at his friend.

"I have another son," Mario said.

"Oh boy." Baatar placed his coffee mug on the floor and sat motionless, starting at the floor too now. "Something that happened recently?" he asked, glancing at Mario.

"Twenty years ago."

Baatar swallowed. "Does Maria know?"

"Hell, no."

"How'd it happen?"

"I remember that bitch," Mario said in a low voice. "We already had Manolo, and Ariana was on the way. One evening after the races, this woman approaches me. Slender, nice looking, Southern accent, big boobs, big smile. Flattered me up and down the ying yang. We had a few drinks, and she pulled me into the stable, and we did it. It just kinda happened. She ran off right afterward. Later I found a thousand bucks nicely rolled together with a rubber band. I felt used, like she had it all planned or something. I didn't even know her name."

"Did you ever see her again?"

"Once, about six months later. She was in the grandstand, pregnant, with a stately man by her side. When she saw that I noticed her, she disappeared. I figured she was just one of those loose chicks, you know."

"You kept the money?" Baatar asked.

"Mario nodded. "I didn't know her. How could I have returned it? Bought a new pony with it."

Baatar grinned. "So, how'd you find out the kid's

yours?"

"I got a weird feeling in my stomach when I heard Ariana talk about this kid she's taking care of at the hospital. I told you she's doing an internship, didn't I?"

"Yes."

"Ariana told us there's this nineteen-year-old guy with leukemia who needs a bone marrow transplant. Mom's a Southern belle. When they did the DNA test for the match, they found out the dad's not the dad. Ariana said she feels awful because the boy looks like he could be her brother."

"But that doesn't mean anything," Baatar said.

"You wanna hear the story?" Mario barked.

"Go ahead."

"So last night after the races, I had a visit."

Baatar stared at Mario. "No!"

"Yup. Same bitch. Still good looking. Told me she'd pay me $10,000 for my bone marrow."

"And?"

"I think she's out of her mind."

"She might be but if he's really your kid and he's dying, and you could save his life…"

"Right," Mario said. "You'd do it, too, wouldn't you?"

"I'd do it without her paying me. I'd just do it for the kid. If it gives him a chance to live."

The two men sat quietly for a while.

"Ariana says he's a shithead."

"What?" Baatar asked.

"Spoiled brat, entitled, obnoxious."

"Yeah, but still, if he's dying…"

"If he's really my son," Mario said, "I'd want to set him straight. Teach him some manners, not just anonymously give him my bone marrow."

"And Maria?" Baatar asked.

"That's the problem," Mario said. "That's the big

problem. Do I tell her or not?"

"She's pretty reasonable, isn't she?" Baatar said.

"She's a woman, Baatar."

"But this happened twenty years ago. Doesn't punishment for a trespass run out after so many years?"

"I don't think that applies in a marriage. After all, I betrayed her," Mario said.

"You were taken advantage of," Baatar defended.

Mario looked at him. "Right. Show me one woman who believes that."

"But if you keep it quiet and Ariana sees you at the hospital? Or the boy comes around?"

"I'll have to tell Maria; I just don't know how," Mario agreed.

"You know her best."

"It's like going to confession, you know, except you're not confessing to some anonymous guy you may never see again, who gives you a couple of prayers to recite. You have to confess to the woman who's the most important person in your life."

Baatar rubbed his chin. "Shit, man."

Mario looked at his watch. "I'll go to the hospital to take the test," he said, "see if I'm a match. Ariana's off today. Maybe that bitch did it with other guys, too." He looked at Baatar as though his friend could dismiss any unreasonable concerns. "If I'm a match," he cleared his throat, "I'll have to tell Maria. Might have to live on the racetrack for good."

Baatar patted Mario's shoulder. "Good luck, my friend."

Twenty-Nine

Mario made an appointment at the hospital, filled out all the required paperwork, and learned about donating bone marrow. The nurse swabbed the inside of his cheeks. The test took less than five minutes. He went back to the racetrack. He didn't speak much. He was moody. He just wanted to be left alone.

A few days later he received the news that he was a match and the doctor explained the procedure. "We'll collect stem cells from your hip bone under general anesthesia," she said. "The process may take up to two hours."

Mario swallowed. *It didn't sound pleasant.* "It takes two hours?"

She nodded. "Yes, approximately. You may have some bruising but you should be able to return to normal levels of exercise within a week to ten days." She looked at Mario to see if he understood and agreed.

He nodded. "How soon will my son receive the stem cells?"

"He's your son?" the nurse asked. She looked at Mario.

"My biological son, yes."

"Probably within seventy-two hours. Then it may take two to four weeks before we know if his body accepts them."

"Thank you, Doctor."

Mario made an appointment for the bone marrow extraction, pondering in his car on his way home how to present this predicament to his wife.

A long conversation with Maria followed, the longest and most dreaded he'd ever had. Maria was surprisingly understanding in view of the boy's condition—understanding of the medical procedure that had to be taken care of—not so understanding of Mario messing around with another woman behind her back, even if it was twenty years ago.

"The question is," Mario asked her, "do you want the $10,000 his mother offered?"

Maria looked at him, eyes squinting. "I don't want that hush money!"

"I'll give him the bone marrow no matter what," Mario said. "It's the decent thing to do. But do you want the money? For revenge?"

"I want nothing to do with that woman, and I don't want her money."

"Should we go and meet the boy together? See what he's all about?" Mario asked.

"He's *your* son."

"I know, but you're my wife."

Maria thought for a moment. "Mario, even if he wasn't planned—at least not by you—and maybe you weren't in love with that woman, he's still your biological son. If you help him stay alive and hopefully get well, then I think he deserves to know who you are."

"Maybe his mother won't want me to get involved. Maybe that's why she wants to pay me hush money."

"She's got some nerve."

Mario looked at Maria. "Do you know how much I love you?"

"You're not forgiven."

He winced. "I know. I'm just saying I appreciate you and I'm grateful I didn't end up with a woman like that who betrays her husband and her kid. What a deranged way to build a life."

"I'm wondering," Maria said, "if she couldn't get pregnant and she knew her macho husband was the problem, so she grabbed another guy."

"But why me?" Mario asked.

"'Cause you were willing?"

"I was drunk."

"Like I said."

Mario rubbed his face. "I'm gonna have to chew on this for a while."

"Should we tell the kids?" Maria asked. "I think they'd wanna know they have a half brother."

"Ariana may find out anyway when she sees the hospital records," Mario said. "Besides, I want to talk to the kid. If he's my son, he'd better learn some manners. I'm not gonna have a spoiled, entitled, bratty kid roaming this earth."

Maria gave Mario a long look and said nothing.

Mario discussed the procedure in private with Manolo whom he would need for backup at the racetrack. Meanwhile, the doctor informed Paul and his parents, and prepared Paul for the procedure.

Mario experienced bruising, and his lower back hurt after he donated his bone marrow. He'd had injuries during his career, and he'd felt pain. It was a small price to pay to save someone's life.

His son's life.

Although Mario had made all arrangements solely through the doctor, when he finally left the hospital, the boy's mother waited outside the door. She wore a tight-fitting pink and purple yoga outfit, with the top being sleeveless and the bottoms reaching all the way to her ankles. Broad accent stripes of pink and purple on each side of the sleek pants highlighted the length of her legs. She paced the hallway. At each turn, she took a sip of water from a thin, dark blue, stainless steel bottle with *peace* written all over it. As soon as she saw Mario, she approached him with a fat white envelope.

"I don't want your money," Mario said.

"But you have to take it," she insisted and pushed it against Mario's chest.

"I don't have to," Mario said, looking straight into the woman's eyes. "What I did twenty years ago was a mistake I regret. I should have never had sex with you. But it happened. You should have let me know I have a son, but you didn't. Why? Do you think you can buy anything and anybody for money?"

"Everybody has his price," the woman said.

"Well, some don't." Mario stuck the white envelope in the woman's hand and turned to leave.

She ran after him all the way into the hospital's parking lot. "You want more money?" she shouted. "How much? Tell me how much!"

Manolo waited in the parking lot, and Mario got into his truck. They drove off. The woman stood in the parking lot in her pink and purple yoga outfit, holding the white, fat envelope, stomping her foot like a two-year-old having a tantrum.

Mario stayed home to rest for four days. He was sore and extremely tired. He slept much more than usual. Despite her resentment, Maria took care of him. As a nurse, she was proud that Mario didn't hesitate, not even for a moment, to donate his bone marrow, no matter what impact it might have on him and his health. But she kept her thoughts to herself. Manolo took over his job as outrider for seven days, while Mario came along to perform whatever work he could.

Two weeks later, Mario, Maria, and the kids sat down in the backyard and held a family council. The older kids, Manolo and Ariana, were quiet as Mario delivered the news that they had a half brother; the younger ones thought it was neat and wanted to meet Paul right away.

Ariana and Manolo lingered and had a lengthy adult conversation with their parents.

"He's not nice," Ariana confirmed again. "It seems his body is accepting the stem cells, and they're beginning to work. It may take a while to know for sure, but the doctors are hopeful he'll recover. When he was at death's door, he turned more authentic, more honest. He was scared; he felt alone. He knew he'd been a jerk for years. But now that he's getting just a little bit better, the entitlement is taking ahold of him again. If it was meant to be a life lesson, he didn't get it."

"Are his parents the same way?" Maria asked.

"His parents are weird. His mom was sobbing when he was really sick, and she was over dramatic whenever one of us entered the room. The volume of her sobs increased, as though she was practicing for an audition for a Hollywood movie. I think her son is a status symbol for her, like a trophy. The dad didn't come around for three weeks. He was traveling for work. His son wasn't important enough to shorten the trip. His business deals were the first priority, can you believe that?"

"I almost feel sorry for the young man," Maria said.

"I want to meet the boy," Mario said. "I don't know if it'll help him to know who I am. Maybe he'll look down on me, but I've got to let him know who he is and where he came from."

Manolo and Ariana agreed. "He needs to know who

his dad is," Ariana said. "I'd want to know. I think deep down he's a very lonely, scared guy, though I doubt he'll be grateful to you, Dad."

A week later, Mario went to the hospital.

Paul was alone when Mario entered the room. One look at Paul, and Mario knew without a doubt that this was his son. He didn't need DNA evidence. Paul's features revealed his origin, particularly his eyes.

"Hi," Mario said and pulled a chair up to the bed.

Paul stared at him. "You don't strike me as a doctor or a shrink," Paul observed. "Are you the guy who gave me the bone marrow?"

"Yes, I am. My name's Mario."

"My mom told me they found a donor. That's awesome you did that. I mean you don't even know me or anything."

"Paul, has your mother told you anything else about me?" Mario asked.

"No, why should she?"

"Doesn't it strike you as peculiar that we live in the same place and we happen to have matching DNA?"

"No, that shit happens, doesn't it?"

"It's not a coincidence," Mario said.

"What do you mean?"

"Your mother tracked me down. You and I, we're related. I thought you should know."

"Huh?"

"Paul, I'm your biological father. I met your mother one time, twenty years ago and apparently you are the result of it."

"Holy shit, that can't be. My dad's Bradley Brooks!"

"I thought it might come as a surprise," Mario said. "I wanted you to know so you don't live your whole life wondering who you are. Apparently your mother didn't tell you, and I don't know if your father knows. I'm married. My wife and I have five children. Ariana is my oldest daughter. If you'd like to meet the rest of the family, our door's always open. We're a close-knit family. It's an open invitation."

Paul stared at Mario. "Who are you?"

"Mario Martinez. You can reach me through Ariana, if you'd like, or I can give you my phone number. No pressure, just an invitation."

"Holy shit." Paul stared out the window. His fists choked the bedspread.

"I know it's a lot to digest," Mario said. "Sometimes in life things happen for a reason. I didn't know you were my son until your mother looked me up a few weeks back, requesting that I get tested."

"You better leave now," Paul said.

Mario stood up and walked toward the door, then turned toward Paul. "And Paul?"

Paul's head turned and he looked at Mario.

"I expect you to be kinder, more grateful, and more polite. Work on that."

Paul's mouth gaped open, but no words came out, and Mario left.

Thirty

Mario shared everything with Baatar, the first meeting with his unknown son, the boy's attitude, how much he looked like Mario. "If we stay connected," he said, "he's gonna be a piece of work."

"Don't let him off the hook," Baatar said. "Sounds to me like you met for a reason."

Mario sighed.

Baatar looked at Mario and nodded, then left for his rounds at the racetrack stables.

"Emmy, good morning."

"Hi, Baatar."

He smiled at her. "How's my daughter?"

"Good. The horses are no longer mean to me. I tell'em what's going on and how I feel, and they're super nice. They're such great listeners."

"Of course, we both know they were never mean," Baatar said, and winked at Emmy.

"Yeah, OK. Guess who I ran into again?"

"Who?"

"Verena."

"Again?" he asked.

"At the grocery store," Emmy said. "She asked me to hang out with her. After all she's done. Can you believe that?"

"Sounds like she's working a steady job and trying to

clean up her life." Baatar said. "And? Do you want to help her?"

Emmy stared at Baatar. "You can't be serious. No way. I'm staying clear of her. Besides, I have no free time with work and school and studying."

"You have time for Manolo," Baatar said, looking at her.

"That's different."

Baatar gave her a quick nod while his attention was drawn to a thoroughbred in the next stall. He bent down and ran his hand along her front legs all the way to her feet and called Jack over.

"This is one of yours, isn't it? Long Strides?"

"Yeah, I train Long Strides. Why?"

"Her stance is a bit off. Look at her front legs. What do you think?"

Jack checked out the legs while Emmy and Baatar watched. "Nothing," Jack said. "I don't see anything wrong. You?"

Baatar looked at her legs again. "There's a tiny nick and a reaction when you stroke the right front leg," he said. "Just a minor tension. I'd observe it closely."

Jack checked again and nodded.

"How'd you find that?" Emmy asked.

"She seems a little bit off," Baatar explained.

"I don't see it," Emmy said, looking at the horse from the front and the sides.

"It's minor," Baatar said. "When you get more experience, you'll see it. Sometimes it's just a hunch."

Emmy remembered what her mom had said about listening to the animals' spirits. She wondered if Baatar knew how to do that. She worked hard while her mind drifted. She couldn't stop thinking about Paul. She remembered how she first encountered him while walking

Bruno, when she heard that familiar whistle and saw him running past her. Then he stopped and looked at her with those steel-blue eyes, and she was mesmerized. And when he invited her to go out on a date, her heart almost stopped beating. Of course, he turned out to be a jerk, but she had feelings for him then, and now he was sick, and his life had so drastically changed.

After her stable work and before heading to class, she drove to the hospital. It was a beautiful, sunny day. She took the coastal road with glimpses of the stark, blue ocean water and cloudless, blue skies above. For a moment, her eyes were drawn to the designated dog beach where large and small dogs played fetch, enthusiastically running in and out of the cascading waves, filled with joy and happiness. She thought of Bruno and smiled.

She reached the hospital and parked her car on the gray cement lot, stall number one hundred and two. The sun was mercilessly beating down on the asphalt, its heat, absorbed for hours, was pushed back into the air, clinging to Emmy's legs with every step she took. She pushed her way toward the long, gray, rectangular six-story building with evenly spaced, square windows, all of them closed, not much different from a large downtown government building or a prison, for that matter.

"Paul Brooks?" she inquired at the front desk.

"Fourth floor, room four-fifty-one."

Emmy took the elevator and found his room. She knocked and stepped inside. He had a private room. His bed stood close to the window. He looked haggard, his previously athletic body thinned to the bones. He had dark wrinkles under his eyes and his blond surfer highlights had turned light brown. His hair had thinned. His collar bones protruded, reminding Emmy of his dieting, thin mother. His eyes looked lifeless.

"Emmy, what are you doing here?" he asked with a raspy voice. If she didn't know him better, she'd have thought he was embarrassed.

"I heard you were sick. I'm really sorry. I hope you get the help you need."

He stared at her.

"I almost didn't recognize you," Emmy said, "without your blue eyes."

Paul cleared his throat. Emmy saw a cup of water on his nightstand and asked, "do you want some water?" He shook his head.

"I always tried to look like my parents," he said, clearing his throat again. "They both have blue eyes. How'd you know I was here?"

"Baatar told me. He works with Mario at the racetrack. They're friends."

"So, you know everything," Paul said. He looked at Emmy as she pulled up a chair and sat down.

She looked at Paul. His brown eyes were Mario's eyes, no doubt.

"I think my dad always knew I wasn't his son," Paul said. "I can't believe my mother did this to me, having an affair with some guy and getting pregnant from a one-night stand. She betrayed me and my father."

"Paul," Emmy said calmly, feeling a surge of anger swirling in her stomach, "do you hear yourself? Why did *she* do this to me? Your mother gave you life. She gave you a beautiful home. She gave you opportunities. She gave you privileges. You're going to Harvard. Without your mom, you wouldn't be here!"

"My dad never wanted kids."

"So, you'd rather be nonexistent?" Emmy asked, feeling that gush of fury creeping up into her throat. "You'd rather never have had this amazing life of yours?"

Paul shrugged his shoulders. "Maybe it's over soon."

"Isn't the bone marrow transplant helping you recover?"

He shrugged his shoulders. "So?"

"Shouldn't you thank your mom for giving you life? Have you asked her why she got pregnant with another man?"

"Isn't it obvious?" Paul said. "Wanting sex while my dad was out of town?" he coughed. "Without considering the consequences?"

"You can't judge her without hearing her side of the story," Emmy insisted. "That's not even done in a court of law, when a crime was committed, and this is your mother we're talking about. She carried you for nine months. She gave birth to you. She raised you."

Paul rolled his eyes.

"I'm sure it wasn't always easy for her," Emmy said, "and, Mario, you should be grateful to him, too. He's a wonderful dad."

"A dad I never knew."

"But now you do. He's an honorable man."

"Honorable?" Paul said, mockingly, while shaking his head. "Obviously, Mario and my mother messed around behind their spouses' backs. You call that honorable?"

"That was a long time ago, once." Emmy said. "It's such a shame your parents raised you feeling so superior, Paul. Do you really think money and privilege make you a superior human being? Hasn't this cruel disease shown you how vulnerable you are, like everybody else? We're all human, Paul, we're all alike. Equal." Emmy took a breath. She looked at Paul.

He stared out the window.

"Now you have an opportunity to get to know Mario," Emmy continued. "He's compassionate and loving. He has a good heart, or why would he have given a bone marrow transplant to a young man he's never met?"

Paul shrugged his shoulders.

"Because he cares, Paul. Do you think your dad is superior to Mario because your dad makes more money?"

"We're just in a different class of people," Paul said.

"You really believe that?" Emmy raised her voice and scooted on the chair. "If your biological father, whom you seem to despise, hadn't had compassion and given you his bone marrow, you'd be dead now, superiority and all."

Paul looked down, tracing invisible lines on the hospital bedspread. As in a daze, he raised his head and stared out onto the gray parking lot with a hundred cars, parked neatly side by side, immovable, with nowhere to go. Stuck.

Emmy observed him quietly.

"I know," he finally said and looked at her. "Do you think I don't know all that shit?"

"Then why don't you act on it?" Emmy asked. "Why don't you thank your mom for giving you life, and get to know Mario and his family? Even though he didn't know you existed until recently, he's opened his heart to you. He could teach you a lot if you could come down from your throne."

Paul looked at Emmy.

"You could be happy," she said.

A slight smile hushed across his face. "You're right, Emmy. I was never happy on my *throne*. I always felt there was something wrong with me, something missing. My dad never spent time with me. He hired people to deal with me, like I was a nuisance, and I tried everything to please him, to be like him, but I failed."

"You've been successful in track and field; you're a great runner. You got a scholarship to Harvard! He didn't appreciate it?" Emmy asked.

Paul shook his head. "He's never really cared about me."

"I'm sorry," Emmy said. "Still, use your privilege. Study at Harvard. Treat others well. You can make life better for others."

"By becoming a patent attorney?" Paul asked.

"Why not?" Emmy asked. "If that's what you want. You could patent new inventions, help get valuable medicines on the market, stuff like that."

"I've never had an interest in law," Paul said. "My dad said that's where the money will be. He knew I wouldn't be a good salesperson like he is. But I bear his name, so I have to become successful in a money-making career."

"What interests *you*?" Emmy asked.

"Nobody's ever asked me that."

"I'm asking you."

"I don't know," Paul said. "Can you believe this self-centered bastard doesn't know?" He smirked.

"Time to find out," Emmy said. "I've got school. I've got to go. Take care of yourself, Paul. Get well. Nothing else matters right now."

After Emmy left, Paul began pestering Ariana with questions whenever she entered the room to take his temperature, pulse, or blood pressure, or when she brought a meal, tea, or just water. Sometimes when he knew she was on duty, he rang for her several times during her shift.

"How's your dad?" Paul asked when she answered his ring.

"He's fine."

"No, I mean how is he as a dad?"

"He's strict but loving," Ariana said. "There's five of us, so we have rules, and we've always had chores. And if we break the rules or don't do our chores, there's consequences."

"Consequences," Paul said. "What does that mean? Does he beat you?"

"My dad would never beat us. We have horses. We take care of them, feeding, cleaning, exercising, training. Horses are a lot of work, and with five kids, there's always housework, laundry, cooking."

"And if you don't do it, what are the *consequences*?" Paul asked.

"A loss of a privilege, something we like or want. Our parents know us well, so they know what would feel like a punishment."

"A *punishment*?" Paul asked.

"I love to watch movies," Ariana said, "I'm addicted to my cell phone; I love seeing my friends, go to parties. If I'm not respectful to my parents or siblings, my parents may take away one of those privileges, or I may be grounded, or my dad may ask me to take on more chores. You know, the typical stuff."

"I never had consequences," Paul said. "We have personnel for everything: a maid, a cleaning woman, a gardener, a handyman, and for social events, my mom hires a chef."

"You never cook or clean?" Ariana asked.

"Never."

"I can't relate to that. And your dad? Didn't he teach you stuff?"

"Like what?"

"I don't know—how to build things or take them apart? Cars, motorcycles, bicycles, plumbing?"

"You're funny," Paul said. "My dad's an executive. He doesn't do that kind of stuff. And besides, he travels all the time."

"No wonder you're so…" Ariana stopped herself in

midsentence. "Sorry."

"So what?"

"Entitled," she said.

"*Entitled*," he mocked. "Such a stupid word. I hear it all the time. People use it as a discriminatory term. Like all teenagers are entitled. What do they mean by that anyway?"

"They mean you have a lack of respect for others," Ariana said. "You think the world rotates around you."

"And it doesn't?" Paul asked with a smug grin.

Ariana turned.

"Hey, are you mad at me?" Paul asked, looking for a moment like a little hurt boy.

Ariana turned to face him once more. "No, I was just explaining to you what entitled means, since you asked. You grew up with great privileges, Paul. Not everyone does."

"You mean I'm a jerk."

"You can be a little prince who thinks everybody should serve him. Look, I'm on shift. There are a lot of other patients on this ward, people who are sick and need help. I can't keep wandering in here again and again because you have questions about my dad. Maybe you should just meet him and have a chat."

"Would he do that? I mean, he doesn't even know me. I'm a stranger to him. Why would he do that?"

"He'd do that because you're his son," Ariana said. "Now that he knows, he'll take care of you."

"But he's already got five kids," Paul said.

"So now he's got six. Here," Ariana said, and wrote her dad's phone number on a piece of paper. "Call him. If he's at work, leave him a message, and he'll call you back."

Ariana left the room and Paul stared at the piece of paper she'd placed on his nightstand. He wondered what he could ask that man. *After all, he'd only contributed his semen, somewhat accidentally, if Paul could trust his mother's story. They'd met at the racetrack bar, got drunk, and it happened. It meant nothing. Except the guy hadn't only given Paul his life, now he'd saved it.*

If Ariana'd gotten leukemia and Paul's dad found out she was his daughter, would he have put his life on hold to give an unknown girl a bone marrow transplant? Probably not. Most likely not, Paul thought. *Definitely not. Dad wouldn't even shorten his trip to see his dying son at the hospital.*

Paul couldn't get his meeting with Ariana's dad out of his head, his donor. "I expect you to be kinder, more grateful, and more polite. Work on that." The man had said it with such authority, it had given Paul goosebumps. Nobody had ever talked to him that way. Sure, Mom whined, *"Paul, honey, would you please be so kind as to let the cleaning woman know to scrub the patio?"* And Dad? Paul couldn't remember Dad ever talking to him much at all. Paul had had a nanny when he was little, tutors for school, and coaches for track and field. Those he remembered.

In his family, life was all about winning, prestige, and image. Nobody talked about kindness or compassion or gratitude. Out of curiosity and boredom, Paul looked up definitions on his phone:

Kindness—the quality of being friendly, generous, and considerate.

Compassion—concern for the suffering or misfortune of others.

The terms were indeed rather foreign to him. Consideration and concern for others didn't make you win. The misfortune of someone else could help you get ahead. "Leave the losers behind," was Dad's motto. *But now that he had two dads, which one was right? Were prestige and image the highest goal in life? If his biological father didn't have compassion, he'd be dead now, as Emmy had so kindly pointed out.*

Why did the man care?

Paul tortured himself with these thoughts during his entire stay at the hospital. He wondered if he could ever become compassionate and kind. It wasn't that he didn't want to. He didn't know how.

He started to express gratitude to the nurses, doctors, and aides whenever they brought him things or helped him. He stopped ringing the bell when he didn't truly need something.

He recovered nicely after the bone marrow transplant and was released from the hospital to recuperate at home. His mother hired a personal nurse to cater to her son's every need. His dad called once in a while to check how soon Paul could return to Harvard and his running career. Harvard wasn't going to wait forever.

Paul thought of Ariana and Emmy often. They knew what they wanted. Emmy had visited him even though he'd been a jerk to her. She was sweet. And Ariana had chosen to become a nurse, to help sick people. He marveled at her discipline, her smiles even when she was at the end of a twelve-hour shift; her willingness to wash him, to clean his butt, if need be. She always listened with a smile. Not only had he learned the meaning of the word kindness from her, he'd seen it in action. He could fall in love with her, but she had shown no interest, and besides, she was his half sister.

He looked out of his bedroom window and watched his mom, sitting in a twisted yoga position on her perfect, thick, purple yoga mat in her perfectly tight, pink and purple yoga outfit, showing off every curve of her perfectly molded body. He felt no emotion.

He still felt physically weak. He still had doctor's appointments. He still had fear.

Fear was entirely unknown in his family. It was denied. A Brooks didn't have fear. A Brooks was a winner. A

Brooks was an executive. A Brooks was one of those at the top who told everybody else what to do. A Brooks had expectations and commanded. There was no room for gratitude, compassion, and kindness.

But now Paul had seen another side of life. He'd seen young kids at the hospital dying of cancer. He'd seen kids with no arms or legs. He'd heard parents' heartfelt sobs in the hallway.

He'd seen death.

He still had the piece of paper Ariana gave him with the man's phone number. His donor. He'd folded it up neatly and placed it in the drawer of his desk. He'd pulled it out twice and started to dial the number but then lost his nerve. *What was he gonna say to the man? I'm scared?*

A Brooks wasn't scared.

Three more weeks passed, and Paul's body became stronger, though he wasn't ready to take up his running practice. "Baby steps," his doctor said. "You're doing well. You've been extremely lucky. Give it time."

But a Brooks didn't have time. A Brooks was on a schedule to perform. And win. Outdo others. Winning was essential to get to the top.

One night, Paul lay awake watching the stars and the moon, wondering about life and death, sickness and disease as he had so many times over the past few weeks. Mom just said, "Oh, honey, you look great," and then wandered off. Dad asked how soon he'd return to Harvard, and Paul smiled, lied, and told them what they wanted to hear. In the darkness of the night, locked away in the privacy of his room, he cried.

He was recovering from leukemia, he had a new lease on life, but he was angry and indifferent. The disease had changed more than he'd bargained for. He ate junk food and frequently visited Mexican fast-food restaurants he'd

286 | MOLLIE MOON

previously scorned. He drove recklessly. He had unprotected sex with strangers he picked up at a bar. He ignored his father's inquiries as to when he'd return to Harvard, repeatedly. His mother, during yoga breaks, told him how thrilled she was that he'd beaten that monster disease; he'd just need to regain a little weight, and he'd be back to normal.

"Normal?" Paul scoffed. "You lied to me all my life. You want to talk to me about normal?"

His mother lowered her eyes and walked into the garden to attend to her roses, and he was alone, alone with his thoughts, alone with his anger, alone with his fear.

Thirty-One

It was only six o'clock in the morning when he took the piece of paper out of the drawer once again. He dialed the number. The phone rang.

"Hello?"

Paul hung up immediately. He hadn't considered the man would pick up the phone, not at six o'clock in the morning. He just wanted to leave him a message. Paul stared out the window, then dialed again.

"Hello?"

"Hi, sir." Paul paused.

"Yes? Who is this?"

"It's Paul. I'm Paul, the guy you gave the bone marrow to."

"Hi, Paul. I'm glad you called."

"You are?"

"Yes, how're you doing?" Mario asked.

"I…I'm fine."

"Are you getting better? Regaining your health? You've been through so much. Ariana couldn't give me any updates since you left the hospital. We're all concerned about you."

"Yes, sir, I'm getting better. I wanted to thank you for saving my life."

"Anybody would have done that," Mario said.

"No, sir, not everybody. What you did was

extraordinary. I'm sorry I haven't thanked you sooner."

"I'm glad I could help, Paul. You're my son, even though I didn't know that until recently."

"Yeah, me too. Would it be…I mean, it's probably a strange thing…I was wondering…" he paused.

"Paul, what is it? You can ask me anything," Mario said.

"Could we meet sometime?" Paul blurted out.

"Of course, I told you our door's open. Would you like to come to Hillside Ranch and meet the rest of the family?"

"No, I'd just like to talk to you, sir, if I may."

"Please, call me Mario, and yes, of course we can meet. When and where would you like to get together?"

"There's a Mexican fast-food place down the hill called *Tacos for All*," Paul said.

"Yes, I know where that is. I'm at work now but I could meet you tonight around six. Would that work for you?"

"Yes, sir, yes, that would be fantastic," Paul said. He hung on every word.

"OK," Mario said. "I'll see you then."

Paul was restless all day. He had hypothetical conversations with Mario. He practiced to look sincere in the mirror. *He was grateful. How could he show the man he was also polite and kind? That he had changed? What should he say? What should he ask? He should ask him about his family, his kids. Ask him about how they lived, how the kids were raised, what it was like to have a big family like that.* He started to take notes, only to throw them into the trash.

At the racetrack, after exercise riding, Baatar walked over to Mario's trailer and poured a cup of coffee. He looked at Mario, who sat quietly on the cot, his hands folded in front of him as though he was praying.

"What's up? Did you run into any problems this

morning? Did the riding go OK?"

Mario looked up. "When you took in Emmy, how'd you first warm up to each other?" Mario asked.

"That girl had a gazillion questions," Baatar said, "her little mouth never stopped. Yacka-di-yacka-di-yack. She wanted to know everything about me."

"Like what?"

"My background, where I was from, what life was like in Mongolia, how I came to America, my family, my life in Alaska and Texas. She even pried my secrets out of me, Jenna, you know. She wanted to know everything."

"And you asked her the same stuff?"

"She mostly volunteered information."

"I see," Mario said.

"What's on your mind?" Baatar sat down next to Mario.

"The boy, you know, Paul. My new son."

Baatar nodded.

"He wants to meet. I've invited him to meet the family, but he just wants to meet me."

"You're his dad," Baatar said, matter-of-factly.

"I'm his biological father," Mario said, "never was his dad."

"Yeah, well, why don't you find out what he wants?"

"I guess." Mario nodded. "It feels odd, you know, like I'm being interviewed for a job and there's already a bias against me 'cause I'm late in the game."

"But you didn't even know he existed. If he has a bone to pick with someone, it'd have to be with his mother."

"Right."

Baatar patted Mario's shoulder. "You'll be fine. You've raised five kids."

"That still doesn't make me an expert," Mario said, "not with this."

Baatar nodded.

"Come on, let's check today's schedule."

"OK."

Luckily, the day at the racetrack went well without any incidents.

When Mario arrived at *Tacos for All*, Paul was already waiting. He'd chosen a table by the window and stood up to shake Mario's hand, but Mario gave him a big hug.

"Hello, sir."

"Paul, call me Mario." Mario looked into Paul's eyes. "You look much better. Last I saw you, I was worried about you."

"You were worried about me?" Paul asked. "How can you say that? You didn't even know me."

"I have kids your age, Paul," Mario said. "I'd be devastated and heartbroken if any of them became so sick that they'd need a bone marrow transplant. I'm happy you called me. I'd like to get to know you better, and if there's anything I can do for you, you let me know, will you? I know you have your own parents and your own life. But if there's anything I can do? Even if I seem to be a stranger, we share the same blood."

"And bone marrow," Paul said. A smile hushed across his face, momentarily. He looked into Mario's eyes. "You're so different from my real dad, I mean, my other dad. You seem to care."

"Yes, I care," Mario said. "I'm sure you're dad does, too. Everybody shows things differently, you know. Some people are stoic when tragedy hits, others weep. In our Mexican culture, we're quite open with our feelings. We talk. We share our experiences, our joys and sorrows, all of life."

"Sir, Mario, are you ever scared?"

Mario leaned back and looked at Paul. "Scared of a

situation like getting so sick or injured you may die?"

"Yeah."

"Of course, everybody's afraid of dying or being disabled. It's the unknown, being out of control. Were you raised Catholic?"

"I wasn't raised with any religion."

What do you believe?" Mario asked.

"I don't know."

"I believe we're here on earth to learn, to become better people, and when we die, we go back to our Maker," Mario said. "What do you think happens when we die?"

"I don't know," Paul said. "We're just gone. Eliminated. We no longer exist."

"We've had long discussions about this in my family," Mario said. "My wife and Ariana are nurses; they tell me there's a lot of scientific evidence now that life goes on. We just change form somehow. Our soul, our mind, and emotions, our spirit lives on."

"Without a body?"

Mario swallowed. "I'm no expert, Paul, but there are many books on this topic. Life after life, life after death. You like to read?"

"I do."

"I'd suggest you read some of the books. The more we know, the less we fear," Mario said.

"But I'm not just afraid of death; I'm afraid I won't be able to fill my dad's shoes. He wants me to study genetics and then go to law school. I'm supposed to become a successful patent attorney."

"Is that what you want?" Mario asked, studying Paul's face.

"I've been programmed for it," Paul said.

"But is it what *you* want? Is it something *you'*d enjoy? It's *your* life, Paul, not your father's. I learned that the hard way. I wanted my oldest son to step into my footsteps, and he told me no. It took me a while to swallow my pride, but I got it eventually. Just because it's a career I love doesn't mean he'll love it. He isn't me. He's my son but he's got his own decisions to make and his own life to live. I feel the same way about you."

"I'm just scared I can't do anything right anymore," Paul said. "My dad was so disappointed when I got sick. I threw off his schedule. He keeps asking when I'll return to Harvard, and I don't even know if I want to return to Harvard. I was a runner at Harvard, I was on the track-and-field team. That was my world, and now I'm weak and tired and scared."

"Have you told your parents how you feel?" Mario asked.

"I can't. They have expectations. They don't care." Paul stared at the burger he'd ordered before Mario arrived.

Mario reached over and touched Paul's hand. "Paul, talk to your parents. The most important thing is that you regain your health. All that pressure you put on yourself isn't helping. You need to heal."

"I'm sure my parents see that differently. They have only one son, and he's meant to succeed."

"Success is living a life that brings joy to you and others, and if you don't know what that'll look like right now, then you need to figure that out," Mario said. "Seeing death in the eye changes people. You've been shook up. Your whole life has been shook up. Talk to your parents. Help them understand where you're at. Get well. Then make new plans. And if I can help, you let me know. As I said, our door's always open. Sometimes it helps to talk, and there's a whole family waiting for you. You already know Ariana and me."

"Thank you, Mario, it really helps to talk."

"We'll do it again," Mario said and stood up. "Call me anytime. Stay in touch, son."

Paul stood up and they hugged.

"Thank you."

Mario left the restaurant, but Paul lingered. He'd been observing the cute, young, friendly waitress. "Miss," he called her over.

"Was something wrong with the burger?" she asked as she approached.

"No, I talked too much, and it got cold. Would you mind bringing me a new one? I'll pay for it, of course."

"I'll be happy to." She took the untouched plate and swung around. Paul watched as she walked away and disappeared through the swinging doors to the kitchen. He felt better. *Maybe*, he thought, *he had a soul, too. He'd have to read up on that.* He missed his talks with Ariana. *The hospital had something good*, he thought. *This whole messy, nasty situation had had something good, even if it had been the most awful experience of his life.*

"What's your name?" he asked when the pretty waitress delivered the fresh burger.

"Verena."

"That's a pretty name. Do you work here regularly?"

"I do."

"I guess then I'll have to come here more often," Paul said and smiled at her.

She smiled back. "We like regulars."

He tipped her generously when he left.

Paul went home to his room, which had become his sanctuary. He ordered a couple of books on life after death online, then sat and stared out the window. He thought about what Mario had said. This stranger, his donor, his biological father, was no executive, but he had authority. He had ethics, the stuff corporations talked about. He had values Paul had never considered. He'd not been raised with those kinds of values, but they'd saved his life.

Mario had saved his life.

He went downstairs and found his mom in the garden, tending to her roses.

"Mom?"

"Yes, dear?" She put down the watering hose.

"Why'd you pick Mario to be my dad?"

"Oh, honey, it was such a long time ago."

"Why, Mom? You knew Dad didn't want kids. Why'd you chose Mario?"

"It's hard to explain, dear. Don't worry about it."

"Mom, he's my biological father. He gave me a bone marrow transplant, so I could live. I need to know."

She picked up the watering hose again. Paul took it from her and shut off the water. "Mom, please!"

She looked at him with her beautiful, sky-blue eyes. "I wanted a child," she said. "I'd been to the races and watched that outrider many times. He was manly. He was young and vibrant and responsible, so one evening after the races, I took him aside and flattered him. I got him drunk and seduced him. I wanted to get pregnant. I wanted to be a valuable woman. You may not understand. Your father was climbing the corporate ladder. I was his trophy wife. He ordered me to attend meetings when he wanted me to. He told me how to dress and what to say—mostly nothing. He wanted to do all the talking. I was to be beautiful, make him look good. My days were empty."

Paul listened quietly.

"I felt ashamed for not having a college degree."

"But you told me you did."

"I lied."

"Mom!"

"I'm sorry. I always felt worthless until I got pregnant.

Knowing I was a whole woman, I could have a baby, gave me a lift. Your father wanted me to abort, but I refused. He didn't talk to me for nine months. When I got you, I was so happy. But your father was furious. He was worried my body would no longer be perfect. I was supposed to look good at his side. That's all he ever wanted from me. He scolded me for having you, and he punished me by hiring all the personnel and demanded I take care of myself."

"Why didn't you divorce him?" Paul asked. His voice was stern, filled with anger, reminding him of his father.

His mom flinched. "Where would I have gone? I had no career; I was a young mother. Nobody would hire an uneducated single mother with a little baby. I focused on *you*. I wanted *you* to have opportunities in life."

Paul stared at his mom. His heart pounded, his jaw muscles cramped. "All I ever wanted was to be loved," he said. It sounded like a reproach.

It was a reproach.

"I love you, Paul, I love you so very much. I've told you that," his mom said, looking at him with slumped shoulders, her arms by her side. Her voice sounded meek.

"Yes, you said the words, but I had nannies and mentors and coaches, Mom. You weren't there for me. I didn't have parents, not really."

Tears welled up in his mother's eyes. "Your dad said that's what privilege means," she said.

"He's hardly ever home," Paul nearly shouted. "Why didn't you love me when he wasn't here?" The veins in his throat became visible.

"He's had such a hold over me, Paul. He controls me. You have no idea." His mother looked down.

Paul took a deep breath in, followed by an even longer exhale. He stared at his mother, a woman he was drawn to and yet despised. "Mom, I'd like to get to know Mario," he said. "He seems nice. He cares. He's only seen me twice, and you know what he called me today?"

"What?"

"He called me *son*. Dad's never called me that, ever."

She nodded. "I'm sorry I wasn't a better mother, Paul. I really am sorry."

He nodded and gave her a hug. She stood like a rock, allowing it, afraid to be seen, to be observed. When he let go of her, she turned around and opened the faucet and continued watering the roses.

Thirty-Two

Baatar and Jenna checked out many houses in the surrounding area and decided their perfect home would be on a bluff above the ocean with a large pool, a grove of trees, and direct, private access to the beach. But such a place didn't exist, and if it did, it wasn't affordable, not in or around Little Oaks. They had to make compromises.

While Baatar was initially mostly focused on a nice lawn for Bruno to run and for kids to play, and a firepit for evening talks, Jenna was focused on the house itself. *Would she want a pantry next to the kitchen? Did they need a washroom where Baatar could drop his dirty clothes and boots when he came home from the racetrack? How many bedrooms and baths were a must, considering DJ, their own baby, and perhaps Emmy, who might like to stay with them if given a choice?*

And what about visitors? Surely her dad would come from time to time, and her aunts? No, she wouldn't consider aunts, uncles, or cousins to stay with them; they could stay at a motel. Baatar's family? She shuddered, *but they'd have to have at least one room they could make available to guests. And then there was her sewing business for which she needed some space.*

House shopping was fun, Jenna thought, *but not under pressure.* She previewed every online ad with photos or videos and flagged only those that had a nice backyard. The real estate agent was willing and ready to have them relocate all the way to Hemet, Palm Desert, Julian, or

Temecula. Jenna just laughed. No, she kept repeating, no, not there either.

They looked at properties in Little Oaks and Hillside Ranch, but none fit their list of desired features.

"Maybe we're just too picky," Jenna said one evening. "We've looked at fifteen properties already, and my stomach is growing."

Baatar sat down and put his hand on her stomach. "Sophie'll have to be patient," he said with his usual calm. "You can't rush these things."

"I don't want to move when I'm eight months pregnant and cannot bend over," Jenna said. "It'll just be too stressful."

"If we don't find a suitable place by the time you're six months pregnant," Baatar said, "we'll take a break and start over after Sophie's been born, OK? Worst case, she'll be spending her first few months here. I don't think she'd mind."

"OK," Jenna said, but she really wanted a house now, a nice, spacious home with enough time to paint the nursery and make it all cozy and perfect.

As if planned, just at her six months mark, they found a lovely property in Little Oaks, a two-story craftsman-style house with four-bedrooms and a loft, a pool and a pantry off the kitchen. The exterior was painted in a light yellow, with white window frames and three steps leading to a dark red entrance door. The red tiled roof matched the color of the door.

On stepping inside, the entryway was filled with light and led into an open floor plan with the living room straight ahead and the dining room and kitchen off to the side. The house had light wood flooring throughout and a marble fireplace that added to the living room's coziness. Next to the fireplace was a built-in, square shelf for firewood which had been stacked with birch wood all the way to the rim. French doors opened onto a large patio. The kitchen had a bay window overlooking the backyard, which had plenty of space to build a swing and a sandbox, and a large grass area for Bruno to run and play. Throughout the house, both downstairs and upstairs, were many windows, giving it an open beach-house feel.

The kitchen, the heart of the house, captured Jenna at first sight. It had the clean look she liked, with plenty of white wooden cabinets with slender, silver handles and a modern, shiny backsplash made of small, glass tile with just a hint of green, a brand-new gas stove, and gray-speckled Caesarstone countertops. It was any chef's dream. It sparkled.

There was one bedroom downstairs, perfect to turn into a guest bedroom.

Jenna looked at Baatar and smiled as they headed upstairs. Each bedroom was spacious, with large windows and white beams meeting at the center of the high ceilings. The master bedroom had its own en suite bathroom with two sinks, an oversized oval tub and a shower big enough for two.

Baatar also liked the house. It was spacious and would fill all their needs. Jenna loved it, and so would he, when she'd put her touch on the rooms' interiors. The two-car garage led into the laundry room, where he could leave his dirty boots when he came home.

They put down an offer the very same day and it was accepted six hours later—a conditional sale. They immediately put Baatar's home on the market.

"Life's been such a whirlwind," Jenna said to Baatar. "Getting engaged, moving to California, selling my Texas home, our international wedding. I'll always remember our honeymoon in Alaska with all the unexpected surprises.

Then DJ joined us, and now I'm pregnant, and we're selling our home. Tell me life will be calmer in the future."

"Life will be calmer in the future," Baatar said and smiled.

"Promise?"

"I can't guarantee it," he said, "but I hope I can make you happy, so you have no regrets."

"I have no regrets," Jenna said and gave him a kiss.

While Baatar pondered how many of his friends and trucks they'd need for a smooth move, Jenna's head was still spinning. "What if we won't sell this house on time, Baatar? What if it takes too long, and the seller of the new home decides to take another offer? And then we have nothing, no place to stay, and we're having a baby! And Emmy has already confirmed she wants to move back in with us."

He looked at her with his deep, penetrating eyes. "Jenna, this place will sell quickly. It's a prime location. It's desirable."

"Yeah, but what if not?"

"If not, then we'll find a solution. I promise you, you won't have the baby in a barn."

She laughed. "Very comforting, Baatar, really."

"I promise I'll take good care of you and the baby," he said. "How can I make you feel more comfortable? Tea?"

DJ's voice came through the baby monitor. "Mommy, Mommy."

"I'll go check on him," Baatar said and stood up. A minute later, he appeared with DJ, who clung to him like a koala bear.

"He had a bad dream," Baatar whispered, apologetically, as he sat down on the sofa with him.

"Oh, poor baby," Jenna said and stroked DJ's head. The boy calmed down and fell asleep quickly in Baatar's arms. He stood up and carried DJ back to bed, tucked him in, and gave him a kiss. Then he walked back into the living room.

"Where were we? Tea?" he asked.

"I'd love some."

Within three days, they received multiple offers on their current home, and accepted the highest bid.

"I'm scared," Jenna said that evening. "Are you sure we made the right decision? I've grown fond of this house and the neighborhood."

Baatar's lips puckered slightly, then he took her in his arms. "We'll have a beautiful four-bedroom house. The kitchen has a pantry, as you wanted, and even a bay window overlooking the backyard. There's a pool and room for me to build a swing and a sandbox. Jenna, this is a dream come true. We're living the American dream, you and me. You can watch the kids play in the backyard, and I'll be home as much as I can. There's room for Bruno to run and play. We can have our friends over, and you have your own space for sewing—indoors!"

She smiled. "I know. That's a big improvement."

"You want to look at the floor plan again and the pictures we've taken?" he asked.

"Yes, they have a video online. I think it's still there."

They sat on the sofa together and watched the video three times in a row, when DJ came walking in with a book under his arm.

"You woke up again?" Baatar asked.

DJ climbed on Jenna's lap and handed Baatar the book. "Read me a story," DJ said, "please." He looked at Baatar with his dark-brown eyes.

"You want me to read you the story while you cuddle with Jenna?" Baatar asked.

DJ nodded while his thumb landed in his mouth.

"We have to pack up the entire house," Jenna said, ignoring DJ's request.

"We have lots of friends who'll help us. Don't worry, love. Everything will work out."

Baatar opened the big picture book and said, "This story is for DJ and Sophie." Then he began to read, "It was already dark, and the stars glistened in the sky…"

Jenna pointed at the pictures while DJ followed along with sleepy eyes, until his eyelids became heavy and his breathing deep and regular.

Baatar stopped reading and closed the book, and Jenna carried DJ back to bed. When she returned to the living room, a nice hot cup of tea awaited her.

"Are you sure everything will go smoothly?" she asked again, as she sunk into the sofa and into Baatar's arms.

"It will," he assured her. "Does Sophie want to hear the rest of the story?"

Jenna nodded, and he opened the book and read it all the way to the end.

Thirty-Three

At Paul's request, Mario and Paul met a few more times and talked. Mario told Paul about his job at the racetrack, the circuit, his ponies and his family. Paul told Mario about his upbringing, his parents' expectations and his inner turmoil.

"Do you like horses?" Mario asked Paul.

"I don't know."

"Maybe you should find out. We're having a barbecue on Sunday. Would you like to come?"

"Why not," Paul said.

Mario prepped his family and invited Baatar and Jenna to come over, too. Emmy and Manolo were also there. They were in the arena where Manolo showed Emmy what to look for in a poorly fitted hoof.

"We'll have to fix this one," Manolo explained. "I can do it tomorrow. Dad mentioned we're having a barbecue. Let's see what we can do to help."

When they walked into the kitchen, Ariana was pouring Paul some water. Maria was putting her finishing touches on a large salad.

"Manolo, Emmy, this is Paul," Ariana said.

Manolo walked over and shook his hand. "Welcome, Paul. It's nice to meet you. This is a pretty unexpected situation for all of us, including you, right?"

"Yeah, unexpected," Paul said and stared at Emmy.

"Paul!"

"Hi, Emmy. Didn't expect to see you here," Paul said and swallowed.

"Manolo and I are together," she said and moved a bit closer to Manolo.

"You're dating him?" Paul asked, staring at Manolo.

"Yes," Emmy said.

"You're dating my half brother? That's awkward," Paul said. He inspected Manolo closely.

"Right, I hear you two know each other," Manolo said.

"We went out a few times, but things didn't work out," Emmy explained.

"I've changed," Paul said. "I'm a nice guy now." He winked at Emmy.

"Good for you," Emmy said. "I'm happy to see you've recovered from your illness." She turned toward Manolo. "Let's check out the barbecue outside."

He nodded, and they walked out onto the patio.

"I told you Paul and I attended junior high together, remember?" Emmy explained. "And when I moved back to Little Oaks last year, we ran into each other and went out on a few dates. He came over to Baatar's house once and made derogatory remarks about the house, me, Baatar, and refused to try the Pozole I made. So Baatar threw him out of the house."

Manolo chuckled. "That sounds like Baatar. I'm glad Paul was a jerk 'cause otherwise, I would've never stood a chance with you."

"Oh, come on, that's not true," Emmy said.

"Emmy," Manolo said, looking at her with a smile, "I couldn't have competed with Harvard. That's way too enticing for you."

"Yeah," she admitted, "Harvard fascinated me but Paul…and besides, you're already a university graduate and a professional farrier, and I'm still in junior college, so please, you're very impressive."

"So, you're not going to dump me for him, now that he's a nice guy?"

"Mano, I love you. Besides, we don't know what his definition of nice is, do we?"

"I love you, too." He gave her a kiss.

Inside the house, Ariana had a long discussion with Paul about Mexican food, their favorite meal—his was lobster—and how to cook for a family of seven or more, when Mario and Baatar walked into the kitchen.

Paul stared at Baatar. "Oh no."

Baatar looked at Paul. "So, you're Mario's son!" He looked at Mario, then back at Paul. "I hear you were sick and have recovered. That's good news. And the illness helped you connect with your biological father."

Paul nodded.

"Mario and I are good friends," Baatar said.

Paul swallowed. The color drained from his face.

"We're happy you've come to meet the family," Mario said, "and that includes our ponies. But first, let's eat."

They headed outside, Mario, Maria, and Ariana up front, with Baatar and Paul following. "You're getting a new chance here," Baatar said to Paul. "Not everybody has two families, one you're born into and one you chose. This is a good one."

Paul nodded.

The entire family gathered. Tina, Daniela, and Miguel were excited to meet their new brother. They asked him lots of questions about how and where he grew up, if he had other siblings, his favorite football team, going to school back east, if he had any pets, and what his future dream was. Paul answered many questions but didn't have an answer to the last one.

"Paul," Mario said after everybody's stomachs were full and the chatter subsided a bit, "mind giving me a hand in the barn?"

"Sure."

Manolo and Emmy helped with the barbecue cleanup, then walked over to the pasture and saddled up the ponies to go for a trail ride, while Miguel ran into the barn to help feed the ponies.

"I know nothing about horses," Paul said to Mario, except that their poop is big and smells."

"Doesn't your poop smell?" Mario asked and looked at Paul, grinning. "Do you want to learn about them?"

"Yeah, it'd be cool to ride them."

"Before you ride them, you'll have to learn about them," Mario said.

"OK."

"Miguel," Mario said, "will you teach Paul what you know about horses? Just the basics."

Miguel came running. "Yeah!"

"I thought you'd teach me," Paul said, looking at Mario.

"I will, too. We're a family. Everybody helps everybody else. Miguel grew up with the ponies. He knows a lot about them. You can learn from him."

Miguel looked up at Paul and smiled.

"He's eight!" Paul said.

"Yes, and he knows a lot about horses. He's your little brother. Give him a chance. I've learned more from my kids than from most adults."

"Half brother," Paul said. He took a deep breath. "OK."

Mario patted Paul on the back. "I have a couple of phone calls to make. I'll be back."

"Do you know about the different kinds of horses?"

Mario heard Miguel ask Paul.

"Nothing."

"This is a palomino. We call her Twinkles."

Mario smiled as he walked out of the barn. *Let an eight-year-old teach you, Paul,* he thought. *A little humility won't hurt you.*

Paul listened to Miguel's horse introductions, then found a reason to step out of the barn. He felt better outside, in fresh air. He walked over to the pasture and sat on the fence, watching Baatar quietly talk to one of his ponies.

When Baatar saw Paul, he walked over to him. "You're lonely and afraid," Baatar said, and sat on the fence, next to Paul.

Paul moved a foot aside as if Baatar was contagious. "You don't know me," he said. "I know I was a jerk when I was at your house. I'm not like that anymore."

"I'm glad to see you've shed the jerk," Baatar said. "Now you're just lonely and afraid."

"How would you know how I feel?"

"Paul, you're not just a physical body that's present here," Baatar said. "You carry all your thoughts and emotions in there, and people who can read horses usually can read people quite well. I can see your loneliness in your eyes, and I can sense your fear. But you have a great family here. They'll take care of you if you let them. You got a second chance in more ways than one. You've just been blessed with five siblings. Get to know them, but most of all, explore the magic inside of you. Fear disempowers us. Knowing yourself gets you centered and present."

Paul looked at Baatar. "I thought you hated me."

Baatar shook his head. "Everybody deserves a second chance. So, what did Miguel teach you about horses?"

"The color of the brown ones is called bay, the weird

spotted one is an appaloosa, and the nice-looking golden one with the white main is a palomino. They have a lot of gut, big teeth, their tails swish to get rid of flies, they eat all day and poop a lot."

Baatar laughed. "Is that what he told you?"

Paul nodded.

"It's true," Baatar said, "but there's a lot more to them than that. Horses are highly intuitive. Their hearing is excellent, their almost three-hundred-sixty-degree vision superior to ours. They're much more intelligent than most people think. They're masters at being present, and they demand that we are present with them. It appears they do nothing but graze, but they're fully aware of their surroundings. And they nurture us. They can read us like a book, and they can help us get in touch with who we are. And Paul, horses never lie."

"Really?"

"Really. If we can believe scientists, animals are much older than we are. Evolution, right?" Baatar said. "Religions state the same. First came the creation of the earth, then the animals, then people. Animals hold an inner wisdom that's much more ancient than ours. They have memories. They've survived tragedies. They have feelings like we do. They have an innate knowledge that goes back thousands of years, and they're willing to share it with us, when we're willing to listen. We can learn a lot from them, but many people feel superior. They lose out. In Mongolia, where I grew up, or in the wild in general, horses are nomads. My people learned to follow them. Our lives were built on their ancient wisdom. "

Paul looked at Baatar, not sure whether he wanted to stay and listen or run off. He glanced at the ponies.

"Horses have the same fight-or-flight mechanism people do," Baatar said calmly. "When the fight isn't worth the risk, they flee, just like we do."

Baatar looked at Paul. "When we fight for something that doesn't match our heart's desire, we may lose the fight; maybe not right away, but it catches up with us at some point. We can only win when our heart's passion is in it."

"What are you trying to say?" Paul asked.

"Wait here," Baatar said and jumped off the fence. He brought Kheer over. "Look into Kheer's eyes. What do you see?"

"Big. Lots of brown." Paul looked at Baatar. "Black?"

"Now look with your heart," Baatar said.

"I don't know what you mean," Paul said.

"Pretend you can see with your heart. Look beyond what your mere physical vision presents. Feel into her."

Paul looked at Baatar.

"No, look at her. Look into her eyes."

Paul took a deep breath. He stared at the pony, then into her eyes. A surge of emotion invaded his chest.

"Breathe, Paul," Baatar encouraged him.

"I don't know. I can't. I don't see anything."

"But you felt something, didn't you?" Baatar asked.

"This is stupid," Paul said, and jumped off the fence and walked away.

Mario came walking toward him. "Sorry, those calls took longer than I thought. Paul, come with me."

Emmy and Manolo returned from their ride. They took off the saddles and bridles, brushed the ponies, and returned them to pasture. "You're nice to him," Emmy said, pointing with her chin at Paul.

"Why shouldn't I be?"

"He mocked us at your place when I invited him for dinner, remember?"

Baatar nodded slightly. "But now he's experienced tragedy, and it shook him up. He says he's changed, and I believe he has."

"You're very kind," Emmy said.

"Don't you think he deserves a second chance?" Baatar asked.

"Yeah, sure, as long as it's not with me. I much prefer Manolo over Paul."

Baatar smiled. "I think you made a good choice, but that young man needs a new start, and new friends." He looked at Emmy closely. "And you? Any more ghost experiences?"

"None," Emmy said with a big smile on her face. "And Axel's behaving, too. He's started going out with Carla. Still, I can't wait till you get your new house, and I can live with you again. I miss you and Jenna," she said, when DJ came running toward them. "And DJ," she quickly added.

"He can be a handful."

"I love kids, I don't mind." Emmy hunched down to be on eye level with DJ. "You wanna go on the swing?" she asked.

DJ nodded and took her hand as they walked off together.

Thirty-Four

A week passed, and Paul accepted another invitation to come and visit the Martinez family. He arrived early and walked over to the arena, where Manolo was training his pony, Rush.

After a short, initial greeting, Paul asked, "You don't use a leash and a whip? How's he going to learn?"

"I've seen many different training methods," Manolo said. "I prefer using intention and trust."

"What?" Paul asked, baffled.

"No lead rope and no whip," Manolo said.

"Why not?"

"In a relationship, would you rather be equal or superior?" Manolo asked.

"Superior of course," Paul said.

"Why?"

"It puts you in control."

"Would you rather control someone like a slave who performs for you grudgingly or a friend who freely gives to you out of love and respect?"

"Is that a trick question?" Paul asked.

"Which relationship do you think carries a greater reward? Which makes both happy? Slave or friend?" Manolo asked, looking at Paul.

"I'd rather have a friend," Paul said. He thought of his mother and how his father had controlled her, and how unhappy she was under his rule.

"Then you must be a friend," Manolo said, "and treat others as equals. Respect them. Big or small. Animal or human."

Paul watched as Rush stopped in his tracks and followed Manolo, his muzzle touching Manolo's shoulder. Manolo put his arm around Rush's neck and petted him. "I teach him, and he teaches me. We learn from each other. We both have our strengths and weaknesses. We have a connection, we're friends. He follows my commands and if there's something he doesn't like or doesn't understand, he lets me know."

"I've never learned how to be a friend," Paul said. There was a sadness in his voice. "My dad commands. He always strictly told me what to do. He's never asked my opinion or how I felt. He intimidates my mom, mocks her in front of others, and she cowers. Sometimes it hurts me to see how he treats her. It's become our way of life. He's a big man. He bellows, and people buckle. That's all I know."

"That's not a good situation," Baatar said, and Paul turned around, facing him.

"You always sneak up on people?"

"I came to check on the ponies."

Paul rolled his eyes. "Sure you did."

"Emotional intimidation," Baatar said.

Paul stared at him. "What?"

"Your dad's mannerism. A child has no means to fight that, but you're not a child any longer."

"What can I do? I rely on him," Paul defended.

"I can't tell you what to do, Paul, but you have choices," Baatar said. "We all do. You can stand up to him and take the consequences. You can tell him how you feel when he intimidates and bullies you and your mom. Most likely, he won't take it well, but it would heal your heart."

Paul stared at Baatar. "Are you a shrink or something?" He turned his back, putting his attention on the ponies.

For Paul, visiting the Martinez family was peculiar. He wanted to be included in the family somehow, find his own place with them, get their acceptance, or perhaps just their attention. And yet he wanted to remain Paul Brooks, the rich kid with privileges; the young promising man who attended Harvard.

He was torn.

At night when he couldn't sleep, he saw Kheer's dark-brown eyes looking at him as though she had a message, she hid a secret. He was baffled. One thing Baatar had said wouldn't leave him alone. *Animals hold an inner wisdom that's much more ancient than ours. They have memories. They have feelings like we do. They have an innate knowledge and are willing to share it with us when we're willing to listen.*

Two weeks passed. Quietly and without an announcement, Paul drove to Hillside Ranch, not to visit the family; he came to visit the horses. Early in the mornings, he drove up, parked the car, and walked toward the pasture. He sat and watched the ponies. Day after day, he came. He didn't ask for Mario, didn't seek out the family, didn't seek any contact.

He sat in the pasture, like a new member of the herd, an outsider, the lowest in the hierarchy, tucked against the fence. He didn't know what he was seeking. Solitude, perhaps. Isolation. A space to be alone, to ponder where he fit into this life, into this world, that was filled with lies and pretense. *Horses never lie*, Baatar had said, and Paul wanted to find out for himself if there was any truth to it. But horses didn't talk. *How could anyone make such a statement?*

Emmy watched Paul, as he sat in the pasture, alone. "I feel for him," she said.

Manolo looked up. "You still like him?" he asked.

"No," Emmy said, "not as a boyfriend. But I know what he's going through." She looked at Manolo. "He's kind of lost everything."

Manolo raised his eyebrows. "He's gained," he said. "He still has everything he had, his parents, his wealth, his privilege. His health has been restored. He gained knowledge of his biological father. He added a few half siblings to his life. He's done nothing but gained."

Emmy slowly shook her head. "His foundation's gone," she said.

"What do you mean?"

"His entire life was built on him being a Brooks," she explained. "All he wanted deep inside was to please his dad. But his dad isn't his real dad. His real dad is an outrider, a man of Mexican descent, someone without the kind of status Paul was taught one needs to feel valuable. Suddenly Paul is half of a culture he knows nothing about, including a family with five kids he's never known. His real dad works with horses—a species unfamiliar to Paul. He's lost. He's only half of who he used to be, or less."

"What do you mean, or less?" Manolo asked.

"His mom."

"What about his mom?"

"Paul thought his mom was a perfectionist, a socialite who enjoyed the glamour of being seen. But it wasn't her true self. It's her survival mechanism. She performs a role for her husband, an image he wants her to uphold. Paul feels like his whole life has been a lie. Everything crumbled, like a sandcastle that was rained on and collapsed."

Manolo nodded.

"He's grieving," Emmy said. "I want to help him. I know what grief feels like, Mano. I'm not going to get involved with Paul, but I've got to help him. Can you understand that?"

Manolo nodded. "Go to him."

Emmy walked outside.

The air was cool, the setting sun cast shadows on the barn, the horses, and Paul. Slowly, Emmy approached the pasture. She stood at the fence, watching Paul. He didn't look up when she approached. He just sat, quietly, forlorn, in the dirt, that held on to him and crawled up his legs all the way to his hips, somehow trying to ground him in its reality.

Emmy climbed onto the fence and sat in silence, a few feet away from Paul, close enough to hear him breathing, and to see his tears that sporadically wetted his cheeks. She didn't speak. She just sat and listened to the silence between them. Her heart ached for him. She noticed a hazy light around his body. It looked grayish and muddy like a dirty pond that had been stirred. She didn't know what it meant. She just observed.

The horses grazed and chewed methodically, hypnotically, their tails routinely swishing off flies without disturbing the eating ritual. Everybody was in their place, peacefully coexisting, as in a Monet picture.

Paul didn't budge until an hour later when he stood up and walked to his car. He glanced at Emmy before he took off to drive home for the night.

Emmy persisted. She repeated her silent offering, her presence, at various times in the early evening hours after class. She watched the light around his body, as it shifted from dark gray to light gray. Some days there were streaks of brown in it, some days she noticed a small swirl of blue or red or green.

Eventually she moved into the pasture and sat next to Paul. "I know about grief," she said. "I lost my parents and sister when I was twelve. They all died on the same day and I remained. I lost everything, except my life. Some days, I still cry. I don't think the pain will ever fully leave, but life also brings me joy. It seems impossible, but it does."

Paul looked at her, then looked down. He didn't respond. He stared at the horses and one of Mario's ponies, Twinkles, came and stood in front of him. She tucked her head into his chest and his silent tears wetted her face.

"He's an odd guy," Manolo said over dinner one evening, while Baatar and Jenna were visiting.

"He's trying to make sense of his life, son," Mario said. "He lost his stability. He had a life-threatening disease and while he recovered, he found out he's not who he thought he was. He's struggling. Let him be. Give him time to figure himself out."

"As much as I disliked his behavior when I first met him," Baatar said, "I can relate to him. When my friend Damdin died so unexpectedly, my life turned upside down. I bought a motorcycle and rode from Texas to California. I spent many days riding lonely roads for hours on end, thinking nothing, just letting the wind hit my face and my eyes take in the scenery. I was completely unable to share my inner turmoil. I put my whole life in question, everything I'd ever done. I can see the same distress in Paul's eyes."

Miguel, on the other hand, watched Paul with the innocence of an eight-year-old. "Dad, why doesn't he talk to us? Why doesn't he want to visit with us?" he asked.

"He needs to sort things out for himself, son," Mario explained. "He's hurting inside."

"But we can help him, Dad," Miguel said.

"No, son, we can't help him right now, but the ponies can. Just let the ponies help him."

Miguel conceded, but sometimes he sneaked out and sat next to Paul; sometimes he brought him carrots to feed to the ponies. He just dropped them into Paul's lap and smiled at him. Then he left and Paul would feed the carrots to Twinkles.

Tina also came with questions. "Shouldn't we invite him in, Dad?"

"We've offered him our hospitality," Mario said. "We've told him he's welcome in our family, and that's all we can do. We can't force him to participate."

"But why does he want to be alone, Dad?"

"He's got a lot on his mind, Tina. He needs to sort it out."

"You always tell us to talk things out, Dad; you make us talk to you when we have a problem."

Mario grinned. "It's because I know you well, and I can help you when you share what's bothering you."

"But why can't you do that for Paul?" Tina asked.

"He's a grown boy, and he's not ready, Tina. Give him time."

"What if he's never ready, Dad?"

"Then we'll have to accept that, but I think he'll come around."

One evening, Tina watched Paul for a long time from her window. Then she ventured out. She walked into the pasture and sat next to him. He glanced at her but remained quiet. "Why do you come here?" she asked.

He sighed and looked at the ponies. They were grazing, all at their own pace, knowing their place in the herd, knowing where they belonged. Ranch smell hung in the air, a mix of horses, hay, and the faint scent of fly spray. It had become his tranquilizer, calming his mood and appeasing his senses.

Tina slipped her hand into Paul's, her new big brother. She didn't understand him or his behavior, but he seemed lonely, and she could be with him. She patiently sat with him for quite some time before she stood up and returned to her room. *Dad was right*, she realized. *Paul wasn't ready.*

Some days, Paul came early in the morning and watched Maria and the kids as they rode the ponies for exercise. Every member of the Martinez family knew how to ride, even little Miguel. They enjoyed it. They chatted with each other, they smiled, and they laughed.

Paul tried to remember when he'd seen his mom laugh. She did yoga every day, but she did it without joy. It was a discipline, as his running had been. *He was done with speeding through life,* he decided; *he was done outrunning others; he was done chasing yet another trophy.*

Twinkles liked him. She became his mentor and therapist. The mare watched him carefully with her big brown eyes that reflected tranquility and understanding. When she looked at him, it felt as if she truly saw him as he was, flaws and all, and she seemed fine with it. Sometimes she walked over to Paul as he sat in the pasture and nuzzled him. Her presence was bold and gentle, her muzzle soft. She tucked her big head into his chest, and the pure and unambiguous gesture of this majestic animal touched his heart deeply. She accepted him. She invited him into the herd. She coaxed him to participate in life, to walk with her, to take his place and belong.

Paul tried to make sense of the myriad feelings inside him. It was the grief he struggled with the most. He grieved over parents who'd been nearby but forever unreachable. He grieved for a loving dad he'd never known. He grieved for a childhood he couldn't enjoy because training schedules and success were forced on him from a young age. He grieved having lost everything he knew when he got so sick he was certain he'd die.

At night, Paul had vivid dreams and recollected every detail upon awakening. He saw himself as a youngster and Mario teaching him about horses and about the kind of values that mattered. He saw himself playing with his siblings, the dog and the ponies. There was no pressure to perform out at the ranch. In his dreams, he laughed, and he could fly. He could see into houses as if there were no roofs. He flew over different countries, witnessed different lifestyles. He saw lush green pastures and dried-out forests. He saw people controlling others. He saw wealth, and he saw hunger. He saw sick people in hospitals. He saw suffering.

His heart stirred, and he wept.

Out in the pasture, he watched Manolo or Mario or Baatar as they took a pony out into the arena or round pen for training. They'd nod at Paul, and he'd nod back, like old cowboys in the wild. He was grateful they didn't bug him with prying questions. He had enough of that at home.

Watching the men train their ponies made him reminisce how he was trained when he was young. While his dad never spent time with him, his nannies, coaches, and mentors received instructions. Drill him. Push him hard. He's a Brooks. Brooks men perform. A Brooks achieves. A Brooks exceeds.

He watched as Baatar held eye contact with his pony, Kheer, during training sessions. It seemed he could guide the horse with his eyes, or his body stance, or his mind. It took Paul a long time until his gut told him Baatar used his heart. Rarely did Baatar speak to his ponies and when he did, it was only to praise.

Emmy didn't give up on Paul either. One evening, as she approached, she carried Pia's potion in her pocket, wondering if she could spray it on Paul to help him with his struggles, to remove the darkness, his pain. She wanted to sit next to him in the pasture, as she had in the past, but something kept her from doing it, and she sat on the fence instead. Like him, she just sat and watched the herd.

Dusk enveloped the valley, slowly dimming the light of day, as the sun dipped into the ocean in the west, it's orange and pink light reflecting in the sky, the same color that had accompanied Emmy the day she'd escaped from the city to Little Oaks after her years in foster care had ended.

She remembered walking all night into uncertainty and how, without any assurances from anyone, she'd known it was where she needed to go. She noticed the colors around Paul's body were turning lighter and more vivid. The brown and gray had lifted. Now she saw yellow, light blue and green and a very light pink. Sitting on the fence in silence, she smiled at no one in particular, except at life itself, when she felt a presence.

She looked to her right and saw her mom. "You can't see into the future, don't always know what's coming or how things will develop," Mom said, "but that doesn't mean you're not guided."

Emmy stared at her mom in disbelief. "Mom, I can hear you, I can see you *and* I can hear you." It was a thought rather than spoken words.

Mom smiled. "We're both learning," she said. "Our communication skills are increasing. We're evolving. And so is he," Mom said, looking at Paul. "He was in a dark place, but he's coming out of it. What you've done here, all of you, is a beautiful thing. You gave him the space he needed to heal. Sometimes healing can be achieved through talking and listening, and sometimes it requires silence and space."

"But how long does it take, Mom?" Emmy asked. "Paul's been coming here for weeks."

"You can't rush the healing process," Mom said. "You just have to allow it."

"But what can I do to help?" Emmy asked.

"You can witness it, like you do a stream in the woods, but you can't force it to slow down or speed up. You can only be present. Your presence alone is all it takes."

"Like when I want Manolo to be here with me, close by, even when we're not doing anything together," Emmy pondered.

"Just like that," Mom said and smiled. "You love him."

"I do."

"You are where you're supposed to be, Emmy. You'll do a lot of good in this life, a lot of good. We'll talk again soon." Her image began to fade. "And, Emmy, you don't need Pia's potion, just being here is enough."

Emmy smiled. "Thanks, Mom."

She hadn't considered her presence could be healing, but she understood. A presence could make all the difference. The presence of Carla, Mark, and Axel had become uncomfortable. Thessaly's presence had given her the creeps. Baatar on the other hand, made her feel calm and loved and understood, even when he was just sitting in front of the TV watching a wrestling match or walking through the stables, checking on horses. And Manolo? She smiled. Manolo was everything.

She watched Paul get up and leave for the day. He nodded her way, and she nodded back.

Thirty-Five

It took Paul weeks until he no longer felt forced to follow the path his father has planned for him. When he let go of the programmed identity, that he had accepted as a child and followed rigorously as a teenager, there was only emptiness left inside of him. Even the fear left him. His life presented only a blank. There was nothing. Nothing to be proud of, nothing to look back on, nothing to look forward to. All plans had shattered. His future became unknown.

Baatar and Mario discussed the situation, sitting on the patio in the evening while Maria and Jenna went shopping. "It's hard just watching him sit there, struggling with himself," Mario said.

"There's so much more happening with him than just sitting there," Baatar said. "He watches not only the ponies but also us, and we watch him. He sees us interact, he sees the kids, the family. He sees how we train the ponies. He sees us talking, teasing each other, and laughing. He sees Manolo and Emmy being in love and what that can be like. He sees how you and I treat our women and how they treat us. He's learning about horses, their connection, their affection, their hierarchy, their pecking order. He's learning the rules of life that were never before presented to him this way."

"He's gotten quite fond of Twinkles," Mario said. "The kids are learning to respect him, to give him space, to be patient with him. They're learning that everybody's different, and sometimes you can't help, even if you want to. You have to wait until the time is right." He took a deep breath and sighed. He looked across the hills and the valley, the chaparral that had dried out in the heat of summer.

"We're all learning from this," Baatar said. "Paul is nineteen. Physically, he's a grown man but inside he's still a boy. I was seventeen when I left home. I was much more stable than Paul is, emotionally, but like him I thought I was accomplished. I thought the world waited for me. Then I found out it wasn't so, but I was no longer home where people could catch me. I was in a foreign country and had to fight my way through, take dirty jobs if I wanted to eat, be bullied or mocked. In a way, Paul's still lucky. He's got all the support waiting for him when he wants it. And I'm sure he'll want it."

Mario nodded. "He'd be a fool not to. We can give him all the things he's never had. The kids have been great. I see them sitting on the fence, sneaking into the pasture to sit with him, to just let him know they're there, even Emmy."

This is a great place for therapy," Baatar said.

"Is that why you come up here?" Mario teased.

"And it's quiet and peaceful," Baatar pondered aloud, "the ranch overlooking the hills. Nature. I love nature."

One evening, as Paul sat in the pasture, Twinkles approached him. Paul stroked her neck. When it turned dark, he climbed on the fence and then on her back. She stood quietly. He encouraged her calmly to walk and she did. She took him for a slow ride all alongside the inner periphery the pasture. He felt the warmth of her body, her steadfastness and her purpose. She gave him confidence. She gave him trust. She'd given him her love, her friendship. *Oh my God*, he thought, *I've fallen in love with a horse.* He shook his head in disbelief and smiled broadly at himself.

When Twinkles stopped, he dismounted and hugged and kissed her. He rubbed her neck and her face. She nuzzled him and looked at him, patiently, calmly. She was present. Her kindness made him cry. Her kindness made him laugh. He looked into her beautiful, big brown eyes and he could see his future laid out before him. The path wouldn't be easy but satisfying. He felt passionate about the choice that life presented. Thank you, Twinkles," he said, "thank you very much."

The next morning when he awoke, life was different. He was different. His mind was profoundly clear, his heart filled with an unknown but electrifying energy, an inner force that pushed him out of bed. He couldn't explain it but there was no need to explain—only to act. His entire body tingled. Instead of being pushed from the outside to perform, he was pushed from the inside. His own voice spoke to him, and it was a voice of authority. He'd connected with his core. He could see how his life would unfold. His path had become clear.

He wouldn't return to Harvard. He wanted to stay in California, close to Mario and his siblings and the ponies. He could go to school here and live the life meant to be lived by Paul Brooks Martinez.

His father returned from a trip that same day and bullied his mother, and for the first time in his life, Paul stood up to him. His father rampaged through the house, and Paul stood firm. He didn't raise his own voice, but he stood tall. He stood in front of his mother. He told his father what he thought of him and his behavior. He had no fear.

That afternoon, Mario's phone rang.

"Hello? Paul?"

"Mario, will you be around today? I'd love to come and visit if that's OK."

"Yes, of course that's OK. I'm in town."

"This evening?" Paul inquired.

"I'll be home by seven."

"OK, thanks. Can you invite Baatar, too? I'll bring dinner. I'll see you in Hillside Ranch at seven."

Mario was perplexed. He invited Baatar who agreed to come.

Paul arrived on time and brought steak and chicken fajitas with beans and rice for the whole family. Maria and the kids gathered in the kitchen and unwrapped the meal. Tina was setting the table when Mario and Baatar walked in.

"Paul," Mario said and gave Paul a hug, then looked at the ample food delivery. "What are we celebrating?"

Paul gleamed. "I had a breakthrough."

"You're all healed?" Mario asked. "No more leukemia?"

"Yeah, that too, but more."

"Please tell us."

Paul looked at Baatar. "I know we didn't have a good start, you and me, but what you said, it really hit me hard. It had an impact."

Baatar raised his eyebrows and looked at Paul.

"My dad's intimidation, his commands, me being no kid anymore," Paul said. He scratched his ear. "Today my dad came home from a three-week trip and immediately nagged my mom, asking if she'd gained weight. She's a stick. All she ever eats is salad. She exercises all the time. She's beautiful."

Paul looked in the round. All eyes were on him.

"Then he started with me," Paul continued. "Am I wasting my money at Harvard? Are you ever going to continue your running career? I thought I raised a champion." Paul swallowed. "So, I stood up and faced him calmly. I told him I'd been deathly sick and recovered, not thanks to him or his money. I recovered because strangers cared. All my life, he knew I wasn't his son, but instead of being honest and expressing his discontent with the situation, he pretended I was his kid and ignored me. He punished me all my life for something I hadn't caused. I told him he didn't raise me. Nannies did. Mentors did. Coaches did. I told him I've given up my running career. I'm done running. And I won't be a patent attorney because that's not something I want to be.

I told my father to quit bullying my mom and treat her with respect or divorce her and let her live in peace. I told him his demeanor was unacceptable."

Paul took a deep breath and sighed heavily. "Both my parents stared at me in disbelief. My dad'll probably disinherit me, but for the first time in my life, I feel alive. I feel empowered. I don't know how to describe it. Like I woke up from a very long, bad dream, because of you, all of you." He looked in the round.

"Baatar, you cared enough to talk to me like a friend even though I'd been a total jerk at your house. And Mario, you put your life on hold to save mine. And the whole family took me in like I was a part of you. I've never met people like you."

He took a breath and swallowed. "I want to become a doctor. I'd be good at it 'cause my heart would be in it."

Mario walked over and hugged him.

"I've never been so emotional," Paul added.

"Welcome to the family," Mario said and smiled. "We're all emotional, it's OK. I'm proud of you, son. You've been through a lot, and it's changed you. You've shed your old beliefs about yourself, about life, and have defined your own path. Today you stood up for what you believe in. That's not easy to do."

"I'm proud to be a Martinez," Paul said, "although I'm still rattled that my half sister wiped my butt at the hospital, when I was really sick." He looked at Ariana, somewhat embarrassed.

She shrugged her shoulders.

"Better her than a complete stranger," Manolo said and winked at Ariana.

"Mario," Paul said, "I can finally answer the question you asked me a while back at the restaurant. I love horses, particularly Twinkles. Weird name for a horse, but she's absolutely beautiful."

"Miguel named her," Mario said.

"Oh, sorry, it's a cute name," Paul said, looking at Miguel.

Looking at Paul, Manolo asked, "You wanna go for a ride with us? Ariana and Emmy are coming, too."

"I'm not good at it," Paul said.

"You're not gonna get good at it by standing around," Manolo said. "You coming or not?"

"I'm coming. But I don't have riding boots or a helmet."

"We've got you covered. What size?"

Baatar and Mario looked on as the four saddled up the ponies, chatting and laughing. Paul had chosen Twinkles.

Mario settled in a big easy chair when Miguel climbed into his lap. "Is Paul all better now, Dad?"

"Yes, son, he's all better."

"And we can talk to him now?"

"Yes, Miguel, looks like he's ready to be integrated. He's part of the family now."

"Then I can go out riding with him sometimes, too?" Miguel asked.

"I'm sure he'd enjoy that."

When the four returned from riding the trails, Manolo showed Paul how to give the ponies a bath and brush them down. Paul volunteered to help and came back to the house with wet clothes. He sat down at the table with Baatar, Mario, and Miguel.

"I may have to sleep in the barn for a while and find a job, with my father being mad and all," Paul said, "but I'll find a way. I'll pull this through."

"You can sleep in my room," Miguel offered. "I don't mind sharing."

Paul shook Miguel's hand and thanked him for his generosity.

When Paul returned home, his father had left. His mom cried. They both expected to hear from his father's lawyer.

It took a week before they heard from his father, who came home to address them in person. He didn't want to lose his only son. He'd gotten used to having a boy, and how was he going to explain to his peers and business partners that his son walked out on him, or his wife, or both?

Paul applied at UCLA and switched his major from law to medicine.

"You've got a long path ahead of you," his academic counselor said.

"I know."

"You say your goal is to become a physician?"

Paul nodded. "I was sick and had a dedicated team of doctors and nurses. I have an amazing dad who saved my life. I know what it's like to taste death and be given a second chance. I want to be able to give people that second chance."

***

The following Sunday evening, the Martinez family invited Baatar and Jenna, Emmy and Paul, and of course DJ. Numerous dishes were placed side by side on the kitchen island for self-service. The air was filled with the smell of Mexican delicacies. When everybody had arrived and the crowd gathered at the table, Mario stood up and spoke.

"This year has brought us a lot of changes," he said, "among them Baatar and Jenna's wedding, DJ, Manolo and Emmy dating, and the arrival of Paul in our lives. In all these events, love is the binding factor."

He looked at Paul. "Paul, we never had a chance to celebrate your birth or your nineteen birthdays after that. But after seeing you sit in the pasture for weeks on end, and our ponies taking you into the herd, we've come to the decision that it's time we officially integrate you into the family. Today, we've gathered to celebrate you."

Paul grinned.

"The ponies have had their chance to get to know you," Mario said. "Now it's our turn. As you can tell, in a Mexican family there's always a feast connected with any kind of celebration. We've all contributed to it today. So, let's sit and eat while the food is warm."

As they ate, there was a lot of chatter, mostly questions for Paul to answer. "Do you like riding Twinkles? What do you like about her? What's it like at UCLA? Will you commute or live up there? How long does it take to become a doctor? Tell us how you grew up."

Paul did his best to answer all the questions. Every so often, Mario reminded the kids to give Paul a chance to eat.

When everybody was full and the table cleared, the family brought gifts for Paul to unwrap.

"Wow, this is like a birthday party," Paul said, smiling.

"Go ahead, unwrap your presents," Ariana said.

Paul unwrapped a big box containing riding boots and a helmet, because, as Mario explained, every Martinez should have his own. Next, Paul unwrapped a pair of jeans with no side-seams, perfect for riding. Maria handed Paul a small box with a keychain with a big silver M for Martinez, and Mario handed him a key to the house.

"You're a member of the family now, Paul," Mario said, and as Miguel previously offered, there's always a place to sleep for you here. And since you've befriended our pony, Twinkles, or perhaps Twinkles befriended you, you're always welcome to ride her."

"But before you get too comfortable with all these presents and privileges, remember that as your dad, I expect you to keep the family rules and uphold our values."

"Family rules?" Paul asked.

"Be polite, and say thank you," Miguel said.

"Be kind," Tina chimed in.

"No backtalking to your parents," Daniela said and made a face.

"The ponies always come first," Manolo said. "They're our lifeline. We make sure they're healthy and safe; we feed them before we feed ourselves."

"We all support each other," Ariana added, "always. If one of us needs something, you help them without a big discussion."

Mario looked in the round and smiled. "Of course, that means if you need anything, Paul, we're here for you, too. It's a mutual arrangement. We're family. And you already know my values. I expect all my kids to be kind, grateful, and polite. Can you live with that?"

Paul smiled. "I can," he said, "and I've been working on that."

Mario stood up and walked over to Paul. "Come here, son." He gave him a big hug, then Maria hugged Paul, and all the kids stood in line to hug their new brother.

"We've got one more thing to do," Mario said. He motioned his head for Paul to follow. Everybody tracked along to the front of the house. Mario picked up a small tree to be planted next to the other five that had taken root, the biggest at Manolo's birth twenty-two years ago; the smallest at Miguel's, eight years ago. Mario cut the first hole into the ground with a big spade, then handed it to Maria, Manolo, Ariana, Paul, Daniela, Tina, and Miguel. Each of them dug the hole a little deeper. They let Paul put the tree in the ground and they all shoved dirt around it. Paul got to water it for the first time, then the watering would become part of the daily chores for those who lived at home, until the roots grew, and the tree could pull water from the ground all by itself.

Baatar took a family picture in front of the trees.

They all returned to the backyard with its beautiful view of the panoramic, sloping hills, now sleepily resting under the protection of the mountain range, whose peaks formed a wave pattern with natural highs and lows against the dark horizon.

They talked about love and grief, each of them sharing memories of a loved one: Jenna's mom, Maria's favorite aunt, Baatar's friend Damdin, Emmy's parents and sister. Mario talked about his first pony that he had to put down when she was twenty-eight. Paul talked about the loss of his dog, Buster, and Miguel about his guinea pig, Stinky. They felt empathy and compassion for each other.

Baatar spoke about leaving behind the Mongolian steppe, his parents' lifestyle, the culture, and language that was all he'd ever known.

"I feel the same," Paul said. "I've left my parents' lifestyle, the culture of pushing and bullying to get to the top, which is all I've ever known, until now." He looked at

Baatar. Their eyes met and Baatar nodded in acknowledgment.

"It's so comforting, sitting around a firepit and telling stories," Paul said. "Can we do that again sometime?"

"We do it all the time," Mario said. "Old horsemen tradition, and now you'll be part of it. Do you play an instrument?"

Paul shook his head. "I can pull up a music video on my phone," he said, and everybody laughed.

Mario brought out his accordion and handed Maria a pair of maracas. They started to play and sing Mexican songs, and the family joined in.

"You'll have to learn some Spanish," Ariana said to Paul, "just the songs."

He smiled and nodded in agreement.

"And what language do I have to learn for the horses?" Paul asked.

"I thought you'd learned it," Mario asked, looking at Paul, "while you sat in that pasture for weeks. Didn't Twinkles teach you?"

Paul smiled. "Some."

Thirty-Six

Baatar and Jenna's new house turned out to be perfect. They painted the nursery yellow, so the little girl, once born, would be welcomed every morning to the color of sunshine. Tina, who was an artist at heart, painted a tree with birds on the wall opposite the crib. It was a cheerful mural. They painted DJ's bedroom in a soft, soothing green, like a pasture, and Tina painted a mural with horses, a rendering that could compete with any professional artist.

Emmy was exuberant when she got to check out the new house for the first time and claim her room, and Manolo transported all her furniture from her rental to Baatar and Jenna's new home. Emmy used the *curandera's* special potion throughout the house, to protect it and bring lots of love inside.

Baatar built a swing and a sandbox for DJ, and the boy and Bruno spent a lot of time in the backyard. Everybody loved the pool, which they used daily. Even Bruno liked to swim.

After two months in their new home, Jenna's water broke. She called out to her husband, and Baatar, who'd been swimming in the backyard pool after work, came running into the house, leaving wet footprints everywhere.

"Are you OK, love?"

"Yes, honey, I'm OK. Get my bag, will you?" Jenna asked.

"Your bag, yes, of course, your bag." Baatar ran upstairs and roamed the bedroom. No bag. "Where is it, love?"

"In the closet."

"Yes, of course, in the closet." While still wet, he got dressed as quickly as he could. He found the bag and rushed downstairs. Car keys in hand, he ran outside, placed the bag into the trunk and helped Jenna into the car. He started the car.

"Honey, haven't you forgotten something?"

"What?"

"DJ. We can't leave him here by himself."

"Oh, yes, DJ." Baatar stopped the car and ran into the house.

"Honey, he's in the sandbox!" Jenna shouted.

Baatar ran into the backyard and scooped up DJ. He placed him into the child's seat in the back of the car when Jenna moaned.

"Jenna, are you OK? We better go!"

They rushed to the hospital. The contractions and labor pains continued. Baatar called Emmy and asked her to come pick up DJ and take care of Bruno. An hour later, he was alone with Jenna at the hospital.

The labor lasted eight hours. Then it was over, and they heard the first cry, and all strain and tension and stress of the last few hours was forgotten. They had a beautiful, healthy baby girl. The doctor placed her into Jenna's arms, and she smiled.

"Sophie," she said softly and looked at Baatar. "Can you believe we made her?"

"Well, mainly you made her," he conceded. "I didn't have that much to do with it."

"You gave her half her chromosomes," Jenna said. "Without you, she couldn't have been created."

"That doesn't sound very romantic, does it?" Baatar said. "She grew inside of you for nine months."

"No matter how you look at it," Jenna said, "you're her dad."

He smiled. "Yes, I am," he said, proudly. "We're her parents, Jenna." He gave her and the baby a kiss, and sat quietly by Jenna's side, holding her hand, counting back the months when she'd been most likely created, in Alaska, on their honeymoon. He took pictures of Jenna and Sophie.

Jenna called her dad, although it was in the middle of the night, and Baatar called his parents. He also called Emmy, his brother and his sister, and woke up Mario to tell him the good news.

In the early morning hours, he left the hospital to get a few hours of sleep, then came back with DJ. He held him in his arms. "Look," he said. "This is Sophie. She's your little sister. Always be kind to her and love her. We're all family."

"Sophie," DJ said.

"Yes," Baatar nodded.

Baatar looked at Jenna. "I'm so proud of you," he said. "Look at her. That tiny face and those tiny hands. She's so perfect. She's very pretty. We're gonna have to watch the boys around her. They'll be after her in no time."

Jenna chucked. "Do you want to hold her?"

"Yes."

DJ took a seat on the bed and Jenna gently placed the baby into Baatar's arms. He smiled and rocked Sophie. "She's beautiful, our little Sophie," he said, "just like you."

Life, he knew, would never be the same. It'd be better.

"We'll have to have a baby welcome party," he said.

"Absolutely. Let's have a housewarming party and introduce Sophie to our friends."

A few weeks after Jenna came home from the hospital,

they invited Jenna's dad, Emmy and Manolo, Mario and Maria and the kids, and all their friends with wives and kids.

Paul came with his new girlfriend. "This is Verena," he proudly announced.

"Verena," Emmy said, sighing deeply inside, "I didn't know you and Paul knew each other."

"Yeah, we're dating," Verena said and placed a hand on his arm. "Looks like you and I are meant to be in the same family, doesn't it? Though I understand Paul's really got a much richer background. I just draw men with money." She gave Paul a flirtatious smile.

Verena was wearing a see-through blouse in a deep red with a tight, black, leather miniskirt and her favorite red lacquered stilettos. Her fake eyelashes had miraculously reappeared.

"Emmy, ya need some serious fashion advice, don't ya?" Verena offered. "Look at ya. Ya barely wear any makeup, your nails are short and plain. Ya have a cute dress, but ya're wearing it with cowboy boots?"

"I love my boots," Emmy said. "They were a birthday present."

"Well," Verena said with a look of disdain on her face, "they kind'a suit ya." She glanced at the horses in the pasture. "It's dull up here, isn't it?" She looked back at Emmy. "Land, wind, and dust—don't you find it boring?"

"I love the ranch and the horses and the people," Emmy said. "They're sincere and down-to-earth. The horses are beautiful. I don't see anything boring out here."

"Maybe we don't have as much in common as I thought," Verena said. "Ya can have the dusty grass-eating things over there; I'll head up to LA with Paul in his Porsche anytime." She seductively leaned over the table, sticking out her rear, and picked up a couple of bottles of beer. She handed one to Paul with a big smile. "You wanna sit down, Superman?"

Manolo approached Emmy as Verena and Paul walked off. He put his arms around her and gave her a kiss. "I love a girl with cowboy boots," he said.

"See why I don't wanna be friends with her?" Emmy whispered.

"She doesn't make it easy on you, does she?" Manolo observed. "But I bet underneath all that glamour is a scared, insecure, little girl. Paul's come around; maybe she will, too."

Emmy rolled her eyes. *Why couldn't people see that Verena was nothing but trouble?*

"You wanna sit by them?" Manolo asked.

Emmy stared at him with wide-open eyes, her head cocked slightly. Her mouth opened with an audible exhale.

"I guess not," Manolo said, smiling. "Let's sit by Baatar and Jenna.

"I can't get rid of her," Emmy whispered to Baatar, pointing with her chin toward Verena.

"Perhaps there's a reason," Baatar said and looked at Emmy.

"Like what?"

"Perhaps there's something she can teach you, or something you need to teach her. There's a reason when people keep popping up in our lives, people or situations."

Emmy looked at him. "OK, Baatar, sometimes I really don't like what you tell me."

"I know," he said and winked at her. "Look how much Paul has changed. He needed that shift, and life gave him a chance to get it, to understand that there was a better path for him."

"You think I need a shift?"

Baatar smiled. "Emmy, we all get pushed around by life

all the time. It's not my decision or yours. Life presents lessons, whether we like them or not."

She sighed and leaned into Manolo. She felt good with him. *There'd be many changes in her life, from junior college to veterinary school, from graduating to being a practicing veterinarian, from being a girlfriend to being a wife, Manolo's wife if she could help it, and from being a wife to also being a mother, someday,* she hoped.

Sometimes it felt as though she'd known him before. Pia, the *curandera*, would say, in another lifetime, if those existed. She'd have to find out more about that. When Thessaly had spoken of her life with Axel in Ireland, it had sounded so natural. Thessaly's memory had been so clear, so historic, so real. And Thessaly knew everything about Axel, his likes and dislikes, his moods, his character, his allergy to avocados.

Emmy's life had turned for the better once again, living with Baatar and Jenna. Bruno slept on her bed again, and her vivid dreams continued. The whisperings from her mom became steady. She didn't even have to go to the cemetery any longer to hear her. She could call on her and connect with her wherever she was. There was a subtle shift in energy, in her head, or maybe it was in her heart, or in her solar plexus. She couldn't pinpoint it. But she knew when it happened. She could feel it. She could make it happen.

Consulting with her mom was starting to be a normal part of Emmy's life. *She wasn't a curandera,* Emmy thought, *but she could hear spirits. She could feel the horses' needs as well, their desires, and at times even feel their inner gifts. Some were runners, some sprinters, some jumpers.* She couldn't explain how she knew. She'd looked at Baatar for these insights, admired him for his wisdom, and now, somehow, sometimes she knew.

***

Emmy joined Jenna on her first visit to the races since Sophie's birth. They hadn't been to the races for some time together. Jenna's dad was visiting and had offered to watch Sophie for the afternoon.

It was Saturday, and the races were well attended. Visitors from all around the world came to this event. The grandstand was packed, as was the restaurant. Jenna, Emmy, and DJ had prime seating, close to the winner's circle. They also had privileges to go to the turf, something most visitors were denied. They'd already been to the stables and could go and greet Baatar when he came riding through the tunnel in between races.

The third race was in progress, with nine thoroughbreds rushing down the main stretch at great speed. The announcer excitedly shouted out the horses' numbers and jockeys' names as they raced down the track, side by side. Jenna watched the outriders more than the race.

Meanwhile, Emmy went to the stables where Manolo had been asked to fit shoes for one of the thoroughbreds. The horse had encountered problems with one foot that needed immediate attention, but the racetrack farrier unexpectedly had been taken to the hospital with a high fever. Manolo filed down the hoof, as he'd been taught. He was confident, dependable, trustworthy. He was firm but gentle.

And he was gorgeous.

He was young but he knew his job well, Emmy thought as she watched him closely. *The sick farrier could rely on him. The horse's trainer could rely on him. Emmy knew, she could rely on him, and she was proud of him.* She remembered the night before, that they had spent together, and her heart beat a little faster at the memory. She thought of blue-eyed Axel and

Harvard-driven Paul. Nobody could make her as happy as Manolo. He had charisma, charm, and a heart of gold.

While the winner of race number three was announced, Jenna had eyes only for Baatar. When she saw him sitting on his pony, all saddled up, it stirred something in her, something primal. She wondered if she'd known him hundreds of years ago, when he rode a horse as a Mongol warrior under Genghis Khan. There was a soul connection between him and her that seemed to be as old as life itself. She swore to herself she'd never let him know how sentimental she was about him.

He noticed her staring at him. Nothing escaped his dark eyes, trained to calmly peruse the horizon for trouble or the slightest move that could cause an incident. He noticed a breeze developing from the ocean, the far-off laughter of a little boy not his own, and the look of a woman he loved.

When the races were done, and the racetrack cleared, Baatar, Jenna, and DJ met up at the barn. DJ proudly wore his helmet. Baatar smiled toward them, as they approached. He lifted up DJ and gave Jenna a kiss.

"I love you," she said.

"That feeling is mutual," he said and pulled her into his arms. It felt like the love between them had lasted for millennia and would continue from here on out. To have such love was magical, and they both knew it. It wasn't something one could demand or search and find. It wasn't something they could teach or explain. Their love was a bond of two souls on one path, a path, it seemed, they weren't walking together for the first time, and probably not the last time either.

The End

About the Author

Mollie Moon's life has been filled with travels throughout Europe, the U.S. and South America, which has given her exposure to many lifestyles and cultures. The immigrant is usually at the center of her novels, reflecting her own history and experience. She resides in Southern California.

All of Mollie's novels can be found on Amazon.

Visit Mollie's website at www.MollieMoon.com and feel free to email her with comments and feedback at mollie@molliemoon.com.

Made in the USA
Columbia, SC
18 September 2021